THE KINGSTONE OF AIRMID

THE KINGSTONE OF AIRMID

A NOVEL OF ALASTRÍONA

SECOND EDITION

BY
WILLIAM SPEIR

Progressive
RISING PHOENIX PRESS

Text Copyright © 2015, 2024 William Speir

All rights reserved.
Published 2015, 2024 by Progressive Rising Phoenix Press, LLC
www.progressiverisingphoenix.com

ISBN: 978-1-944277-04-8

Second Edition

Printed in the U.S.A.

Cover Artwork by Gordon Napier, Buckinghamshire, UK (http://dashinvaine.co.uk). Used by permission of the artist, © Copyright 2013 Gordon Napier.

Interior Artwork by Gordon Napier, Buckinghamshire, UK (http://dashinvaine.co.uk). Used by permission of the artist, © Copyright 2015 Gordon Napier.

Map of Alastríona Illustrations by: Mag. Robert Altbauer, Cartographer and Illustrator, Salzburg, Austria (http://www.fantasy-map.net).

Book and Cover design by William Speir
Visit: http://www.williamspeir.com

DEDICATION:

Deepest gratitude goes to my wife Lee Anne for putting up with being married to a writer. Every day I love her more than I ever thought possible. I am also grateful for my children: Sonya and her husband Tom, and Brad and his wife Susie. Without my family, there would be no words worth writing.

I want to express my gratitude to Gordon Napier for his cover art and illustrations, and to cartographer Robert Altbauer for his map of Alastríona (pronounced *al-is-TREE-nah*). I have never worked with two such professional illustrators who helped take my vision and turn it into a reality!

Special thanks goes to my sister and editor, Linda Speir, for her tireless work in helping me shape my draft manuscripts into a polished, finished version worthy of being read!

Additional thanks go to my beta readers for their valuable suggestions: Diana Beebe, Robert Box, Janet Broussard, Leo Bush, Raine Carter, Celia Eidex Ciemnoczolowski, Jennifer L. Cook, Eric Dossa, Jan Eldritch, Larry French, Joe Hoeddinghaus, Ellen D. Hosafros, Daniel Kaplan, Zame Khan, James Kirkland, Evergreen Lee, Ann Meyer, Susan Miner, Dean Murphy, James Newman, Amy Paulshock, Charlie Philippin, Pat Russell, Jim Schnetzler, Lindsey Schnetzler, and Amy Townsend.

To Colten Alexander Speir, my first grandson. Welcome to the world!

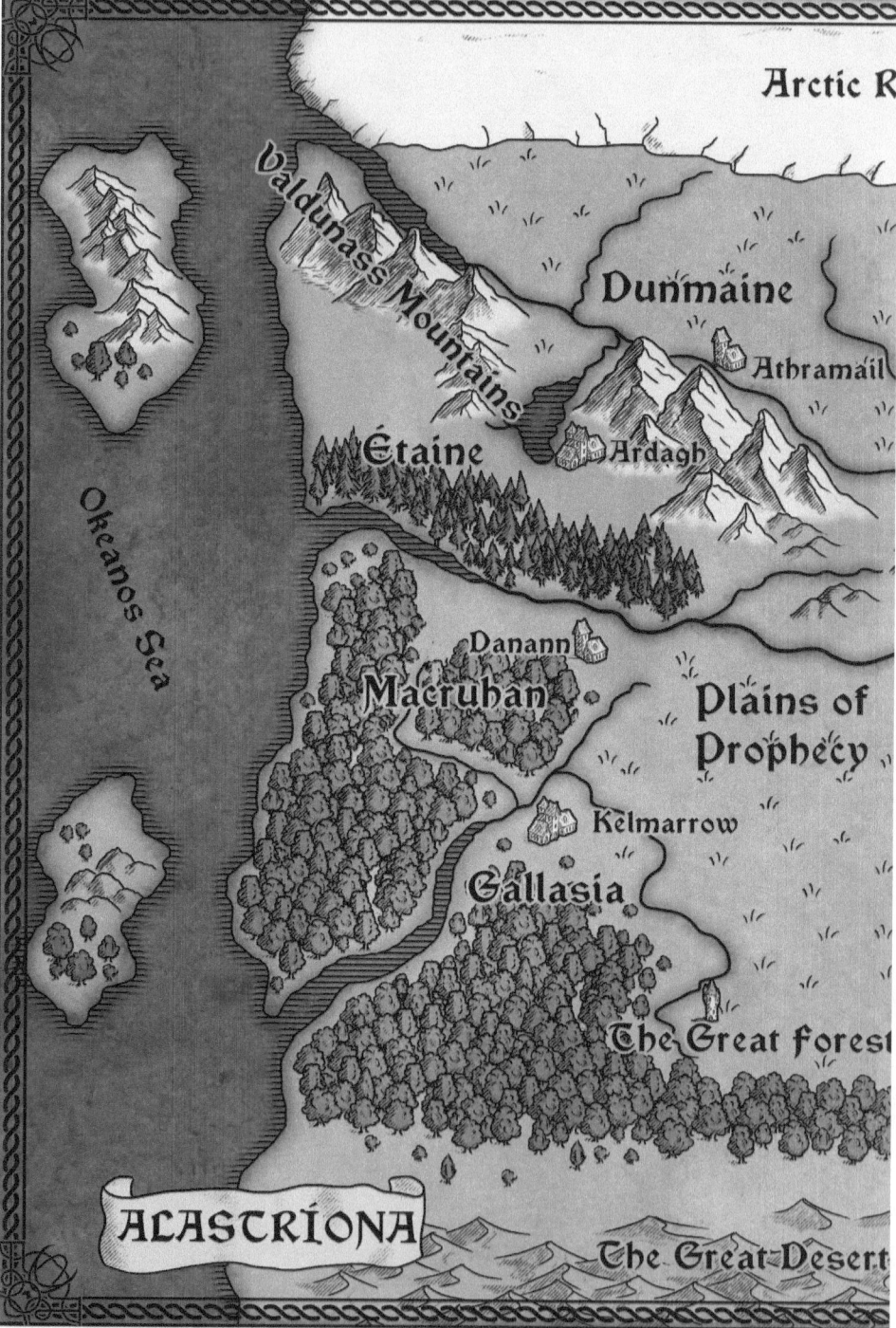

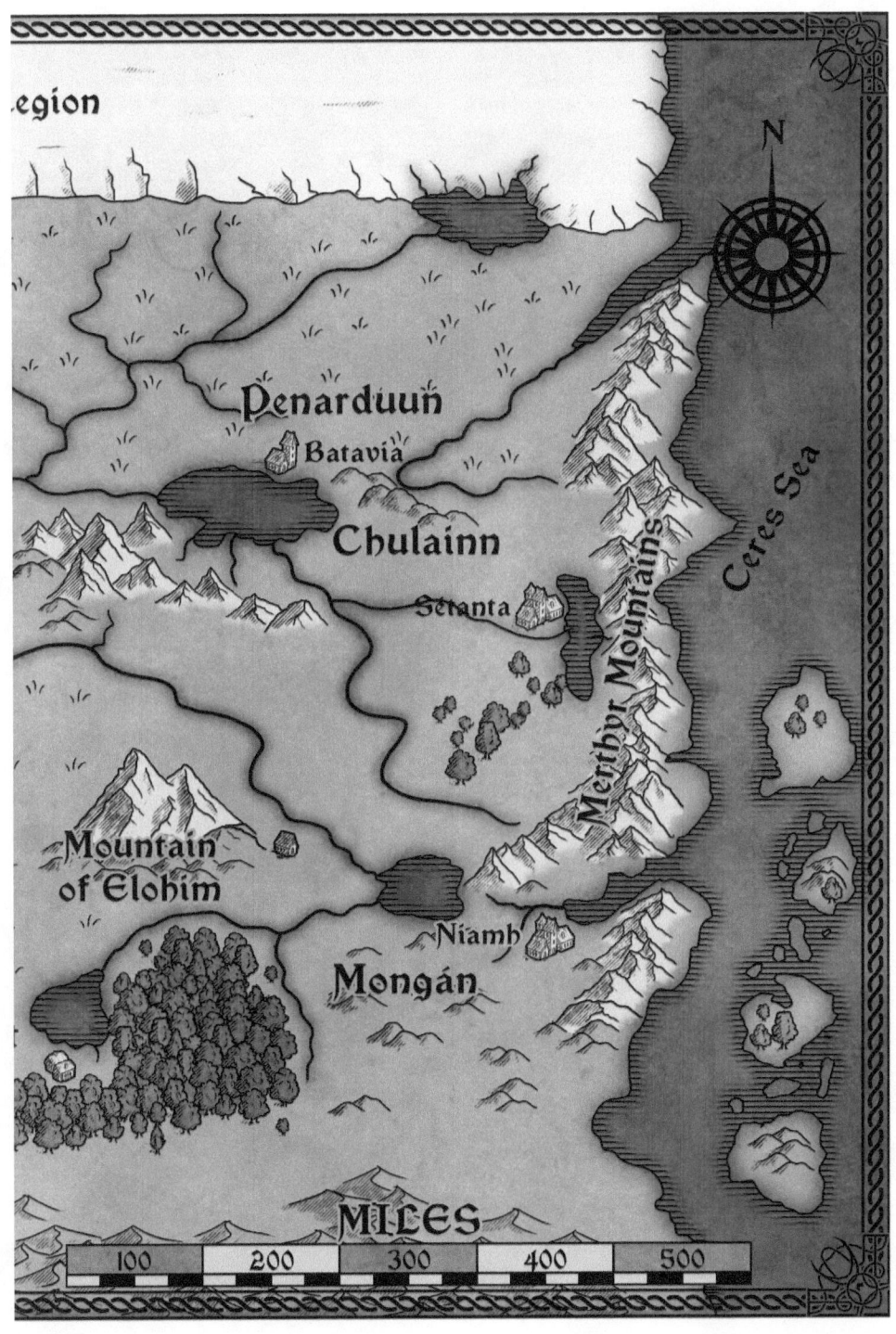

he sentry ran through the halls of the palace toward the great hall where the King of the Étaíne tribe waited. For three days, the sentry had been standing at his post on the palace wall that overlooked the lake, waiting for the arrival of King Taranus' guests. A few minutes earlier, three longboats reached the lake and approached the docks of the capital city.

An unusual sight had appeared in the sky above Alastríona. The path of one of the two moons took it in front of the sun at midday, causing the sky to go dark for several minutes. This wasn't the first time that one of the two moons had crossed in front of the sun, but it was something that hadn't happened in over a century.

Mider, the god of the Étaíne tribe, believed that the eclipse might be the first sign mentioned in the prophecy, heralding the birth of the three orphans who'd overthrow the gods and unite the tribes. He had instructed King Taranus to send for the kings of the Étaíne tribe's allies to discuss the situation in case the red moons appeared two weeks later.

The sentry entered the great hall and waited by the entrance for King Taranus to summon him forward to deliver his message.

"Don't just stand there," Taranus grumbled when he saw the sentry. "What news do you bring me?"

"My King," the sentry said as he approached the dais where Taranus sat, "the longboats are on the lake and will be docked within the hour."

"It's about time," the king muttered to himself. Looking at the sentry, he said, "Have my escorts fetch our guests and bring them here quickly."

"Yes, My King." The sentry turned on his heel and exited the chamber to carry out his orders.

An hour and a half later, the king's chamberlain announced the arrival of the kings of the Mongán. Gallasian, and Chulainn tribes.

"Did we get here in time?" King Ocelus of the Mongán asked as he strode into the great hall with his purple war cloak billowing behind him. His laced sandals made a strange tapping sound on the floor as he walked.

"Barely," Taranus replied, stepping down from the dais so he could greet his guests. "The moons are supposed to rise within the hour."

"And if they're red?" King Latobius of the Gallasians asked. The reflection of the torch light in the chamber glistened from the heavy gold chain he wore around his neck.

"Then we have much to discuss."

"Only if they cross paths," King Grannus of the Chulainn reminded them. The jewels lining his cloak sparkled and clinked together as he walked up to his host. Even the hand he extended in greeting had jeweled rings on three fingers.

"That's true," Taranus admitted. "The moons have to be red *and* cross paths for this to be the sign of the births of the three orphans from the prophecy."

Taranus led his guests out of the great hall and up the stairs that led to the roof of his palace. The palace was built into the side of a mountain, and the roof of the palace where Taranus led his guests extended far enough away from the mountain to provide an unobstructed view of the two moons as they rose.

Normally, the two moons of Alastríona looked white or light grey in the sky, although sometimes they had a pale blue or orange appearance. The four kings hoped that today would be no different. If the moons were any color other than red, it meant that the events mentioned in the prophecy weren't yet going to happen. However, if the moons *were* red and crossed paths, it would signal that changes were coming – changes that none of the four kings wanted.

Taranus was about to say something when he heard one of his captains shout and point toward the western horizon. There, rising slowly over the mountains, was a blood red moon. Another shout went up from the southern wall of the palace, and the kings saw Alastríona's second moon rising over the Great Forest. It, too, was red as blood.

The kings watched as the two moons rose higher in the sky. Servants brought chairs and a table so the kings could eat and be comfortable while they watched the sky. The four kings talked for several hours, glancing up at the sky often to see whether the paths of the moons crossed each other.

2

When the moons reached their zenith, the paths of the moons crossed, and for several minutes, it appeared as if there were only one moon in the sky.

"There can be no doubt," Grannus whispered, sounding awestruck at the implication of the celestial event the kings had just witnessed.

"None," Taranus agreed. "The orphans of the prophecy have been born. If they succeed, all of the tribes will become one tribe, and we'll all worship only one god. Everything we've built, and everything our families have achieved, will be undone. We'll no longer be kings over our people. We can't let that happen!"

"What can we do to stop it?" Latobius asked as the four kings left the palace roof and descended the stairs to Taranus' Council chamber.

"Find the orphans and kill them, of course," Taranus replied.

"But who are the orphans?" Ocelus asked. "Where are they?"

Taranus ushered his guests into the Council chamber. "I don't know."

"Does Mider know?" Ocelus asked.

"Not yet, although I know Mider's working on it."

"How do we kill three children if we don't know who they are or where they are?"

"If we kill every boy born this week, the orphans will die, too, won't they?" Taranus asked.

Latobius gasped. "You can't be serious!" he said.

"Of course I'm serious," Taranus snapped. "Do you want the prophecy to succeed?"

"Well, no, of course not," Latobius replied. "But..."

"What do you propose we do to stop it?" Taranus interrupted. "A living orphan could grow up to unseat us all. A dead orphan won't fulfill anything. Is there any other choice?"

The other kings looked at each other for a minute and slowly shook their heads.

"Then it's agreed. We'll send soldiers out across Alastríona and kill every boy born this week. Mider hasn't found them yet, but he told me he'd know if they're killed. Until then, we do whatever is necessary to keep the prophecy from being fulfilled."

"What about the other tribes?" Ocelus asked.

"What about them?" Taranus asked.

"Won't they object to our soldiers entering their territories and killing their newborns?"

"I'm sure they would if they knew we were doing it. The soldiers we send out can't wear any insignia or uniform that would identify who they are or who sent them. They'll attack in secret like assassins, rather

3

than soldiers. The other tribes won't have any idea who they are."

"What about girls?" Grannus asked.

Taranus and the other kings laughed. "Girls?" Taranus asked. "Why would we need to kill girls? The prophecy says one of the orphans will be the king of the world. How could a girl become king?"

"Actually, the prophecy says that one of the orphans will become the Ruler of the World," Grannus countered.

"What's the difference?" Ocelus asked.

"None," Taranus stated. "Mider hasn't said anything about girls, so all we have to worry about is boys."

The other kings nodded, but Grannus wasn't looking comfortable with the plan. "What about the parents?" he asked.

"We'll need to tell the soldiers to avoid killing the parents if they can," Taranus replied. "We don't want to accidently create any orphans."

"And if the parents try to prevent us from killing their newborns?" Grannus asked.

"Then we kill the parents and all of their children, just to be safe."

By the end of the day, the kings sent orders to their soldiers to hunt down and kill any boys born that week. The great slaughter had begun, marking the early days of the fulfilling of the prophecy with bloodshed.

CHAPTER 1

rawn, Cerridwen, and Amaethon were born on the day that the two red moons crossed paths in the skies over Alastríona.

Arawn was born in Kelmarrow, the capital city of the Gallasian tribe. His parents were traders who used their wagons to transport other people's goods to market.

Arawn's father was not there for the birth. He was bringing a load of timber up from the southern end of the Gallasian territory, and weather delayed his arrival. When he finally returned home, his wife presented his new son to him.

"He looks just like you," she said, smiling at her husband.

Arawn's father looked at his son with an expression of wonder on his face. "He's the most beautiful baby I've ever seen," he said.

Cerridwen was born in Danann, the capitol city of the Macruhan Tribe. Her twin brother Callum was born a few minutes before her. As her mother rested, holding the newborns, Cerridwen's father came into the room with the oldest son, Duncan.

"Look Duncan," Cerridwen's father said. "You have a baby brother and a baby sister now."

Duncan looked at the twins and giggled. "They look funny," he said before he scampered out of the room.

Cerridwen's father chuckled and left the room to find Duncan before the child found something new to break.

Cerridwen's mother looked at the newborns and smiled contently. "My precious little ones," she said softly.

Amaethon was born in Athramail, the capital city of the Dunmaine tribe. His father was a baker and his mother was a singer who performed in the city choir. Amaethon was their first child.

Athramail was a quaint walled city located on the north bank of the river at the base of the Valdunass Mountains. The river formed the border between the Étaíne tribe's territory to the south, and the Dunmaine tribe's territory to the north. Amaethon's parents had lived in Athramail their entire lives, and their home was on the western edge of the city near the river.

Amaethon's parents loved going for walks in the evening. Just after Amaethon's supper feedings, they bundled him up and took him on their walks around the city until he started getting sleepy. Their lives were happy.

From the moment that Arawn, Cerridwen, and Amaethon came into the world, their lives were in jeopardy from the enemies of Airmid.

"Our time is at hand," Alaunus said to the other elders selected by the god Airmid three centuries earlier to protect the orphans. "The children of the prophecy have been born and are already in danger."

"From whom?" Belenus asked.

"Taranus and the others," she replied, looking into the fire she had lit to keep herself warm in the chilly evening air. "As we expected, they've sent soldiers to kill the orphans."

"How could they know who the orphans are?" Nemausus asked. "*We* don't even know who they are yet."

"They don't know either," Alaunus replied. "The soldiers have orders to kill all the boys born this week."

"Even in the territories of the other tribes?" Tridamus asked.

"Yes. The soldiers will wear no markings that identify them as Mongán, Gallasian, Étaíne, or Chulainn. Their orders are to kill all newborn boys no matter where they are."

"How can we sit by and let all those innocents die?" Nemausus asked. "We need to do something!"

"We will do something," Alaunus stated. "We'll obey Elohim and protect the orphans until they're ready to retrieve the Kingstone and unite the tribes."

"Is the Kingstone still safe?" Belenus asked.

"It's safe. No one knows its hiding place, and even if someone discovered where it's hidden, he could never reach it."

Alaunus watched the flames' frenzied dance in the evening wind, grateful that the time of the fulfilling of the prophecy had finally arrived. She and the others had been waiting a very long time for this day, and now that it was here, she felt a great sense of urgency. Time was running out.

"Is there no way to save the other children?" Tridamus asked.

"No, old friend. If we move openly against the soldiers, we risk revealing ourselves, and that would put the orphans in even greater danger. We have a sacred task to perform, and it must be our only focus. We'll all mourn the loss of life caused by the other tribes, but it's the orphans who must be protected at all costs. If they fail, or if even one of them dies before the prophecy is fulfilled, it would be catastrophic for Alastríona. I know it's hard, but we must look to the task we all accepted and never lose focus. On this, everything depends."

Alaunus waited patiently as the other elders thought about what she had said. She felt their anguish about allowing the deaths of so many children whose only crime was the day of their birth, but she trusted Elohim and knew that there was no choice in the matter. She stared at the fire, and after a few minutes, she continued.

"Belenus, you'll be responsible for Arawn, who's a Gallasian. Nemausus, Amaethon will be your responsibility; he's a Dunmaine. Tridamus, you'll be responsible for Cerridwen, who's a Macruhan. I don't have any more information to give you at the moment, but Elohim will tell you what you need to know when the time is right. I'll keep an eye on the others and let you know if anything happens that might put the orphans at risk. We should communicate with each other often. I think it'll be good to keep each other informed about how the orphans are doing. Are there any questions?"

"Isn't Cerridwen a girl's name?" Tridamus asked.

"Yes," Alaunus replied. "Apparently, Taranus and the other kings aren't even considering that possibility. It'll be her greatest protection. Mider may eventually realize his mistake, but until then, her identity will be the easiest to conceal. Are there any other questions?"

No one spoke. Alaunus broke the mental connection with the other three elders and looked up from the fire. Apart from her horse tethered nearby, she was quite alone on the plains below the western face of the Mountain of Elohim.

After checking on her horse, she pulled her cloak tightly around her and lay down near the fire. Looking up at the stars, she felt the peace of Elohim all around her, calming her as she thought about the task she and the other elders had to accomplish.

CHAPTER 2

elenus stood by the banks of the lake on the night that the blood-red moons rose and crossed paths. He knew Alaunus was right about having to focus on the children of the prophecy, but it pained him to think of the other children that would die at the hands of the soldiers.

Looking up at the stars, he knew he had a task to perform. But Alastríona was a large place, and he wasn't sure where to look for the orphan that would be placed into his care. He calmed his mind and listened.

The answer finally came to him as an image in his mind. He saw a long caravan crossing the central plains to the south of the Mountain of Elohim, which was just across the lake from Belenus' farm.

Twice a year, a great caravan carried goods between Kelmarrow, the capital city of the Gallasia tribe, and Niamh, the capital city of the Mongán tribe. The next caravan would be leaving Kelmarrow in three months, taking it past the lake about three weeks later. Belenus understood that he needed to meet the caravan when it reached the northern edge of the lake.

The next morning, Belenus spoke to his factor, who was the person responsible for the day-to-day operation of the farm and for selling its wares at the region's markets. "Gareth, I'll be taking a trip away from the farm in a few months. I should be back in less than three weeks, but I can't be certain."

"Another rescue mission?" Gareth asked.

Belenus nodded. He had taken many trips to find orphans and bring them back to the farm in the thirty years since Gareth lost his parents and came to live on the farm. "For some reason, I'm feeling pulled to meet the caravan going from Kelmarrow to Niamh. I don't know why exactly, but I guess I'll find out when I get there."

"Why do you have to drive the wagon yourself this time?" Arawn's mother asked her husband a week before the caravan left Kelmarrow. "Can't you get one of the men to drive it and stay here with me?"

"My customers won't trust anyone but me to carry their cargo. I'll only be gone three months. You'll barely notice I'm away."

"I don't want to be here for three months taking care of the baby by myself," she protested. "You've heard the rumors. You know baby boys born around the time of the blood red moons are being murdered. So are their families. Who's going to protect us while you're away?"

Arawn's father thought about this for a moment. He had heard the rumors, but didn't realize his wife had heard them. He knew she'd never forgive him if he left her alone. Making a quick decision, he asked, "Why don't you come with me?"

"And bring the baby?"

"Of course," he said smoothly. "There'll be room in the wagon for you and the baby. We can even use one of the empty trunks to make a crib for him to sleep in during the day. You won't have to take care of him by yourself, and I'll be there to protect you both from any harm."

Arawn's mother thought about this. She had accompanied her husband on the caravans before, but she was worried about bringing a baby on such a long journey.

"Do you think the baby can handle the bouncing of the wagon?" she asked.

"I'll come up with a way to make it as comfortable for our baby as possible. Remember, he's going to grow up to be a wagon driver someday, and the sooner he gets used to the sounds and the movement, the sooner he'll be ready to help me drive."

His wife smiled. "If you can rig something for the baby to ride in on the trip, then we'll come with you."

Arawn's father kissed his wife. "I promise I will. Trust me. Everything will be just fine."

The caravan left Kelmarrow just before dawn. Arawn was asleep in a trunk just behind the driver's bench. The lid was open, and he was lying on a stack of blankets to absorb some of the jostling of the wagon. His mother looked at him from the driver's bench, happy to be with her husband.

As the sun rose higher in the sky, Arawn's father reached back and turned the trunk so that the lid blocked the sun. "You see?" he said, pointing to the sleeping baby. "He's going to be just fine back there."

Arawn's mother patted her husband on the hand.

Belenus rose before dawn, packed his supplies into two large bags designed to hang from his saddle, and walked across the compound to the stables. His horse, whom he named Thunder after the sound his hoofs made at full gallop, seemed anxious to leave. One Thunder was saddled, Belenus mounted his horse, and they rode north around the lake to meet the caravan.

There were wild flowers blooming everywhere on the central plains, covering the ground with various shades of green, red, blue, purple, white, yellow, and orange. In sharp contrast, the granite slopes and snow-capped peaks of the Mountain of Elohim, which looked immense even from this distance, reflected off the calm and glassy surface of the lake.

Belenus reached the northern bank and set up camp three days before the caravan was due to arrive. He knew that the caravan normally stopped at the lake to rest for at least a day. He sat calmly next to the lake. There was nothing to do but wait for the caravan.

As he sat, he saw glimpses in his mind of mounted troopers following the caravan. He saw the caravan stopping at the lake, and he saw the troopers attacking a wagon. As he watched the wagon, he sensed the name "Arawn." Belenus bowed his head in gratitude that he had been shown where he needed to go.

"What's that over there?" Arawn's mother asked, pointing to the northwest.

There was a cloud of dust that looked like it was approaching the caravan. "Looks like riders," he replied. "Lots of them."

"Could they be coming to rob us?" she asked, suddenly afraid for her baby.

"No, they look like soldiers."

"Are they an escort?" she inquired.

"We don't usually have an escort through this region," her husband replied.

"What do they want with the caravan?"

"I have no idea," he said, staring at the rapidly approaching dust cloud.

Belenus saw the caravan approaching. He tied Thunder to the branch of a nearby tree and walked toward the place where the wagon he had seen in his vision would be. He carried a shoulder-height walking stick but no other weapons. Belenus had never studied warfare and never carried any

10

weapon other than the walking stick, which, as he had proven on many occasions, was more than enough to keep him safe from harm.

"I don't recognize their uniforms, do you?" Arawn's mother asked.

The troopers were dressed in black and wore no badge or other device to show their tribe. "No," her husband replied.

As he watched the troopers, he saw them draw their swords. "Get in the back!" he said to her as he reached behind him and closed the lid on Arawn's trunk.

Belenus was about a hundred yards from the wagon when he heard the troopers riding toward the caravan from the north. He heard shouts from some of the caravan drivers, followed by screams as the troopers attacked. *The troopers are attacking the wagons. Mider must have told them which ones are carrying babies.* He broke into a run and arrived at the wagon just as three of the troopers were attacking.

He ducked under the lead horse of the wagon and swung his walking stick at the nearest trooper. The trooper, who was using his sword to attack the wagon's driver, slumped forward in his saddle as the walking stick hit the exposed back of his head. The trooper's horse went wild, racing off to the north with the unconscious trooper barely staying on its back.

The horse going wild alerted the other troopers to Belenus' presence. One of the troopers wheeled about and raised his sword to attack Belenus while the other trooper continued to attack the wagon's occupants. Belenus waited for the right moment to thrust his walking stick directly into the face of the approaching trooper. The trooper fell backward onto the ground, and his sword went flying off underneath the wagon. The trooper's horse ran away, and Belenus quickly moved toward the fallen trooper to see if he were still conscious.

The trooper lay on the ground without moving. When Belenus bent down to check on him, there was blood pooling underneath him. Belenus realized that the trooper was dead. His head had hit a rock when he fell, killing him instantly. Belenus quickly stood up and approached the last trooper, who was still attacking the wagon's occupants.

Belenus saw that the remaining trooper had already killed the driver. Belenus watched as the trooper's sword slid into the stomach of the woman trying to fight off her attacker with what looked like a large iron skillet. Belenus struck the trooper's sword arm with his walking stick and hit the trooper again in the neck. Dazed, the trooper turned to face Belenus, but all he saw was the walking stick as it plunged directly into his left eye. Screaming out in pain, he wheeled his horse around and took off toward the north, shouting to the other troopers to follow him.

The rest of the troopers broke off the attack and followed the trooper that Belenus had just injured.

Belenus ran forward to check on the occupants of the wagon. As he climbed up onto the driver's bench, he saw the murdered driver lying across the seat. Looking back, he saw the woman, still holding the large skillet, lying across several trunks. He heard shouts coming from all around as the members of the caravan inspected the damage from the troopers' attack, but he continued searching the wagon for any sign of a child.

Belenus stood still for a moment and closed his eyes. Stepping forward, he grasped the woman by the shoulder, moving her onto a different trunk. He opened the trunk she had been lying on, and there, wrapped in a blanket, was a baby boy. She had died protecting the child.

Belenus reached down and carefully lifted the child from the trunk. Closing the trunk's lid, he grabbed his walking stick and jumped down off the wagon to return to his campsite where Thunder was waiting.

No one noticed him as he walked back toward the lake, and no one saw him riding off to the south with the child. When the other caravan drivers discovered the dead man and woman on the wagon, Belenus was already several miles away.

Belenus traveled home much faster than he had traveled north to meet the caravan. He had a precious passenger with him who needed to reach the protection of the farm as soon as possible. Thunder seemed to know that it was important to travel much faster than before, and he crossed the distance to the farm in less than three days.

As Belenus rode into the compound, he looked down at the small baby sleeping in his arms. "You're home, Arawn, and you're safe. This is where you'll live until you're ready to seize your destiny and fulfill your part of the prophecy."

CHAPTER 3

ridamus was sitting on a large rock on the hill overlooking his smithy when he felt Alaunus break the connection with the rest of the elders. *One of the orphans is a girl!* He looked up at the Mountain of Elohim, wondering where he'd find the orphan he had been tasked with protecting.

He closed his eyes and saw the image of a young girl, with flaming red hair, hammering hot metal on the anvil in his smithy. He opened his eyes and smiled, knowing that the image was from Elohim.

I've never heard of a woman blacksmith before. The soldiers are looking for boys, and even if they were looking for girls, they'd never attack a blacksmith. This must be the reason she's been assigned to me. He found himself looking forward to teaching Cerridwen about jewelry-making and the other crafts of a blacksmith.

Jumping down from the rock, he returned to the smithy, confident that Elohim would show him where to find the young girl when the time came.

Every year, Tridamus loaded his creations into a large wagon and attended the artisan fairs around Alastríona. Even though people visited the smithy to purchase his wares, most of his annual sales and commission orders came from these fairs. The next fair was in four months near Danann, and Tridamus kept busy getting ready to attend.

"Are you sure you still want to go to the fair next week?" Cerridwen's father asked his wife.

She nodded. "I need to get out of the house and stretch my legs," she replied. "I've been cooped up here for months with Duncan and the twins. Besides, we never miss the fair and I don't want this to be the first year we don't go. You and I have both talked about getting a rug from that weaver we saw last year, and I want to find something for the nursery."

Her husband nodded. "Do you want to take the children or find someone to stay with them while we go?"

"I'd like to make it a family outing, if you don't mind," she replied. "We haven't been anywhere with the children since the twins were born, and I think it's time."

He kissed his wife. "Anything you want," he whispered in her ear.

Tridamus rode into the fairgrounds just outside Danann, the capital city of the Macruhan tribe. The city lay on the northern edge of the Great Forest, just south of the Great River that separated the territories of the Macruhan tribe from the Étaíne tribe.

As Tridamus arrived at the fairgrounds, he saw several of the other craftsmen, artisans, and vendors setting up their tents and displays. He waved and shouted to a few familiar faces as he guided the wagon to his usual spot along the southern edge of the fairgrounds.

Once Tridamus had his tent set up and his wagon unloaded, he made his rounds to see old friends and to meet new ones. Craftsmen, artisans, and vendors who attended fairs travelled widely around all of the territories of Alastríona, and fairs were a great place to share and learn information about what was happening across the world.

As Tridamus moved from tent to tent, he heard several stories that confirmed what Airmid had said. Boys were disappearing or being killed along with their families across the territories. The only thing that these boys had in common was that they were all born in the same week as the rising of the blood-red moons. He even heard people speculate that someone was trying to make sure that the prophecy couldn't be fulfilled.

He returned to his tent and set up his traveling forge so he could take custom orders during the fair. He'd be at the fair for two weeks, and there were typically several orders that he could fill before it was time to return home.

The organizers of the fair always made sure that there was plenty of wood and charcoal available. Tridamus brought back to his campsite enough wood and charcoal for the next three days before sitting down and eating a light supper. Once the sounds of the other craftsmen, artisans, and vendors faded in the darkness, Tridamus checked his area one more time before going into his tent to get some rest.

It was well before dawn the next morning when Tridamus woke up from a dream. He was at the fair, and a young family was watching him make some jewelry. The father, who had shoulder-length reddish blonde hair, held a baby boy in his left arm. His right hand held onto an older boy to keep the boy from touching any of the shiny things around Tridamus' area. The mother, who had pale skin and long, straight red hair pulled back by a leather clasp, held a baby girl with bright red hair. The girl couldn't have been more than a few months old.

Tridamus held up the piece he had been working on so the family could see it. Suddenly, a shrouded figure came up behind the young family. A blade flashed in his hand as he stabbed the father, the baby boy, and the older son several times in quick, controlled thrusts. The figure pulled the mother's head back, exposing her throat. She tossed her baby to Tridamus just as the blade slid home. Tridamus saw the life go out of her eyes as he caught the baby. The figure ran away and left Tridamus standing there with the baby in his arms and the family lying dead on the ground. He looked at the baby girl's face, and the name "Cerridwen" came to his thought. The baby girl spoke to him and said, "Find me, Tridamus."

Shaking the image of the dream from his mind, Tridamus knew he'd find Cerridwen at the fair. It wasn't the first time he had been given instructions in the form of a dream, but there had never been such a sense of urgency before.

He got up and started building the fire in his traveling forge.

Over the next week, Tridamus did more business than usual with the patrons of the fair. His swords and armor sold well, and many of his commissions were for more of his swords and daggers. His jewelry also sold quickly, and he spent several hours a day making more to keep up with demand. While he worked, he watched for any sign of the family from his dream.

"Where's Duncan?" Cerridwen's mother asked.

"He was just here a moment ago." Cerridwen's father looked around and shouted, "Duncan!"

He heard a giggling sound coming from under the bed in the next room. He ran into the room, reached under the bed, and pulled out a struggling Duncan.

"I swear, Duncan, if you run away today I'll leave you at the fair and let one of the vendors sell you."

Duncan just giggled and tried to squirm away from his father. Cerridwen's father picked him up and gripped him tightly.

"I think we're ready," he said when he rejoined his wife. Cerridwen's mother was holding the twins and was standing at the door. "Do you want me to take one of the babies?" he asked as he followed her outside.

15

"Not yet," she replied. "I need to get used to walking with them. But I may need you to take one of them if I start getting tired."

Her husband nodded, and the family started walking to the city gates and the fair beyond.

On the second-to-last day of the fair, Tridamus put out the fire in the forge so it would have time to cool down before he had to load it back into the wagon for the trip home. He still had a few pieces to sell, and the remaining work on his commissions didn't require the forge to be lit. He spent most of the day wrapping the handles of the swords with leather and wire to make them easier to grip, stitching the leather scabbards for the swords and daggers, and braiding gold and silver wires to create intricate jewelry designs that looked like knots.

Toward the end of the day, he saw familiar faces approaching in the crowd. It was the family from his dream. They showed no sign of recognizing him, but he knew them instantly.

When they arrived at his area, Tridamus showed them several of his pieces while trying to appear calm. When he heard the baby girl whimper slightly, he asked, "What is her name?"

"Cerridwen," the mother answered, smiling as she pulled back the corner of the deep green blanket wrapping Cerridwen so Tridamus could see her face. "And this is her twin brother Callum, and her big brother Duncan," she added, pointing to the baby in the father's arm and the older boy trying to break free from his father's grip.

"Beautiful names for beautiful children," Tridamus said pleasantly, hiding the fact that he already knew the girl's name.

The mother continued looking at the jewelry made with the braided metal. Tridamus suggested several pieces, scanning the surrounding crowds for any sign of the assassin from his dream. The mother selected a necklace made of pale gold with several knots worked into the design. Tridamus walked around and put it on her neck while the father, releasing his hold on Duncan, handed his pouch of coins to Tridamus.

Tridamus reached into the leather pouch and pulled out the correct sum for the necklace. He was about to hand the pouch back to the father when Duncan started running toward the side of the fair opposite the city of Danann. The father took off after Duncan, and the mother, still holding Cerridwen in her arms, followed her husband and escaping son.

Something told Tridamus that he needed to follow the family, so he put the coin pouch in a pocket, grabbed one of his knives and thrust it into his belt, and threw a canvas covering over his remaining items before setting off after the young family.

The sun was getting low in the horizon as Tridamus searched for the family. He grew increasingly concerned when he entered the part of the fair where some of the more unscrupulous vendors had set up their tents. These were the vendors who were mainly thieves and charlatans, promising the highest quality but selling the cheapest junk imaginable. Tridamus knew that this was no place for a young family after sunset.

Even over the sound of the crowd, Tridamus heard something that sounded like a whimper coming from his left. He turned and followed the sound into an area where two rows of tents backed onto each other. In the low light, Tridamus saw a figure wearing a black traveling cloak and hood standing over a grisly scene.

The young mother's throat was cut, and she lay dead on the ground next to the body of her son, Duncan. She was still clutching Cerridwen tightly in her arms. Her husband, bleeding from several wounds, tried unsuccessfully to shield Callum from the assassin, but the assassin continued to slash at father and son with a large knife.

Without hesitating, Tridamus pulled out his own knife from his belt, took aim, and threw it directly at the exposed back of the hooded assassin. The assassin, who must have somehow sensed the knife, quickly rolled out of the way, jumped to his feet, and ran off.

Tridamus raced forward. He checked Duncan and the mother first, confirming that they were dead. The mother's face looked almost peaceful, but the blood on her new necklace made the metal look crimson in the fading light. Looking over at the father and Callum, he saw that the baby boy was dead. The father's eyes began to close as his life drained out of him onto the ground. A moment later, he joined his wife and sons in death.

Tridamus carefully took Cerridwen from her mother and made sure that the baby girl wasn't injured, grateful that the assassin didn't understand that Cerridwen was the orphan in the prophecy. Seeing that she was uninjured, he stood up, retrieved his knife, and hurried back to his tent with the baby girl in his arms.

When he returned to his tent, he looked around and made a quick decision. He set Cerridwen down on his bed and began loading everything into the wagon. He wouldn't wait for the last day of the fair as he normally did so he could deliver his completed commissions. He'd leave immediately.

The vendor from the next tent came over to see what was going on, and Tridamus arranged for the vendor to deliver the rest of the completed commissions the next morning. Tridamus was glad that he always insisted on payment in full when patrons placed commission orders so there'd be no issues with collecting the money he was due.

17

Once all the tools and the few unsold items were loaded, Tridamus rigged a hammock in the front of the wagon for Cerridwen. He gently wrapped her in an extra blanket to keep her warm in the cool night air and placed her in the hammock. He took down his tent and loaded it and the bed into the wagon.

By the time the sun rose over the fairgrounds, he was several miles away traveling east along the Great River toward the Mountain of Elohim, which was visible even from this great distance. It was over three hundred miles from the fair to the Mountain of Elohim, and another one hundred and fifty miles to the smithy. It would take close to three weeks to get home, and Tridamus made sure that his remaining swords and daggers were within easy reach in case something happened along the way.

CHAPTER 4

emausus was standing on the roof of his tower, staring at the stars in the sky, when he felt Alaunus break the mental connection with the rest of the elders. As he stared into the night, he felt a sudden desire to travel to Athramail. He was grateful for the sign telling him where to find Amaethon. He immediately prepared to leave at first light.

Nemausus arrived at Athramail during the Dunmaine's annual Harvest Festival, which was when the bakers and brewers that made the Dunmaine famous would create their most elaborate delicacies. He found a room at one of the nicer inns near the river and began searching the city for any signs of Amaethon.

Amaethon's father had been busy all week with the Harvest Festival. He had to leave early in the mornings to prepare the day's breads and pastries, but he always made it home in time for supper and his evening walks with his wife and son.

Toward the end of the festival, he arrived home, ate a quick supper, and helped his wife bundle their son for the evening walk. They left their house and walked to the center of the city, where revelers were enjoying the latest creations of the city's breweries.

The noise made Amaethon fussy, so they walked toward the river where the streets were less crowded. Neither of Amaethon's parents noticed a person wearing a black hooded cloak and following them through the crowds.

As they walked through the city, Amaethon's father looked at his son and saw that the baby was falling asleep. He smiled at his wife, and they started walking back to their house. They were about to pass a side street when someone grabbed them roughly from behind and forced them into the dark alleyway. Once they were away from the prying eyes of witnesses, their attacker pushed them to the ground.

Amaethon's father hit his head on the ground and lay there moaning. His wife clutched their baby tightly and looked up at the person standing over them. She saw something long and shiny in his hands. It caught the light, and she saw that it was a wicked-looking knife.

Nemausus had just left the home of one of his former students, the chief healer to the King of the Dunmaine tribe, and was heading back to the inn where he was staying. He reached the street where the inn was located, but as he started to turn to the left to make his way through the crowd of revelers, he felt a strong urging to turn right instead. Nemausus was accustomed to feeling the pull of that inner voice and instinctively turned right.

As he walked toward the river, he felt that familiar sensation telling him he was near someone who had the gift of sorcery. It was a stronger sensation than he had felt before. As he approached a side street, he sensed that the person he sought was close by.

Looking down the alleyway, he saw a shadowy figure, wearing a hood that covered its head and face, standing over something lying on the ground. He couldn't tell if the figure were male or female. As he approached to see what was going on, he saw the flash of a knife blade in the figure's hand and watched as the blade was plunged several times into what was on the ground.

"What's going on there?" Nemausus shouted. He ran forward toward the figure, and with a thought, he sent the knife flying out of the figure's hand.

The figure whirled around and saw Nemausus approaching. Unable to reach the knife, it stood and ran down the side street in the opposite direction. Nemausus focused on the fleeing figure, intending to use sorcery to pull the figure back, but he felt a jolt of energy go through him like lightning had struck him. It was the sensation caused by someone using sorcery to block him.

The figure disappeared in the distance. Nemausus wanted to pursue the figure, but he felt a strong compulsion to remain where he was. *The attacker is clearly a sorcerer, and it wouldn't be a good thing to get into a sorcery duel here in the city. The Dunmaine don't like magic and don't trust those who practice magic in their midst. I don't want to find myself banned from the city because someone sees me using sorcery.*

As Nemausus retrieved the knife, he noticed a bundle on the ground. He reached for the bundle, picked it up, and felt movement. He opened the bundle and saw a baby boy inside – no more than a month

20

old. He quickly rewrapped the baby to keep him warm.

A young man and woman lay on the ground nearby. Nemausus carefully set down the knife and the baby, and he checked to see if the baby's parents were still alive. The man was dead from a stab wound to the heart. The woman was still alive, but Nemausus could feel her life quickly slipping away.

"My baby?" she gasped, clutching Nemausus' cloak with a trembling hand.

"He's here, and he's safe," Nemausus replied, trying to comfort her in the final moments of her life. "What is his name?"

"Amaethon," she said in a whisper.

"Do you know who attacked you?" Nemausus asked.

The woman shook her head. Nemausus heard the woman gasping for air and knew that she wouldn't last much longer.

He placed a hand on her forehead and concentrated. He attempted to read her thoughts to learn as much as possible about the couple and their attacker. He felt her slipping away, but in that moment, he saw her entire life. He watched as she met the young man lying dead next to her, joined with him, and gave birth to their first child. Neither she nor her husband had any other family. He learned nothing that would help identify the attacker. He felt her last breath and knew that she was gone. He removed his hand from her forehead and closed her eyes.

Straightening up, Nemausus was suddenly aware that he still felt the sensation of being near someone with the gift of sorcery. He had assumed the sensation was because of the shadowy figure, but looking down, he realized that the baby was the source. He picked up the baby and stared into his eyes. The baby looked back and smiled at Nemausus, drooling slightly.

"Well, Amaethon, you're all alone in the world now," Nemausus said, gently wiping the drool away with a corner of the swaddling cloth. "I was supposed to find you today, but I'm sorry you lost your parents. Since you have no family to take you in, you'll come and live with me. I'll teach you everything I know to help you fulfill your destiny."

Nemausus picked up the knife again and looked at it carefully. It was unlike anything Nemausus had seen before. Normally, he could sense things about whoever had just handled an object, but for some reason he couldn't sense anything clearly from this knife. The images were all blurred and shifted rapidly. Nemausus realized that strong magic infused into the knife was preventing him from discerning anything about its owner.

I'll need to study this knife more carefully. He put it in the pouch on his belt and left the narrow street. He quickly walked back to the inn, collected his belongings, and left the city to return to the safety of his tower.

CHAPTER 5

ridamus was of average height and had unusually broad shoulders. The years of forging and hammering metal had made his upper body muscles huge and his skin well-calloused. His hair and long beard were the color of fire, but there were silver streaks running throughout. His face had a somewhat leathery look that was common among people who had spent years working near the tremendous heat of a blacksmith's forge.

The smithy where he brought Cerridwen to live stood at the base of the Mountain of Elohim, between the eastern face and the Great River that flows through the middle of Alastríona from the Okeanós Sea in the west to the large lake in the Mongán tribe's territory. The smithy was comprised of three buildings around a square courtyard. Tridamus' house was across the courtyard from his workshop. Between the house and the workshop, forming the third side of the open courtyard, were the stables where Tridamus kept the wagon that he took to fairs and the team of horses he used to pull the wagon. Just behind the workshop were several piles of metallic ore and other materials that Tridamus used to make the metals he needed for tools, implements, blades, and armor. Miners from across Alastríona delivered the ore on a regular basis so Tridamus always had a good supply on hand when he needed it.

Tridamus thought it was strange to have a baby at his smithy. He knew that he had to keep a close watch on Cerridwen, but he also knew that there was no one else around to watch her while he was working.

Shortly after he returned from rescuing Cerridwen at the fair, he came up with what he thought was a workable plan. He sectioned off a corner of his workshop away from the forge where she could sleep and play while he worked.

He constructed the area like an oversized stall. The solid wood walls on either side were as high as Tridamus' chest. The end facing the forge had a gate made of iron that Tridamus could easily see through, but would keep Cerridwen from crawling out. Tridamus also rigged a hinged wooden flap to the ceiling that he could lower over the gated end of the stall to muffle the sound of Tridamus working when Cerridwen was sleeping.

Several of Tridamus' neighbors and regular patrons noticed the changes to the workshop. Tridamus usually lowered the flap when people stopped by, but he knew people were bound to discover the baby girl that had come to live with him eventually. He decided he'd try to pass her off as his niece if anyone asked. Tridamus and Cerridwen both had red hair, which made the story more plausible.

It took several weeks for life to settle into a new routine around the smithy. Tridamus typically worked from sunrise to sundown, but now he had to stop frequently to check on the baby. He didn't mind feeding her, but changing her diapers was another matter altogether.

"Why did you have to be orphaned when you were just a baby?" he lamented one evening as he changed her diaper for the fifth time that day. "Why couldn't you have come to me when you were six or seven?"

Cerridwen looked up at Tridamus with a big smile and reached for his beard. He pulled his head back and she let out a little laugh. Tridamus smiled and forgot about being frustrated with the little orphan. He finished changing her and pulled up her blanket to keep her warm.

Cerridwen cooed softly as Tridamus gently patted her head. "Sleep well, little one," he whispered as she drifted off to sleep.

For the first several months, Cerridwen spent most of the day sleeping in the crib Tridamus had fashioned in her stall. She ate and had her diaper changed frequently, but in between those times, she lay quietly in her crib. Tridamus thought it was strange that she could sleep through the hammering and other sounds of a blacksmith at work, but it seemed to sooth her. She was usually the most fussy when the workshop was quiet. Tridamus had to create a mechanical noisemaker for her bedroom, powered by counterweights and pulleys, so she'd sleep through the night.

As the months passed, Tridamus noticed that Cerridwen was sleeping less during the day. She lay in her crib without crying unless she was hungry, needed her diaper changed, or wanted Tridamus to pick her up. He also noticed that she was watching him work. When he used the bellows, she'd get a look of wonder in her face, and when he hammered hot metal on the anvil, she'd grin and laugh. In time, Tridamus looked at having a baby at the smithy as a joy rather than a burden.

Cerridwen learned to walk much faster than Tridamus expected. She also learned to climb. After Tridamus caught her climbing up the iron gate at the end of her stall for the tenth time, he made some changes to the gate to keep her from reaching the top and falling out.

Tridamus decided it was time to learn a new skill: making toys to keep Cerridwen busy and happy. His first efforts were rather plain, but as he gained more practice, his toys became both intricate and beautiful.

In time, toys filled Cerridwen's stall. As he worked, Tridamus would look over to her stall and see her sitting on a blanket and playing games with her toys that he couldn't figure out but evidently made perfect sense to her.

On more than one occasion, he saw her with a stick imitating him shaping hot metal with his hammer. Finally, he made her a toy hammer and a small anvil made of wood. After that, he frequently heard her hitting things with her little hammer.

One afternoon, he heard her hammering and turned to look at what she was doing. She had one of her toys on the anvil and was hammering it with a look of deep concentration.

Is that how she sees me when I'm working? He tried not to laugh at the toddler sharing his workshop.

Cerridwen looked up at Tridamus and saw him watching her. She held up the toy and smiled at him. Then she put the toy back on the anvil and started hammering it again.

Tridamus chuckled and went back to his own hammering.

Cerridwen eventually reached the age where she was too big to spend all day in the stall. Tridamus removed the gate and took down the two walls. He moved most of the toys into her bedroom, but the toys that looked like Tridamus' tools stayed in the workshop.

"You're old enough now that you can be in the house if you want," he told her when he showed her the changes to the workshop, "or you can be in the courtyard. If you want to be in here, that's fine as long as you keep away from the forge and don't touch any of my tools or any of the pieces I'm working on. But whatever you do, don't leave the smithy unless I'm with you. Okay?"

"Yes, Tridamus," Cerridwen replied.

Tridamus patted her on the head and turned to start heating the forge. When he looked around a few minutes later, he saw her sitting on a large stool where her stall had been, swinging her legs and watching him work.

"Don't you want to go and play?" he asked.

"I want to watch you, Tridamus," she replied, still swinging her legs.

He shrugged with amusement and went back to work.

There weren't many people Cerridwen's age who lived near the smithy, so she didn't have playmates to spend time with during the days. Tridamus knew that the fewer people who knew about her, the better. But he was sad that his life as a blacksmith meant that she didn't have the chance to interact with other children.

Cerridwen didn't seem to mind. She was hungry for knowledge, and it was clear to Tridamus that she wanted to learn how to be a blacksmith. He had never trained a woman before, but he found himself looking forward to the day when she was old enough to begin learning his craft.

As she grew older, Tridamus wondered how much Cerridwen had learned just by watching him work. When she turned seven, he sat down with her and showed her the art of making jewelry by braiding wires of gold and silver together into knotwork designs. Cerridwen had slender and nimble fingers, and was soon copying his designs. Her first efforts were rough, but he was patient, and she was a fast learner.

Just before her eighth birthday, she came into the workshop and walked to the table where Tridamus kept the gold and silver wire. Looking around, she noticed that Tridamus wasn't there.

"Tridamus?" she called.

"Out here," she heard him reply.

She followed his voice outside. Tridamus strode out of the stables with his arms filled with tanned animal hides. He carried them into the workshop with Cerridwen following close behind.

"What's that?" she asked.

"Leather. I have to make some scabbards for the blades I've been working on before the patrons come to pick them up.

"Can I help?"

Tridamus put the leather down and looked at her. "It's not easy. Do you think you're ready?"

"I don't know. I've never tried."

"Well, let me show you how it's done, and we'll see if you're ready."

He showed her where he kept the patterns for each type of blade. The knives used to cut the leather were large and sharp, and Tridamus wouldn't let Cerridwen handle them. Once the pieces were cut, he showed her how he made the spacers that would keep the blade from cutting into the scabbards, and how the scabbards and spacers were laced together with long, thin leather laces.

26

Tridamus reached over and pulled out the small chest that was underneath the table where they were working. When he opened it, Cerridwen saw a number of intricate tools and small mallets.

"What are these?" she asked with wide eyes.

"I use these to put designs into the leather before I stitch up the leather pieces." He picked up one tool and showed it to her. "This is my stamp. I put it on every belt, scabbard, jerkin, or any other leather item I make."

He demonstrated by placing the carved end on the leather and hitting the other end with one of the mallets. It left an indentation in the leather that Cerridwen recognized immediately.

Tridamus reached for a piece of scrap leather and put it on the table. "You try it," he said, handing her the mallet.

Cerridwen selected one of the other tools and hit it with the mallet the way Tridamus showed her. He nodded approvingly. He showed her the rest of the tools and demonstrated how to use multiple tools to make complex patterns and designs.

Cerridwen watched Tridamus make scabbards for the rest of the day. There were several pieces of scrap leather left over when he was finished, and Tridamus gave them to her and told her to practice making designs with the tools.

Over the next several years, Cerridwen proved herself a worthy student. She continued to be a quick learner and soon was making small pieces of jewelry and tooled leather scabbards. Tridamus noticed that she had a look of complete concentration while she worked, and he appreciated that she took her work seriously. He was amused at some of her early work, but as her skills improved, so did the quality and intricacy of the pieces she created.

Each morning, Tridamus sat with her and told her what she needed to do that day. She gathered the materials and tools she needed, organized them so that everything was within easy reach, and prepared her worktable. Her long red hair often got in her way, so she had a piece of scrap leather cord that she used to tie her hair back. Once her hair was in place, she was ready to work.

Most days around the workshop, she wore loose-fitting leather trousers to protect her legs from flying metal. She also wore a leather halter that kept her arms free to work. Even though she worked with tools every day, her hands didn't have the same roughness as Tridamus' hands did. He had made her a pair of leather work gloves that she always wore, and those protected her hands.

As Cerridwen approached her eleventh birthday, she noticed changes happening to her body. Tridamus had explained them to her, but knowing what was happening and seeing it reflected in the burnished metal oval on her wall were two different things.

She had just finished bathing one evening, and as she combed her hair in the lamplight, she looked at her reflection. Her arms were strong and muscular, but her fingers were still long and slender in spite of the work she did with them each day. Her hips were beginning to widen slightly, and her chest was gaining curves that had never been there before. Even her face was beginning to take on a leaner look. She wasn't self-conscious about her body at all, and she found that she liked the feminine features that were starting to develop.

The craftsmanship of Cerridwen's jewelry pieces weren't quite as good as Tridamus', but her designs were more intricate and sought after. Tridamus always took her with him to the various fairs around Alastríona to keep an eye on her and protect her, but after her eleventh birthday he let her set up a separate area to show and sell her own work. Patrons loved her creations, and she usually sold out quickly. They made a good team, but Tridamus knew she really wanted to learn how to use the forge and anvil to make swords and armor.

As Cerridwen's feminine features continued to develop and show, Tridamus noticed that the boys at the fairs were paying too much attention to her. Cerridwen didn't understand why they wouldn't leave her alone, and she found it very annoying. Tridamus knew that he needed to explain what was happening, but he wasn't sure how to start the conversation.

Tridamus was wrestling with these thoughts as he and Cerridwen sat at the table one evening eating dinner. *Maybe the conversation can wait another few years.*

"No it can't," a voice inside his head stated firmly.

Tridamus' shoulders dropped. He took a deep breath and looked across the table. "Cerridwen, there's something we need to talk about."

Young Cerridwen Learning the Blacksmith Trade

CHAPTER 6

ive years after he came to live with Nemausus, Amaethon sat in the grass below the round stone tower that had become his home. He glanced up at the window of Nemausus' study, wondering if Nemausus were sitting at his desk or pacing around as he often did.

The tower was located on a hill to the southwest of the Mountain of Elohim and north of the Great Forest along the eastern bank of the river that marks the border of the Gallasia tribe's territory.

Nemausus' study was on the top level of the tower. This is where he taught, wrote, meditated, and relaxed. On the far side of his study from the stairs was a ladder that led to the roof. The roof was surrounded by a stone wall and a walkway that went all around the outer edge of the roof. From the walkway, one could see for miles in every direction, and there was a clear view of the night sky.

Stairs built along the inside wall ran up all four levels of the tower. Amaethon's room and a classroom were on the third level. There were guestrooms and rooms for studying on the second level. The kitchen and dining area filled the first level. The stables were in a separate building built just behind the tower.

Amaethon practiced making rocks levitate the way Nemausus taught him. The sunlight hit his blond hair and made it shine almost white. Amaethon had the typical Dunmaine features: light blue eyes that always looked inquisitive, blonde hair like his parents, bushy eyebrows, and a strong chin and jawline that made him look older than he was. He was a handsome boy.

The afternoon shadows were beginning to lengthen when Amaethon looked up and saw Nemausus standing there. The sorcerer, a tall man with piercing blue eyes, black and silver hair, and a close-cropped beard, was looking up at the sun. Amaethon looked up and saw one of the moons passing in front of the sun, making the sky go dark.

"What's happening, Master?" Amaethon cried out.

"It's something that happens every now and then," Nemausus replied casually, smiling at his young student. "There's no harm, and it'll be over soon. It's no different than when I walk between you and a candle at night. There's a moment of darkness, and you see the light again once I've passed. Only this time, one of the moons is crossing in front of the sun. When it passes, the sunlight will come again. You're not afraid of a bird flying in front of the sun, are you? Don't be afraid of a moon moving in front of the sun either."

Amaethon felt better, and when the sun reappeared several minutes later, Nemausus motioned for Amaethon to continue with his studies.

"When was the last time that happened?" Amaethon asked as he made four rocks rise in the air and hover just over his head.

"Partial eclipses like this occur every couple of years," Nemausus replied. "That's when a moon crosses in front of the sun but doesn't block all of the sun's light. There was a full eclipse about five years ago when one of the moons completely covered the sun, and it was like nighttime all around."

"Do the moons ever cross each other?" Amaethon asked. Alastríona had two moons that circled the world from different directions. Amaethon was curious to know if the paths of the two moons ever crossed, making it look like there was only one moon in the sky.

"Interestingly enough, that also happened five years ago. In fact, it happened on your birthday. That was the first time in over a century it had happened."

Even though Amaethon was only five, he sensed that there was something unusual about a total eclipse of the sun and the two moons crossing each other so close to the day of his birth. Ever since he had started studying with Nemausus, Amaethon discovered that he knew much more than he should for someone his age. And he could sense when someone was telling the truth and when someone was hiding something.

He was a quick learner, but it was as if he already knew the material Nemausus was teaching, which both pleased Nemausus and confused him. No other student had learned things so quickly, and for a five-year-old to be so gifted was remarkable indeed.

Amaethon was making the levitating rocks move around in a circle when Nemausus picked him up. The rocks fell, and Amaethon laughed in delight as Nemausus put him on his shoulders and walked out into the

31

fields below the tower.

When they reached the top of a nearby hill, Nemausus let Amaethon climb down from his shoulders. Amaethon looked up at Nemausus and saw a strange look on his face. "Did something special happen when the moons crossed five years ago, Master?"

"You mean besides you being born?" Nemausus asked.

Amaethon nodded.

"As a matter of fact, something quite remarkable did happen that day. The moons were red as blood when they rose. No one had ever seen two red moons before."

"Red moons? Was it a sign?"

Nemausus nodded. "Yes, it was a sign. We're on the edge of great things happening, and there's a lot we need to do to get ready. I need to speed up your training. There's so much to do and so little time left to get it all done."

"I'm to be part of the great things, Master?" Amaethon asked with a sense of wonder in his voice.

"Possibly," Nemausus replied. "Who knows? Maybe you're going to be right in the middle of it all."

Nemausus picked up Amaethon and walked back to the tower.

Over the next several years, Nemausus found his young student to be hungry for the opportunity to learn. Nemausus taught lessons that he rarely taught to students twice Amaethon's age. The lessons weren't just about magic and the control of the elements. Nemausus taught how to calculate the exact position of the stars and the moons of Alastríona a hundred years into the future, he taught about how the gods had created the world and had amused themselves by pitting the tribes against each other, and he taught the healing of both man and beast.

Nemausus' student proved to be an excellent scholar, but it was Amaethon's creativity and sense of humor that Nemausus enjoyed the most. Rather than begin a new lesson with the steps needed to follow to solve a problem, he'd give Amaethon the problem and see what kind of solution he'd devise.

Several months after Amaethon's twelfth birthday, Nemausus summoned his student to the kitchen.

"We need more water," he said, pointing to the large wooden casks along the far wall of the stone kitchen used to store water. "I need you to fill up the two water casks with water from the stream."

The stream, which connected to the river that formed the border of the Gallasia tribe's territory, was only two hundred yards down the hill from the tower. Nemausus filled the casks at least once a week, but in the twelve years that Amaethon had lived in the tower, he had never seen how Nemausus did it.

"Do you have any questions?" Nemausus asked, trying to hide his amusement.

"When do you need the casks filled, Master?"

"Before nightfall. Do you know how you're going to get it done?"

Amaethon shook his head. "Not yet. If I can't figure it out by mid-afternoon, I'll come and find you."

Nemausus nodded and turned to walk up the stairs to his study.

How am I going to fill the casks with water? Amaethon had asked himself this same question twenty times.

He had been staring at the casks for almost thirty minutes, but no ideas were coming to him. Amaethon knew that Nemausus would give him hints when he was stuck trying to solve a problem, but only when the task was particularly difficult would Nemausus have to provide the complete solution. This was the normal game the two played at least once a week, and Amaethon enjoyed finding solutions to problems on his own and presenting them to Nemausus for his judgment.

Amaethon realized he was thirsty and decided to get himself a drink. He reached a ladle into one of the casks and filled it with water. As he poured the ladle into a tankard, an idea came to him.

If I can pour water out of the cask, can't I pour water into the cask?

Amaethon smiled, *Okay. How do I pour water into the cask? Do I levitate the ladle and send it back and forth between here and the stream until it brings back enough water to fill the casks? That'll take all night.*

He had another idea. *What if I levitate the water and bring it up here?*

He concentrated on the stream below the tower and tried to get water to rise from the stream and fly up the hill. But as soon as the water rose out of the stream, it flew in all directions. Amaethon couldn't figure out how to keep the water together, and after several attempts, he abandoned that idea.

Amaethon stared at the casks for several minutes, thinking about the problem.

What if I take the casks down to the stream, fill them down there, and bring them back here already filled?

Amaethon cleared his mind and concentrated on one of the casks. It wobbled for a moment before lifting off its base, floating toward Amaethon, and coming to a stop in the center of the room. Amaethon shifted his focus, and soon the second cask was hovering beside the first one.

Amaethon smiled. *I think this will work.* He opened the front door of the tower and walked outside with the two casks following him.

Amaethon led the casks down to the stream, feeling satisfied with his solution to the problem. But when he reached the stream, another thought hit him. *How do I get the water into the casks?*

When Nemausus reached the top floor of the tower, he looked around the room. His desk stood on the far side of the study from the stairs, but there were several smaller tables, chairs, and cabinets around the room. Even though the room was quite large, there were few surfaces not covered with tools, scrolls and papers, and other items he kept handy in case he ever needed them.

As Nemausus walked over to his desk, he noticed something catch the light from underneath a stack of papers on the table closest to him. Reaching for the papers, he saw a black-handled knife underneath, where he had left it twelve years earlier when he brought Amaethon home to live with him. He picked it up and sat down in his chair behind his desk, looking at the knife intently.

Nemausus had always intended to study the knife more closely when he had time, but over the years, he kept putting it off until eventually he forgot about it. It was as if the knife itself were keeping him from trying to uncover its secrets. He sensed Amaethon still in the kitchen and returned his attention to the knife.

It was a simple knife with a sharp curved blade and a black wooden handle. Normally, Nemausus had no difficulty sensing information about whoever had last used an object. Most humans tended to leave a mental imprint on things that they touched or handled, but for some reason, the wielder of this knife didn't. Nemausus knew that only someone highly trained in the magical arts could keep from leaving a clear imprint behind, and Nemausus was determined to discover more about this person.

For the next several hours, Nemausus wrestled mentally with the knife. Every time he thought he had broken through the knife's protections, the magic infused in the knife threw up another shield to block Nemausus from learning about the knife's previous owner.

The shadows were getting longer when Nemausus realized that he could no longer sense Amaethon in the area, but he felt another sensation – the same sensation that he had when he first found Amaethon. Looking out the window of his study toward the hill where he and Amaethon had watched the partial eclipse seven years earlier, he saw a shadowy figure.

Even from that distance, Nemausus felt the presence of the shadowy figure and felt its thoughts reaching out to search the tower. He felt a strange tingling in the hand that was holding the knife, and when he turned to look, the knife suddenly vaporized into a fine white powder and disappeared. Nemausus quickly turned back to the window, but the shadowy figure had disappeared, and Nemausus could no longer feel its presence anywhere in the area. He climbed the ladder to the roof and looked out in all directions with his eyes and his mind. His mind touched on Amaethon down by the stream, but he couldn't detect anyone else for several miles. He stayed on the roof, searching for several more minutes, before turning to climb back down to his study.

Movement coming from the stream caused him to stop and remain on the roof. He leaned on the wall and watched intently. Several minutes later, he saw Amaethon coming up the hill. He had the two casks with him, but they were floating about two feet off the ground on either side of him. Amaethon's outstretched arms directed each of the casks up the hill, and it was clear that he was concentrating hard on what he was doing.

Nemausus appreciated the simplicity of Amaethon's solution. He chuckled and left the roof of the tower so he could meet Amaethon when he reached the kitchen.

Nemausus was sitting at the kitchen table when Amaethon arrived and began mentally directing the two casks back to their bases. He was concentrating so hard on the task that he missed the fact that Nemausus was in the room with him, watching him the whole time.

Once he had returned the two casks to their proper places, Amaethon turned and saw Nemausus. He sat down across the table from his master, feeling quite tired and successful at the same time.

"I filled the casks with water as you asked, Master," he said, breathing heavily from the exertion.

"I see that. What made you decide to take the casks down to the stream? Why not just bring the water here?"

"I tried that," Amaethon explained, "but I couldn't figure out how to the get water to stay together. I could get water out of the stream, but it flew apart when I tried to move it. So I decided to take the casks down to the stream. I levitated them like you taught me, and that worked fine."

Nemausus nodded.

"Master, may I ask how you do it?"

"Certainly. I just bring the water up here."

"How do you keep it from flying all over the place?"

"I mentally create something that'll hold the water and carry it back in that. The water needs to be contained, but that doesn't mean you can't create the container in your mind and use it. Things you create in your mind can be just as real, just as tangible as you want them to be. Tomorrow, I want you to try that. I want you to take all the water in the casks back to the stream, and bring the water back and refill the casks without using anything other than your mind. I want you to keep doing it until you can do it without any difficulty."

"Yes, Master."

The next day, Amaethon rose early, prepared a quick breakfast for Nemausus and himself, and started working on how to move water without using the wooden casks.

If I can't use the casks as the container for the water, and using a ladle is still too small, what should I use for the container?

Staring at the casks, an idea came to him. *Why not build a cask in my mind to carry the water?*

Amaethon looked at the cask and thought about how barrel-makers built casks. *If I don't construct it in my mind just right, the water will leak out. Maybe I should try to make a smaller container until I get everything figured out, and then I can make a full-size cask to move the water.*

For his first attempt, he tried to make a container the size of a bucket. It took a while to concentrate enough to make a bucket in his mind that was complete and could hold water.

He built the image in his mind the way Nemausus had taught him, but this was different from creating an illusion that only appeared to be real, which was something Amaethon had mastered years earlier. He had to build the mental image of the bucket just like a real bucket. Every seam had to be sealed, each stave had to be tight against the next, and the bands had to be tight to help maintain the tension between the staves so that the bucket wouldn't leak.

Once Amaethon had the bucket ready to test, there was one more problem to tackle. *How do I get the water into the bucket?*

Amaethon tried to have the water fly into the bucket, but instead it went everywhere like it had at the stream. He tried two more times and watched bitterly as the water sprayed all over the walls and floor of the kitchen for the third time. *All right, clearly I'm not getting anywhere trying to make water fly. I guess I can dip the bucket into one of the casks and lift the water out that way.*

After a few mental adjustments, he had a bucket that could hold the water. Amaethon was elated at his success. He mentally lifted the bucket to the ceiling and set it down on the floor. He sent it flying around the room, but none of the water leaked. He was about to put the water back in the cask and start working on a larger container, when he heard someone behind him.

He turned and saw Nemausus watching him. He had been concentrating so hard that he didn't sense his master come down the stairs. The sight of Nemausus startled him. He lost control of the bucket and sent the water flying all over the kitchen, soaking both of them.

Nemausus and Amaethon burst out laughing. Nemausus flicked a finger, and all the spilled water on the floor and on their clothing flew off through the kitchen window into the garden outside.

"A bucket?" Nemausus asked when he finally stopped laughing. "You spent all morning trying to create a bucket to hold the water? Were you planning to move the water to and from the stream one bucket at a time?"

"No, Master, I was just trying to start small before creating a larger container to hold all of the water."

"You were going for a full-size cask?" Nemausus asked, stifling another laugh.

"Yes, Master," Amaethon answered, wondering what was so funny.

"Why did you come up with such a complex container to carry water? Why not create a simple tube?"

Amaethon was dumfounded at the idea. "I got lost in the idea that I had to create a container for the water, so I tried to create containers like the ones I use every day."

Nemausus smiled and nodded. "When I get the water, I create a tube that carries the water from the stream directly into the casks. That way, I don't have to worry about the water going everywhere when I try to get it into and out of the container. Try that and see how it works."

"Yes, Master," Amaethon said, feeling somewhat downcast and embarrassed at how much time he had wasted on the bucket.

Nemausus looked at his student and sensed his discouragement. "Look at me, Amaethon," he said, smiling proudly.

Amaethon looked up at his master.

"While you may not have chosen the simplest solution, your solution would've worked. It required ten times the mental effort of a tube, but you were successfully able to create a complete bucket in your mind that could carry water over great distances, and that's quite an accomplishment. Not many of my students could have created as complete an object as you did. I have no doubt you'd have created a complete cask in your mind as well. You had a workable solution, and had I not distracted you, you'd have been able to do what I asked you to do.

"There will be times when creating a highly complex object in your mind will be necessary, and now you know you can do it. But never forget to look for the simplest solution before beginning such a difficult one. Don't let yourself get bound by what you've seen and done in the past. Focus on the simplest and quickest way to solve the problem whenever possible. In a crisis, seconds count, and creating a simple solution could mean the difference between life and death.

"Generally speaking, the outcome is more important than how you reach the outcome, so don't let yourself get hung up on trying to do things mentally the way you'd do things physically. Let your mind explore solutions that only the mind can create. You're not bound by physical limitations, only mental ones, so think in terms of what's possible, not just what's practical. Understand?"

"Yes, Master," Amaethon said.

After Nemausus left the kitchen, Amaethon felt much better. He set about mentally creating the tube he'd use to get the water to and from the stream. Creating the tube was easy enough, but getting the water in and out of the tube proved more difficult. In time, he had it worked out and soon was moving water between the casks and the stream, which was two hundred yards away.

Nemausus came down to check on him and was pleased with Amaethon's progress. "Well done," he said after watching Amaethon drain the casks and refill them a moment later. Looking around the kitchen, he added, "We also need some more wine. Do you think you could refill that cask as well?"

"Yes, Master," Amaethon said with a twinkle in his eye. "Just tell me where the other end of the tube needs to go."

Young Amaethon Practicing Sorcery

CHAPTER 7

rawn was growing up to be a handsome boy. Even if Belenus didn't know that Arawn was a Gallasian, he'd have figured it out after a few years. He had many of the Gallasian features, including his dark hair and eyes. He was always alert and aware of what was going on around him. Gallasians were great hunters and trappers, and Arawn displayed similar qualities at an early age, even though he hadn't been raised around other Gallasians.

Belenus watched Arawn closely as the boy grew up. No one noticed another orphaned boy on the farm, but Belenus stayed vigilant just the same. If the troopers he had encountered when he rescued Arawn had been after the boy, then their work wasn't finished, and it was possible that they'd continue to search for him.

None of the workers on the farm, including Gareth, had any idea who Arawn was. To them, he was just another orphan that Belenus was raising on the farm. Belenus thought about asking some of the farmhands to help watch Arawn but decided against the idea. He didn't want anyone to notice Arawn being treated differently from the other orphans who had been brought to the farm over the years.

Belenus was a slightly pudgy man of medium height, with close-cropped graying hair and a face that was always clean-shaven. His farm, the largest in the region, consisted of several large fields that stretched from the Great Forest to the large lake south of the Mountain of Elohim. The fields surrounded a central compound, comprised of several buildings arranged in roughly the shape of the spokes of a wagon wheel.

At one end of the compound were stables for the horses and oxen. Next to that were the storage sheds for the wagons and farm tools. On the other side of the stables were the storage sheds for the food. Across from the stables were the four long bunkhouses where the farm's workers and their families lived, a kitchen, two smokehouses, and the main house where Belenus lived. At any time of the day, there was a menagerie of small animals running around the compound.

There were more than a hundred people living and working on the farm, including men, women, and children. Some were hired workers who were given free room and board as part of their wages, but many were orphans that Belenus had found over the years and brought back to raise on the farm. Some of the orphans moved on once they were ready to start their own families, but others, like Gareth, stayed on with Belenus.

There was a seven-year-old cat on the farm that helped keep rodents from eating the food stored in the sheds. He was a large cat, easily weighing over twenty pounds, but he was a great hunter and jumper. Many of the children had tried to catch him over the years, but no one was fast enough.

One morning, while almost everyone was out in the fields or working in the kitchens, Belenus watched Arawn playing in the center of the compound. After a few minutes, he realized that Arawn was imitating the cat. The cat was carefully creeping toward a mouse that was near one of the storage sheds, and so was Arawn. Both the cat and Arawn pounced at the same time. The mouse, startled at the sudden appearance of the cat, scrambled to get away and ran right into Arawn's outstretched hands.

Arawn grabbed the mouse and rolled away from the cat. The cat looked bewildered at the man-child who had managed to sneak up on him and steal his prey. His fur fluffed out and the tip of his tail twitched left and right as he meowed loudly at Arawn. Arawn sat on the ground, facing the cat, and allowed the cat to see the mouse in his hand. The cat approached cautiously with its tail down, suspicious of the man-child. Belenus watched as the cat touched Arawn's hand with its paw. Arawn opened his hand and gave the mouse to the cat.

The mouse tried to scamper away, but the cat pounced and soon had killed the mouse. The cat looked back at Arawn, wondering if the man-child would interfere, but Arawn just sat and watched. When the cat finished its meal, Belenus saw something he had never seen before: the cat curled up in Arawn's lap and took a nap. The cat stayed in Arawn's lap for quite a while as the young orphan gently stroked its fur. Then the cat stretched, got up, and started making its rounds again to see if there were any more rodents lurking around.

There were many times, while Arawn was still small, that Belenus watched the young orphan chase and catch some of the other small animals that inhabited the compound. He seemed to have a gift for following animals silently and unnoticed. Sometimes he'd catch one of the chickens, other times he'd catch one of the dogs that helped guard the smaller animals from the scavengers that lived in the Great Forest on the southern edge of the farm.

The summer after Arawn's sixth birthday, Belenus was exiting one of the storage sheds when he saw Gareth on the far side of the compound, talking to a stranger. Belenus watched for a moment before walking over to the stables to check on one of the mares who was about to deliver her first foal.

When he entered the stables, he could tell that the mare was anxious. Thunder watched the mare over the wall of his stall, and Belenus patted Thunder's nose as he walked past. "Don't worry, Thunder. I'll make sure nothing happens to her or the foal."

Thunder whinnied and nodded his head. Belenus smiled at him and entered the mare's stall, stroking the side of her head reassuringly. "It's all right," he whispered to her. "Everything's going to be just fine."

The mare looked at him and calmed down immediately. Belenus called for Ethan, one of the stable boys, to fetch the groom from the horse paddock to assist with the birth.

While Belenus waited for the groom to arrive, Gareth entered the stables. "Do you have a minute, Belenus?" he asked.

"Make it quick, Gareth," Belenus replied, keeping his eye on the mare. "Her foal is coming very soon."

"I was just taking to a young man who's looking for work. We're down about three men since Dougal and his brothers left to join up with the army of the Followers of Elohim. He seemed a pleasant-enough person and looked fit enough for the work. What do you think?"

Belenus stroked the mare's head and neck to reassure her. "If you like the look of him, go ahead and try him out, Gareth. What's his name?"

"Torkall."

"Do you know what his tribe is?"

"If I had to guess, I'd say he's a Gallasian originally, but his accent sounds more like a Penarduun or a Chulainn."

"Did you tell him we follow Elohim here?"

"I mentioned it, and he didn't seem to have a problem with that."

"Then I leave it to you," Belenus said as Ethan returned with the groom. Gareth left the stables to tell Torkall that he was hired and to show him where to put his belongings.

Later that day, Belenus left the stables with a look of satisfaction on his face. Both the mare and the foal were doing well, and while Belenus dried his hands on the towel he was carrying, he offered his thanks to Elohim for the birth of the farm's newest young colt.

As he walked across the compound, he saw a stranger coming out of one of the bunkhouses and decided it must be Torkall. He stopped and waited for the young man approaching him.

"You must be Belenus," Torkall said pleasantly when he noticed Belenus standing there.

"And you must be Torkall," Belenus replied. "Welcome to the family."

"Thank you, sir," Torkall said. "I'm glad you were hiring. I was getting tired of walking."

"Where were you before coming here?" Belenus asked.

"I was a guard for a village near the Chulainn border, but I wanted to be in a warmer climate."

"Have you ever done any farming?"

"When I was younger. My parents owned a farm, but they died when I was sixteen, and my uncle took over. He and I didn't get along, so I left to have some adventure. It didn't take long to find that adventure is overrated, so I've been looking for farm work here in the south ever since. I've never seen a farm this large before."

"It's large, but we all still act like family. When you get to know everyone better, you'll see what I mean."

The two talked for a while longer. Belenus sensed no deception or danger from Torkall. He thought Torkall was a friendly and polite young man, but he felt there was more to the young man's past than he was admitting.

Belenus walked back to his house. *He's entitled to his privacy. Maybe when he gets to know us better he'll open up more about who he is and what he has done.*

Torkall watched Belenus walk away, feeling like he'd fit in on the farm quite well. As he walked back to the bunkhouse, he found himself liking the elder gentleman quite a bit. *It's nice to work for a trusting person for a change.*

Torkall rose early each morning to exercise, unable to shake the discipline that comes from having served as a soldier for several years. In addition to exercises designed to keep his muscles toned for hand-to-hand combat, Torkall also practiced with the sword, spear, and bow.

Belenus, who was always the first person on the farm to rise, watched Torkall each morning. It was several weeks before he realized that someone else was also watching Torkall.

43

Arawn, who often rose early, watched intently as Torkall practiced. After a few more weeks, Belenus saw Arawn begin to imitate Torkall's exercises in the shadows of the farmhouse. Belenus was certain that Torkall must have seen Arawn watching and imitating him, but he assumed the young man was pretending not to notice.

One morning, after Arawn had been imitating Torkall for almost a month, the young man stopped his exercises unexpectedly and stared at Arawn. He motioned for Arawn to step out of the shadows. Arawn walked over to Torkall, and Torkall began teaching Arawn how to perform the exercises properly.

That was the beginning of their friendship. Each morning, Arawn joined Torkall in the compound to exercise. Belenus watched Arawn learn everything he could from the young man, happy that Arawn had found a new mentor.

Arawn wanted to learn how to use weapons, and one morning Torkall decided to teach Arawn how to use a fighting spear.

"There are several ways to use a spear," Torkall said, demonstrating each to Arawn. "You can throw it, you can stab with it, or you can brace it and let your prey impale itself. The third way works best when the prey is a large animal like a bear, or is a person riding a horse at you. Their speed and size does all the work if you can hold the spear steady."

"Have you ever used a spear in a fight?" Arawn asked.

"No, but I was trained how to fight with a spear when I was a village guard. I've hunted with spears, though."

Torkall let Arawn practice with the spear for a while, and noted that Arawn learned quickly. After only a dozen tries, Arawn was able to throw the spear and hit a target that Torkall had set up a few feet away.

Over the next several months, Torkall and Arawn continued to practice with the spear. Torkall gradually moved the target farther back to help Arawn improve his throwing skills. It took a while, but Arawn finally learned how to control the spear when throwing over greater distances.

There were two other orphans close to Arawn's age, and the three of them were the best of friends. Ethan, one of the stable boys, was from the village two hours from the farm. Mongán soldiers killed his father in a skirmish a week before Ethan was born. His mother went into labor when she received the news, and she died a few minutes after giving birth. Belenus arrived the same day and brought Ethan back to the farm.

Atrius, who was from the Mongán tribe, had been orphaned when he was three years old. Belenus rescued him from a fire at an inn near the

Mongán border. The fire claimed the lives of Atrius' parents, but fortunately, he had no memory of the incident. It never seemed to bother Ethan that Atrius was a Mongán. The two boys accepted each other as brothers.

Ethan, Atrius, and Arawn were well-known for getting into mischief, but they never did anything that would get them into serious trouble. When they were finished with their chores, or when no one was paying attention to what they were doing, they'd sneak into one of the storage sheds or behind the stables and pretend to be great warriors. They made swords out of sticks, and in their minds, their battles were epic struggles between good and evil.

Arawn was the undisputed leader of the group. It was nothing that they ever discussed between them, nor did Arawn ever try to take the leadership role. Ethan and Atrius simply followed where Arawn led and did as he asked them to do.

In spite of the mischief they enjoyed getting into, the one rule that Ethan, Atrius, and Arawn never broke was going into the Great Forest without an adult. The forest was filled with dangerous animals, not to mention thieves and smugglers who traveled the old soldier paths that still existed underneath the thick boughs of the ancient trees. To the three youngsters, the edge of the forest was an impenetrable wall they couldn't breech.

Belenus never let Ethan, Atrius, or Arawn celebrate their birthdays on the actual anniversary of their births in case someone should notice that Arawn was born on the day of the red moons. All three boys celebrated their birthdays together on the same day. This made the boys feel even more like brothers.

For Arawn's ninth birthday, Torkall approached Belenus about making a special present.

"Do you mind if I make a bow and a quiver of arrows for his birthday?" Torkall said when he asked Belenus for his permission.

"Not at all," Belenus said. "Will you also teach Arawn how to use it properly?"

"Of course," Torkall replied.

Belenus was grateful that Torkall was teaching Arawn how to hunt and defend himself. In the three years that Torkall had been on the farm, he had proven himself a great worker and a valued member of the farm's family.

Arawn was delighted with his birthday present, and he practiced with Torkall and some of the other men of the farm as often as he could.

It was almost two years later when Arawn found himself faced with his first chance to prove his skills.

Young Arawn Practicing with the Bow

CHAPTER 8

A fox snuck into the compound and killed two of the chickens before the dogs chased it away. This happened three more times that same week. Arawn knew that something needed to be done to protect the rest of the chickens and their hatchlings. He was getting quite good with the bow and arrows Torkall gave him, so even though he wasn't quite eleven years old, he decided to take care of the fox himself.

Arawn rose early one morning and got dressed as quickly and quietly as he could. He took his bow and arrows and crept toward the front of the building. When he reached the doorway, he listened carefully for sounds of anyone else moving around, but there was only the sound of animals stirring in the low light preceding the dawn. He grabbed a spear that Gareth used for hunting boars and slipped into the courtyard.

Arawn saw Torkall exiting one of the bunkhouses and ducked into the shadows to hide. When Torkall began his morning exercises, Arawn crept away from the courtyard between two of the buildings. Once past the buildings, he looked around to make sure that no one was following him, and he started running south toward the Great Forest.

The Great Forest stretched almost the entire width of Alastríona. It was ancient, dating all the way back to the creation of the world by the gods. Several of the gods dwelled inside the forest, preferring the beauty of the great trees to that of the open plains or the mountains. Many of the trees were hundreds of years old, wider than ten men, with branches stretching high into the air. The forest was home to uncounted varieties of animals, including many that hunted man.

When he reached the edge of the forest, he stopped. He had been in the forest before, but it was always in the company of men from the farm.

Belenus has never allowed me to enter the Great Forest alone. He'll be mad that I disobeyed him, but that fox is killing our animals and needs to be stopped.

Arawn hated the idea of disobeying Belenus, but he knew he couldn't stand by and let more the farm animals get killed. He had no desire for glory; he just needed to keep the farm animals safe. Tightening his grip on the spear, he took a deep breath and entered the forest, hoping that Belenus would understand.

It didn't take long to pick up the trail of the fox, and soon Arawn was deeper into the forest than he had ever been before. He carefully followed the trail the way Torkall had taught him.

After a couple of hours, Arawn stopped next to a large tree to rest for a few minutes. He was about to put down his weapons when he thought he heard something approaching. He hid behind the tree and listened. As he waited to hear if the sound came closer, he hoped that the wind wouldn't reveal his scent.

Arawn suddenly wished that he hadn't come alone. *I'm not an experienced hunter yet, and I'm a long way from home. If this isn't the fox, I could be in worse trouble than Belenus being mad at me.*

Arawn heard the sound coming closer and steadied his nerves. He peered carefully around the tree and looked in the direction of the sound. He was relieved to see a fox on the trail, heading in the direction of the farm.

Careful not to make any noise, Arawn leaned the spear against the tree and drew an arrow from his quiver. He set the arrow in place on the bow and pulled the bowstring back. As the fox neared his hiding-place, it stopped and sniffed the air as if it detected that there was something nearby. Arawn took aim and let the arrow fly.

The arrow hit its mark at the base of the fox's neck, and the fox immediately fell to the ground. Arawn grabbed the spear and jumped out from behind the tree. He approached the fox and could tell it was still alive. Not wanting it to suffer any longer, he took the spear and stabbed the fox, killing it instantly.

In that moment, Arawn felt sorry that the fox had to be killed. *The animals on the farm needed to be protected,* he reminded himself. Feeling conflicted, Arawn offered a silent prayer to Elohim. He hoisted the spear, with the fox still impaled on it, over his shoulder and began the long walk back to the farm.

The farm was still in an uproar when Arawn exited the forest shortly before midday. Belenus had gone looking for Arawn several hours earlier when Torkall mentioned that Arawn had missed their morning exercises and weapons practice. When Arawn couldn't be found, Belenus went looking for Ethan and Atrius, assuming that the three boys were off somewhere playing. Atrius was working in the stables and Ethan was feeding the chickens in the compound. Neither boy had seen Arawn all day.

Belenus grew concerned and asked several of the farmhands to help him look for the young orphan. They searched the entire compound thoroughly, they searched along the lake, and they searched each of the fields, including the rows of corn, which were just tall enough to conceal a young boy who was hiding. Arawn was nowhere to be found. Belenus and the farmhands were getting ready to search inside the forest when Arawn appeared carrying the fox.

"Arawn, where have you been?" Belenus asked as he ran up. "We've been looking everywhere for you."

Arawn saw the concern on Belenus' face and immediately felt bad about having gone after the fox without letting anyone know where he was.

"I'm sorry, Belenus. I should have told you where I was going. I took care of the fox problem we were having."

Belenus looked at Arawn, feeling impressed, concerned, and frustrated at the same time. There was no pride or triumph in the boy's face. Only the grim satisfaction that he had successfully done something that needed to be done.

Belenus was surprised that Arawn would have done something as dangerous as tracking and killing a wild animal in the forest so far away from the protection of the farm. Before Belenus could say anything, Gareth, Torkall, and some of the other farmhands ran over to see what Arawn was carrying. Belenus decided that this wasn't the right time to chastise the young hunter.

"Arawn was in the forest solving the problem of the fox that was attacking our chickens," Belenus said to the others.

Arawn looked at Belenus with surprise. He had thought that the elder gentleman would be angry at him for leaving the farm and going into the forest by himself. Looking at Belenus' face, he knew he'd be having a conversation with the man later, but for the moment, the farmer was letting him be a hero to the others on the farm.

After everyone had made Arawn tell the story of how he killed the fox, Gareth took the fox and buried it. Arawn cleaned and returned the spear and his bow and arrows to their proper places.

Torkall found Arawn coming out of the bunkhouse and congratulated the orphan on his first solo hunt. Arawn thanked the young man. "I couldn't have done it if you hadn't taught me how."

Torkall smiled. "It's impressive how well you used what I taught you – especially with an animal as difficult to sneak up on as a fox!"

Knowing that he needed to have a conversation with Belenus, Arawn excused himself. He looked around the compound quickly, but he thought he knew where Belenus would be waiting. He walked out of the north end of the courtyard and found Belenus in his favorite place – standing by the banks of the lake, looking at the Mountain of Elohim in the distance.

Belenus heard Arawn approaching, but he didn't turn around.

"I'm sorry I disobeyed you, Belenus," Arawn said as he reached the Belenus' side.

"Why did you do it?" Belenus asked calmly.

"Everyone was busy with other chores, and I felt I could handle it. Someone needed to protect the chickens."

Belenus appreciated the innocence of that answer. Arawn was someone who looked at the world in a special way. Belenus had taught Arawn that the people and animals of the farm needed protecting, and Arawn took it to mean that he was to be their protector. He'd never do anything to hurt the animals on the farm, but he'd kill without a second thought anything that threatened one of those animals. Belenus knew that Arawn's Gallasian blood contributed to his outlook. It was a trait shared by many other Gallasians. Belenus didn't blame Arawn for what he had done, but he knew he needed to help Arawn understand the danger involved.

"You knew you were breaking the rules when you left the farm this morning?"

"Yes, sir."

"And you left anyway?"

"Yes, sir."

Belenus turned to face Arawn. "Do you know why I told you to never leave the farm or go into the forest without an adult with you?"

"No, sir."

"Because of the danger."

"But Belenus, I was never in any danger in the forest. I got a little nervous, but the fox is the only animal I saw, other than some birds. I know how to hunt, and I know how to hide. I can also run fast when needed. I don't see what danger you're talking about."

Belenus just shook his head. Then he heard a voice say, *"Tell him."*

51

He looked up at the Mountain of Elohim and nodded.

Turning back to face Arawn, he said, "Walk with me for a while, Arawn. There are things I need to tell you that'll explain what I mean when I say 'danger'."

They walked along the banks of the lake. "Have I ever told you about how you came to live on this farm?" he asked after a minute.

"No, sir. Other than to tell me that my parents died and that you were there to make sure I was taken care of."

"There's a bit more to the story than that," Belenus said. He told Arawn about the dream he had, about the caravan, about the troopers who killed his parents, and about how he had found Arawn in a trunk and had taken him back to the farm for protection.

Arawn was quiet for a while after Belenus finished telling the story. "So troopers killed my parents. Why do you feel I still need to be protected?"

"Because I believe the troopers were there to kill you."

"Me? Why would they want to kill me? I was just a baby."

"Do you remember when I told you about the Prophecy of Airmid?" Belenus asked.

"Yes, sir. I remember that there's something about three orphans who will be born on the same day, and one of them will become the Ruler of the World."

"Do you remember anything about the sign that'll announce when the three are born?"

"Something about the moons being red and crossing their paths in the sky. Why?"

"Because you were born on the day of the red moons, Arawn. There are people who don't want the prophecy fulfilled. They've been hunting and killing all the children born around that time to make sure that the orphans mentioned in the prophecy never grow up to become the Ruler of the World. The troopers who attacked the caravan and killed your parents somehow knew that you were traveling in that caravan, and they know they didn't find you there. If I'm right, that means they're still out there looking for you. That's why I don't want you to leave the farm or go into the forest without an adult with you. It's not because the animals are dangerous, even though some are; it's because there are people out there who are hunting you, and I don't want them to find you with no one there to protect you."

"Do you mean I'm one of the orphans in the prophecy?"

Belenus stopped and faced Arawn. He saw the look in Arawn's face and knew that he needed to be as honest as possible. "Yes, you're one of the orphans in the prophecy. I had a dream that I was supposed to find you, and Elohim led me to you. That means you must have been touched by a great destiny, and because of when you were born, there's only one destiny it could be."

Arawn looked out over the lake, deep in thought. He tried to remember everything that the prophecy said about the orphans, but he couldn't recall most of the details. Belenus stood silently by his side – waiting while Arawn processed the information he had been given.

After several minutes, he asked, "Do you know who the other two orphans are?"

"No, but I know who's taking care of them. They're safe, and there will come a day when the three of you will be together."

"What do we do until then?" Arawn asked.

"Well, first of all, you must promise me that you'll ask me before doing anything that breaks any rules, agreed? We must also look to your training. There's much you need to learn before you can fulfill your role in the prophecy, and you need to know how to defend yourself in case someone on the farm or nearby is working with the people who are trying to kill the three of you. And finally, you must promise that you'll never tell anyone about what we've talked about here until I tell you it's safe to do so. Do you understand?"

"Yes, Belenus. I promise."

Over the next year, Arawn kept his promise to Belenus. When leaving the farm or going into the forest, Arawn made sure he was always in the company of several of the men from the farm. He also trained harder with Torkall each morning. As Arawn's skill with the sword and other weapons improved, Torkall began teaching Arawn how to fight from horseback.

"A fighter on the ground is at a disadvantage when facing an opponent on horseback," Torkall explained. "The opponent on horseback is not only harder to reach, but he has an additional weapon – the horse itself. I'm going to show you how to fight on horseback, but I'm also going to show you how to fight against someone on horseback. Whether you're on the ground or on a horse, you need to know how to fight a mounted opponent. It's different than being on the ground and fighting someone else who's on the ground. You need to understand how to keep a horse under control while you handle your weapons, and you need to know how to use your horse against your opponent as well."

Arawn had to admit that learning to fight from horseback was hard. He didn't ride that often, and he had trouble controlling the horse. Torkall decided to teach Arawn basic horsemanship first. Once Arawn had mastered the basics, Torkall began showing how to use weapons on horseback.

"Attack me with your sword," Torkall shouted to Arawn.

Arawn and Torkall were inside the horse paddock behind the stables. Torkall sat on his horse at one end of the paddock with his practice sword drawn. Arawn was at the other end. The groom was leaning against the paddock fence railing, watching the two men closely to make sure that the horses didn't get injured. Ethan, Atrius, and some of the farmhands were also watching to see what would happen.

Arawn adjusted his grip on the reins and drew his sword. He pressed his heels into the side of the horse the way Torkall had demonstrated, and rode toward Torkall. As he approached Torkall, he raised his practice sword so he could bring it down on Torkall's unprotected head.

As he drew up beside Torkall, he swung his sword downward, and… found himself in mid-air with the ground rushing to meet him. He landed with a loud "thud" and his practice sword went flying out of his hand.

"Ouch!"

"Are you all right?" Torkall asked, looking down at his student from the back of his horse. Just as Arawn's practice sword had come down, Torkall had raised his sword like he was going to block Arawn's blow, but he dropped the reins and shoved Arawn off his horse instead.

Arawn heard Ethan and Atrius laughing and shot them an angry glance. He rolled over and reached for his practice sword, wincing from the pain in his left hip. "I wasn't expecting that," he replied, standing up and brushing off the dirt from his clothes. This wasn't the first time that Arawn had fallen off a horse, but it was the first time that he had been pushed off, and the ground seemed harder and the pain more intense. He bent down and stretched, trying to work out the pain in his hip.

"I know. That's why I pushed you. When fighting on horseback, you have your weapon, you have the horse, but you also have height to work with. Sometimes the best defense isn't using your weapon or even a shield. It's using the fact that you and your opponent are well off the ground and sitting on animals that are distracted by the fighting."

Arawn walked over to his horse, took the reins, and led it back to Torkall. He checked the saddle and the bridle, mounted his horse again, and turned to face Torkall. *I hope I'm going to learn something other than how to fall off my horse.*

"You don't have to kill your opponent to win a fight," Torkall continued. "You just need to keep him from killing you. If you push him off his horse, like I did with you, you have a chance to ride away and escape. He might get back on his horse and follow you, but then again he might not. Deal with the problem that's facing you at the moment. If your opponent is a superior fighter, the unexpected may be your only way to beat him."

Arawn nodded. He knew that, in order to survive in the heat of battle, every potential advantage had to be pressed. He turned his horse and rode to the opposite side of the paddock.

"Try and stay on your horse this time," Ethan said. He and Atrius laughed.

"Maybe you'd like to try this?" Arawn asked sarcastically, and he rode past the two boys.

"No, we'd rather just watch you," Atrius replied with a grin. "It looks too painful."

Arawn shook his head. He reached the far side of the paddock and turned his horse around.

"Again," Torkall shouted.

Arawn pressed his heels into the sides of the horse and rode toward Torkall.

It took a while, but Arawn finally began showing some improvement. He still found it hard to focus on fighting and controlling his horse at the same time. Torkall held back on his attacks so Arawn wouldn't get badly hurt. Arawn knew this and wondered how many more times he would've been knocked off his horse if Torkall wasn't being so kind.

Just before Arawn turned twelve, the groom ran up to Belenus one morning and asked if he had seen Ethan. "I can't find him anywhere," he said, looking worried.

"Has anyone else seen him?" Belenus asked.

"Not since last night. I've looked in all the normal places a twelve-year-old might get into, but he's not here."

"Was anyone out of the bunkhouses late last night?"

"It's not like we keep everyone locked in at night, Belenus," the groom said. "People come and go all the time. All we ask is that they do so quietly so they don't disturb anyone else."

"What I meant was: did anyone see someone leaving the bunkhouse with Ethan last night?"

"No."

Belenus looked at the groom for a moment and could tell the man was genuinely concerned. "Tell Gareth to select ten to fifteen farmhands to start looking for Ethan."

"Thank you, Belenus," the groom shouted over his shoulder, running to find Gareth.

Two hours later, one of the farmhands ran up to Belenus, who was watching Arawn practice using a rope to catch animals. The look of shock on the farmhand's face told Belenus all he needed to know.

"Where?" he asked softly, so Arawn wouldn't hear.

"Just inside the forest," the farmhand whispered. "You'd better come and see."

Turning to Arawn, Belenus said, "Arawn, please go into the stables and get started clearing the stalls. I'll be back in a little while."

"Okay, Belenus," Arawn said. He coiled up the rope and put it away before walking across the courtyard to the stables.

Belenus followed the farmhand across the southern fields to the tree line that marked the edge of the Great Forest. They entered the forest and walked for almost ten minutes before arriving at a small clearing. Gareth, the groom, and two other farmhands were already there, looking at the gruesome scene.

Ethan, the stable boy, lay on the ground in a pool of blood. At first glance, Belenus saw that someone using a knife or a short sword had cut the boy's throat. He knelt down and looked for anything on Ethan's clothing or on the ground around the body that might give him some clue as to who committed the murder. There was nothing to find.

"Who could have done this?" the groom demanded. Even though Ethan had been an orphan, the groom treated him like his own son.

"It has to be someone who slipped into the bunkhouse and took Ethan in the night against his will, or else it's someone that Ethan knew and willingly followed here into the forest," Gareth speculated.

"Why would someone sneak onto the farm to murder a stable boy?" the groom asked, disturbed at the very idea.

"Why would one of us bring him here and murder him?" one of the other farmhands asked.

Belenus stood up, wiping the tears from his eyes, and looked at the others. "We're not going to find the answers here," he said hoarsely. "We need to give Ethan a proper burial, and we need to question every person on the farm to see if anyone saw or heard something last night."

The groom knelt down and picked up Ethan's lifeless body. As they carried it back to the farm, Belenus reached out with his mind to Alaunus.

"A young boy was murdered here on the farm last night," he said.

"Is Arawn safe?"

"Yes, but the boy who was killed is about Arawn's same age."

56

"Do you know who did it?"

"No. It could have been someone from the outside, or it could have been one of the farmworkers. I'd hate to suspect any of them, but I can't rule out the possibility."

"I think you may need to speed up Arawn's training," Alaunus said.

"I agree."

"Are there any others around Arawn's age on the farm?"

"Just one," Belenus replied.

"Then watch them both. This could be unrelated to Taranus' attempts to interfere with the prophecy, but with soldiers still hunting the orphans, we can't be too careful.

"I will."

Belenus felt Alaunus break contact, and he suddenly felt a great need to be near Arawn.

CHAPTER 9

The celebration for Arawn's twelfth birthday was marred by circumstances that had everyone at the farm on edge. Atrius had disappeared two days earlier, and no one knew where he was. The farmhands searched everywhere on the farm and had even gone deep into the Great Forest, but they couldn't find his body or any indication of where he might have gone. There was no evidence that someone had taken him, but no one believed that Atrius would wander off. He knew the rules about staying close to the compound and was too obedient of a boy to break those rules.

Several weeks after Arawn's birthday, someone noticed something floating in the lake. Belenus and Gareth rowed a boat out and discovered the body of a boy. Looking at its face, they knew it was Atrius. He had been dead a long time.

There were marks around his ankles. Belenus surmised that someone tied the boy to a rock before throwing him into the lake, but that somehow the body had come loose and floated to the surface. Belenus and Gareth brought Atrius' body back to the farm and buried him next to Ethan near the edge of the Great Forest.

The morning after the burial, Arawn skipped his morning exercises and training with Torkall and walked down the lake to be alone. He didn't want to be around anyone. He sat down on the banks of the lake and stared at the Mountain of Elohim.

"Why are they dead?" he asked the mountain, knowing that it wouldn't answer him.

Arawn picked up a rock and threw it into the lake, watching the ripples spread from where the rock had hit the water. He thought about how many times he had come to the lake with Atrius and Ethan to fish, the games they had played around the farm, and how they always found something to laugh about when they were together.

Now his two closest friends were dead. *They're gone. There's nothing left to laugh about.* He buried his head in his hands and cried.

He spent the day on the banks of the lake, throwing rocks and staring at the mountain in the distance. He never heard Belenus, who came to check on him but didn't say a word.

As the sun began to set, Arawn returned to the farm. He didn't speak to anyone. He just walked with his head down to his room and closed the door.

Belenus brought Arawn something to eat, but Arawn had no appetite. He just left the food on the stool by the door where Belenus had put it. He rolled over in his bed with his back to the door, wondering how to make the pain go away.

Torkall saw him entering the courtyard the next morning. "Would you like to get some practice in this morning? It looks like it's going to rain this afternoon."

Arawn just shook his head and walked out of the north end of the courtyard toward the lake.

The groom found Arawn a few hours later, sitting on the banks of the lake. "Hey, Arawn, a couple of the horses jumped the paddock fence and ran toward the Great Forest. Do you want to go with me to bring them back? We need to get them indoors before the storm reaches us."

Arawn just shook his head and continued staring at the mountain in the distance.

Dark grey clouds moved over the lake and the farm that afternoon. The rumble of thunder echoed all around, and soon Arawn saw lightning flashes in the distance.

Gareth saw Arawn sitting on the banks of the lake as he was riding to make sure the farmhands were indoors before the storm hit. "Arawn, it's getting ready to rain," he shouted. "You should get back to the farm before it starts."

Arawn waved to Gareth. He heard Gareth's horse ride away, but he didn't move. A few minutes later, the rain started falling, but Arawn kept sitting on the banks of the lake, watching the patterns of the rain on the surface of the lake.

Arawn was soaking wet. A lightning bolt hit the ground nearby. The boom of its impact was deafening, and Arawn felt a tingling sensation all over his body.

For the first time since the burial, Arawn felt something release inside himself. He looked up at the mountain, which was hidden by rain and mist, and shouted, "Am I the reason they're dead?"

Arawn's tears mixed with the rain pouring down his cheeks. *Were they killed because someone thought one of them was an orphan in the prophecy? Did they die because I'm still alive? Will they come for me next? What am I supposed to do when that happens? Will others die because of me?*

Arawn stared at the mist hovering over the lake and felt anger boiling up inside.

"Answer me!" he shouted toward the mountain.

The only sound was the thunder and the rain hitting the ground and the water in front of him.

"Did he eat anything last night?" Belenus asked the cook.

It was two weeks after the burial, and Belenus was concerned. The cook, the groom, Torkall, and Gareth were with Belenus in the stables, keeping the elder informed about what was happening with Arawn.

"He took a couple of chunks of cold bread, but nothing else," the cook replied with a worried tone of voice. "It's not natural for a boy that age to be eating so little."

Belenus nodded. Turning to Torkall, he asked, "Has he shown any interest in exercising or practicing with weapons since the burial?"

"No, Belenus. He doesn't even speak to me."

"I understand that he feels alone in the world with his friends gone," Gareth spoke up. "He's an orphan, and now he feels like he has no one."

"He has us," the groom objected.

"It's not the same for an orphan," Gareth stated. "No matter how much you make an orphan feel at home, he still feels like a guest in someone else's home. Trust me. I know this. Arawn knew Ethan and Atrius since he was a baby, and he thought of them as brothers. Now they're gone, and he doesn't know who he is anymore."

Belenus listened to Gareth, but said nothing. He had been standing in the rain two weeks earlier, watching over Arawn. He overheard Arawn shouting at the mountain. He knew what was tormenting Arawn the most.

"We need to find something to keep him busy so he can work through his grief," Gareth added.

"I agree," Belenus said. "And I think we need to accelerate his training. If he knows how to defend himself, perhaps he won't be afraid that someone will try to kill him like Ethan and Atrius."

"Do you think Ethan and Atrius were killed by the same person?" the groom asked.

"It doesn't matter what I think," Belenus answered carefully. "It only matters what Arawn thinks. Two of the three boys born around the same time were murdered. If you were the third boy, what would you think?"

Everyone nodded.

"We have men on the farm who have served in the army and cavalry," Gareth said after a moment. "Torkall has been training Arawn with weapons, but what if some of the men with military experience work with Arawn to train him how to fight as a unit? If he's worried that someone may be after him, changing his focus to protect the farm, rather than just himself, might help him work though what he's going through."

"That is an excellent idea, Gareth," Belenus said, smiling.

The next morning, Arawn woke up and decided to walk down to the lake again. He turned over to get out of bed and saw Belenus sitting on the stool by the door.

"How are you this morning, Arawn?" Belenus asked.

"How do you think I am, Belenus?" Arawn retorted as he got out of bed and dressed himself.

"I think you're in pain over the loss of your friends. I think you blame yourself for their deaths because you were all orphans around the same age. And I think you're worried that the murderer, or murderers, will come after you next. Am I leaving anything out?"

Arawn looked at Belenus with an expression of shock.

"They didn't die because of you, Arawn," Belenus said quietly. "But I'm certain they did die because of the prophecy, or rather because of some people who want the prophecy to fail. And if that's the case, then you have every right to be worried that they'll come after you. So what do we do about that?"

"I don't know," Arawn said, sitting down on the edge of his bed.

"Well I do. But first, you need to eat. You can't concentrate without food, and you need to get your strength up. Let's get some breakfast, and I'll show you what I have in mind."

Before Arawn could ask any questions, Belenus had stood up and left the room. Arawn stared at the empty stool for a moment.

"Now, Arawn," he heard Belenus' voice say calmly from down the hall.

Arawn jumped up and followed Belenus.

After breakfast, Belenus led Arawn to the horse paddock where several of the farmhands were waiting.

"You're worried that someone may be after you. I'm worried

because someone managed to take two boys from the farm and kill them. You need to continue learning how to defend yourself, but I need the farm defended so what happened to Ethan and Atrius will never happen again."

Gesturing to the men waiting at the paddock, Belenus continued. "These men have all been in the army or the cavalry. They've seen combat, and they know how to fight as individuals and as a unit. In addition to your lessons with Torkall, which I want you to resume immediately and work on every day, I want you to work with these men to learn how to how men fight as a unit. I also want you to work with them to look for ways to defend the farm. Do you understand?"

Arawn nodded. "Yes, Belenus."

"Good," Belenus said. He put his hand on Arawn's shoulder. "I'm not doing this so you'll forget about your friends. I'm doing this so you won't spend so much time thinking about their deaths that you forget to live. They'd never have wanted you to do that. Honor their friendship by living the life you were destined to live."

Arawn flashed a tired smile and nodded. For a moment, he looked like his old self, and Belenus felt relieved for the first time since the burial.

The new training seemed to help Arawn deal with his grief. In addition to his normal chores, Arawn spent as much time as possible learning from the men and practicing with the sword, bow, and spear. He was grateful that by staying busy, he didn't feel the pain of his friends' deaths as much. He still missed them, but each day he found it easier to get on with his own life.

Arawn found himself spending more time with Torkall than before. Belenus was happy that Arawn had a friend who was keeping him distracted from thinking about Ethan and Atrius. But Belenus continued to keep a close watch on Arawn.

What Belenus didn't realize was that someone else was also keeping a close eye on Arawn.

CHAPTER 10

By the time Cerridwen turned twelve, she had grown into a lovely girl. Her fiery red hair was naturally wavy, unlike her mother's, which had been straight. Her skin was smooth and tanned, in spite of the fact that pale skin was typical of the people from the Macruhan tribe. She had a slender athletic build, but her curves had become more pronounced.

She was also fearless. She was not supposed to leave the grounds of the smithy, so she learned to climb. There were several times when Tridamus heard something on the roof of the workshop, only to see Cerridwen swing in through one of the open windows a moment later.

Tridamus had not taught her how to ride horses yet, but a few weeks before her thirteenth birthday, he discovered that she already knew how to ride.

He had driven the wagon to the closest village to pick up some provisions, and he returned to the smithy as a storm approached from the north face of the Mountain of Elohim. He put the first horse in its stall, and he had just unharnessed the second horse when lightning flashed and the sound of thunder spooked the animal. It reared back and pulled free from Tridamus' grasp. It reared again just as Cerridwen came out of the workshop to see what was happening.

The horse bolted toward the open side of the smithy's courtyard. Before Tridamus could move, Cerridwen started running. She reached the horse just as it was racing past her. She jumped, seized the horse's mane, and pulled herself onto the horse's back. As the horse ran out of the courtyard, Tridamus saw Cerridwen lean back while still clutching the base of the horse's mane.

"Cerridwen!" Tridamus shouted, concerned.

He started running after her, but the horse walked into the courtyard with Cerridwen on its back. It stopped in front of Tridamus and lowered its head. Cerridwen slid off its back and caressed its neck, whispering softly as she stepped forward.

Tridamus stood there with his mouth open. He couldn't decide if he were delighted or furious with her.

"How did you do that?" he sputtered as he reached for the horse's harness.

"I don't know. I didn't want the horse to get hurt, and I knew we need it to pull the wagon. It just came to me."

"You could have been seriously hurt," he said more calmly.

"I know, but the horse could have been hurt worse."

Tridamus stared at her for a moment. "Was that your first time on a horse?"

Cerridwen nodded.

"How did you know what to do?" Tridamus asked as he led the horse into its stall.

"I watched how you and your patrons handle horses, and I imitated it. It's how I learn everything."

Tridamus nodded. He decided he was delighted with her and didn't want to hurt her feelings by chastising her any further. Without saying anything else, they led the second horse to its stall, brushed the two horses, cleaned and put away the tack, covered the wagon, and took the provisions into the house.

Two days later, Tridamus was saddling the horses when Cerridwen came out of the workshop to see what he was doing.

"Both horses?" she asked when she walked into the stables.

"Yes, I thought you could ride with me today."

Cerridwen was thrilled that Tridamus was allowing her to ride one of the horses. "Where are we going?"

"There's a mill on the edge of the village. The miller needs some new parts for the windmill, and I'm going down to take measurements. Since you've already shown me that you know how to ride, it makes sense for you to come with me."

Tridamus showed her the proper way to mount and dismount a horse, and soon they were riding toward the village. Cerridwen kept begging Tridamus to let the horses go faster, and once he felt comfortable that she could stay in the saddle, he showed her how to make the horse speed up and slow down. Soon they were galloping down the road, and Cerridwen was squealing with delight.

The grain mill was a tall building that used wind power, rather than water or oxen, to turn the grinding stones inside that changed the grain into meal or flour. As Tridamus and Cerridwen rode up to the mill, she saw the miller's house next to the mill and several outlying buildings where the grain was stored.

The miller came out and greeted them, followed by two children. Tridamus jumped off his horse and handed the reins to Cerridwen before disappearing into the mill with the miller to see what parts were needed.

The boy and girl were twins and were about the same age as Cerridwen. She noticed that the girl was dressed very differently from Cerridwen's leather work clothes. She also noticed that the boy couldn't take his eyes off of her.

"Your name is Cerridwen?" the girl asked as Cerridwen dismounted. "My name is Elise."

"Hello, Elise."

"And I'm Siegfried," the boy said, taking the reins from Cerridwen and walking toward a nearby hitching post. "Let's put your horses over here."

"Thank you," Cerridwen said, glad that Tridamus had explained why boys stare at girls.

"You work as a blacksmith?" Elise asked.

Cerridwen nodded.

"I've never heard of a girl as a blacksmith," Siegfried said as he tied up the horses.

"You have now," Cerridwen said.

Siegfried looked up at her sharply, but relaxed when Cerridwen smiled.

"I've never been to a grain mill before. Can you show me around?"

"Sure," the twins said at the same time.

It was almost thirty minutes before Cerridwen caught up to Tridamus, who was taking detailed measurements of the iron bands that held the turning mechanism together. In that time, she had met the miller's wife and seen all of the other buildings at the mill. But she found the windmill fascinating.

"How does it work?" she asked.

"The wind hits the blades of the windmill and makes them turn," Siegfried answered excitedly. "The windmill is connected to those gears above the grindstone and makes it turn in a circle and crush the grain."

It took Tridamus another hour to finish taking measurements and sketching the shape of the parts that the miller needed. As they left the grain mill, Elise and Siegfried ran after them, begging Cerridwen to come back and visit them soon. Cerridwen turned and waved to them as she and Tridamus rode back to the smithy.

After their visit to the mill, Tridamus decided to let Cerridwen start exercising the horses every day. He allowed her to ride to the village and back, but other than the mill, she was not to ride anywhere else.

"No one is foolish enough to try and harm a blacksmith," he told her, "but when you're out there, no one knows you're a blacksmith. There are ruffians who travel the roads looking for easy prey. If you see anyone approaching you, hide. If you can't hide, run away from them as fast as you can."

"I promise, Tridamus."

It didn't take long for Cerridwen to become an accomplished rider. She exercised the horses daily, and rode to the village a couple of times a week. She frequently stopped at the mill to visit Elise and Siegfried when she had enough time, and soon they became great friends.

Elise and Siegfried were a typical brother and sister. They loved each other, but they also bickered with each other constantly. On more than one occasion, Cerridwen arrived at the mill and found them either arguing or not speaking to each other at all.

Cerridwen had a gift for getting them to stop fighting and be civil to each other. She could quickly pacify whichever of the twins refused to give in or apologize. Then the three of them would laugh and have fun until it was time for Cerridwen to return to the smithy.

Tridamus was happy that Cerridwen had made some new friends, but he worried about Siegfried. He knew that Cerridwen had a destiny to fulfill, and the miller's son didn't figure into that destiny.

I'll need to keep an eye on them and make sure that the boy doesn't become a distraction to her. There's too much at stake.

CHAPTER 11

everal months after the discovery of Atrius' body in the lake, Arawn participated in his first boar hunt in the Great Forest. Boars not only made a fine meal, but because they're one of the most aggressive animals in the forest, they're a danger to livestock and the farmhands. Twice a year, the men of the farm would enter the Great Forest to kill as many boars as they could find. Afterwards, they'd feast on the meat.

Hunting boars was dangerous work. Unlike most animals, which fled from hunters, boars charged at their attackers. The razor-sharp tusks could slash a man, causing him to bleed to death before anyone could help.

Boar hunters broke into two groups. The first group made as much noise as possible, driving the boars to a place where the second group was waiting. The second group, with their spears braced against the ground, would allow the boars to impale themselves as they ran from the first group. If any boars got past the waiting hunters of the second group, the hunters would have to use bows or spears to track down the boars and kill them before they could attack any of the hunters or reach the animals on the farm.

Belenus wasn't thrilled at the idea of Arawn going on the hunt, but he knew the other farmhands would question why a boy of twelve wouldn't be allowed to participate. When Torkall promised to stay with Arawn and watch over him, Belenus reluctantly agreed to let Arawn go.

"We're going to be with the group driving the boars toward the hunters," Torkall told Arawn as they walked with the men to the edge of the forest. "Hopefully the boars will run away from us, but we have to be ready in case they charge us instead. Are you ready?"

Arawn nodded excitedly. He was happy to be on his first boar hunt in the Great Forest with the rest of the men from the farm.

"Good," Torkall continued, handing a strange metal clapper to Arawn. "Keep your spear in one hand and this noisemaker in the other. When Gareth gives us the signal, we'll walk forward, shaking the noisemakers. The sound should infuriate the boars and make them run right into the waiting spears of the other group. We won't need our spears unless one of the boars decides to turn and attack us instead."

The men entered the forest quietly so the boars wouldn't hear them approaching. Torkall and Arawn kept walking forward with their group as the other group broke off and moved around to the left. Arawn knew the hunt couldn't start until the other group was in position on the far side of the low brush where the boars were resting.

Arawn and Torkall reached the place on the far left of the first group where they were supposed to wait for the signal. Torkall knelt behind a bush and gestured for Arawn to do the same.

Arawn looked around at the other members of his group. Most of the men appeared calm, but Arawn could see some of the men shifting nervously. Arawn was apprehensive, like he was just before he shot the fox, but he was also excited.

When Gareth whistled loudly, Arawn and the rest of his group stood up and started shaking their noisemakers. Arawn watched as the bushes in front of them started shaking violently. The boars were running to get away from the sound. Arawn saw several medium-sized boars running away from him, and he moved forward after them.

After about ten minutes, Arawn entered a clearing and realized that he couldn't see the rest of the men in his group. He turned to ask Torkall a question and found himself falling to the ground – his face hurting from where something had struck him. His spear fell out of his hand, and as he reached for it, he felt something press against his throat.

"What are you doing, Torkall?" Arawn demanded when he recognized who was standing over him, feeling more angry than afraid.

"What I have to do, Arawn," Torkall replied, throwing down his noisemaker and reaching into his pouch.

"What do you mean?" Arawn asked, still not sure what was going on.

Torkall, looking frustrated, said nothing. A moment later, he pulled what looked like a boar tusk from the pouch and held it in his hand.

"What are you going to do with that?"

"There's always someone who gets seriously hurt on a boar hunt,"

Torkall replied. "Sometimes there's even someone who gets killed. If the boar's tusk catches you in just the right place, like the upper part of your inner thigh, you'll bleed to death in just a couple of minutes. When they find your body, it'll look like you let a boar get too close to you. I'll be distraught that I couldn't get to you in time to save you. No one will suspect that this was anything other than a tragic accident."

"Why?" Arawn asked. He tried to move slightly to reach his spear, but Torkall saw what he was doing and pressed the shaft of his own spear harder against Arawn's throat.

"Don't try that again," he said, looking troubled. "It'll just make this harder on you. What I'm going to do won't hurt much. You'll feel cold, but there's no real pain apart from the initial slash. I did the same for Atrius and Ethan. I don't want you to suffer."

"You killed Atrius and Ethan?" Arawn spat out. "Why?"

Torkall nodded sadly. "All three of you are the right age. It's nothing personal against any of you."

"What does our age have to do with anything?" Arawn demanded, realizing that Torkall was working with the people who killed his parents.

"It's the reason you have to die, Arawn. There are people who want to kill all the boys born when you were born. I didn't want to be the one to do it, but they made me. I made a terrible mistake when I was younger, Arawn. I killed my uncle because he was terrible to me after my parents died, and I ran away to keep from being punished. Some men found me working here who knew what I had done. They told me I had to kill the three of you or they'd expose me as a murderer. They paid me enough to get far away from here when this is over – enough to make a new start. I never wanted to kill you. That's why I killed Ethan and Atrius first. I was hoping I could find a way to spare your life, but they found me a few days ago and told me that if I didn't finish this, they'd kill me and then kill you in a horrible way. I couldn't let them do that."

Torkall adjusted his grip on his spear and knelt down next to Arawn. He held the boar tusk next to Arawn's inner thigh. Arawn felt it touch him and fought the urge to flinch in case the movement would cause Torkall to plunge the tusk into his leg.

"Relax, Arawn," Torkall said softly. "It'll all be over soon. If things were different, you and I would have remained the best of friends."

Arawn felt the tusk press against his leg and braced himself.

A loud sound distracted Torkall. A boar had escaped from the hunters and was racing toward Torkall and Arawn. When it burst through brush on the far side of the clearing, it charged them, mad with fear. Torkall shifted his spear toward the boar to protect himself. Arawn, sensing his chance to escape, grabbed the tusk, pulled it away from his leg, and scrambled away as Torkall engaged the boar with his spear.

Without looking back, Arawn ran as fast as he could away from the clearing, leaving his spear on the ground behind him. He stumbled and heard a whizzing sound over his head. Torkall's spear flew past him and imbedded itself in a tree right in front of him. He ducked under it and kept running, knowing that Torkall had another spear to throw.

Arawn wondered if there were boars in the brush around him, but he decided it was better to risk the possibility of running into boars than face the certainty of death at the hands of Torkall. His eyes teared up as the pain of Torkall's betrayal hit him. *He was my friend! How could he be a murderer?* Arawn kept running.

Arawn didn't know if he were running deeper into the forest or toward the farm. He heard sounds behind him, but he didn't turn; he didn't want to trip and fall, allowing Torkall to catch him.

Arawn began to tire, and he didn't know if he could keep running for long. He knew he was slowing down, and the sounds behind him were getting louder. A moment later, he was knocked to the ground.

Torkall tried to pin him down, but Arawn kept struggling to break free. "Stop fighting this, Arawn. I promise it'll be quick," he said, trying to get a firm grip on Arawn.

"I don't want to die, Torkall!" Arawn shouted. He continued to fight Torkall with all his remaining strength.

Torkall pulled a dagger from his belt and put it against Arawn's throat. Arawn fought to control his anger and froze, knowing that Torkall might kill him accidently if he kept moving around.

"Good-bye, Arawn," Torkall said sadly, breathing heavily from the chase. "Forgive me."

The sound of twigs snapping distracted Torkall. His head shot up as he looked for the source of the sound.

Arawn saw his chance. He grabbed Torkall's hand and pulled the dagger away, twisting Torkall's wrist so the point of the dagger pointed upwards.

Torkall looked down at Arawn and tried to regain control of the dagger. Arawn, using both hands, pushed with all his might. The dagger slashed Torkall in the face, just below his left eye.

"Aaahh!" Torkall cried out in pain, loosening his grip on the dagger.

Arawn slashed at Torkall again, cutting the young man along his jaw. Torkall raised his left hand to protect his face, and Arawn thrust the dagger into Torkall's forearm.

Torkall released the dagger and rolled off Arawn, clutching his left arm. Arawn hacked at Torkall with the dagger and cut the young man across his upper right thigh. Blood poured from the leg and arm wounds, and Torkall's neck and cheek were bleeding freely.

Torkall got to his feet, and Arawn jumped up and lunged at the man. Torkall grabbed Arawn's hands and forced the dagger away before it could cut him again. The two of them struggled for control of the weapon.

"Arawn, drop!" Arawn heard someone shout.

Arawn recognized Gareth's voice and didn't hesitate. He dropped to his knees, keeping both hands on the hilt of the dagger.

Torkall looked up at the four hunters running toward him. Before he could turn and run, he felt a sharp pain in his neck. Torkall's hands went slack, and he fell backward. He was dead before he hit the ground.

Arawn looked up and saw the arrow sticking out of Torkall's neck just below the skull. He turned and saw Gareth and three of the other hunters running toward him. He dropped the dagger.

"Are you injured?" Gareth asked, kneeling next to him.

Arawn shook his head, looking over at the man who had been his friend. "He killed Ethan and Atrius. He was going to kill me!"

"Why?" Gareth asked as one of the other hunters made sure Torkall was dead.

Arawn shook his head. "I don't know," he said, knowing that Belenus wouldn't want Arawn to mention anything about the prophecy. "He was going to make it look like a boar slashed me, but I escaped from him and ran as fast as I could. He caught up to me and was about to kill me with his dagger when he heard you approaching. I grabbed the dagger, and we fought. That's when you arrived and shot him."

Arawn gave Gareth a hug, shaking as the memories of the ordeal flooded into his consciousness. "Thank you for saving my life!"

"You're welcome, Arawn. Belenus wanted me to keep an eye on you, and when I saw you and Torkall moving farther away from the rest of us, we came looking to see what was going on."

One of the hunters ran back to the farm to get Belenus. Arawn felt too shaken to walk, so the hunter promised to bring back a horse for Arawn to ride. Less than forty minutes later, Arawn heard a horse approaching. Thunder charged into the clearing a moment later carrying the hunter and Belenus. Belenus jumped down and knelt next to Arawn, who sat on the ground, staring at Torkall with a look of anger and disbelief.

"Are you all right, Arawn?" he asked, the concern evident in his face.

Arawn nodded. Belenus looked up at Gareth, who told Belenus the whole story. Belenus looked at Arawn when Gareth mentioned that

Torkall had killed Ethan and Atrius, but he said nothing until Gareth was finished.

"I'm sorry, Belenus," the factor said. "I'm the one who hired him."

"Don't think that this is your fault, Gareth," Belenus said, reaching up and putting his hand on Gareth's. "He was with us for six years, and none of us saw anything in him that would make us think he could be a murderer. I thought I was an excellent judge of character, but he fooled even me. This is not anyone's fault."

"Yes, sir," Gareth said, looking upset.

"Look at me, Gareth," Belenus said.

Gareth looked at Belenus.

"This is not your fault," Belenus said to his factor. "You saved Arawn. Think on that instead."

"But Ethan and Atrius are dead."

"Because of what Torkall did, not because of anything you did. Today you saved a life and ended a threat to Arawn and to others. Don't torture yourself with what someone else did. Celebrate what you did. You saved Arawn. You killed Torkall. That's what you did."

Gareth nodded and flashed a tired smile, but Belenus could still see that it would take a while for Gareth to stop blaming himself.

Belenus stood and helped Arawn onto the back of Thunder. He mounted up and slowly rode back to the farm.

"Did Torkall tell you why he was trying to kill you?" he asked once they were out of earshot from the hunters.

"Yes. He said he killed his uncle years ago and ran away to escape punishment. Some men found him working here and paid him to kill the three of us. They said if he didn't kill us, they'd expose him for what he'd done and kill us themselves."

Belenus nodded. "Did he say who these men were who made him do this?"

"No, sir. Just that he didn't have any choice. He had a boar's tusk and was going to make it look like a boar killed me. Belenus, what if the men who paid Torkall come after me?"

"I think we can assume that they will, Arawn. And if they come for you on the farm, others could be hurt. I think it's time to move you somewhere away from here where they can't find you."

"And leave the farm unprotected?" Arawn asked indignantly. "Even if I'm gone, they'll come looking for me here. And if they found me here, they'll eventually find me somewhere else. I'm not going to spend the rest of my life running, Belenus. We need to find a way to defend the farm from anyone trying to get to me."

"It's too dangerous," Belenus said softly.

"I don't care. My place is here, and it's my responsibility to protect everyone else."

"Why?"

"Because they're in danger because of me whether I'm here or not."

"Let me think about it, Arawn."

"Fine," Arawn said, feeling tired and hungry. "But I've made up my mind."

As they approached the farm, Arawn saw that the hunt had been successful. Several boars were being prepared for the smokehouse, while others were on spits for roasting. He knew he'd feel better after he ate. Then he'd start working on how to keep everyone on the farm safe.

Later that night, after everyone had gone to bed, Belenus stood along the banks of the lake.

"He had been with us for six years, and we never suspected a thing," he told the other three elders.

"Is Arawn all right?" Alaunus asked.

"He's shaken, but physically he's fine. He was close to Torkall, and this is affecting him greatly. I told him I need to move him to a safe place, but he won't go. He wants to stay here and defend the farm from anyone who comes after him. There's no talking him out of it. So starting in a couple of days when the shock of the betrayal wears off, I'm going to have him continue working with some of the farmhands – the ones who have served with the military – on the defense of the compound. I'm also going to have them step up his training."

"Good," Alaunus said. *"These are skills he will need when the time comes for him to fulfill his destiny. What do we know about the people who made Torkall do this?"*

"Nothing yet."

"Is Mider still unaware that one of the orphans is a girl?" Tridamus asked.

"Yes, but we need to prepare for the day when he finds out. Cerridwen also needs to learn to fight and take care of herself. Amaethon needs to know how to fight as well, but not in the same way as the others. His gifts give him a weapon that none of the others has. You all need to put more effort into having them trained to defend themselves. If we lose just one of them, the prophecy will fail, and all of Alastriona will pay the price."

Torkall Betrays Arawn at the Boar Hunt

CHAPTER 12

maethon went down to the stream below the tower to practice his lessons in one of his favorite places. There was a large rock where the stream bent, and Amaethon sat on that rock for hours trying to master Nemausus' latest challenge. As the shadows began to lengthen, he decided it was time to return to the tower.

When he stood up to climb down from the rock, he felt someone staring at him. Looking around, he noticed someone standing on the hill overlooking the other side of the stream, but he couldn't see the person's face.

Amaethon stared at the person and saw the hint of a beard sticking out from underneath the hooded cloak he was wearing. The man on the hilltop didn't move.

There's something familiar about him. I know I've seen him before.

Amaethon continued staring and started seeing images in his mind. At first, he saw someone who looked like Nemausus confronting someone in a dark alley. Then he saw himself making rocks hover. Several other images flashed through his mind, and Amaethon recognized himself in most of them.

Amaethon wanted to find out why the person was watching him, but the sun was setting, and he needed to get back to the tower. When Amaethon finally jumped down and looked up toward the hilltop again, the person was gone.

Nemausus was waiting outside the tower entrance for his student to return. "How did you do today?" he asked.

"I'm starting to get the hang of making objects change their shape, but I still need to work on it."

Nemausus nodded and smiled at Amaethon. As Nemausus turned to enter the tower, Amaethon added, "Master, there was someone watching me at the stream."

Nemausus looked at his student. "Who was it?"

"I don't know, but I feel like I should know. I sensed him before I saw him, and it felt familiar somehow. Not like the way I can sense you, but still familiar."

"What did he look like?"

"He was wearing a dark cloak with a hood covering his head and face. I couldn't see anything except for a beard sticking out of the bottom of the hood. I was standing on the big rock – staring at him. Then I started getting these flashes like memories. When I jumped down off the rock, he was gone. I feel like I've met him before, but I don't know where."

Nemausus nodded. "I've seen him, too. I felt him watching the tower when I was examining the knife that killed your parents. I turned to look at him, and somehow he made the knife disintegrate. It's almost like he knew I was trying to learn the knife's secrets, and he came here to make sure that I didn't discover anything useful."

"Did you learn anything at all, Master?"

"Only what I already knew. The knife was infused with a powerful magic to keep anyone from learning about the person who had used it."

"So we still don't know who killed my parents?"

Nemausus put his hand on Amaethon's shoulder. "No, we don't. Believe me, if I could have saved your parents, I'd have done so without hesitation, but it seems clear to me that I was supposed to find you and raise you as my own, and that could only be done if you were an orphan. I don't completely understand why things happened the way they did, but I have no doubts that you were meant to be here, learning what you're learning. I understand the desire to know who and why, and I hope someday to give you that answer or to help you find the answer yourself. Until then, we'll have to keep looking for the truth wherever it may be hiding."

Amaethon looked at his teacher. "Thank you, Master," he said softly.

Nemausus nodded. "For now, let's make supper. I'm suddenly very hungry."

The next morning, Nemausus sat down next to Amaethon at the table. "We need to add something to your training starting today."

"What are we adding, Master?"

"I need to train you to fight and to defend yourself."

"With human weapons or magic?"

"You need to learn both, but I'm going to teach you how to fight with magic. I'm going to send for some of the soldiers who patrol this area to help teach you human weapons."

Later that morning, Nemausus and Amaethon stood on a hilltop near the tower. "Dueling with another sorcerer is similar to dueling with swords," Nemausus began. "One side attacks, and the other side defends. This goes on until one side surrenders, escapes, is killed or otherwise incapacitated. Understand?"

Amaethon nodded.

"Good. The real difference is the weapons that you use and how you defend yourself against the enemy's weapons. If your enemy throws something at you like a boulder or a tree, you need to be able to deflect it before it hits its target. If your enemy reaches out with his mind and stops your heart from beating, you have to be able to break his hold on your heart without ripping your heart apart in the process. No sword or other human weapon can stop an enemy from doing either of these, especially if he's several miles away at the time.

"In the heat of battle, you need to be calm if you're going to figure out how to get out of a situation or if you're going to make the best attack. Confusion, anger, distractions… these cloud your judgment and make it harder to focus your thoughts in the right place."

For the rest of that day, and for several hours each day after that, Nemausus attacked Amaethon and showed his student how to block the attacks. At first, the attacks were simple and not very dangerous. In time, though, they became more difficult to block.

Nemausus also taught Amaethon how to attack by focusing his will on making something happen that would injure or kill an enemy.

"Just as in human warfare, it's best not to reveal your full strength at the beginning of a battle," Nemausus said. "Let the enemy see exactly what you want him to see, and when he gets overconfident, show him something he doesn't expect and can't defend himself against easily. An enemy having to defend himself cannot attack, so keep the enemy on the defensive as much as possible. The goal is to stay alive by any means necessary. But be careful about the destruction or loss of life around you. Anyone getting too close to a sorcery duel could be injured or killed accidently."

As Amaethon grew more comfortable dueling, Nemausus tested him frequently and without warning. Sometimes the attacks came while Amaethon was sleeping, while he was eating, while he was practicing his other lessons, and even while he was bathing in the stream below the tower. Amaethon never knew when or how the attacks would come, and eventually he grew used to being ready for an attack at all times.

One day, while Amaethon was watering and feeding the horses in the paddock near the tower, Nemausus attacked by lifting Amaethon in the air and hurling him toward the haystacks next to the stables. Unable to focus his thoughts in time due the suddenness of the attack, Amaethon flew past the haystacks and hit the stones at the base of the tower, knocking him unconscious.

Seeing his student fall to the ground, Nemausus ran down the stairs to check on him. There was a large gash above Amaethon's left eye and several scratches where his face hit the rocks. Nemausus checked for any serious injuries, and when he discovered that Amaethon had a concussion, he placed his hand on Amaethon's head for a moment and concentrated. Then he carried Amaethon into the tower and placed him in his bed. Nemausus sat with him for several hours until he regained consciousness.

"How are you feeling?" Nemausus asked anxiously when he saw Amaethon's eyes open.

"Everything hurts," Amaethon replied, wincing as he tried to sit up. "What happened?"

"I attacked you, and you weren't prepared. You were supposed to land in the haystacks, but somehow you hit the tower pretty hard instead."

"That explains why it feels like the tower fell on me."

Nemausus gave Amaethon a reassuring smile. "There were no serious injuries, so you should recover completely in a day or so. Rest for now, and when you're ready, we'll start practicing again."

Two days passed before Amaethon was able to venture outside again. Nemausus was in his tower when he heard a loud explosion coming from the base of a nearby hill. Looking out the window of his study, he saw fireballs and lightning materializing and striking the ground all around where Amaethon stood.

Nemausus descended the stairs to the first level, exited the tower, and walked toward Amaethon. It took more than a minute before Amaethon realized that anyone was standing next to him.

"What are you doing, Amaethon?" Nemausus asked.

"As it turns out, I seem to be fairly good at making things blow up. I thought I'd practice that for a while. It makes my head hurt less."

Nemausus nodded and left his young student to blow up the hillside in peace. After a few hours, he heard Amaethon climbing up the stairs to his study.

"Master, may I disturb you?" he asked before entering the top floor of the tower.

"Certainly," Nemausus said, putting down the scroll he had been reading.

Amaethon was about to say something when they both heard a loud sound coming from outside the tower.

"Did you do that?" Nemausus demanded.

"No, Master," Amaethon replied, looking in disbelief out the tower window.

Nemausus turned and saw green energy bursts lighting up the sky to the north of the tower. Walking over to the window, Nemausus saw a hooded figure standing on a nearby hillside with its arms outstretched. More energy bursts sounded and lit up the sky as some unseen barrier kept the energy from reaching anywhere near the tower.

Amaethon watched in fascination. "What's happening?" he asked.

Pointing to the figure on the hill, Nemausus said, "It looks like our watcher is back. He's trying to attack the tower, but I have a protective barrier around the area that magic cannot penetrate."

They watched as the figure on the hill tried for nearly an hour to find a weakness in the barrier around the tower. Then, in the blink of an eye, the attack ended and the figure was gone.

"No one has ever tried to attack this tower before," Nemausus said darkly as he sat back down behind his desk. "I never thought anyone would be that bold."

Looking up at Amaethon, he added. "We need to accelerate your training on fighting and defending yourself. You've seen what our watcher is capable of, and without the protective barrier, he could easily obliterate you."

"Yes, Master," Amaethon agreed.

Another month passed before Amaethon was finally able to pay Nemausus back for being slammed against the tower. Nemausus attacked Amaethon in the same way as before, and Amaethon flew into the air and hit the side of the tower again, falling unconscious on the ground.

"Not again," Nemausus muttered as he raced down the stairs to check on his student.

When he bent over Amaethon to check for injuries, he quite suddenly found himself several hundred feet in the air. He felt Amaethon pushing with his mind and defended himself against being hurled off into the distance. A moment later, Nemausus felt Amaethon's attack disengage, and he began falling. Just before he hit the ground, Nemausus focused his thoughts and began to hover. He lowered himself to the ground next to his grinning student.

"I see you weren't seriously hurt by hitting the wall again," Nemausus said, hiding his amusement.

"But Master, I never hit the wall. I just made it look like I did so you wouldn't expect my counterattack."

"Nicely done, Amaethon," Nemausus said, holding out his hand to help his student get up from the ground.

Amaethon practiced daily with Nemausus and with a company of soldiers that had started patrolling around the tower on a regular basis. In time, Amaethon became an accomplished swordsman. But Nemausus was most impressed with Amaethon's ability to duel with magic.

Their watcher tried to attack the tower two more times that year, but he had no success breaching the barrier. Amaethon started keeping a close watch for the figure wherever he went, but the figure didn't reappear.

CHAPTER 13

After the attack on Arawn, Tridamus kept an even closer eye on Cerridwen until he could arrange for her to learn how to fight and defend herself properly.

The morning of her thirteenth birthday, Cerridwen walked into the smithy, put on her leather gloves and apron, and sat down to begin working on some new scabbards. By the time Tridamus joined her, she was concentrating so hard on the design she was making that she didn't realize there was another person in the workshop.

When she finally looked up and saw that Tridamus had a guest with him, she quickly stood up and bowed, assuming the guest was a patron.

"Is that her?" the stranger asked Tridamus.

"Yes, it is. What do you think?"

"Would you ask her to take off the apron and turn around for me?"

"Cerridwen, would you mind doing as the gentleman asked?"

Cerridwen obeyed, but with a sense of alarm. *What is Tridamus doing? Is he trying to join me to this stranger or bartering my services in return for something?* Cerridwen knew that many young maidens around her age were already betrothed, but she felt that sure Tridamus would have said something to her if he were going to do that.

When Cerridwen finished turning around, the stranger asked, "Has she ever handled a blade before?"

"Other than to take measurements for the scabbards, no," Tridamus replied.

The stranger looked like he was deep in thought as he stared at Cerridwen. Cerridwen was beginning to get uncomfortable, but she remained silent and still. Finally, the stranger said, "Very well. It's an unusual request, but I can spare two hours each morning. Have her fitted with a leather jerkin today, and I'll be back in the morning to get started."

"Thank you, William. I really appreciate this."

"You're welcome, Tridamus. Just make sure the blade you promised is as good as you claim it will be."

The stranger and Tridamus clasped each other's right forearm. The stranger left, and Cerridwen just stood there staring at Tridamus with a dozen questions swirling in her mind.

"You're probably wondering what that was all about," Tridamus said once the stranger had left.

"Yes, sir, I am," Cerridwen replied, sitting back down on her stool.

"It's all part of your birthday present," Tridamus stated with a smile.

"My birthday present?" Cerridwen asked, feeling completely bewildered at the statement.

Tridamus pulled a stool over and sat down across from her. "Yes. I know you've wanted to learn to use the forge and start making armor and blades, right?"

Cerridwen nodded, and Tridamus continued. "I believe that you can never *make* a weapon properly if you don't know how to *use* it properly. So before I let you start making weapons, I need to make sure you know how to use them. The name of the man who was just here is William, and he's the master-at-arms for the soldiers in this district. In return for a sword that I'm going to make him, and that you're going to help me embellish, he's agreed to teach you how to fight with swords and daggers."

"I'm going to learn to swordfight?" Cerridwen asked, wide-eyed.

Belenus nodded. "Once you understand how swords and daggers are used, I can teach you how they're made. I'll let you try your hand at making a few pieces in addition to your other work around here. If you show promise, I'll let you keep doing it. But if I don't think that you have the potential for making swords and armor, you'll go back to just making jewelry, scabbards, and embellishing sword and dagger hilts, and we'll never discuss using the forge or the anvil again. Agreed?"

Cerridwen was thrilled that she'd finally get to use the forge and anvil, and she was excited to learn how to fight using swords and daggers. This wasn't something that girls typically learned, but she hadn't been raised to be an ordinary girl. She leaped off the stool and threw her arms around Tridamus' neck.

"Thank you, Tridamus!" she squealed with delight, hugging his neck tightly.

"You're welcome," Tridamus said, patting her back with his large hands.

When she released his neck, he added, "Now before you start learning how to use the sword, we need to make you a jerkin."

"What's a jerkin?" she asked.

"You've seen the soldiers wearing them. It's the thick leather vest or coat that protects the upper body. It's what soldiers used before plate armor was developed, and archers and other soldiers who don't typically get near the enemy still use them. I've never made one for a woman before, so we may have to modify it once you've started practicing, but we can at least get you one that'll work for your first lesson tomorrow."

Tridamus and Cerridwen spent the rest of the day fashioning a leather jerkin for Cerridwen to use during her lessons. It was bulky and didn't allow her to move freely, but when Tridamus gently poked her a few times with a sword while she was wearing it, she appreciated how it worked and why she needed to be wearing it while learning to fight.

Tridamus also made her two leather wrist guards to cover her wrists and forearms. "There are twelve primary kill zones on a body," he explained to her as he fitted the wrist guards. "Two are on either side of your neck, which is why jerkins and armor have high collars. Two are each wrist, which is why some jerkins have full sleeves or why you need to wear wrist guards. One is your stomach, one is anywhere along the spine in the center of your back, and one is on either side of you just below the ribs. The next two are your inner thighs, which is why many jerkins either go down to the knee or why there is separate leg armor made of metal plates or leather. You won't need that for your lessons, but if you ever go into battle, you will. These nine kill zones are slow killers because it takes a while to bleed out and die."

"What are the other three kill zones?" Cerridwen asked.

"One is your heart, here," he said, pointing to a place just to the left of the center of her chest. "That's why there's extra leather or thicker armor plating there. If a sword hits your heart, you're dead."

He pointed to the soft part underneath her chin. "One is an upward thrust here into the center of the skull. That kills instantly as well. Some helmets have a part that wraps around the chin to protect that area, but it's hard to protect it with a jerkin or armor because it would restrict head movement, making it hard to see someone attacking you from the side."

"What about wearing a separate collar that protects beneath the chin?" Cerridwen asked.

"Everyone should use them, and some people do. Others can't stand having anything around their neck because it gets tight and feels like it's squeezing. Which brings me to the last zone."

"What is the last zone?" she asked.

Tridamus tapped Cerridwen on the back of her neck. "Cutting off the head. That's another instant killer, but if everyone would wear armor collars, it wouldn't happen on the battlefield."

Cerridwen nodded. She loved the look of armor, but this was the first time she began to understand how it worked.

Cerridwen barely slept that night. She was too excited for the morning and her first lesson. As she tossed and turned in her bed, she heard Tridamus call to her from his room at the end of the hallway.

"Morning will come quicker if you get some sleep!"

She forced herself to try, but she was still too excited. She finally managed to get a couple of hours of sleep, but when the first rays of the morning sun hit her windowsill, she bounded out of bed, fully awake. She quickly straightened up her bed and her room, put on her clothes, picked up the jerkin and wrist guards, and ran down the hall to the kitchen to grab a quick bite to eat.

After Cerridwen ate and set out some food for Tridamus, she ran outside to take care of the horses. She heard a sound coming from the workshop as she entered the first stall, and she knew that Tridamus was using the giant bellows to blow air into the forge to build up the fire. She led each of the horses to the paddock behind the stables, and she made sure that the water trough was full before putting a grain mixture in the food trough. Then she cleaned out the stalls and put down fresh straw in each stall.

As she walked out of the stables thirty minutes later, she saw William approaching the compound. He saw her and raised a hand in greeting. He motioned for her to join him in the field next to the house. Cerridwen ran to him and saw him unrolling a leather bundle that contained several practice swords and real swords.

Sizing her up as he had done the day before, William watched her put on the jerkin and the wrist guards. Satisfied that she understood their purpose, he selected one of the swords and handed it to her.

"This is called a broadsword because of the width of the blade and because both edges of the blade are sharp. This sword can cut and stab. Some will tell you that there's no 'style' in using a sword to cut, but the first lesson I want you to learn is that style has nothing to do with fighting. When you're fighting for your life, you do what you have to do to stay alive. That means cutting, stabbing, or even using the sword as a club. If you fight, fight to win."

William showed her the other swords and instructed her on their use and the circumstances where one was better suited than another. There

84

were one-handed swords and two-handed swords, there were swords that were more effective in battle, and there were swords that were more suitable when the fighting was between just two people.

He showed her some of the basic moves, but they didn't spar during the first lesson. "I need to make certain you understand the basics before I show you how they're used together," he explained as he rolled up the swords in the leather bundle.

Over the next two weeks, they practiced with the swords every morning. Cerridwen spent the rest of the day doing her normal chores and work. She stayed in the smithy until much later at night to keep up with her work, but she didn't mind at all. She was too excited to be learning something new, and she looked forward to what Tridamus had promised to teach her when he felt she was ready.

Toward the end of the second week of Cerridwen's training, Tridamus watched from the courtyard as Cerridwen and William were sparring. They were using wooden practice swords, and Tridamus was impressed at Cerridwen's reflexes as she tried to keep William from getting through her defenses. William always managed to get through, but Cerridwen was improving nonetheless.

Once the lesson ended, Tridamus walked over to talk to William as Cerridwen hurried to the workshop to finish a jewelry commission that a patron was picking up later that day.

"How is she doing?" he asked the master-at-arms.

"Quite well, for a girl," William replied. "She's a good student and a quick study. If we continue the lessons, I'm certain that someday she'll be able to hold her own in a fight against any swordsman that comes along."

"Will you continue teaching her?" Tridamus asked.

"Certainly. For a twin to the sword you're making me already."

"Deal," Tridamus said with a smile. It was a fair price to make sure that Cerridwen could protect herself and be ready to fulfill her part of the prophecy.

CHAPTER 14

rawn and the men with military training were beginning to act more like a military unit protecting the farm, rather than just a collection of farmhands. He continued to improve his skills with the sword and bow, and he frequently accompanied the men from the farm on hunting trips into the forest for fresh meat. After a few months, he didn't seem to be haunted by the memories of his lost friends and his first boar hunt.

"How do you lead men, Belenus?" Arawn asked one night after he returned from his patrol of the compound.

"There are different qualities that a leader has," Belenus replied. "A soldier fights and obeys commands. A leader decides when and where to fight, and when to avoid fighting. A leader leads by example. He embodies the qualities he wants in his men. He makes the welfare of his men the first priority, but he knows that some must die for others to live. Most of all, a leader is honest, courageous, and compassionate. Men will know if their leader is lying, and they'll lose respect for him. A leader must have courage in a fight, but he must also have the courage to stand by his convictions even if it seems hopeless. And he must be compassionate toward his enemies. Any butcher can kill, but a true leader must also forgive. The true test of a leader is to bring the peace, not just win the battle."

Arawn nodded thoughtfully as Belenus stood up, patted Arawn on the shoulder, and went to get both of them something to eat.

When Arawn was fourteen, Belenus found Arawn on one side of the courtyard, discussing something with several of his military teachers who were instructing him on how armies moved together in battle.

"I don't understand why it's necessary to fight in the open like this," he said, pointing to the diagram that had been drawn in the dirt depicting two armies moving toward each other. "If you're marching in the open toward them, they can see you, they can see how you're organized, what your strength is, what weapons you have with you... there's no surprise and no advantage once you commit yourself in the open."

"There are times when the goal is to intimidate the enemy with a show of force, letting fear break the enemy's will," one of the men commented. "Sometimes fear makes the enemy easier to defeat, and sometimes it makes the enemy decide not to fight at all."

"How would you do it, Arawn?" Belenus asked, joining in the discussion.

"When you hunt, you approach your prey with stealth from a direction that makes it harder for the prey to see you. Why don't armies do the same thing?"

Arawn erased the diagram in the dirt with his hand and drew a new diagram showing a small force in the face of the larger enemy force, and two other forces approaching the side of the enemy force.

Belenus pointed to the new diagram. "If your forces are hidden, how do you get them to attack and spring your trap?"

"I'd give the enemy something to see that lets them believe exactly what I want them to believe. Let them see a smaller force with simple weapons and let them think that's all I have with me. While they're focusing on what they can see, my other two forces that they can't see will be approaching from the sides. The enemy's overconfidence in the size of their force compared to what they can see of mine will be their undoing, and once they commit to attacking my smaller force, my other two forces will attack and destroy them."

"So it would be like hunting boars in the brush?" one of the others asked. "Your small force in front of the enemy would flush them out and make them attack using one of the traditional tactics for attacking a smaller force, and then your larger forces would move in once the enemy had committed to a specific tactic?"

"Exactly," Arawn stated, happy that someone understood what he was saying. "If you show the enemy everything you have, they know exactly how to come at you. If they don't know what you have, they might not come at you at all. The trick is to make them think they know what you have when they really don't. It's how you hunt boars and how you hunt bears – both of which are extremely dangerous to attack head-on. You have to trick them into attacking you before they know how large your force really is."

Belenus saw the others begin to nod. "So you're tricking them into falling for a defensive strategy, when you're actually fighting an aggressive offensive strategy?" Belenus asked.

"Yes, sir," Arawn answered. "I just can't see any reason to put your whole army in the field at one time and let the enemy see everything you have to throw at them. The only time I'd let my entire army be seen is if I had no intention of fighting."

"But what if the enemy is doing the same thing to you that you're doing to them?" Belenus asked, bending down to adjust Arawn's diagram so that both armies had small forces in front of each other and larger forces hidden on each side.

Arawn stared at the diagram in silence and admitted, "I'm not sure. Depending on where the soldiers were hiding, you might end up having three battles going on at the same time or having some of your forces surrounded and cut to pieces."

Belenus stood up and wiped the dirt off his hands. "You may want to think about that. You might fool an enemy once with what you suggested, but could you use it on the same enemy twice? Battles aren't hunters against prey. They're hunters against hunters. How do you hunt something that's hunting you? That's a strategy you need to work out."

Belenus walked away and left the group to consider his suggestion.

With Torkall dead, it fell to the other men with military experience to train with Arawn each day. This gave Arawn the chance to practice fighting against multiple opponents at the same time, both mounted and on the ground.

Frequently, Arawn and the other men would divide into two teams and attack each other. Arawn learned how to fight together as part of a unit, and he learned how disorganized things become once a battle begins.

"You can have a great strategy going into a battle," one of the older cavalry veterans told him one morning. "But once the battle begins, everything changes. You can't predict everything that'll happen, so the general needs to be able to read how the battle is going so he can make adjustments and either press an advantage or avoid disaster."

Arawn's skills on horseback improved along with his skills as a fighter. He and the other men patrolled along the perimeter of the farm several times a day on horseback. As part of Arawn's training, some of the men would turn around without warning and attack Arawn.

One afternoon, Arawn found himself facing five of the other men with no one else there to help him. Two of the other men were working their way around him, and he knew if they succeeded in surrounding him, he couldn't escape.

Arawn adjusted his grip on the reins and drew his sword. He pretended he was going to attack the man on his left, but he pulled the reins to the right and made his horse rear up. The man on his right was getting ready to attack, but the horse kicked him with its front hooves and knocked him off his horse. Arawn gave his horse the cue, and the horse bucked and kicked at the man behind him, causing the man's horse to bolt.

With two men out of the fight, Arawn turned and attacked the three remaining men. He pushed the first man off his horse and moved around to the right so the other two couldn't get around him. After several minutes of maneuvering his horse to keep him safe, he saw all five men regrouping for another attack. He turned his horse and pressed his heels into its sides.

The men chased him back to the farm. They deployed in a way that kept him from being able to turn left or right. The horse paddock behind the stables was right in front of him.

Arawn thought about his options. *They'll block me if I try to turn, and if I stop at the paddock fence, they'll have me trapped. I can't dismount while the horse is running this fast, and if I slow down, they'll catch me.*

There was only one option left, but Arawn had never jumped a fence before. He leaned forward in the saddle, clutched the lower part of the horse's mane, and stood up in the stirrups, hoping the horse wouldn't stop and send him flying over the fence into the paddock.

Belenus watched from the rear of the stables as Arawn raced toward the farm with the five men chasing him. "Looks like they've got him trapped," he commented to the groom, who was standing next to him.

"I don't think so, Belenus," the groom replied. "He's not stopping."

"What, you mean he's going to jump?" Belenus asked, surprised.

"I think so. Look how he's riding."

"Does he know how?"

"I showed him how to jump over bales of hay a few months ago," the groom replied, "but never anything as high as a fence."

Arawn's horse reached the fence, and Belenus held his breath as he saw the horse leap up into the air, barely clearing the top of the fence with its hooves. The horse landed inside the paddock, and Arawn quickly turned the horse around to face his attackers.

Belenus watched the men react to Arawn's unexpected escape. Four of them turned in time to avoid the fence, but the fifth was too close. His horse slid to a stop just short of the fence, sending him flying over the fence. He landed near Arawn's horse, stunned.

Arawn jumped off his horse and put his sword to the man's chest. "Do you yield?" he asked the man.

89

"Y y y yes, I yield," the man panted.

Arawn helped the man up and looked at the other four men, who were sitting on their horses on the other side of the fence.

"Nice jump, Arawn," the older cavalry veteran said. "I didn't think you knew how to do that."

"I didn't," Arawn replied. "But you didn't leave me much choice."

The older man nodded. "And that's the real lesson. When you don't have a choice, sometimes the impossible is the only acceptable alternative."

The groom stepped forward. "Okay, you've had your fun. Now tend to your horses and put them in the stables for the night. They're thirsty and need to eat."

Arawn and the men did as they were told.

Arawn and the men met several times a week to discuss defensive and offensive strategies. Sometimes they'd discuss fighting in great battles, but mostly they discussed ways to keep the farm safe from raiders.

Shortly after Arawn turned fifteen, Belenus received reports of troopers in the area who were raiding some of the local farms and villages. From the reports, it was clear that these troopers were looking for a tall, dark-haired boy around Arawn's age.

Arawn and the men wasted no time preparing to defend the farm. The biggest problem they faced was how to protect all of the ways in and out of the compound.

"There are just too many ways in and out," one of the men pointed out early one morning. "We don't have enough men to protect them all, and we don't have enough time or lumber to build a wall around the compound."

"And wood walls can be burned down," one of the other men commented. "They won't stop a determined enemy."

Arawn looked around the compound, thinking about the problem. "What if we block most of the entrances?" he suggested after a moment. "We can cover them with the wagons, crates... anything that will keep them from entering that way. Then we control where they can enter and exit, and we don't need more men to cover the other entrances."

"Great idea, Arawn," several of the men said.

They pulled the wagons out and moved them between several of the buildings, blocking all but three entrances to the compound. They turned the wagons onto their sides so the troopers wouldn't be able to move them easily. Once the other entrances were blocked, they started planning how to deploy the defenders.

"Do you think they'll ride into just one of the entrances, or split their forces and come in from all sides?" Belenus asked after inspecting their defenses.

"I'd split my forces," the older cavalry veteran replied. "That way, they cut off our escape. They'll think they have us trapped."

"What about the people on the farm?" Belenus asked.

"I think we need to send the women and children into the Great Forest as soon as the troopers are sighted," Arawn stated. "We need to get them away from the fighting. As for the rest of the farmers, I say we give them farm tools to use as weapons and tell them to wait in the center of the compound for the troopers. Once all the troopers are inside the compound, we can attack them."

"You mean the men with military experience will attack?" Belenus asked.

Arawn nodded.

"So you're going to let the troopers see a group of simple farmers, while keeping your real fighting force hidden until the last minute?"

Arawn smiled. "They'll expect to see the famers with farm tools. They won't expect the real attack and won't know how to react until it's too late."

Belenus nodded, as did the other men.

"How will we know they're coming?" the older cavalry veteran asked.

Pointing to the roof of the kitchen, Arawn said, "I'll be up there as lookout. It's the tallest building in the compound, and I can hide behind the chimney and still see anyone coming long before they get here. I'll have my bow with me, and I can signal when to start the attack."

Belenus nodded. "It's a good plan."

The next day, Arawn was in position behind the chimney on the roof of the kitchen. Around mid-day, he saw a cloud of dust in the distance that indicated a large number of riders approaching.

"Here they come," he shouted.

"Women and children to the forest," Belenus shouted, coming out of the main house with his walking stick. "The rest of you grab your weapons."

The women and children left the compound and made their way south toward the Great Forest, making sure to stay low so the troopers wouldn't see them escaping. The farmers joined Belenus in the center of the compound, and the men Arawn had been training with hid out of sight.

Arawn watched the troopers approach and let everyone know when they were about to reach the compound.

"How many are there?" Belenus asked.

"About twenty," Arawn replied.

"Are they wearing any markings?"

"None that I can see."

Arawn watched as the troopers split their ranks. "They're coming in from all sides," he said before ducking back behind the chimney.

The troopers entered the compound through the three remaining openings. They were dressed in black leather tunics and head coverings, but they wore nothing that could identify who had sent them. They quickly encircled Belenus and the other farmers in the compound.

When the troopers saw the weak defense being offered by the farmers, they laughed. "What do you think you're doing?" the leader shouted once he had Belenus and the others surrounded.

"We're defending what's ours," Belenus replied.

"We're not interested in what's yours," the leader sneered at Belenus. "We're interested in a boy of about fifteen who has been seen living around here."

"There's no one here of that age," Belenus said. "Ride on and leave us alone."

The leader drew his sword, as did the other troopers. "We can't do that. You understand it's nothing personal."

The leader raised his sword and approached Belenus, but the horse had only taken two steps when suddenly there was an arrow sticking out of the leader's chest. His eyes opened wide, he fell sideways off his horse, and didn't move.

The troopers looked around, but saw no one. "Who did that?" one trooper shouted at Belenus.

A second arrow was released, and another trooper fell dead to the ground.

The troopers wheeled around on their horses, looking for the source of the arrows. Two more troopers fell in less than a minute, but no one could tell where the shooter was hiding.

"Spread out and find him!" a trooper shouted to the remaining men on horseback.

Several of the troopers dismounted and moved toward the buildings to search them. The rest remained in the center of the compound to watch the farmers and Belenus.

Arawn stood up from his hiding place and whistled. He let two more arrows fly, and as the troopers fell, the rest of the armed farmers who had been hiding jumped out of their hiding places and attacked.

Using their spears like pikes, the men ran forward, each impaling the trooper nearest to him. Arawn continued shooting arrows at the mounted troopers while the men fought with the dismounted ones. Once all the mounted troopers were on the ground, Belenus gave a shout and the farmers attacked the troopers who were still fighting. Overwhelmed by the farm's defenders, several of the troopers tried to escape, but found the exits blocked. Those who managed to get back on their horses were soon lying on the ground – killed by Arawn's arrows.

Arawn's quiver was empty, and there was only one trooper left alive. Arawn whistled loudly to get the attention of one of the men holding a pike. When the man looked up, Arawn motioned for the man to attack the trooper.

Arawn watched as the trooper pulled something from his belt that looked like a small hatchet. Just before he was stabbed to death with the pike, the trooper threw the hatchet directly at Arawn.

Arawn could barely see the hatchet spinning in the air toward him, and he waited too long to duck out of the way. He felt a tremendous pain in his left shoulder. He lost his balance and fell backward on the kitchen roof. He felt himself sliding down the roof followed by the sensation of falling through the air. He felt another sharp pain and blacked out.

"Arawn!" Belenus cried as he ran to the young man lying on the ground, bleeding from the gash on his shoulder.

Belenus tore open Arawn's tunic and looked at the wound. He applied pressure to stop the bleeding and called for one of the farmhands to bring fresh towels and a bucket of water. He cleaned the wound and discovered that it wasn't deep enough to cause any permanent damage. Relieved, he had three of the farmhands carry Arawn to his bed while Belenus checked on the other wounded.

The battle with the troopers hadn't lasted long. All twenty troopers were lying dead on the ground, and only three of the farmers were injured. The injuries weren't serious, and Belenus tended to the wounds immediately. All but eight of the troopers' horses had escaped, and the eight that remained were taken to the stables.

Belenus went back to check on Arawn, who was still unconscious. He stitched the wound and covered it with a bandage. Then he checked Arawn again for any other injuries. After an hour, Arawn opened his eyes and looked around the room.

"What happened?" he asked when he saw Belenus sitting next to him.

"One of the troopers threw a hatchet at you, and you fell off the roof. The wound isn't bad and will heal quickly.

"How did we do?"

"Your plan worked," Belenus said.

Arawn nodded with a tired smile. "I'm just worried there are more of them out there."

"I agree. I think it might be a good idea to patrol the perimeter of the farm more frequently so we'll know when more are approaching. In the meantime, I suggest building permanent barricades to limit the ways into the compound. We need to use the wagons to get our goods to the market."

"I'll get right on that," Arawn promised. He tried to get up to let the men with military training know what Belenus had suggested, but Belenus gently pushed him back down.

"For now, you need to rest and give your shoulder time to heal. I want you to stay in bed until at least tomorrow afternoon. There's plenty of time to start on the barricades."

"Yes, sir," Arawn conceded.

From that moment on, Arawn and the men with military training set up a regular patrol of the farm's perimeter. They used the captured horses so the farm's horses could continue to work the fields and pull the wagons. Movable barricades were built between most of the buildings. The barricades couldn't be moved from outside the compound, but they could be moved from the inside in case anyone needed to escape.

Belenus was impressed with the simplicity of the barricades' design and the release mechanism that allowed the people on the farm to escape if necessary. He was still worried, and hoped the men working with Arawn would be enough to keep the rest of the people on the farm safe.

Troopers attacked the farm two more times during the next year. In both attacks, at least one trooper tried to kill Arawn; and in the last attack, one of the troopers tried to seize Arawn and drag him out of the compound. The defenders of the farm were able to rescue Arawn before the trooper could get away with him, and everyone thought it was strange that the troopers would risk so many men just to capture a farmer.

The bodies of the dead troopers were taken deep into the Great Forest and left there for the animals to dispose of. None of the farmers wanted to waste time and space to bury the bodies near the farm where someone might notice or where they might serve as a reminder to the farmers of the attacks.

It didn't take long for the men with military training to recognize Arawn's skills as a leader and to begin deferring to him in discussion about defending the farm. Arawn had a gift for planning and for deploying the men, as was proven by the success of the first several attacks. Belenus never appointed Arawn as the leader, and the men never discussed it, but it was clear that Arawn was in charge of the men defending the farm.

Arawn and his men began training more of the farmers to fight, and many of the farmers went out to work the fields each day wearing swords from the fallen troopers. Thanks to their attackers, the farm now had a wide array of weapons, including swords, pikes, bows, and daggers.

Belenus watched the change in Arawn as the young man assumed the responsibilities of leadership over his men. Arawn seemed to be handling the responsibility well, but Belenus instinctively knew that there were greater tests of the young man's skills yet to come.

Will he be able to handle failure and loss as well as he handles victory? Will he be able to handle all the things his enemies decide to throw at him?

Belenus was all too afraid that he was about to find out the answers to these questions.

CHAPTER 15

ridamus and Cerridwen loaded up the wagon and took a trip to the fair located near the eastern tip of the Valdunass Mountains on the edge of the Chulainn tribe's territory. They had created more items to sell than normal, so there was little room left for a passenger in the wagon. Cerridwen rode one of the horses while Tridamus drove the wagon. She loved being in the saddle, and Tridamus told her it was fine if she rode well ahead of him as long as she never left his sight.

Apart from having to wait for several hours for the ferry to take them across the Great River, the two hundred mile journey from the smithy to the fairgrounds was quick and uneventful. Cerridwen kept up with her sword practice in the evenings when they stopped to make camp, but Tridamus kept the swords in the wagon while they were traveling.

"I don't want anyone seeing us to notice a girl wearing a sword," he explained when she complained about not getting to wear her sword. "It might call too much attention to us, and I don't want people to remember us or start asking questions we don't want answered."

Cerridwen nodded. She knew that if patrons saw her practicing with the sword at the smithy, they'd think it was odd for a girl to be learning how to fight. She liked the fact that learning to sword fight was a secret she shared with Tridamus and William.

When they arrived at the fair, Tridamus and Cerridwen set up their camp and their displays. Tridamus allowed Cerridwen to set up her own space to sell her jewelry. In fact, Tridamus had not brought any of his own jewelry on this trip. He decided to focus on blades and armor, letting Cerridwen handle the jewelry.

Each morning, before the patrons began making their way through the fair to visit the various craftsmen and artisans, Cerridwen practiced with her sword using makeshift targets that Tridamus set up behind the wagon. She kept a close watch for patrons and other vendors, and when she saw someone approaching, she quickly hid her sword and pretended to be feeding the horses or gathering firewood.

Cerridwen's jewelry was popular as usual and quickly sold out. She spent most of her days making more jewelry items to sell and working on commission pieces. There were several times during the fair when she found herself surrounded by patrons who wanted to watch her work.

There were also several times when she found herself surrounded by young men who just wanted to watch her. On one occasion, Tridamus had to bring one of his hammers down hard on the anvil as a warning to them that Cerridwen was under his protection and off limits to their advances.

As the young men scattered, Cerridwen looked over at Tridamus and silently thank him for handling her would-be suitors. She was flattered at the attention, but annoyed at the same time. She couldn't understand what all the fuss was about.

"I'm just a girl, after all," she said that night as she and Tridamus were eating supper. "What's so special about that?"

"Could it be because you make jewelry?" Tridamus asked.

"There are other women here at the fair who make things. They make soap, they weave rugs and other fabrics, they make clothes… it can't be because I'm a jewelry-maker."

"You don't look like the girls from this region. Maybe what's want intrigues them."

"How am I different?" Cerridwen asked.

"Well, for one thing you're not voluptuous like many women in the region seem to be. You have more of an athletic build, and some boys find that attractive. And then there's your hair."

"What about my hair?"

"There aren't many redheads around here, you know. It marks you as a Macruhan, and they live far to the west. Many folks in this region have never seen a redhead before – especially one who makes jewelry with a blacksmith. Boys are attracted to things that are unique, and you are unique."

"That's silly."

"Get used to it," Tridamus commented. "It's only going to get worse as you get older."

"How do you think they'd act if they knew I could fight with a sword?" she asked, taking another bite of her food.

Tridamus smiled. "A few would find that irresistible and want to marry you on the spot, but most would run away as fast as they could."

"Why?"

"Because boys think they're superior to girls. They're wrong, but it's been that way for centuries. Seeing a girl working with a blacksmith, which people think is a man's job, is strange enough. It means she's independent because she works at a craft or trade, and she's strong and good with tools. But a girl who can fight is truly terrifying because boys know they can't control a girl who can fight with a sword."

"Is that important?" Cerridwen asked.

"For many boys, yes. They've been raised to think that they're the dominant ones. To meet a girl who can challenge that dominance is more than their minds can take."

"Are all boys like that?"

"No," Tridamus said, leaning back in his chair. "There are some who have been raised to understand that men and women are equal. They appreciate strength in a girl. They want to be with someone who can keep up with them, not someone who only knows how to cook, clean, and raise children."

"Do you think I'll ever meet someone like that?"

"Yes, I do," Tridamus replied as he watched Cerridwen finish her supper.

And if I'm right, I even know who he is.

CHAPTER 16

The sun was setting as Tridamus and Cerridwen returned home to the smithy after the fair. Tridamus unloaded the wagon while Cerridwen took care of the horses. Once everything had been put away, they went into the house to eat a quick supper and get some sleep. The next day was going to be a big day for Cerridwen, although she didn't know it yet.

When she woke up the next morning, she got dressed quickly, made breakfast for herself and Tridamus, took care of the horses, and performed her other morning chores. She then met with William to continue her sword lessons. The master-at-arms was pleased that she had continued her lessons on her journey.

By the time she entered the workshop later that morning, she was surprised to find that Tridamus had not yet lit the forge. In fact, it looked like he hadn't started working yet.

"What's going on?" she asked as she tied her hair back and started preparing her worktable for some new projects.

"You're not going to be working on jewelry today. You've kept your end of our bargain, and now it's my turn. Today, you're going to start learning how to use the forge and the anvil. Once you understand how they work and how to use them to make the metal do what you want it to do, then I can show you how to make blades and armor."

Cerridwen's eyes lit up as she heard this. She ran forward and gave Tridamus a hug.

"Thank you, Tridamus!"

"Don't thank me yet. It's hard work, and it may prove too much for you. But the only way to find out is to give it a try."

Tridamus took her outside to the rear of the smithy where miners deposited wagonloads of metal ore on a regular basis. Walking over to the largest of the piles, he picked up a handful of dark gray ore. "This is iron ore. It's the ore we use to make steel." Gesturing at the other piles of ore, he added, "Sometimes, we mix ores together to create metal with different properties and patterns, but mostly we work with iron."

He put the ore down on a rock, took a hammer, and smashed the ore into smaller pieces. Then he placed the ore into a clay pot about the size of a water pitcher. He walked over to another pile, which contained charcoal mixed with cow bones that had been burned. He pulverized a bone with the hammer and crushed the pieces with a rock before putting the powdered bone and some of the charcoal into the pot with the ore. Next, he walked over to a pile of sand and filled the pot with the sand. "This is how we make crucible steel," he explained. "We put the ore in a clay pot. Then we add burned bone and charcoal, which makes the iron harder than it is by itself. Last, we add sand. We close up the pot with wet clay and put it in the kiln. We'll use the bellows to heat it for several hours. When the pot's glowing a bright orange, we take it out and break it. The sand melts into glass, and the impurities in the ore, called slag, will stick to the molten glass and the sides of the pot. What's left is an ingot of nearly pure steel, which has to be hammered for several hours while it cools to turn it into a hardened steel bar that we can use in the forge to make anything we want to make."

"I've always wondered what you used the kiln for." Cerridwen watched Tridamus seal the cover of cover the pot with wet clay. "Is this how you made the metal bars stacked on the far side of the forge?"

Tridamus nodded. He placed the play pot into the kiln and filled the kiln with coal. Then he lit the kiln, and he and Cerridwen started working the bellows to push air into the kiln to heat it much hotter than the forge would ever be heated. For hours, they worked the bellows to keep the heat as high as possible. When Tridamus carefully removed the pot with a pair of tongs, Cerridwen saw that it was glowing bright orange. Placing the pot on the ground, Tridamus let it cool for several minutes before taking his hammer and breaking the pot open. The clay and slag fell away from the glowing steel ingot at the bottom. Tridamus picked up the ingot with the tongs and motioned for Cerridwen to follow him inside. For the next several hours he beat the ingot with his hammer until it was the shape of a long bar. Then he placed the bar with the other bars along the wall.

Tridamus showed her how the forge worked, what it took to light it, and how to use the bellows to make it hot enough to soften metal so it could be flattened and shaped into blades, armor, tools, and implements.

He took a piece of scrap metal and showed her how to heat it. Then he showed her how to use the different hammers on the hot metal to bend it on the anvil into any shape desired.

100

Cerridwen could barely contain her excitement. *I'm finally learning how to be a real blacksmith!* She watched Tridamus intently, trying to memorize everything she saw and heard.

"Are you ready to try using the forge and anvil?" he asked her.

Cerridwen nodded enthusiastically.

Tridamus motioned for her to come closer and told her what he wanted her to do. He took a seat away from the heat of the forge to watch her work.

She started using the forge to heat up a long piece of metal he wanted her to use to make a dagger. She pulled on the chain that operated the giant bellows, which forced air into the forge and heated up the coals. The air in the workshop became oppressively warm as Cerridwen heated the forge hotter and hotter.

Once the metal was glowing reddish-orange, she removed it from the forge with a pair of iron tongs and took it to the anvil to start working the metal with the hammer. When she tried to pick up the hammer, though, her excitement turned into disappointment.

"I can't pick up the hammer, Tridamus," she said after trying to lift it several times. "It's too heavy."

Tridamus looked at her arms and understood the problem immediately. Cerridwen didn't have the upper body strength that Tridamus did, so she couldn't use the tools that he used for his work.

"I'm sorry, Cerridwen," he said, walking over to her. "I made all the tools in here to fit my hands. I'll need to make a set of hammers and tools that you can use."

A few days later, Tridamus was waiting for Cerridwen when she entered the workshop. When she walked over to him, he presented her with a new set of tools that he had made for her. "Give these a try," he said, pointing to the forge. "I still want you to make that dagger."

Cerridwen picked up each of the hammers and tools to make sure she could handle their weight. She gave Tridamus a hug and ran over to the bellows to heat the forge.

When the metal was glowing reddish-orange again, Cerridwen brought the metal to the anvil and selected the largest of her new hammers. Tridamus watched her closely as she worked the metal with the hammer. Cerridwen heated and hammered the metal several times, folding the metal to give it greater strength.

"What am I doing wrong, Tridamus?" she asked several hours later. The metal looked crude and not well made, and Cerridwen was frustrated.

"It's your first time, Cerridwen," he said as he came over to look at

101

her work. "You're not used to working with metal like this, and you're using smaller hammers than I do. You need to find a way with your tools to make the metal do what you want it to do."

Cerridwen threw the metal she had been working on into the scrap pile, and Tridamus selected another piece so she could try again.

It took several weeks for her to understand how to heat, fold, reheat, shape, quench, temper, and polish the metal, but she eventually found a way to use her new tools to create weapons and armor.

Tridamus kept his word and showed Cerridwen the secrets of making blades and armor that were strong and beautiful at the same time. He showed her how to take measurements of a patron wanting armor, how to design the individual pieces, how to make the pieces, and how to attach the pieces to the body so they remained in place while fighting. He also showed her how to create perfectly balanced blades that were the best length for the patron to use.

As a result of using smaller hammers and tools, Cerridwen was able to include more details in her work. Her armor was as strong as Tridamus' but incorporated several design changes that made them easier and safer to wear in a fight. The armor that Tridamus made was comprised of several large pieces linked together with leather straps. Cerridwen's armor still had a large piece in the center to protect the chest, but was comprised of several smaller pieces that overlapped so they moved with the body while still protecting the kill zones effectively.

At first, Tridamus was skeptical about her design, but when Cerridwen demonstrated how it worked during one of her morning lessons with William, he was forced to admit that it worked very well.

Cerridwen continued making jewelry and scabbards; those pieces were constantly in high demand. Tridamus unveiled her armor for the first time at the annual fair near Batavia, the capital city of the Penarduun tribe's territory. It sold quickly, and she soon found herself with several commissions for armor of the same design.

Cerridwen's reputation as a blacksmith grew with each fair they attended, but Tridamus began to worry that the popularity of her work might lead to unwanted attention.

If the enemy stops looking at her work and starts looking at her, they might figure out when she was born, and that could make her a target.

102

CHAPTER 17

hen Amaethon was fifteen, Nemausus presented him with a new challenge. "There will be times when you need to disguise that you're using magic to get things done. Some people fear magic and will attack anyone caught using it. Also, sometimes it's better if people believe that things happened for natural reasons, rather than from magical ones. Some people could try to force you use your magic for their purposes, making you little more than a slave. Do you understand?"

Amaethon nodded.

"Good. So today I want you to set fire to the stack of wood on that hill," he said, pointing to a small hill about half a mile away. "You cannot get any closer to the hill than you are now, and it needs to be done in a way that would keep the average person from ever knowing you were the one who started the fire."

"How long do I have?"

"Twenty minutes."

"Yes, Master."

Amaethon sat down and thought about how to set the wood on fire. He knew he could have a fireball or lightning fall from the sky, but it was a cloudless day, and creating a sudden storm wouldn't look natural. He closed his eyes and pictured the wood on fire. Then he thought about how to deliver that fire. A moment later, he smiled and started focusing his mind on creating the solution.

Nemausus watched Amaethon carefully, trying to guess what the solution might be. The situation Nemausus described was a real one that he knew Amaethon might face when it was time to help fulfill the prophecy. As Nemausus waited, he began speculating on the various ways Amaethon might solve the problem.

Nemausus noted that the twenty minutes had almost elapsed when he suddenly heard a loud shrieking sound behind him. Turning, he saw something he hadn't seen in a very long time. The beast was making wide circles in the distance, but its shape was unmistakable. The great wings cupped the air, keeping the large beast flying – its long neck turning as if looking for something specific. It let out another shriek and flew directly for Nemausus and Amaethon.

As the beast approached, Nemausus heard its wings beating against the air, sending chills down his back. The beast moved faster toward the master and his student, and as it passed overhead, Nemausus felt the heat of its breath. He saw the muscles of the beast rippling underneath the rust-colored outer skin and the translucent quality of the edges of the wings as it flew past. The long tail was stretched straight back, which helped the beast turn to the left or the right like the rudder of a boat.

The beast approached the hill where the wood was stacked, banked into a circle around it, opened its mouth, and turned its head to face the wood. A moment later a huge fireball flew out of its mouth and hit the wood, setting it on fire immediately. The beast shrieked in triumph and circled the hill one more time before turning northward and flying out of sight.

For a moment, Nemausus stood in shocked disbelief at what he had just seen. *He's never seen a dragon before, and he created one perfectly. Is this what the other prophecy was talking about?* He looked at Amaethon with a mixture of surprise and admiration.

"A dragon?" he exclaimed. "Of all the ways to start a fire, you chose a dragon? What made you think of that?"

"Well, there are no clouds in the sky, so I thought a fireball or lightning wouldn't seem natural, and neither would a sudden thunderstorm," he answered with a smile. "A brush fire would be too hard to contain, and I'd still have to create a natural way for a brush fire to have started. If the goal was to start a fire so that it didn't look like a human had set it, a dragon seemed a plausible solution."

"But you've never seen a dragon before, have you?"

"No, Master, but I think you described them to me once."

"For something that hasn't been seen for many centuries in this part of the world, you created it perfectly – right down to the sound and the breath." Nemausus shook his head, feeling a sense of wonder and pride in his student's accomplishment. "Impressive!"

"Thank you, Master."

"Now I need for you to put out the fire in a way that seems natural as well."

"I thought you'd say that," Amaethon replied with a grin just before the thunder announced itself from behind them.

Nemausus turned and saw the storm clouds moving in from the south. Turning back toward Amaethon, he was about to ask a question when the rain hit. Nemausus raised his hand and directed his mind toward the rain, keeping it from falling on himself and his student, and watched as the storm moved toward the hill. In a few minutes, the rain had completely doused the fire and moved toward the north in the same direction as the dragon. The ground all around them was soaked, but where they were standing was still dry. The clouds broke up, and soon the sun was shining again.

"Now why didn't you use that to start the fire?" Nemausus asked.

"Because you only gave me twenty minutes to get the fire started, and the storm took longer than that to create. It took thirty minutes just to gain enough strength to put out the fire. I actually created both at the same time."

Nemausus was pleased with his student's solution. "Outstanding! Truly outstanding!" he said. "Now if you don't mind, could you create a dry path for us back to the tower?"

Amaethon closed his eyes for a moment, and Nemausus saw the water on the ground fly off to the left and the right, leaving a dry path directly back to the tower.

"Anyone watching would know you did that," Nemausus said as he began walking.

"You didn't say I had to do it in a way that seemed natural, Master," Amaethon said as he followed his teacher back to the tower.

"I thought it was understood given my initial instructions," Nemausus replied, hiding his amusement.

"If you don't specify how things are to be done, I believe I'm free to use any method available. However, if you want it to appear natural, I'm sure I could get the dragon to come back, but it would probably scorch the grass between here and the tower, and I don't think you want that, do you?"

Nemausus glared back at his young student, but seeing the overly-innocent look on Amaethon's face, he burst out laughing.

"Highest marks, Amaethon," Nemausus said as the two made their way back home. "Highest marks."

CHAPTER 18

hortly before the summer of her fifteenth year, Cerridwen rode one of the horses along the road that led from the village, past the smithy, and around the northern face of the Mountain of Elohim. She had ridden to the village early that morning to pick up some supplies, including spools of wire that had finally arrived, which she needed in order to finish several sword hilts.

As she started for home, she thought she smelled smoke. The village produced a variety of smells, including smoke from the bakery and the smokehouses, but this was different. Looking around, she saw black smoke rising in the distance. At first, she couldn't figure out where the smoke was coming from, but as she continued riding, a thought struck her.

The grain mill!

She pressed her heels into the sides of the horse to make it go faster. The grain mill was close to the village, and it only took a few minutes to reach it. As she got closer, she saw the smoke getting thicker and knew that this was a large fire.

She reached the fork in the road that led to the grain mill and pulled on the reins to stop the horse. The miller's house was on fire, as were several of the outlying buildings where the grain was stored. Cerridwen was about to ride forward until she saw the source of the fire.

Men dressed in black uniforms were throwing torches into the open windows of the house and the outlying buildings.

Cerridwen angrily watched the men. *What are they doing?!*

Realizing that she was exposed, she slipped off the horse and led it into the tall brush on the side of the road so she could see what the men were doing. She also wanted to see what had happened to the miller and his family.

She couldn't see the miller or his family anywhere, and she

wondered if they had escaped before the fires were started. She also couldn't see any of the men who were holding the torches.

Looking at the house, she saw movement in one of the second floor windows. Smoke poured out of the windows, but it looked like someone was in one of the upstairs rooms. She kept watching, and she saw Siegfried climb out the window and drop to the ground. Elise climbed out the window next, and Siegfried caught her as she dropped next to him.

Cerridwen wanted to shout to the twins, but she didn't know if the men were still around, and she didn't want them to see the twins trying to escape. Siegfried and Elise looked around and started running down the road away from their burning house.

Cerridwen knew that she had to help her friends, but they were still too far away from her hiding place to see or hear her. She decided to mount her horse and ride to meet them. Her plan was to pull them up onto the back of her horse and ride as fast as she could to the village. Before she could move, something caught her eye.

She saw three of the men with the torches coming out of the mill. They saw the twins running and started chasing them.

What do they want with Elise and Siegfried?

As the men got closer to the twins, Cerridwen saw them draw their swords. She watched, horrified, knowing that there was nothing she could do at that point. The twins were too far away from her to save them from the men.

Cerridwen saw one of the men catch up to Siegfried, but rather than grab him with his free hand, the man swung his sword, catching Siegfried's shoulder. Siegfried fell, shouting for Elise to keep running. The man stood over the miller's son and, to Cerridwen's dismay, plunged his sword into Siegfried several times.

Elise looked back once but kept running as fast as she could. Two of the men were gaining on her. Cerridwen wanted to ride to her, but she was still too far away.

One of the men clutched the hilt of his sword with both hands and swung it at Elise's head. Cerridwen saw the miller's daughter fling her arms out as she fell forward to the ground. The men plunged their swords into her several times like the first man had done to Siegfried.

Cerridwen heard the men laughing as they rejoined their comrade and strode back to the inferno that had once been the miller's house.

Tears flowed down her face. She couldn't take her eyes off her friends lying dead in the road that led to their house. She wanted to ride after the men, to punish them for what they had done to the twins, but she was unarmed. All she could do was watch.

She saw more men near the mill. Some were mounted, and the others were bringing up the rest of the horses. The leader of the men whistled, and the men mounted their horses and rode toward Cerridwen's hiding place. She made sure that she and the horse were well-hidden. She didn't want the men to see her and kill her like they had killed the twins. She watched the men trample Elise and Siegfried's bodies as they rode away. Cerridwen bit her lip in rage, but remained silent as they passed her.

The miller's house and grain storage buildings were burning out of control. The roof of the house collapsed, sending a shower of sparks up into the air. Cerridwen stayed hidden until she felt it was safe to head back to the smithy. As she mounted her horse, all that remained was the stone structure of the mill with its giant blades turning in the wind.

When she reached the smithy, she ran into the workshop to find Tridamus.

"It was terrible," she said when she finished telling him what had happened. "They murdered Elise and Siegfried right in front of me, and I couldn't do anything to stop it!"

"And they killed both of them?" Tridamus asked, concerned at the implication.

Cerridwen nodded, still shaking with rage and horror.

Tridamus hugged her for several minutes before sending her into the house to rest for a while. Once Cerridwen had disappeared inside, he cleared his mind and reached out to the other elders.

"Soldiers killed the children who lived at the mill near the smithy today – a boy and a girl who were both close to Cerridwen's age."

"I feared this might happen," Alaunus said. *"Mider recently told Taranus that one of the orphans might be a girl. Now it looks like the soldiers will be killing girls born around the time of the red moons in addition to boys."*

"Do you think they know about Cerridwen yet?"

"I don't know, but I wouldn't take any chances. Do whatever you have to do to protect the smithy and keep her safe."

Alaunus broke the connection and Tridamus decided to have a quick conversation with William in the morning to see if he'd increase patrols around the smithy and push Cerridwen to improve her skills with the sword.

CHAPTER 19

erridwen trained for several hours a day with William and the other soldiers who began spending time around the smithy. The new soldiers, who claimed that they wanted to barter their services for new swords or pieces of armor, were excellent teachers. It never occurred to Cerridwen that the soldiers might actually be there to protect her and the smithy.

Several months after the destruction of the miller's home, Cerridwen was sparring with one of the soldiers while three other soldiers stood by and watched.

"Have you ever fought more than one opponent at the same time?" she asked the soldier.

"Many times," he replied. "Combat is rarely with a single opponent."

"How do you fight more than one person at a time?"

"The key is to keep them from surrounding you. You need at least one way that's open for you to move and escape. Some people carry a shield on one arm to protect the side of the body opposite their sword. Some fight with multiple weapons. However you do it, remember to keep the enemy from getting directly behind you. It's your blind spot, and nothing you do can protect you against an attack from that direction."

The soldier called over the others who were watching, and they demonstrated what he had just taught her. She immediately understood what he meant about an opponent getting directly behind her. As hard as she tried, she couldn't keep from being surrounded unless she stood with her back to a tree, but the tree interfered with her fighting. She tried using a shield, but it wasn't enough to keep an opponent from getting behind her.

After several weeks of trying new techniques, only to have all of them fail, she decided to try using multiple weapons at the same time. She picked up two swords and faced the four soldiers who were teaching her that day. She motioned for them to attack her.

It took a while for her to make both swords move separately. The sword in her weaker hand kept moving in the same direction as the sword in her stronger hand, and she realized she had never before tried to make both hands move independently. Over time, she managed to improve. She still couldn't prevent some of the opposition from getting behind her, but she found that, by using two swords, she could keep them from getting behind her as quickly.

Tridamus watched her practice from the workshop. Some days, he'd stop working and come outside to see how her skills were improving.

"Why did you start practicing with two swords?" he asked her one morning after her teachers had left for the day.

"Because I want to keep my opponents from getting behind me."

"That assumes you'll always be fighting alone," Tridamus pointed out.

Cerridwen looked at him. "That's the only way I've been trained."

Tridamus nodded thoughtfully. "Why don't you have your teachers start showing you how to fight with allies? If you ever find yourself in a fight with people who are trying to help you, you might end up killing or injuring them by accident."

Cerridwen nodded.

The next morning, Cerridwen asked for one of the soldiers to fight with her against the others. As the fight began, she quickly realized that Tridamus had been right. She wasn't used to having someone next to her who wasn't an opponent, and it made her rethink most of the ways she fought multiple people at the same time.

It took several practice sessions, but eventually she was comfortable fighting alongside allies and fighting alone against multiple opponents.

Tridamus watched from the workshop with satisfaction. The swords he was providing to the soldiers as payment for practicing with Cerridwen every morning was a small price to pay for getting her ready to fulfill her destiny.

As Cerridwen's fighting skills improved, she began making subtle changes to the designs of her weapons and armor to see if they'd perform better in a fight. Tridamus encouraged her to try new designs and test them with the soldiers.

At first, the soldiers didn't think much of her armor designs. They were accustomed to more traditional designs and couldn't understand the need for any changes. As they practiced with her, they realized that her changes made the armor easier to fight with while covering the kill zones more effectively.

Cerridwen made modifications to her designs based on the soldiers' suggestions. After several experiments, she created a design which increased the protection to the wearer while reducing the overall weight and bulkiness of the armor. Once the new design had been tested and proven effective, several of the soldiers placed commission orders for sets of her new armor.

Cerridwen was working on a commission for one of the soldiers when she heard horses approaching the smithy. She glanced up and saw Tridamus looking toward the courtyard.

"Tridamus," she heard someone shout,

"Pasquale!" Tridamus bellowed. "It's been years, my old friend. What brings you to my smithy?"

Cerridwen watched Tridamus walk to the workshop entrance and embrace a distinguished looking older gentlemen. There were three other men standing nearby – all looking like younger versions of the man Tridamus was greeting.

"It's been too long, Tridamus. Too long indeed," she heard the gentleman say.

"And are these your sons?" Tridamus asked. "The last time I saw them, they were barely as tall as your chest. Now look at them!"

"They're why I'm here," the gentleman said. "I need them outfitted with armor and swords. I want them to have the best, so I came to see my old friend."

"I'm glad you thought of me, Pasquale," Tridamus said, ushering the group into the workshop. "Let me show you some of the design samples I have, and then we can take measurements and work out a price."

"I see you have a new apprentice," Pasquale said once he and his sons were inside the workshop.

"Yes, I do," Tridamus said proudly. "The best one I've ever had, in fact. Cerridwen, come here, please."

Cerridwen stood up and walked over to Tridamus.

"Pasquale, this is Cerridwen, my apprentice. Cerridwen, this is Pasquale, one of my oldest customers and dearest friends. And these are his sons, Gorlan, Collin, and Tristan."

111

"How do you do," Cerridwen replied. "I'm pleased to meet you."

"It's a pleasure, my dear," Pasquale said. Turning to Tridamus, he added, "A female apprentice, Tridamus? That's a bit unusual, isn't it?"

"Unusual, yes, but her talent is beyond what any of my other students possessed."

Tridamus pointed to the armor that Cerridwen was working on for the soldiers. "Cerridwen, why don't you show Pasquale and his sons the armor you've been working on?"

Cerridwen nodded and brought over one of the completed sets. She explained her design and how it was different from the traditional armor that Tridamus made. She let Pasquale's sons try it on.

"She designed and made that armor?" Pasquale asked.

Tridamus nodded. "It's entirely her design. She's been working with some of the local soldiers to experiment with different configurations, and this is what she's come up with. The sets she's working on are commissions for the soldiers."

Tridamus and Pasquale watched Cerridwen demonstrate the armor with each of the sons. When she helped the last of Pasquale's sons remove the armor, Tridamus asked, "What else would you like to see?"

Pasquale looked at his sons for a moment. Turning back to Tridamus, he said, "I think my sons like the armor they just tried on. I'll need three sets with matching helmets, shields, and swords. When can you have them completed and what will it cost me?"

Tridamus produced several cups and a jug of wine, and poured his guests a drink. Cerridwen put the armor away while Tridamus and Pasquale started negotiating the price. She appeared calm, but inwardly she was ecstatic. *Three armor commissions from one of Tridamus' long-standing customers!* She tried to hide her smile. Her mind was already focusing on the work required to get the armor finished when she rejoined Tridamus and the others.

"We're agreed, then?" Pasquale asked.

Tridamus nodded and shook Pasquale's hand.

Turning to Cerridwen, Tridamus said, "Cerridwen, please take the boys' measurements and see which swords will work best for them."

For the next hour, Cerridwen took detailed measurements of Pasquale's sons for the armor. She showed them several of the swords on hand to see which ones suited their style of fighting the best. In the end, Gorlan selected one of Tridamus' swords, while Collin and Tristan each selected one of Cerridwen's.

"We'll make scabbards for the swords and you can pick them up when you come back for the armor," Tridamus said once they were finished.

"Excellent," Pasquale said as he led his sons out into the courtyard. "Until then, be well, my old friend."

"You, too, Pasquale," Tridamus said.

Tridamus and Cerridwen watched Pasquale and his sons ride out of the compound. As the sound of hoof beats faded in the distance, Cerridwen asked, "Do you mind that they wanted my designs instead of yours?"

"Of course not," Tridamus said with a wide smile. "I'm thrilled beyond words that they saw the value of what you've created. If I didn't want you to be successful, I'd never have trained you to make armor and blades in the first place!"

"Thank you, Tridamus," Cerridwen said, feeling relieved.

"You're welcome. Now what can I do to help you get this order finished?"

Between Pasquale's sons and the soldiers who had commissioned armor from Cerridwen, it didn't take long for people to become aware of her armor design. As more people saw the armor in action, the demand for her armor grew. In spite of the fact that her pieces were entirely unique from the ones Tridamus made, she soon found herself with almost as many armor commissions as he had.

Cerridwen enjoyed the increasing demand for her pieces, but she never felt she had found the perfect design. At night, she'd sketch out ideas for a new design of armor that still protected the kill zones and used smaller, overlapping pieces to increase flexibility and range of movement without allowing an enemy's blade to slip between the overlapping pieces and get stuck or damage the integrity of the armor. She worked on this for months in her spare time, which was minimal, but the more she experimented, the better her armor became and the more orders for her designs she received.

One evening, several months after Cerridwen's seventeenth birthday, Tridamus sat down next to her at the kitchen table while she worked on a new sketch for her armor. The light from the candles on the table danced as an evening breeze blew through the open windows into the kitchen, giving the room the illusion of movement.

"How's the latest design coming?" he asked.

"I'm getting closer," she answered, looking up at Tridamus with a tired smile. "I have an idea that I'm working on, but I'm not through testing it in my mind."

"What has you worried about it?"

Cerridwen showed Tridamus the sketch and pointed to two places where the metal plates overlapped. "There's still a way for a sword or dagger to get between these pieces and either cut the straps or penetrate the skin. It's a small weakness, but it's a weakness I want to eliminate."

Tridamus looked at the design for a few minutes. "I see you're using leather straps to hold these pieces together. What's worn underneath this armor? Padded wool or canvas so the straps and armor plates don't dig into the skin?"

"Whatever the wearer wants," Cerridwen replied. "The armor should work equally well regardless of what's worn underneath."

Tridamus took a piece of paper from Cerridwen and drew a quick sketch. Then he showed her what he had in mind. "Rather than have these pieces all fitted together on a series of leather straps that attach the pieces to the body and to each other, why not have them attached to a vest-style or half-sleeve leather jerkin? That way you can eliminate the straps in the areas where the armor overlaps, and you can strengthen the part behind the overlaps with a thicker piece of leather for extra protection."

Cerridwen looked at the sketch for a minute. "Most people wear either leather or metal, but not both. It's never been done that way before," she commented.

"And why is that a problem for you?" Tridamus said with a grin, knowing that Cerridwen's gift was doing things in new and bold ways that went against what was considered normal.

Cerridwen stared at the sketch for several minutes without speaking. She reached for another piece of paper and began a new sketch. Tridamus quietly stood up, walked across the kitchen to the cupboard, and took out two tankards. He filled them both with ale from a small cask that had been a gift from a grateful patron. He came back to the table and set the tankards down between Cerridwen and himself before taking his seat again. He waited for her to finish the sketch.

He was watching the sunset through the window and sipping his ale when he heard Cerridwen softly say, "I think this will work!"

He turned and looked at her. She was nodding and looking excited with her latest sketch. After a moment, she handed the design to Tridamus and asked, "Is this what you were thinking?"

Tridamus looked over the design with great interest. He saw how she had incorporated his suggestion, but he noticed that she had made several other subtle design changes to take advantage of presence of a leather jerkin underneath. The armor protecting the arms, sides, waist, and the center of the back were attached to the jerkin. The center chest plate was attached by leather straps at the shoulder so it could be lifted up to put on the jerkin and strapped down in place once the jerkin was cinched up. Put together in this manner, the armor would be almost impenetrable. He put the paper down and closed his eyes for a minute, trying to envision the completed armor in action. After a while, he opened his eyes and smiled.

"I think you have it," he said proudly.

Cerridwen smiled. "Do we have enough materials to try and make one?"

"We actually have enough to make three, and that's what I came in to talk to you about."

"What do you mean?" she asked, reaching for the tankard that Tridamus had brought her and taking a drink.

"I have a commission that I want you to take. I need three complete sets of armor using your new design, including helmets, shields, and swords. There needs to be some ornamentation on the chest pieces that I'll sketch for you, and the helmets need to indicate that the wearers are of highest rank and have similar ornamentation as the chest pieces. Apart from one major difference, the three sets are to be identical."

"What difference?"

"One of the sets is for a woman," Tridamus replied. "The wearer is about your size and build, so you can use yourself as the pattern."

Cerridwen was surprised. She had never heard of armor being made for a woman before, and she knew that the additional curves in the chest area and the hips would require some changes to the overall design, but she was excited at the challenge. "When do you need everything completed?"

"Three months at the latest," Tridamus replied. "It needs to be finished before your eighteenth birthday. There are things happening in the world that were set in motion a long time ago, and this commission is necessary for those things to be completed successfully. Your other work can wait. This is the most important thing for you to be working on right now, along with your sword training. I need you to train harder starting tomorrow."

"Why?"

"Because the things that are happening in the world will involve you, and I need to make sure that you're ready for whatever may be required of you in the months ahead."

Cerridwen asked Tridamus for more information, but he just shook his head and finished his tankard of ale. He got up and went back to his bedroom, leaving Cerridwen sitting at the table with her sketches in the dancing candlelight.

Cerridwen Learning to Fight Multiple Opponents.

CHAPTER 20

wo months before his eighteenth birthday, Arawn was patrolling along the edge of the Great Forest when he heard one of the men shout out a warning. He and the other men, who were patrolling different parts of the farm, rode quickly to see who raised the alarm.

"There's movement in the forest over there," the man who had shouted said to Arawn, pointing to the south.

"Did you see anyone?"

"No, but I heard the horses. They were moving fast, and it sounded like they were chasing someone."

Arawn didn't want to leave the farm undefended, but if there were horsemen out there chasing someone, he needed to help.

Arawn pointed to the men next to him. "You four come with me. The rest of you stay here and protect the farm. If we're not back in two hours, come looking for us."

Arawn turned his horse and rode for the forest. The men he selected followed him, and the rest returned to their positions around the farm to make sure no one tried to attack from a different direction.

Several trails ran through that part of the forest. In centuries past, soldiers used these routes to move in secret during the wars between the tribes. Now smugglers, thieves, and others who didn't want their passage observed used them – especially people who wanted to take a less-exposed route between the Gallasian and Mongán territories.

It only took Arawn about ten minutes to find evidence of several horsemen riding through the forest on one of the trails. There were dozens of fresh hoof prints in the ground, and bent and snapped branches showed the way the horses had gone. He and his men quietly followed the horsemen's path, hoping it wasn't a trap.

Several minutes later, he heard people shouting ahead and silently motioned for the others to get ready. As the horsemen came into sight, Arawn raised his hand and signaled the men to stop. In the clearing ahead, a dozen horsemen were attacking three men and a young woman on foot who were trying to defend themselves with sticks and branches.

"What's going on here?" Arawn shouted.

The horsemen turned their heads at the sound of Arawn's voice, and one of the horsemen shouted an order. Several of the horsemen broke off the attack, wheeled around, and rode toward Arawn and his men with their swords pointing forward. Arawn and his men drew their swords and charged into the clearing at the advancing horsemen.

Just as Arawn reached the first horseman, two of the other horsemen raced forward and pulled Arawn off his horse. Arawn fell to the ground, pulling one of his attackers down with him. Arawn landed hard, and his sword flew out of his hand, landing several feet away. He crawled toward his sword, but his attacker grabbed his leg and pulled him back.

Arawn's men were too busy fighting with the other horsemen to notice that Arawn was no longer on his horse. The other horsemen saw Arawn on the ground, but were unable disengage from Arawn's men and press the advantage.

Rolling out of the way to keep from being stepped on by one of the nearby horses, Arawn tried to kick his attacker to free himself. The attacker held on and pulled a long dagger from its sheath. He stabbed at Arawn's leg, but Arawn continued to kick his attacker.

Another horse started backing up, nearly stepping on Arawn's attacker. He released Arawn, who immediately crawled for his sword again. The attacker, seeing Arawn reaching for the sword, rushed forward and landed on Arawn, knocking the sword away with his free hand.

Arawn twisted around and faced his attacker. His attacker raised the hand with the dagger, and Arawn grabbed the attacker's wrist and held on with all his might so the horseman couldn't stab or slash him.

One of Arawn's men, seeing that Arawn was in trouble, wheeled his horse around and rode to help. He swung his sword and hit Arawn's attacker in his exposed back, killing him. Arawn pushed the horseman off of him, crawled toward his sword, and retrieved it. He got to his feet and ran for his horse, which stood near the edge of the clearing.

As Arawn reached his horse and climbed into the saddle, one of the horsemen hit the woman in the head, and she fell to the ground, unconscious. The men who were with her threw their sticks at the horseman and ran for one of the trails leading away from the clearing. Four of the horsemen rode after the men and disappeared into the forest.

Arawn looked around the clearing. Four of the horsemen were lying dead on the trail, and the rest turned their horses and followed their comrades deeper into the forest. Arawn ordered one of his men to stay with the woman, and he and the rest of his men raced after the surviving horsemen.

Arawn had never followed this particular trail so deep into the forest and didn't know what lay ahead. After a few minutes of following the horsemen, he rounded a corner that was shielded by a large boulder and quickly had to pull back on the reigns of his horse. The trail ahead was blocked by the horsemen, who were waiting for him and his men.

The horsemen attacked, and Arawn and his men fought back ferociously. Several more horsemen fell, and when the surviving horsemen fled, Arawn decided it was too risky to follow them further. He turned his horse and rode back to where they had left the woman. He and his men had suffered cuts and bruises in the skirmish but were able to ride back to the farm.

When they arrived back at the clearing, Arawn jumped off his horse, threw the reins to one of his men, and ran over to the young woman, who was still lying unconscious on the ground. There was a small cut on her forehead that was bleeding, but there didn't appear to be any other injuries.

Arawn looked at the woman closely but didn't recognize her. He carefully picked her up and carried her over to where his men were waiting with his horse. He handed her up to one of his men and mounted his own horse. He and his men rode back to the farm along with several horses in tow that had belonged to the dead horsemen.

When they arrived at the farm, Belenus ran out to meet them. "What happened?" he asked.

"We found horsemen attacking some travelers on one of the old trails in the forest," Arawn replied. "We killed several of them and took their horses. The rest escaped and chased after the other travelers. One of the travelers was injured and left behind. We brought her back with us."

Arawn described the fight and how he had been pulled off his horse.

"Could you identify the horsemen?" Belenus asked, looking at the unconscious girl.

"No," Arawn replied. "They wore no uniforms or other markings that would indicate who they were."

"Do you think they were connected to the troopers who have been attacking us?"

119

Arawn thought about this. "It's possible. They were dressed differently, but that doesn't mean they weren't troopers in disguise.

Looking up at the girl again, Belenus said, "You'd better bring her into the house."

Arawn climbed down from his horse, took the girl from one of his men, and carried her inside while his men took care of the horses.

When Arawn entered the front room of the house, Belenus motioned for him to place the girl on a cushioned bench near one of the windows. Arawn set her down, and Belenus removed her deep maroon traveling cloak so he could check for injuries. He motioned for Arawn to bring the basin of water and a towel from its stand by the door.

Belenus dipped the towel into the water and used it to clean away the dirt and blood from the woman's face. Arawn was finally able to take a long look at the women he had rescued. She was beautiful, even after being attacked and knocked unconscious. He guessed she was around his age, but she wasn't as tall as he was. She was slender in an elegant sort of way, and her long raven-colored hair framed her striking face. She had high cheekbones, and the corners of her full lips were turned up, making it look like she was smiling.

She was dressed in tight black leather trousers, knee-high black boots, and a black vest over a dark green tunic that was cut to show off the curves of her chest. Arawn saw the hilts of several small daggers protruding from her vest and leather gauntlets. Arawn pointed them out to Belenus, who nodded thoughtfully.

Once her face was cleaned and Belenus saw that the wound on her forehead was small and had stopped bleeding, he took out a small vial from his vest pocket, opened it, and placed it under her nose. Arawn saw her head shake and heard her gasp. She opened her eyes and tried to sit up.

"Easy, girl. Easy," Belenus said, putting his hand on her shoulder to keep her from sitting up too quickly. "You've had a rough time."

"Where... where am I?" she asked, looking around.

"Somewhere safe," Belenus said. "We found you in the forest and brought you here."

The woman reached up to her forehead. "What happened?"

"What do you remember?" Belenus asked.

"We were on our way west. I'm a dancer, and I paid three men to make sure I got to the next settlement safely. We were about halfway there when some people rode up and tried to rob us. I remember grabbing a stick and swinging it around, but nothing after that."

"We rode up just as you were knocked out," Arawn said. "I saw them hit you in the head. We killed several of them, and the rest took off after the men you hired. We decided to bring you back here."

"Thank you," she said softly, looking at Arawn with gratitude.

Arawn blushed furiously. He had never had a girl look at him that way before. He stammered for a moment before Belenus interjected, "I think he's trying to say 'you're welcome'."

The girl just smiled at Arawn, which made him blush even more.

"What is your name?" Belenus asked so that Arawn could regain his composure.

"Siena."

CHAPTER 21

elenus knew that Arawn had done the right thing in bringing
her back to the farm, but he was troubled about the effect this
exotic young woman might have on the men who lived and
worked on the farm – especially on Arawn. He couldn't put his
finger on exactly what bothered him. He sensed that Arawn
was physical attracted to her, and he knew he needed to watch that
carefully. Since Arawn was one of the orphans mentioned in the
Prophecy of Airmid, he didn't need the kinds of distractions that Siena
could cause while he was striving to fulfill his destiny.

Belenus helped Siena back to one of the guest rooms in the farm's
main house. She fell asleep as soon as she lay down on the bed and
didn't get up again until the next morning.

Belenus decided that he needed to find something for Siena to wear
in case she wanted to change out of her traveling clothes. He borrowed
some clothes from the wife of one of the farmhands that looked like they
might fit, and he placed them in Siena's room. He checked on her every
few hours and brought her food to eat when she got hungry. He refused
to let anyone else be with her, including Arawn, until he learned more
about her.

Arawn spent most of his days patrolling the perimeter of the farm in case
troopers attacked the farm or the horsemen who had attacked Siena and
her companions decided to try to take her. He occasionally caught
glimpses of Siena through her window as he rode past but had seen little
of her since her rescue.

Belenus sat at his kitchen table a few mornings later when he looked up
and saw Siena walking down the hallway toward him. She had changed
into a simple dress but had put back on her leather vest over the blouse.

She wasn't wearing any shoes, and Belenus could tell from the way she moved as she walked that she was indeed a dancer. Her bare feet made almost no sound on the floor, and when she entered the kitchen and saw Belenus watching her, she flashed a big smile as she twirled around, holding out her skirt as a way of thanking her host for the clothes.

"How are you feeling this morning?" he asked pleasantly.

"Much better, thank you. And thank you for the clothes."

"Has your memory returned?"

Siena shook her head. From the couple of times Belenus had spoken to her, it had become clear that parts of her memory were missing. She remembered childhood things, and she remembered that she was a dancer on her way to a new village to entertain the men in that area, but most of the rest of her memories were jumbled up in her mind, and there were gaps that she seemed unable to fill. Belenus was aware that some head injuries caused memory problems, but he had never seen so many gaps from such a slight wound before.

"It's still a blur," she said, pouting as she sat down across from her host. "I get flashes, but nothing that makes any sense to me."

"Well, don't worry too much about it," Belenus said softly. "I'm sure the memories will return in time. For now, enjoy the hospitality of my farm until you feel well enough to travel again. I'll find you a proper escort to take you on to your destination or back to your home if that's what you'd prefer."

"Would it be that young man who rescued me?" she asked as she dropped her eyes so Belenus wouldn't see the twinkle in them.

Belenus smiled, knowing exactly what she meant. "No, he has other duties around the farm. I meant some of the local soldiers who are stationed in the village about two hours from here."

"There are soldiers stationed that near?" she asked with a frown.

"Of course there are. Military patrols stay close to farms like this to keep us protected from raiders."

Siena nodded slowly. "Have there been raiders around here?"

"You mean like the ones that attacked you in the forest? There have been a couple of raids, but nothing serious."

Belenus watched Siena's face as he answered her questions. He purposely misled her about the military patrols and the raids that had been made on the farm – partly to keep her from feeling nervous, and partly because he was curious about the emotions she was clearly trying hard to hide from him.

He suddenly stood up, startling her somewhat. "Where are my manners? You must be hungry. Let me fetch you something to eat."

"Oh, no," she said with a big smile. "I'm still full from last night.

Just some water to drink, please."

Belenus took a tankard from the shelf that ran along the kitchen walls just below the ceiling. He filled it from a cask kept in the corner and brought it to her before taking his seat again.

Siena took a long drink. "That's good water!" she said. "Is it from the lake I saw?"

Belenus shook his head. "No, we have a well behind the house that's tapped into an underground spring."

Siena took another drink and set the tankard down. She opened her mouth to say something, but Belenus saw her face suddenly change. She was no longer a young woman having a pleasant conversation with an elder gentleman. She was a seductress who had sighted her prey. Belenus knew instantly that she must have seen Arawn in the courtyard, and when he turned to look out the open door where Siena was watching, he saw that he was right.

Arawn had been on patrol since shortly before dawn. He tied his horse to a ring attached to the wall of the stables next to the main door and crossed the compound to get something to eat.

Even though Arawn had a room in the main house, he usually ate in the bunkhouse with his men. It seemed important that he spend as much time as he could with the ones who had taught him so much about the military arts, and Belenus didn't mind. He was pleased that Arawn was growing up into a fine young man and was taking his responsibilities seriously. The farm provided many distractions, especially with so many orphans coming and going, and Belenus appreciated the way Arawn maintained his focus without being aloof or distant from the others who lived in the compound.

Belenus saw Arawn approaching the house instead of the bunkhouse. *Is he hoping Siena's awake and out of her room?*

"There's no sign of any raiders this morning," Arawn said as he entered the kitchen and saw Belenus sitting at the table. He was about to say something else when he saw Siena sitting at the table as well.

"Good morning," Siena purred softly with her eyes wide open and fixed on Arawn's face.

"Good morning," Arawn replied, blushing. He quickly turned to get a tankard and a piece of freshly baked bread that had come from the oven about thirty minutes earlier. "Feeling better?"

"Much better, thanks to you," she replied in the most innocent voice Belenus had ever heard. He began to wonder if, as a dancer, Siena manipulated men like this and didn't give it a second thought, or if she were actively pursuing Arawn out of a sense of gratitude for her rescue.

Either way, he knew he needed to watch her even more closely.

Arawn joined Siena and Belenus at the table, and Belenus watched the two young people talk with each other. Arawn was innocent when it came to women and seemed unsure of himself in the face of a striking woman giving him all of her attention. Siena clearly wasn't innocent when it came to men, and as Belenus watched her, he grew even more concerned about her intentions.

Belenus had many gifts, not the least of which was the ability to find and rescue orphans, but he didn't have the gift of looking into someone's mind and knowing their thoughts. However, he knew someone who did possess that gift. Belenus decided that he'd summon his old friend and see if his friend could help unravel some of the mysteries about this young woman.

After a few minutes of talking with Siena, Arawn stood up. "Excuse me, Siena, Belenus," he said to the two people at the table. "I need to get back to my duties. I'll see you both later this afternoon."

Arawn left the kitchen and crossed the courtyard to retrieve his horse. He quickly climbed into the saddle and rode away, sending up a small cloud of dust from the horse's hooves.

"I need to check on some things, my dear," Belenus said, standing. "Please make yourself comfortable. I'd suggest remaining inside the compound, and whatever you do, don't go into the forest without someone with you. I think it's still a bit too dangerous for you out there."

Siena nodded. Belenus took his walking stick, left the house, and made his way across the courtyard toward the lake.

When he reached the banks of the lake, he stared at the Mountain of Elohim and quieted his mind, focusing his thoughts.

"My old friend. Can you hear me?"

A moment later, he heard the familiar voice in his mind. *"It's been a while since I've heard from you. Is everything all right with Arawn?"*

"Yes, the boy's fine. How is Amaethon?"

"He's well. Is it time?"

"I'm not certain, but that's not why I need to talk to you. There's a young woman staying at the farm, and she troubles me."

Belenus shared his thoughts about Siena and how she came to be at the farm.

"And she has gaps in her memory?"

"Yes, and she's having quite an effect on Arawn as well. There's something about her that bothers me, but you're better at these things than I am."

"You want me to come there the normal way, or do you need me to

125

come there faster?"

"I think the normal way is fine. I don't want you to reveal that ability to anyone who might be watching. Also, I think it might be good for Amaethon and Arawn to meet each other. Their destinies are intertwined, and the sooner they know about each other, the better."

His old friend didn't respond immediately.

"Are you still there?" Belenus asked.

"Yes, I was just concerned that if we bring them together too soon, it might create a dangerous situation. Two of the three children of the prophecy in once place might be tempting to whoever has been watching and hunting them all these years."

Belenus was about to say something when he heard another voice in his mind join the conversation. *"It is time,"* the voice stated calmly with a gentle authority that erased all doubt from Belenus' mind.

"We have our answer," Belenus said.

"Yes, we do," his old friend agreed, having also heard the voice. *"We'll leave tomorrow and try to be there in a week or so. Will you inform the others?"*

"Yes, I'll let them know right now. See you soon."

CHAPTER 22

emausus leaned back in his chair and looked out the window of his study. He had been preparing for this day for a long time, but now that it was here, he had difficulty grasping that the quest to decide the fate of the world was finally beginning.

Knowing that there were things to be done before they set out in the morning, he called out to Amaethon, but there was no reply. In fact, he couldn't sense his student anywhere.

I haven't taught him to hide himself from me. Standing, he crossed the room to the ladder and climbed up to the top of the tower to see if he could find out where Amaethon was and what he was doing.

Amaethon had been practicing his lessons down by the stream all morning. He stood on a rock where the stream bent and concentrated on levitating the water out of the stream, raising it over his head, and lowering it so that it flowed around the other side of the rock instead. Nemausus had taught him how to lift water so that it continued flowing as if it weren't being moved. Amaethon was getting better at keeping the water from dripping on his head as it passed over him.

Amaethon had just put the stream down when he heard someone clapping. Looking in the direction of the sound, he saw a figure standing on the opposite bank of the stream. The figure in the dark traveling cloak with the hood pulled over his face was all too familiar.

"Well done, Amaethon," the figure said with a nod. "I see you've been well trained to be a great landscaper someday."

"Who are you, and why have you been watching me?"

"Who I am is unimportant, but if it's a name you want, you may call me Athanaric. I've been watching you because I want to know if you're the one I've been searching for during the past eighteen years."

"Why have you been searching for someone for eighteen years?"

"Because we have unfinished business."

"You've been watching me for years. I've seen you. Why are you approaching me now?"

"Because I finally know it's you I need to find," Athanaric replied.

"To do what?" Amaethon asked.

"To kill you. You escaped me when you were a baby, and you've been too closely guarded since then. But there's no time left. Are you ready to die?"

"Do you think you can?" Amaethon said grimly.

"Oh, I admit you have power, boy. I've watched you practice your landscaping and rock rolling for many years. But if you think your skills impress me, then you have no concept of what real skill is."

Athanaric unclasped his cloak and let it fall to the ground. Amaethon crouched down on the rock and watched Athanaric, wondering what skills his opponent might possess. Athanaric was tall and looked much older than Amaethon. His silver-streaked black hair, bushy eyebrows, and piercing black eyes gave him an eerie look. His black and silver chin beard was long and curled at the bottom like a pig's tail, adding to his sinister look.

Amaethon thought back to when Nemausus had started the lessons about how to fight with magic and against magic. "There may come a time when you'll meet another person trained in the magical arts, and you need to know how to defend yourself and fight back," he had said when the lessons began. Amaethon was grateful that he and Nemausus had practiced fighting and defending with magic every day for the last several years.

He tried to call for Nemausus in his mind and heard Athanaric laugh. "He can't hear you. I've seen to that. I put a barrier of strong magic around his tower that'll keep him from hearing or sensing anything that's happening down here. We're quite alone, and there's no one who can help you."

Amaethon suddenly felt afraid, but he quieted his mind the way Nemausus had taught him. "When your mind is quiet," he had said many times before, "you can hear the universe speaking to you, telling you what you need to do and when you need to act. Be still and listen."

Amaethon remembered something else Nemausus had taught him. "At the beginning of any conflict, unless you're in a position to crush the enemy with little effort, never let your opponent see everything you can throw at him. Let him see what he expects, and surprise him when he gets overconfident."

Amaethon relaxed a little. If Athanaric thought of him as a mere landscaper, he'd use that. Turning his mind to the pebbles at the bottom of the now-dry streambed below the rock, he mentally selected the flattest ones and, after sharpening their edges, sent them flying quickly toward Athanaric from several directions.

Athanaric anticipated the attack and lifted his hands casually. The rocks changed direction and flew off harmlessly into the woods along the stream.

"So you like rocks?" he asked, mockingly. "Let's see how you like this."

Athanaric made a sudden motion, and the next thing Amaethon knew, the rock he stood on exploded, sending him flying several feet into the air and cutting him with the shards of rock that were flying out in all directions. He crashed into the stream, which followed its new course behind the rock. The cold water snapped his mind off the pain and helped him focus on his next move.

Before he could act, he felt a force like a giant hand pushing his head back below the water. No matter how he tried to free himself, he couldn't move. He started to panic, knowing he couldn't hold his breath much longer, but he managed to quiet his mind again and listen for a solution.

In that instant, he remembered the tube that Nemausus taught him to make to move water between the tower and the stream. He knew it could just as easily move air instead of water, so he focused his thoughts and created a tube that went from his mouth to the surface of the water several yards downstream.

Once he was able to breathe again, he decided to play dead and trick Athanaric into thinking he had drowned. Amaethon assumed that Athanaric could come closer to check on the body, and when he did, Amaethon would unleash his next attack.

Amaethon flailed his arms and legs for several moments, and then became still. He tried to control his breathing so Athanaric wouldn't see that he was still alive.

Athanaric watched as Amaethon stopped moving. He continued holding Amaethon's body under the water until he was sure that the young man was dead. After another minute, he moved closer to make sure the boy didn't escape him again.

Amaethon felt the force that had been holding him underwater begin to lift, and he steadied himself. Thinking about the day he had conjured the dragon for Nemausus, he wondered how Athanaric would feel about being struck by lightning and fire.

When he finally felt Athanaric release him and allow his body to float to the surface, Amaethon leapt up and launched a vicious attack on his opponent. Without even bothering to use storm clouds, Amaethon created lightning from the air and focused it directly at Athanaric. Six bolts of lightning hit Athanaric at the same time, giving Amaethon time to jump out of the stream and face his opponent on dry ground.

He saw Athanaric writhing in pain and fighting to push the lightning away. Amaethon stopped the lightning with a thought and sent a hail of fireballs from the sky to rain down on Athanaric.

The ferocity of Amaethon's attack caught Athanaric off guard. He had to use all of his power to protect himself, giving Amaethon the advantage.

Amaethon summoned all the force he felt he could contain and, when he stopped the fireballs, he unleashed the force at Athanaric, lifting his opponent high into the air and hurtling him at tremendous speed toward the west. As he watched Athanaric's body spinning off into the distance, he wondered if Athanaric would reach the Okeanós Sea before he finally fell back toward the ground.

Amaethon bent over, panting from the exertion of fighting Athanaric. He felt hot and had trouble catching his breath. When he was able to breathe easier, he straightened up and wiped the sweat and water from his face. A moment later, he felt Nemausus calling to him in his thoughts and realized that Athanaric's barrier was broken.

"*I'm by the stream, Master,*" he called out in his mind.

"*What happened?*" Nemausus demanded, sounding concerned. "*I couldn't hear you or sense you anywhere.*"

"*My watcher returned. He told me his name is Athanaric, and he tried to kill me. He almost succeeded.*"

"*Where is he now?*"

"*Probably halfway across Gallasia by now, Master,*" Amaethon replied. "*I hit him with more force than I've ever released before, so there's no telling where he might land.*"

"*Come back to the tower and tell me all about it. I have some news for you as well.*"

"*Yes, Master.*"

By the time Amaethon reached the tower, he felt light-headed and dizzy. Looking down, he saw that the cuts from the exploding rock had stopped bleeding, but he felt weaker by the step. By the time he entered the tower, he felt like he was about to pass out.

Nemausus caught him as he fell and helped him to a chair. He checked Amaethon for any injuries and cleaned up his wounds from the exploding rock. Amaethon was in no condition to answer any questions, so Nemausus placed a hand to his forehead and concentrated. In a flash, he saw the entire encounter with Athanaric and understood why his student was so weak. He placed his hand on Amaethon's heart and closed his eyes. After a minute, he opened his eyes and pulled over a chair so he could sit down opposite his student. A moment later, Amaethon opened his eyes and sat up.

"How are you feeling?" Nemausus asked with a concerned smile.

"Better, but still a little tired. What happened to me?"

"It's my fault," Nemausus said, leaning forward in his chair. "I should have warned you about it before. When you build up the kind of force you used to send Athanaric flying off into the air, that force has to come from somewhere. If there's a storm nearby, a fire, or some other source of energy, you can use that energy to build the force you need. But if there's not enough energy around you to build the force, the force gets taken from you.

"You spent almost all of your life-energy to release that much force against Athanaric. Frankly, I'm amazed it didn't kill you! If you hadn't gotten back here when you did, you'd be dead by now. You had little life-energy left. I had to give you some of mine."

"Thank you, Master."

"In the future, you need to learn to control how you build and release energy. Try to take the energy from everything around you so that you don't use up your own. It's not hard, and I can show you how to do it in a way that doesn't damage the life around you. It's safe to draw from your own life-energy for many things. The magical arts you've learned have infused you with greater amounts than the average person has. When dueling with another sorcerer, try to take the energy from your opponent and turn it back on him. However, an experienced sorcerer will know how to block you from taking his energy, so I need to show you how to protect and replenish your own. We'll start on that tomorrow."

"I look forward to learning that, Master."

"Good. By the way, we're going on a journey at first light, so I need you to get some rest and have your things ready to take with you before dawn."

"Where are we going?"

"To visit an old friend who goes by the name Belenus. He has a situation he needs my help with, and there's someone there I want you to meet. It may be quite some time before we return, so make sure you don't leave anything behind that you might need."

"Yes, Master."

131

Nemausus stood up and smiled at Amaethon. "I want you to know how proud I am of you for the way you handled yourself against Athanaric today, Amaethon. Not many others could have done what you did their first time against another sorcerer, and while I can't shake the feeling that you'll have to face him again someday, you proved that you are a far more powerful opponent than he anticipated. The next time he sees you, he'll be afraid."

Nemausus put his hand on Amaethon's shoulder and squeezed it reassuringly. He walked over to the cupboards to begin putting together the supplies they'd need for the journey to see Belenus. It was almost two hundred miles across the plains from the tower to the farm, and two men and two horses would need food and water for many days.

Athanaric Attacks Amaethon by the Stream.

CHAPTER 23

By the time Amaethon woke up the next morning, Nemausus had already saddled the horses and loaded all of the supplies. Amaethon grabbed his sword belt and travel bag, which had his heavy cloak and changes of clothes rolled up tightly, and raced down the stairs in the dark to join Nemausus in the kitchen. He poured himself some water, took a few sips, and splashed the rest in his face to wash away the sleep from his eyes. He nodded to Nemausus, and the two of them exited the tower, walking in the pre-dawn stillness to the horses.

Once they mounted their horses, Amaethon watched Nemausus hold out his hand toward the tower. A moment later, he saw candlelight appear in the windows and saw shadows moving inside. Nemausus nodded to himself and pressed his heels into the sides of his horse. The horse seemed anxious to be getting the journey started, and Amaethon had to kick his horse lightly so he could catch up.

"What did you do back there, Master?" he asked when he finally caught up to Nemausus.

"It seems to me that it's better if no one knows we've left. I created the illusion that we're still there and going about our normal daily chores. That illusion will last for a couple of weeks, and by the time anyone realizes that we've gone, they'll have no idea where to start looking for us."

Turning in his saddle to face Amaethon, Nemausus said, "You're still in danger, Amaethon. You have a destiny, and there are people out there who are determined to see that you fail or are killed before you can fulfill that destiny."

"Why?"

"Do you remember what I told you about how your parents died?"

"Yes, Master."

"Well I believe it was Athanaric who was responsible for their deaths. He tried to kill you then, and he's been trying ever since. My protection has been around you since you came to the tower, but yesterday he found a way to neutralize that protection and keep me from hearing or sensing you. Any sorcerer that powerful won't stop until he kills you or is killed himself."

"But what's so special about me? What destiny do I have that he doesn't want me to fulfill?"

"You remember the prophecy, don't you?"

"The Prophecy of Airmid? Of course. You made me memorize it."

"Think about it for a minute."

Amaethon began repeating the prophecy softly to himself. Suddenly, he stopped and looked at Nemausus. "Am I one of the orphans?" he asked.

Nemausus hesitated answering this question. He had purposely avoided discussing Amaethon's role in the prophecy, but recent events made Nemausus realize that it was time to reveal what he believed. "Yes, you are. I was given the task of raising and training you."

"What about the other two orphans?" Amaethon asked, his mind reeling from the revelation about his part in the prophecy.

"All three of you were born the same day. Do you remember when I told you about the blood red moons rising? That was the sign of your births, and people have been trying to kill the three of you ever since. Belenus, whom we're going to see, was also tasked with protecting, raising, and training one of the orphans. You'll meet him when we arrive. There have been several attempts to kill him, and they almost succeeded. But so far, no one has tried to kill the other orphan."

"Why is that, Master?"

"Because that orphan is hidden in a way that no one would ever expect. Most of those who are searching for the orphans have never even considered the possibility, which shows their limited understanding of the universe and its plan for all living things. I blame their gods for that, since the four gods who refused to obey Elohim never really understood the universe and their part in the plan. That'll change soon, one way or another, and you'll be at the center of what's going to happen. The universe has a plan for you, and it's been my job to make sure you're ready. I've done my part. The rest is up to you."

"You make it sound like you're going to leave me."

"When this is all over, I will. I have another purpose, you see, and it's time I got back to it."

Amaethon asked Nemausus to explain what he meant, but Nemausus just shook his head and continued riding east in silence.

135

Amaethon's mind filled with questions, but he kept them to himself out of respect for his teacher.

Over the next several days, Nemausus taught Amaethon how to shield his own life-energy while drawing energy from other sources. Amaethon had to be careful not to take energy from the horses or from Nemausus, but after several attempts he understood how it worked. At one point, he focused his mind on a nearby tree and pulled all of the life-energy from it. He sent that energy back at the tree and watched it burst into splinters.

"Very good!" Nemausus said approvingly.

"Can you put life-energy back into something once you've removed it? Could I have given life back to that tree once I had drained it out?"

Nemausus nodded. "As long as there is even a spark of life-energy remaining, you can replenish it even if you're using the life-energy you took to do so. But once all life-energy has been removed, there's no way to revive something or someone. You can't bring anyone back from the dead, but you can keep someone from dying if there's still some life left in him."

"But you must be careful," Nemausus warned. "If you replenish someone with your own life-energy, it could weaken you or even kill you. Always try to pull energy from all living things around you so that you only take a little from each."

Amaethon nodded. He practiced what Nemausus had taught him as the two of them continued their journey to Belenus' farm.

CHAPTER 24

he next attack on the farm was the worst one by far. It was the largest force that had been sent against the farm, and it appeared without warning just before dawn as most of the workers were getting ready to leave the bunkhouses to start their morning chores. The two men who watched the compound at night were heading back into the bunkhouses to get some sleep.

Arawn and his men were getting ready to begin the first patrol of the farm's perimeter when he heard the dogs barking furiously. He grabbed his sword and bow, and motioned for his men to take their weapons and follow him out into the courtyard.

An arrow whizzed past his head and embedded itself in the doorframe behind him as he stepped outside. In one quick motion, Arawn rolled to the right, placed the notch of an arrow against the bowstring, and drew the bowstring back as he ended up in a crouched position. He let the first arrow fly at the closest trooper in the compound. He quickly fired two more arrows at other troopers to give his men cover as they ran out of the bunkhouse and counter-attacked.

Arawn saw one of his men collapse from a head wound. He aimed his bow and shot an arrow at the slayer, killing the trooper instantly.

Arawn reached for another arrow, but a movement to his right distracted him. A trooper on horseback was getting ready to ride him down. Having nowhere to run, he dropped his bow and leaped into the air. He clutched the horse around the neck and swung his body up, knocking the rider off and sending trooper's sword flying into the melee that was taking place a short distance away.

Arawn spun the horse around, swung down to retrieve his bow, and rejoined the fight. Several of his men had fallen, and his face flushed with anger as his pulse quickened. He emptied his quiver of arrows, and, discarding his bow and drawing his sword, charged at the closest trooper. He killed the first trooper and took his sword, continuing the fight with two swords.

Several of the farmworkers ran out of the bunkhouse to join in the fight. They picked up swords from the dead and rushed several troopers fighting on horseback, pulling them off their horses. The farmworkers couldn't fight as well as the troopers, and several were injured, but the troopers who were pulled off their horses were overcome quickly by the farmworkers who fought more like an angry mob than a disciplined fighting unit.

Siena heard the commotion outside as she was getting dressed. She grabbed the leather vest and gauntlets that held her daggers and ran down the hallway toward the kitchen.

Arawn saw her exit the house and look around at the fight that was taking place in the courtyard. He saw her eyes open wide with recognition when she saw one of the troopers close by.

Siena saw Arawn across the courtyard watching her, and she reached for one of her daggers and threw it at the trooper. She threw daggers at two more troopers before Arawn fought his way back across the compound and moved his horse between her and the attacking troopers.

"Get back inside," he shouted as two troopers attacked him from either side.

Siena watched as Arawn fought two troopers at the same time. He had his back to her, but he felt her watching him. He stabbed the trooper on his right before turning to fight the trooper on the left with both swords. Soon the second trooper was on the ground. Arawn moved to protect one of the farmworkers who was surrounded.

Siena continued to watch and was getting ready to throw another dagger when suddenly Belenus appeared and pulled her back into the main house. "Stay here," he said firmly as he ran back outside, using his walking stick to knock unsuspecting troopers off their horses.

The farmworkers and Arawn's surviving men began to turn the tide of battle away from the troopers. Thirty troopers were already dead, and the remaining troopers knew that their advantage of numbers had been lost.

The leader let out a loud whistle, and the troopers broke off the attack. Each of the troopers still on horseback seized the hand of a trooper who had been unhorsed and pulled him up as they rode out of the compound.

Arawn lept onto the back of a nearby horse that had belonged to one of the fallen troopers. He shouted for his men to mount up and follow him, and he dug his heels into the side of the horse. The horse reared back – its front hoofs pawing the air as Arawn adjusted his grip on the reins. The horse leaped forward and took off after the escaping troopers. Arawn raced out of the compound with his men following close behind.

Belenus looked around the compound with a sense of sorrow. More than twenty of the farmworkers and four of Arawn's men were dead or dying. Belenus silently mourned the loss of his friends and faithful workers – many of whom had been on the farm since Belenus had brought them there as children.

As he looked around, he saw Siena walk out of the house and approach the first trooper she had killed with one of her daggers. Once she finished recovering her daggers, she walked back to Belenus and asked, "What can I do to help?"

Belenus appreciated her offer, and he grudgingly admitted to himself that he was impressed with the way she had fought during the battle. He put his hand on her shoulder and said, "Thank you for helping us against the raiders. You were very brave. Go put your daggers away and bring some towels from the house. We need to tend to the wounded first."

He watched her run back into the house and realized she that she had been fighting barefoot. He still had lingering concerns about the way she flirted with Arawn but hoped it was just because Siena was raised around different customs, rather than something more sinister. Still, he knew he had to keep a close eye on her and Arawn until he could feel comfortable with her presence on the farm.

Arawn and his men returned an hour later. They had chased the troopers into the forest but turned back when Arawn grew concerned that he and his men were being drawn into an ambush.

The dead troopers had already been loaded into one of the large wagons so the bodies could be dumped in the forest, but the fallen farmworkers and those of Arawn's men who died were laid out on the ground in the shade of the storage sheds.

Arawn dismounted to check on the wounded, and he was pleased to see that most would make a full recovery. Then he walked over to the bodies of those who had fallen. Siena and some of the other women had cleaned them up and were getting ready to wrap the bodies in canvas for burial.

Arawn knelt beside each of the fallen farmworkers and his comrades. He had never experienced loss like this before. It tore him inside. He felt a deep sense of personal responsibility for their deaths, and he was angry with the troopers and with himself for failing to keep the farmworkers and his comrades safe. He began to weep inconsolably.

Belenus walked over and knelt next to Arawn.

"I let them down, Belenus," he said after several minutes.

"No you didn't. You protected everyone. Some were lost, but more were saved thanks to you."

"But I should have been more prepared. I should have made sure we were ready."

"And would you have seen them approaching in the dark? Would your patrols have raised the alarm in time for you to get everyone into position? No. It's fortunate that almost everyone was already awake when they attacked, or we all could have been killed. You and your men gave the others time to get ready and join the fight with you. You inspired them to defend this farm against a vastly superior force, and you succeeded. The farm is still here. Most of the people are still here. Most of your men are still here. Mourn the loss of these friends who have left us, but don't forget why and how they died, or you'll dishonor them. They died to save the others, and the others are safe. You and your men did well, and you can't be a leader of men if you can't remember the triumphs even in the midst of the tragedies. Go. Be with your men and help them with their grief. Help them see what they accomplished so they don't get blinded by what they lost."

Arawn dried his eyes and looked at Belenus. Belenus had never spoken with such authority before, and it was exactly what Arawn needed to hear. He nodded, stood up, and went to find his men who were putting the horses away in the stables.

By sundown, the bodies of the dead troopers had been taken into the forest, and those who died defending the compound had been buried along the tree line to the east of the farm.

Arawn had just finished moving the wagons into position to block the three remaining ways into the compound as the sun set in the distance. Rather than have patrols riding around in the dark, he felt it was better to secure the compound and place guards on the tops of three of the buildings to raise the alarm if any troopers were heard approaching in the night.

The horses were put in the stables for the night, and Arawn felt the compound was secure from any attempt at a night raid. As Arawn walked toward the kitchen, the cook came out and handed him a small basket of food. Arawn took it from her gratefully and climbed up to the roof of the kitchen to take his position for the first watch. Two of his men were already in position above the stables and on top of a storage shed.

Arawn was glad that the moons were up so he could see what he was eating. The cook had given him a roasted chicken quarter, steamed vegetables, and fresh bread. For dessert, she had made a small cake that smelled of oranges. The food was delicious, and Arawn ate quickly so he could focus on watching for raiders. One of his men would relieve him after midnight so he could get some sleep. The other two men standing guard around the compound would be relieved at different times.

Arawn stood up and stretched, looking around the compound briefly before returning his attention to the approaches outside the compound that the troopers might use for another attack.

Within two hours, the compound grew quiet, and the lights were extinguished. Soon the only sounds were those of the nocturnal creatures that were beginning to move about in the darkness. The moons moved toward the horizon, making it harder for Arawn to watch the approaches on his side of the compound.

About thirty minutes later, Arawn thought he heard a sound. He looked around but couldn't see anything moving. He listened intently, but the sound didn't repeat itself. He relaxed, deciding it must have been an animal.

A dark figure carefully crept through the barricade between the main house and the first bunkhouse. The figure moved silently, and with the moons setting behind the trees, it would have been difficult for anyone to see the figure moving across the south fields toward the forest.

The figure entered the forest and walked in the near-darkness for several minutes. After a while, a light became visible in the distance. The figure walked quickly in that direction.

As the figure approached the light, it saw about two dozen troopers sitting in the clearing with three torches stuck in the ground to provide light and to ward away any prowling beasts. The figure crept toward the clearing, trying to avoid making a sound that would startle the troopers.

"How long do we have to wait for the assassin?" one of the troopers asked softly.

"For as long as it takes," the leader whispered irritably. When he looked up, he saw the figure standing in the clearing staring at him. He reached for his sword, but recognition flashed in his face, and he moved his hand away from his weapon.

"We were worried you wouldn't come. Why did you have to kill poor Drickso like that?"

"Because he got too close, and it would look strange if he didn't

141

attack me and I didn't defend myself. It's not like he was any great loss. And besides, the raid worked."

"For you, maybe, but I lost a lot of men, you Étaíne harlot."

"That doesn't matter, you Chulainn dog. You're following King Grannus' orders, who's following Morrigan's orders, just like I'm following King Taranus' orders, who's following Mider's orders. If it weren't for Mider, none of us would know who the orphans are or where they're hiding. He's the only god who had the foresight and the wisdom to put this plan in motion and save us from Airmid's little prophecy. That means my mission is what matters now. You missed your chance to kill the boy too many times. Be glad Grannus hasn't killed you for your failures."

"I don't care if you are Taranus' favorite assassin and Grannus' favorite plaything," the leader spat angrily. "I don't have to take that from you."

"Yes you do, and you know it. Also, I need you to stop the raids until you hear from me again."

"Why?"

"Because it's not enough to kill just the boy. I need to make sure that all three are together before we strike again. Mider's not sure that he read all the signs properly. If the boy and the two others are together, we'll know we have the right ones. Understood?"

"I understand," the leader grumbled. He didn't like being bossed around by this Étaíne assassin, but he had his orders, and he was sworn to obey them.

"Good. I need to get back before someone notices I'm missing. Keep a close watch on the farm, and don't let the patrols see you. We need stealth to make this work, not brute force."

The assassin turned and disappeared into the forest. The leader couldn't contain his sarcasm as he muttered, "As you command, *Siena*."

Siena crept back across the fields of the farm and approached the barricade that she had propped open when she left the compound earlier in the night. She closed the barricade quietly and crept back to her window, climbed inside, and stood in the darkness listening for any sounds from the guards. Hearing nothing, she quickly undressed and crawled into bed, making sure that the daggers in her vest didn't hit the floor and make a sound. She went to sleep with a look of smug satisfaction on her face.

CHAPTER 25

wo days later, shortly after noon, Belenus and Arawn were walking together by the lake. Arawn was about to ask Belenus a question when he heard one of the patrols shouting, "Riders spotted west of the farm." Belenus and Arawn ran across the fields to investigate.

Arawn saw that there were only two riders, and they didn't look like troopers. But he unslung his bow and reached for an arrow just in case. He was about to put the arrow in place when suddenly he heard Belenus laugh.

"Welcome my old friend," Belenus shouted with his arms open wide. "You made good time!"

Arawn stared at Belenus with surprise. Not only did Belenus know one of the riders, but he seemed to be expecting him. He lowered his bow but kept the arrow in place until he knew what was going on.

"We had the wind at our back and the promise of a fine meal before us," the elder of the two riders shouted back with a wide smile.

The elder rider dismounted and ran to Belenus. The two men embraced each other and touched their foreheads together in a sign of greeting.

Arawn looked at the two men and at the other man still on his horse. He slowly put the arrow back in the quiver and slung the bow across his shoulder. Whoever these men were, it was clear that they posed no threat as far as Belenus was concerned.

"Come here, Arawn," Belenus said, gesturing for Arawn to join him. "I want you to meet one of my oldest friends and one of the greatest sorcerers in the history of the world."

Turning to his old friend, he said, "Nemausus, this is Arawn. Arawn, this is Nemausus."

Arawn bowed to the sorcerer. "I'm honored to meet you, sir."

Placing a hand on Arawn's shoulder, Nemausus closed his eyes. Arawn had the sensation of wind blowing, but before he could ask a question, Nemausus opened his eyes and smiled. "The honor is mine, Arawn. Please allow me to introduce my finest student, Amaethon."

Amaethon dismounted and walked over to the others. He held out his hand, and he and Arawn grasped each other by the right forearm. "My pleasure," Arawn said with a nod.

"Mine, too," Amaethon said. Turning to Belenus, he added, "I'm pleased to meet you, sir. My Master has told me many things about you and your role in what's to come."

Belenus nodded and motioned for everyone to follow him back to the compound.

Arawn helped Amaethon lead the horses across the fields. "I notice the sword and the bow," Amaethon commented as he watched Belenus and Nemausus walking ahead of them. "Strange for a farmer, isn't it?"

"We've had some raiders lately. I spend most of my time patrolling and fighting rather than farming. Two days ago, they hit us at dawn, and it was the worst raid yet. I never go anywhere without the sword and the bow anymore."

Amaethon nodded. "How much do you know about what's coming?"

"You mean the prophecy?"

Amaethon nodded. "I'm assuming you're one of the orphans mentioned in the prophecy."

"And I'm assuming you're also one of the orphans," Arawn responded.

"Any idea who the other orphan is?"

"Not a clue," Arawn admitted. "Belenus doesn't talk about it much, but I get the feeling that's about to change."

"Me, too."

Belenus turned and said, "You two take the horses to the compound. Nemausus and I are going down to the lake for a little while. We'll be along shortly."

Arawn and Amaethon nodded. When they entered the courtyard, Arawn led the way to the stables and found stalls for the two additional horses. He introduced Amaethon to the men guarding the compound and to the farmworkers who were nearby. He showed Amaethon the defensive barricades and led him to the main house so Amaethon could put his and Nemausus' things away and get something to drink.

Arawn grabbed two tankards and filled them. He motioned for Amaethon to sit down at the table and took a seat across from the young sorcerer. For both Arawn and Amaethon, it was like meeting a long-lost

144

brother. Even though they weren't related as far as they knew, their shared destiny made a bond between them that felt stronger than blood ties.

Arawn finished telling Amaethon about the raiders and the tactics that he and his men used to protect the compound. Amaethon had started telling Arawn about his dealings with Athanaric when he stopped mid-sentence and stared out the doorway into the compound. Arawn smiled. He didn't even have to turn around. He knew the look on Amaethon's face was one he had made himself a number of times.

"She's quite beautiful, isn't she?"

Amaethon didn't answer immediately, and Arawn turned around to see what Siena was doing. She was barefoot, and it looked like she was dancing to some unheard music. She swayed gently like a reed in the wind, and her arms cupped the wind as she spun and turned in circles, her feet making interesting patterns in the dirt.

"She does that a lot," Arawn commented.

"Who is she?" Amaethon finally asked.

"Her name's Siena. We rescued her from thieves in the Great Forest not too long ago. She's a dancer and had hired some guys to escort her to the next village, but the thieves attacked, and her escorts ran, leaving her behind."

"She's the most beautiful woman I've ever seen," Amaethon said, taking another drink without taking his eyes off her.

Arawn nodded. He thought he should feel jealous about Amaethon's reaction to Siena, but for some reason he didn't. Amaethon was a brother, and Arawn was so grateful to have someone like that in his life that the effect Siena usually had on him seemed diminished somehow.

Arawn was about to get up and take Amaethon outside to make the introductions when he heard hoof beats approaching the compound rapidly. "It never fails," he said to himself, getting to his feet and motioning for Amaethon to follow.

As he stepped outside, two of his men rode into the compound and stopped between Arawn and Siena. Arawn caught a disappointed look on her face, but he noticed she was inching closer to overhear what the riders had to say.

"We found a party of troopers watching the farm just inside the tree line of the forest to the southeast."

"How many were there?" Arawn asked.

"About twenty, as near as we could guess. We were paying our respects at the graves we dug the other day when we heard voices. We snuck up on them so they wouldn't see us."

"What did they say?"

"We couldn't make out most of it. They said something about having to wait for the 'assassin' to come and give them the order to attack again. We thought we should get back here quickly and let you know, so we snuck back to our horses and rode as quickly as we could."

Arawn nodded with a frown. The compound was still recovering from the previous raid and wasn't ready for another one so soon. He remembered Amaethon standing next to him and made quick introductions, letting his two men know that Belenus had guests who'd be staying for a while. "Go tell the others what you just told me. I want to talk to Belenus, and then we'll figure something out. I'll come find you in a little while. In the meantime, don't do anything that'll let the troopers know they've been discovered."

The two men nodded and rode off to alert the other patrols, kicking up a cloud of dust. As the dust settled, Arawn saw Siena standing there with her hands behind her back, looking at Amaethon.

"Siena, this is Amaethon. Amaethon, this is Siena."

"Pleased to meet you, Amaethon," Siena purred in the way she did when she was trying to get a reaction from Arawn.

"It's my pleasure, Siena," Amaethon replied, stunned at her mannerisms. "I watched you dancing earlier."

"Did you like what you saw?" she asked seductively.

"Very much."

"Well, I'll have to dance for you again when there's not so much going on around here."

Amaethon laughed.

A moment later, Belenus and Nemausus entered the courtyard from the direction of the lake.

"Siena, this is my master, Nemausus," Amaethon said as the two gentlemen approached.

Siena kept her hands behind her back but nodded to the sorcerer. "My pleasure, sir."

"Ah, so this is the young woman who has lost her memories," Nemausus said as he began focusing on her face and her thoughts.

"Yes, sir," she said demurely.

Siena felt Nemausus' mind touch hers and quickly put up the defenses she learned long ago to use when in the presence of a sorcerer. She let flashes of memories slip through on purpose, but she kept most of her thoughts well-hidden.

Nemausus knew what she was doing immediately, and glanced over to

Belenus to let him know he had been right to be curious about her. "Well I'm certain you'll remember everything you should as the need arises," he said cryptically.

"Belenus, may I speak with you for a moment?" Arawn said, interrupting. "Two of my men just brought news, and I need to fill you in."

"Certainly," Belenus replied. "Let's all go inside, and we can talk at the table."

Turning to Siena, Belenus added. "Siena, why don't you go and get something to eat from the kitchen?"

Siena started to protest, but she shot a glance at Nemausus, who was watching her closely, and nodded.

Belenus gestured for everyone to go into the house as Siena turned and walked across the courtyard to the kitchen. Soon Belenus, Nemausus, Arawn, and Amaethon were sitting around the table. No one noticed that Siena had doubled back and was standing just outside the doorway.

Arawn repeated what his men told him. "I just don't think we're ready for another fight this soon, Belenus," he concluded. "I'd like to know your thoughts."

Belenus sat back and stared at Nemausus as if the two men were having a conversation that no one else could hear. "What do you think, old friend?" he asked Nemausus after a minute.

"I think it's time for you to go," he said flatly. "Things are happening too quickly, and you have a long journey to make. You take the boys and find the others. I'll stay here and create the illusion that you're still here. I can protect the farm if it's attacked. I can give you a month's head start before leaving to catch up with you. You three should leave as soon as possible."

"I agree," Belenus said reluctantly. "I was hoping for your company on this part of the journey, old friend, but I think you're right. Time and speed are the most important things now, and you're the better one to have around if there's another attack."

"It's settled then," Nemausus stated. Turning to Amaethon, he said, "You know what to do. Belenus knows where you're going, but you know how to hide any traces of your journey. Do it just like I taught you, and you'll all be fine. I'll see you soon."

"Yes, Master," Amaethon responded.

Siena tried to suppress the feelings of panic that she was having as she slipped through the doorway and stood in the shadows near the end of the table. It never occurred to her that both Arawn and Amaethon would leave the compound so soon. "May I come along, too?" she asked Belenus.

Belenus looked up at her, but didn't act surprised at seeing her inside the house. "No, I think it would be better if you stayed here, Siena. It's a long journey, and it won't take you anywhere near the village you were trying to reach or your home. Stay here for another week, and I'll have Nemausus arrange for an escort of soldiers to take you wherever you want to go."

"But what if I'm the reason the troopers are attacking in such large numbers?" she asked, pushing the one advantage she still had. Looking at Arawn, she said, "You said yourself that the attacks were never this bad before you rescued me. If I stay here, they'll keep attacking, and more of your people will get killed. If I'm gone, maybe they won't attack."

"No, they'll just start following us and overwhelm us where we can't defend ourselves," Arawn pointed out.

"Not if they don't know we're gone." Turning to Nemausus, she added, "If you can create the illusion that we haven't left, then you can give the illusion that I'm still here. If they're after me, they won't know I'm gone, and if they're looking for the rest of you, the same holds true."

"And if they think we're all still here, what would keep them from attacking the farm and killing more innocent people?" Arawn asked.

Siena looked at Arawn and hid her anger. She wasn't prepared for this discussion, and Arawn had managed to turn her own arguments against her. She bit her lip, trying to think of some way to salvage the situation.

Nemausus looked at Belenus and silently communicated with him in his mind. *"There's something not right about her. She seems panicked about you and the boys leaving, but she's blocking every attempt I make to read her thoughts. She's hiding something, and it could be dangerous."*

"I know," Belenus replied in his mind. *"I don't trust her. If we don't take her, she could follow us anyway and give us away without meaning to. But more importantly, if we do take her, it could change the way events are supposed to be played out."*

"It's better if she stays here." Nemausus commented. *"It'll give me more time to observe her and figure out what she's hiding."*

"I agree. And it's safer for the boys if she's kept as far away from them as possible."

Turning to Siena, Belenus said aloud, "I'm sorry, my dear. This journey isn't for you. You'll need to stay here with Nemausus."

"I understand, Belenus," she said, bowing her head to hide her expression.

"Where is it we're going, Belenus?" Amaethon asked.

"You'll know when we get there," Belenus replied cryptically, continuing to watch Siena.

elenus, Arawn, and Amaethon were miles away by the time the sun rose the next morning. Arawn and Amaethon were dressed in loose-fitting trousers, high leather boots, and leather vests and wrist guards. Amaethon wore the sword he brought with him from the tower, and Arawn wore his sword and had his bow slung over his shoulder.

Belenus was dressed as he always dressed and looked every bit like a farmer taking a trip to the nearest village. He tucked his walking stick into the bedroll behind his saddle, but he carried no other weapons – as was his custom. "I prefer not to call attention to myself when traveling," he explained when Amaethon asked him why he was unarmed. "Besides, with the two of you to protect me, I don't need any weapons."

They were traveling to the smithy at the base of the foothills on the eastern face of the Mountain of Elohim. The most direct route from the farm was to go around the eastern edge of the great lake to the south of the mountain. After crossing the river at a ford near the northeastern edge of the Great Forest, the smithy was only a few days' ride to the northeast. It was almost a four hundred mile journey to the smithy, and Belenus expected to arrive in three weeks.

They made good time as they traveled north between the lake and the forest. The Mountain of Elohim rose majestically in front of them, and Arawn was beginning to understand just how large it was. He knew that he was getting closer, but the size of the mountain never seemed to change. When he asked Belenus about it, Belenus replied that the mountain was more than two hundred miles from the farm. Arawn thought about this for a while. He had never traveled more than a day's ride from the farm before, and it was several hundred miles to where they were going. He wondered what the mountain would look like up close, amazed that anything could be that large.

At one point, as they were leading their horses on foot to give them a rest, Arawn asked, "Belenus, I'm still not certain what's happening here. Can you tell me what's going on?"

"There's no easy answer to that question, Arawn," Belenus replied.

"It's going to be a long journey," Amaethon noted.

Belenus nodded. He closed his eyes for a moment to alert Nemausus and Tridamus about what he was going to do. Tridamus replied that he'd do the same with Cerridwen. Belenus sent his thoughts to Alaunus so she'd know as well.

"Where to begin…" he said thoughtfully. "I guess it goes all the way back to the birth of the universe. Elohim created the universe with a single word. Elohim created the universe in thought and made it materialize. The stars were made first to give light to creation. Elohim has a plan for the universe and everything that will ever exist within it. Everything fits together, you see, and everything is equally important."

Belenus paused for a moment before continuing. "Elohim created the gods to help make the worlds that would fill the universe. Twelve were created, and each had a specific purpose. Cerrunos created Alastríona itself. Balor, Llyr, and Camalus worked with Cerrunos to create the ground, the waters, and the sky. Once the foundations of the world were finished, the other gods created life on Alastríona. Mebd created grasses and grains, Branwen created small plants, Lugh created the trees, Manannan created small animals, Mider created fish, Morrigan created birds, and Artio created the beasts."

"That's only eleven, Amaethon pointed out.

"I know," Belenus said. "I'm coming to the twelfth. Once everything else had been created, Airmid created man, and this was to be the universe's greatest creation. Even though everything is equally important to Elohim, it would be primarily through man that the plan would be carried out."

"What is this plan you keep mentioning?" Arawn asked.

"Do you remember when we built the new smokehouse a few years ago?" Belenus asked.

Arawn nodded.

"Do you remember the drawing I made so the men would know how to build it?"

Again, Arawn nodded.

"Well, that drawing is called a 'plan.' It describes what needs to be done and how to do it. Now imagine a plan that encompasses the entire universe! That's a plan that includes every single part of creation from the smallest speck of dirt to a single blade of grass to an individual leaf on a tree to every living creature on every world that has been created and is yet to be created."

Belenus looked at his traveling companions. "Think about it for a moment. You two are here now. Think of all the things that had to happen in just the right sequence to bring you here. Then think about all the things that happened to bring your parents to the point where they met so they could bring you into the world. Then think about their parents and so on all the way back to when Airmid first created man on Alastríona. If any single thing happened in the wrong order or didn't happen at all, nothing that's happening today would be happening in the right way, and the future would be rewritten. That's what Elohim's plan is: the definition, creation, and sequence of each interaction of all life on all worlds so the future happens as Elohim has written it."

"How is that possible?" Amaethon asked. "How could a single plan contain all that?"

"It's hard for humans to grasp the enormity of the plan. Frankly, it's hard for the gods to grasp it either, which is where the problems started."

Belenus fell silent to collect his thoughts. Arawn was about to ask a question, but Belenus resumed his story. "Animals act primarily on instinct, so it was easy to ensure that they'd conform to their part in the plan. But the higher forms of life, specifically man and the gods, were given free will. Now, as you can imagine, it's hard to have a plan that lays out the future when the beings that the plan depends upon have the ability to choose whether or not they'll be obedient and carry out their part. So Elohim's plan had to be self-adjusting, meaning it had to have alternate ways to make the future happen as written should any of the individual things that were supposed to happen not happen."

A large bird flew overhead and landed on the lake. Its head disappeared underwater and a moment later reappeared with a fish in its beak. With a flutter of its large wings, the bird took off for the sky again and disappeared into the forest.

"The gods," Belenus continued, "were supposed to create Alastríona and move on to create other worlds. But ten of the gods disobeyed Elohim and decided to stay here. This was the first world they created, and they fell in love with it. They didn't want to leave, and because Elohim had shared with them only what they were supposed to create and hadn't shown them the entire plan, they didn't understand why it was important for them to leave. Only two of the gods obeyed Elohim. Cerrunos left Alastríona once he had completed his task, and he moved on to create other worlds around each of the stars in the sky. Airmid

152

knew more of Elohim's plan than the other gods. Man had to be created to fulfil Elohim's plan, and Airmid needed to understand the plan to know how man should be created. But Airmid wasn't able to follow Cerrunos and create man on the other worlds. Man is the last act of creation for each world, and with the other gods staying here, there weren't any other worlds finished where man could be created.

"Airmid tried to get the other gods to listen, but they didn't. Then the other gods came in contact with man, and that's when the real trouble started."

"Trouble?" Amaethon asked.

"Yes, trouble," Belenus replied. "Airmid created man according to the will of Elohim. All men and women were created as equals, with no one made superior to another. There was no conflict between people in the beginning. Petty jealousy, the desire for status, the desire for power... none of these existed. People learned how to hunt and fish for food, but killing another person was something that Airmid never taught. All people lived in peace."

"And all that changed because of the gods?" Arawn asked.

Belenus nodded. "People had never seen any of the gods before. They began worshipping whichever god they lived near, and the gods thought this was the greatest thing they had ever experienced. They forgot that they created this world for Elohim and began thinking that Alastríona and its people had been created just for them.

"Over time, people formed tribes and started identifying themselves by the god they worshiped. As the tribes started growing, traveling, and interacting with other tribes, rivalries developed between the tribes over which god and which tribe was greater.

"Eventually, rivalries grew into open conflict between the tribes, and the conflict led to war – something that man was never intended to learn. Several of the gods enjoyed the fighting and pushed their worshippers into attacking the other tribes. Tools became weapons, and man learned the arts of war to satisfy the gods' desire for amusement and dominance. This is when Elohim had to make an adjustment to the plan to keep the universe intact and induce the gods to fulfill their purpose. Elohim spoke to Airmid and revealed much of what was to come. Airmid was given the task of setting into motion the events that would lead to the gods returning to their purpose.

"Airmid began visiting the tribes of man and tried to convince them to abandon the conflict and return to peaceful pursuits. Some followed Airmid and worshiped Elohim, but many didn't. Airmid also kept trying to get the gods to leave and finish their work, and the gods turned on Airmid. After years of fighting, some of the gods realized that Airmid was right, but four didn't, and until those four agree to leave and obey Elohim, the universe can never move forward in accordance with Elohim's plan."

Belenus stopped at a small stream to water the horses. He opened the leather bag underneath his bedroll and pulled out some dried meat and fruit. He shared the food with Arawn and Amaethon, and they ate while the horses drank from the stream. After a few minutes, Belenus led Thunder across the stream.

"Which brings us to where we are now," Belenus said as he got back on his horse and motioned for the others to do the same. "As I said, the plan has the ability to adjust itself, but there are limits. Elohim knew that there'd come a point when the plan could no longer be adjusted for the future to happen as it needed to. The prophecy told of future events that would bring the world to the final moment of decision. When that moment happens, either the gods will decide to obey Elohim, and the universe will begin moving forward again, or Elohim's plan for the universe will shatter and fail."

"What happens if the plan fails?" Arawn asked.

"I don't know," Belenus admitted. "But I doubt any of us will survive the event."

"Would Elohim unmake the universe just to spite the gods?" Amaethon asked.

"Not for spite, no. It's the gods who are treating Elohim with spite through their disobedience. Elohim may decide to take drastic action to bring the universe back into alignment with the plan."

"So Arawn, the other orphan, and I are supposed to get the gods to make the final decision that affects the future of the universe?" Amaethon asked.

Belenus nodded. "You three are the catalyst that'll bring all the gods together in one place at the same time, which hasn't been done since the world was made. This isn't about a battle between the tribes of man, although that may certainly happen as well. The real battle will be between the gods, and the result of that battle will determine the fate of the universe."

"So we're nothing more than tools to bring the gods together?" Arawn asked.

"No, Arawn, you three are much more than that. Remember the rest of the prophecy. It is from the three of you that the Ruler of the World will be chosen. If the gods choose correctly and leave this world, someone will need to unite the tribes of man and lead them according to the plan of Elohim. That's no small task, and it's for that task that the three of you were born. The decision of the gods will determine if you get to perform that task or not."

Looking around, Belenus commented, "It would be a shame if Alastríona didn't survive. There's so much more to it than anyone has discovered."

"What do you mean?" Arawn asked.

"Do you think that where the tribes of man live is all that there is to Alastríona? There's more to the world than that!"

"Where?" Amaethon asked.

"Think about the Great Desert to the south of us. Have you never wondered what's on the other side? Have you never wondered what lies beyond the Okeanós Sea to the west or the Ceres Sea to the east?"

"I know there are islands off the eastern and western coast," Amaethon said, "but are you saying that there are other places like this across the sea and south of the desert?"

"Yes," Belenus replied. "The gods stayed here because this is where it all began. They stood just below the Mountain of Elohim as they created the world, and when they decided to stay, they felt drawn to stay close together – close to where they once stood with common purpose to carry out the will of Elohim. But this place is just one of the places the gods created on Alastríona for man to live. Man just hasn't discovered the other places yet. Once the wars are over, assuming anyone survives, man can start exploring this world and spreading out the way Elohim intended."

"How do you know so much about the world and the gods?" Arawn asked finally.

"Oh, I've met one or two of the gods before," Belenus admitted with a wry smile. "They love to talk, and they love to teach. It's amazing what you can learn when you just listen to others talk."

"Which gods sided with Airmid, and which ones are still defying Elohim?" Amaethon asked.

"There are eight gods obedient to the will of Elohim," Belenus replied. "Cerrunos and Airmid obeyed Elohim from the beginning. Cerrunos left Alastríona once he had finished his work here. Llyr, Balor, and Camalus never had tribes of their own and joined with Airmid to end the conflict between the tribes. Mebd, Branwen, and Lugh eventually grew tired of the fighting and joined with Airmid shortly after the revelation of the prophecy. Manannan, Mider, Morrigan, and Artio are the disobedient ones still defying Elohim, and they're the real problem."

"What's the Kingstone?" Arawn asked. "I remember the prophecy saying something about it."

"The Kingstone is a blue jewel with a golden crown on top that's infused with the spirit of Elohim. Airmid made it, but it was Elohim who commanded that it be made. It was created to help convince the gods to leave Alastríona and return to their original purpose. It'll also help the Ruler of the World, who has the responsibility of leading all of the people of Alastríona once the gods have left, to serve the people of Alastríona wisely and fairly. Elohim ordered Airmid to hide the Kingstone and protect it until the Ruler of the World retrieves it from its hiding place and summons the gods so the final choice can be made."

"So one of us has to find it and use it to convince the gods to obey Elohim?" Amaethon asked.

"Something like that," Belenus replied.

he three rode on in silence for the rest of the day. Every now and then, Arawn looked behind him. He couldn't shake the feeling that they were being followed, but he couldn't see any evidence of anyone. While looking back, he suddenly realized that he couldn't see any tracks on the ground from their horses.

"It's all right," Amaethon said when Arawn pointed it out. "I've been erasing our tracks ever since we left the farm so no one can follow us."

"You can do that?" Arawn asked.

"Sure. It's an easy thing that Nemausus taught me. But I can't erase every sign that we've passed this way. If we rub up against a branch, fibers from our clothes can be left behind. Leftover food can also leave a trail that an expert tracker can follow. And if another sorcerer is out there, he can follow the trail of the magic I'm using to obscure our path."

"Are there other sorcerers in the world?" Arawn asked.

Amaethon nodded. "I've met one. He's the one who killed my parents, and he's tried to kill me. Nemausus told me that Mider trained a couple of sorcerers to help make sure the prophecy would never be fulfilled, and some of the former students of Nemausus have trained their own students in the magical arts. I doubt there are more than a dozen, but Nemausus and I know for certain that at least one is actively working against us. I'm just hoping he doesn't know that we've left our tower yet. Nemausus left behind an illusion to make people think we're still there, but I don't know if another sorcerer would be fooled by it."

That night, they camped in the shelter of the forest, but decided not to make fire in case anyone was watching. Arawn couldn't shake the feeling that they were being watched, but there was no indication of anyone nearby. Arawn mentioned his concerns to Amaethon and

Belenus, and he offered to take the first watch. Amaethon and Belenus agreed and cleaned up the campsite so the trio could leave quickly the next morning. Amaethon and Belenus then went to sleep.

The attack came about three hours later. Arawn kept a close watch for any movement in the dark, but he couldn't see anything once the moons had set. As he bent down to brush a large insect off his boots, he heard the whizzing of the arrow just miss his shoulder and imbed itself in the tree next to where he was leaning.

Arawn dropped to the ground, grabbed his bow and an arrow, and sent the arrow flying in the direction where he estimated the shooter might be. He heard a grunting sound and knew that his arrow had hit someone. More arrows flew into the campsite.

"Wake up," Arawn hissed at his two companions, nudging Amaethon with the tip of his bow.

"What is it?" Amaethon asked, wiping the sleep from his eyes.

"Keep quiet and take cover," Arawn whispered, letting another arrow fly into the darkness. "We're under attack!"

Amaethon wondered if the attackers were moving to surround the campsite, using the darkness to cover their position. He quieted his mind and focused for a moment. Suddenly, the woods were filled with a pale green light coming from the treetops. The attacking troopers were suddenly visible, and Arawn was able to fire his arrows with greater accuracy.

Several troopers fell dead before they could react to the fact that they were visible. The leader let out a loud whistle, and the troopers retreated deeper into the forest.

The trio wasted no time. While Arawn retrieved his arrows from the fallen troopers, along with some of the weapons the troopers had been carrying, Belenus and Amaethon quickly saddled the horses. When Arawn returned, he mounted his horse, and the trio rode northward as quickly as they dared in the darkness. With no light shining from the two moons, they had to use caution so the horses wouldn't stumble or bump into anything.

It was well after sunup when the trio finally slowed down and dismounted to give the horses a rest. They had been walking for about thirty minutes when Belenus, who was deep in thought, heard someone yelling his name. He looked around quickly but realized it was the voice of Nemausus in his head.

"I'm here, old friend," he said in his mind. *"Is there a problem?"*

"Are you all right?"

"We were attacked last night, but we're fine. Why?"

"Siena's gone," Nemausus told him.

"When?"

"I don't know. She locked herself in her room after you left and never came out. I went in to check on her this morning, but she was gone and so were all of her things."

"Are any of the horses missing?"

"Not that I can tell. I'm sorry. I should have watched her more closely."

"She wasn't among the attackers we saw last night," Belenus said. *"There must be a reason why she left, old friend. We need to focus on our tasks and let her actions unfold as they will."*

"I wish I could be as calm about this as you are."

"It's not a question of being calm. I'm just being practical. There's nothing that can be done, so there's nothing to get excited about. I doubt she could find us on her own – especially without a horse or wings."

"You're right. But keep a close watch out. Mider's up to something, and I feel the need for great caution now that the days are counting down to the final decision."

"Agreed."

Belenus felt his old friend pull away. He told his two companions about Siena.

"How do you know?" Arawn asked.

"Nemausus has the ability to send his thought to me. He just told me."

"Do you think she's following us?" Amaethon asked.

"I don't know, but we need to see if we can go a bit faster today and be watchful for any troopers following us."

The trio picked up the pace as they continued northward around the lake toward the Mountain of Elohim. As they rode, Belenus found himself answering more questions from the two young men.

"Is there anyone we can trust?" Arawn asked around mid-morning.

"Of course there is, Arawn," Belenus answered. "In addition to everyone who lives in this region, there are three tribes that now follow Elohim and are loyal to Airmid. There's the Dunmaine tribe and their King Vellaunus, the Penarduun tribe and their King Arvernus, and the Macruhan tribe and their King Esus. Amaethon, did you know you're a Dunmaine?"

"No I didn't," Amaethon answered.

"What am I?" Arawn asked.

"You are a Gallasian, Arawn."

"I'm one of the enemies?" Arawn asked.

"No, and you should never look at any of the tribes as enemies. If all goes well, man will be united as one tribe once all this is over. The Ruler of the World will have to lead all peoples equally."

"What is the other orphan?" Amaethon asked.

"A Macruhan," Belenus replied.

"I've met some Macruhans before," Amaethon said. "Fascinating people. They love trees and they're some of the best craftsmen I've ever seen."

"I think you'll find the other orphan every bit of that and more," Belenus said with a smile.

"So who do we need to watch out for?" Arawn asked.

"There are four tribes still warring against the rest of us," Belenus replied. "The Mongán tribe and their King Ocelus, the Étaíne tribe and their King Taranus, the Chulainn tribe and their King Grannus, and the Gallasian tribe and their King Latobius. Taranus is the worst of the lot, but they're all a bit mad if you ask me."

"Why do you say that?" Amaethon asked.

"Because they all think that they're descended from the gods."

"Aren't we all descended from Airmid?" Amaethon asked.

"Man was created by Airmid, but no one is descended from a god in the way that you're descended from your grandparents. Gods and men cannot breed. Airmid made sure of that when man was created. Elohim didn't want there to be a super race of men. Airmid made all men *and* *women* equal in all ways. But somewhere along the line, these kings' families got it into their heads that they had divine blood in their veins, and they used that to claim the kingship over their tribes."

"What made them think they were of divine blood?" Arawn asked.

"Well, let's say that you're the head of an important family in one of the tribes, and you have a beautiful daughter that you love above all things. She comes to you and tells you that she's with child. What do you do?"

"If my family were that important in the tribe, I'd probably find the boy who did that to her and have him killed. I might even punish my daughter just to keep the respect of my peers," Amaethon replied.

"Exactly," Belenus said. "Now suppose that your daughter knows what you'd do. She wouldn't want the father of her baby killed, and she wouldn't want to get punished either, would she? So she comes to you and tells you she's with child, but she says a god visited her and gave her the baby that now grows inside her. What would you do then?"

160

"Well, I couldn't very well go and kill a god, could I?" Amaethon answered.

"Right," Belenus said. "There's no one you could take your anger out on. You couldn't confront the god, and you dare not punish your daughter without risking the anger of the god who visited her. Then you realize the opportunity this presents. Your grandchild will be half-divine. You tell your friends, and soon you get them to accept that your grandchild will be a superior being in their midst. Before that child is even born, it has been proclaimed the king of the tribe. Only your daughter knows the truth, and she has the good sense to say nothing because, as the mother of the king, she'll be in a position of power herself. A royal dynasty is born, and generations follow the commands of the rulers from that family all because of a lie a desperate girl told her father to keep from getting punished."

Arawn and Amaethon nodded. "How did Vellaunus, Arvernus, and Esus become kings?" Arawn asked.

"The Dunmaine, Penarduun, and Macruhan kings used to be selected by their gods from among the greatest warriors. Once these tribes joined in the worship of Elohim, they knew that a new ruler would be coming that would eliminate the need for tribal kings. Now, they're ruled by a Council that's comprised of a representative from each of the major families, and they appoint one of their own to serve as king and handle relations with the other tribes. It's really just a ceremonial position for them."

The trio continued heading northward as quickly as they dared for the rest of the day. The moons rose early, and they made the decision to keep moving as long as the moons gave them enough light to see. It was well after midnight before they stopped to rest. None of them slept, but no attack came that night. By first light, they were on the move again.

CHAPTER 28

he next two days were uneventful, but the trio remained ready for a fight. On the third day, Arawn thought he saw something moving on the lake to the west. Looking again, he was certain that he saw more than one shape moving south on the water. After a while, he realized that the shapes were actually boats.

"Look at that!" he said excitedly, pointing toward the boats.

Belenus looked in the direction where Arawn was pointing. "Warships. Those are Étaíne longboats. What are they doing this far south?"

"Étaíne?" Amaethon asked. "How did they get here?"

"It's possible to follow the larger rivers and waterways from here all the way to the Okeanós Sea without having to take the boats over land," Belenus replied. "Longboats only need about four or five feet of water to maneuver, and the shallowest point of the river leading here is five feet at the ford where we're crossing. But Étaíne warships haven't been seen around here since the last war. I knew Mider was up to something. If he's got Taranus sending ships down here, then he must really be desperate to keep the prophecy from being fulfilled. We need to get out of sight."

"But if the troopers are in the forest, we could get trapped," Arawn noted.

"No choice," Belenus said, dismounting and leading his horse toward the trees. "Those longboats can carry up to a hundred armed men. We can't go up against a force that large."

For the remainder of the day, the trio stayed close to the trees. Whenever they saw one of the longboats, they moved into the trees to get out of sight. Once the longboat moved past them, they moved out of the trees and rode north again as fast as they could.

No more attacks came, but the trio felt certain that the enemy knew exactly where they were. They felt that someone was watching them all the time.

Belenus grew more and more concerned as they approached the ford they needed to use to cross the river. "If longboats are on the lake," he said, "then I think we can assume that they're on the river as well. If there are any longboats near the ford, they'll make it difficult for us to cross the river."

When the trio finally passed the northern tip of the lake and began following the river to the northeast, they saw that Belenus had been correct. There were longboats on the river. The trio decided to stop for the night and decide what to do.

Amaethon had been giving the matter some thought and believed that he had an idea that might work. The next morning, he was up well before dawn. Belenus and Arawn found him standing on the banks of the river, but they didn't disturb him.

Amaethon stood motionless for quite a while. As the sun began to rise over the trees behind them, Arawn noticed that a heavy mist was rising up from the river. A few minutes later, both banks of the river were engulfed in a heavy fog.

"What did you do?" Belenus asked when Amaethon walked back toward them with a smile on his face.

"I took as much energy out of the river as I could," he replied.

"Rivers have energy?" Arawn asked.

"Yes, they have heat from the sun. Heat is energy. I took the energy out, and that made the water much colder. When the warm rays of the sun hit the water, it produced fog. It'll last for four or five hours at least."

"Good thinking!" Belenus said. "Let's get started and see how far we can get before the fog lifts."

The horses didn't like the fog, and the trio had to coax them to keep moving before the fog finally lifted shortly after noon.

"Can you make fog again?" Arawn asked after they stopped for the night.

"If tomorrow is sunny, yes. But I saw clouds moving in, and if it rains I can't make fog."

It rained the next day. The rain was hardest along the river, and Arawn finally realized that Amaethon was using the wind and the rain to make it impossible for the longboats to see anyone on the eastern bank of the river.

A thunderstorm moved into the area, and Arawn saw lightning in the distance. As the lightning moved closer, he saw Amaethon concentrating. A moment later, lightning struck nearby on the river, and Arawn saw a large fire erupt. The lightning had hit one of the longboats. As the trio rode on, Arawn looked back periodically and watched the ship burning out of control.

They made camp just inside the trees that night. Arawn heard the snapping of a twig in the darkness while he was guarding the camp, but there were no other sounds apart from those caused by the rain that fell most of the night. The occasional flash of lightning lit up the woods around the campsite, and Arawn didn't see anyone approaching.

The next morning they ate a cold breakfast and broke camp quickly. The horses shivered in the cold rain, and Arawn wished there was a way to keep them dry as he put the saddle on his horse. *I hope they'll warm up once we start riding.*

Just after mid-morning, a longboat appeared on the river. The trio dismounted and led their horses into the trees until the longboat passed. Amaethon was ready to hit the longboat with lightning if the sailors gave any indication that they had seen the trio, but the longboat sailed on down the river and disappeared into the mist.

They led the horses into the open. Belenus and Amaethon mounted quickly. Arawn shifted the position of his bow and put his foot into the stirrup. Just as he pulled himself up and swung his leg over the horse, he heard a familiar whistling sound. He felt a sharp pain in his back and chest.

Amaethon heard Arawn cry out and saw the arrow sticking through his chest. More arrows flew toward them and Amaethon blocked them.

"Run for it!" Belenus shouted, seizing the reins of Arawn's horse.

Belenus leaned forward and whispered to Thunder. The horse whinnied and raced forward, kicking up mud when its hooves hit the soft, wet ground. Belenus kept a tight grip on the reins of Arawn's horse, and it followed Thunder.

Amaethon concentrated for a moment and sent a shock wave in the direction of the archers in the woods. He heard them scream in pain, and he turned his horse and rode to catch up to Belenus and Arawn.

As he caught up to Arawn, he saw the arrow clearly. The archers had shot Arawn in the back, and the tip of the arrow was sticking out of his chest. The arrow was close to Arawn's heart. Amaethon reached out and caught Arawn, who was swaying in his saddle and almost fell off his horse. Amaethon held onto the unconscious Arawn to keep him upright in his saddle as they rode together after Belenus.

"He's badly injured, Belenus," Amaethon shouted.

"Just a little further," Belenus shouted back. "The trees are a little thicker up ahead and will give us some shelter."

Amaethon felt Arawn's life-energy slipping away. "I don't think he has that long."

"Is there anything you can do for him?" Belenus asked, urgently. "We need him alive. The prophecy will fail if we lose any of you."

Remembering what Nemausus had taught him, he nodded and began drawing energy from everything around him except for the trio and the horses.

He used his mind to probe Arawn's injury. The arrow had nicked the heart, and Arawn was losing blood too quickly. Amaethon knew that Arawn wouldn't make it to the trees ahead.

I need to repair the heart at the same time that I remove the arrow, or he'll bleed to death.

He focused the energy he had been gathering and concentrated. His horse stayed next to Arawn's so Amaethon could keep his arm across the unconscious orphan's shoulder.

Amaethon touched the arrow sticking out of Arawn's back. In a flash, it disappeared. He placed his hand over the wound. With his mind, he stopped the bleeding and repaired the heart, the muscles underneath the skin, and the skin on Arawn's chest and back where the arrow had had pierced.

He felt Arawn's life-energy, but it was still very weak. Just as Nemausus had taught him, Amaethon transferred life-energy into Arawn, careful not to use too much of his own.

They reached a thick grove of trees, and Belenus stopped and dismounted quickly. Coming around to the side of Arawn's horse, Belenus reached up and gently pulled Arawn off his horse. Amaethon dismounted as Belenus set Arawn on the ground and began checking his injuries.

"Where is the wound?" Belenus asked when Amaethon knelt down next to him. "I see the hole in his clothes, but there's not a mark on his body."

"Nemausus showed me how to heal injuries," Amaethon said. "Arawn only had a few moments left to live. The arrow nicked his heart, so I had to remove it and heal the damage."

"He'll recover, won't he?" Belenus asked.

Amaethon nodded. "I restored his life-energy. He'll be good as new once he wakes up."

165

Belenus reached out and put his hand on Amaethon's shoulder. "You did a wonderful thing, Amaethon," he said – his voice shaking slightly. "You saved his life. You saved all of us."

Amaethon was about to say something when Arawn's eyes fluttered open. "What am I doing on the ground?" he asked. "What happened?"

Belenus hugged Arawn. "How do you feel?" he asked.

"A little sore in the chest, but I'm fine. Did I fall?"

"No, you were shot by an arrow and nearly died," Belenus replied.

Belenus let Amaethon tell the story. Arawn listened with a shocked look on his face. When Amaethon was finished, Arawn got to his feet and gave Amaethon a hug.

"Thank you! I owe you my life."

Amaethon smiled. "Don't mention it."

"Should we get going now?" Arawn asked.

"Do you feel up to it?" Belenus asked.

Arawn nodded. "I feel better than I did this morning when I woke up. There's no reason to wait here because of me."

The trio mounted their horses and rode north.

"We nearly lost Arawn today," Belenus said to Nemausus, Tridamus, and Alaunus silently after the trio started riding again.

"What happened?" Alaunus asked.

Belenus told them how Arawn had been shot and how Amaethon saved Arawn's life.

"You trained your student well," Alaunus said to Nemausus when Belenus was finished.

"I knew that it was something he needed to know," Nemausus said. *"I just didn't know he'd have to use it so soon."*

"I'll let you know if anything changes, but for now Arawn seems completely healed," Belenus said. *"Apart from a couple of holes in his clothes, there's no evidence that he was ever injured."*

"Keep them safe, Belenus," Tridamus said. *"I'll be waiting for you at the smithy."*

"We'll be there as soon as we can," Belenus said, breaking the connection with the other elders.

It rained for the rest of the day and all of the next day. Progress was slow because of the mud along the riverbanks. Fortunately, the weather also worked against the troopers and the sailors. The thunderstorms that blew through periodically led to several more longboats catching fire, and Amaethon chuckled softly when the lightning started each fire.

Both Belenus and Amaethon kept an eye on Arawn, but he didn't seem to be experiencing any problems related to the arrow that nearly killed him.

The sky was clear on the third day, and Amaethon made the fog return as soon as the sun's rays hit the water. By that afternoon, they couldn't see the longboats anymore.

Belenus knew that they were getting close to the ford when they reached the northernmost edge of the Great Forest. The trio stopped and tried to detect any sign of the troopers or anyone else who might prevent them from crossing the river.

Around noon, they came into sight of the ford. Belenus motioned for them to dismount and lead the horses into the trees.

The troopers were waiting for them on the southern banks of the river. Instead of following the trio, the soldiers had anticipated where Belenus, Arawn, and Amaethon were heading and set a trap instead.

Looking across the river, Belenus saw soldiers along the northern bank. Looking closely, he recognized them as Mongán soldiers. He pointed them out to his companions.

The Mongán soldiers had a unique look that was unmistakable anywhere in Alastríona. Because they lived closest to the Great Desert and came from a hot climate, their clothing was different from the other tribes' clothes. Rather than trousers, they wore a wrap-around garment called a kilt that allowed the air to flow more freely and keep the wearer cool. Over their kilts, the soldiers wore a belt with studded thick leather straps that hung down to the knees to protect the legs. The soldiers also wore metal shin guards.

Every soldier wore chest and back armor. The armor of the lower-ranking soldiers was made of different pieces of metal that overlapped and allowed the air to flow underneath. They carried a large shield in one hand and a spear or short sword in the other. Their helmets were short and rounded on top.

The officers wore large plumes of colored horsehair on top of their helmets. Their armor consisted of a single piece of armor plating that covered their chest and another piece that covered their back. The higher the rank of the officer, the more ornate the chest piece. Highest-ranking officers wore chest pieces shaped like a human torso, making them easy to spot at almost any distance.

"Both sides of the river are guarded, and there are still longboats on the river somewhere," Belenus said. "There's no way to get to the other side!"

Arawn and the others looked at the soldiers guarding both banks of the river. He knew that three people could never go up against that many soldiers. The trio couldn't cross the river, they couldn't go past the troopers and ford the river farther down, and they couldn't go back toward the farm because of the longboats. They were trapped.

"We could wait until nightfall to cross," Belenus suggested.

"If I were those soldiers, I would expect us to do just that," Arawn pointed out. "I'd light fires and deploy my soldiers so no one would cross."

"Then what do we do?" Belenus asked. "We have to cross the river, and this is the only possible place we can."

Amaethon was quiet for a while – deep in thought. "What are you thinking, Amaethon?" Belenus asked.

"Do we need to cross the river in secret, or do we just need to get across?"

"What do you mean?" Belenus asked.

"Do we need to make it look like we never crossed, or can they know we crossed but couldn't do anything to stop us? I can create enough confusion for us to get across, but it'll be harder if we're trying to get across in secret."

"They're guarding the ford, so they know we're coming," Arawn commented. "I don't think secrecy matters that much as long as they don't follow us once we're on the other side."

Belenus nodded. "Crossing is what's important. What are you going to do?"

"Summon a dragon," Amaethon replied casually.

"You're going to do what?" Belenus demanded.

"Summon a dragon. I did it once before. It won't be a real dragon, but the soldiers won't know that."

Belenus shook his head and closed his eyes, sending his thoughts out to Nemausus.

"Can you hear me, old friend?"

A moment later, he heard Nemausus' voice. *"I'm here. Things have been quiet here since Siena left. How are you?"*

"We reached the ford. Soldiers are guarding both banks of the river, and your student wants to summon a dragon to create a distraction."

Belenus heard Nemausus laugh. *"Good! Enjoy the show. He's very good with dragons."*

"Has he seen a real dragon before?"

"No, but he managed to create the illusion of one several years

ago," Nemausus replied. *"If I didn't know that dragons only live on one island on the far side of Alastríona, I would've believed it was real myself."*

"Fascinating... I always wondered what Alaunus was talking about concerning dragons all those years ago."

"It took me by surprise when Amaethon created that first one, but now the other prophecy makes sense," Nemausus commented.

"I agree. Thank you, old friend. I'll let you know what happens."

Belenus opened his eyes and looked up at Amaethon. "What do you need us to do?"

CHAPTER 29

It was less than an hour until sunset, and the trio was in position in the woods about three hundred yards from the ford. So far, they had managed to remain unseen by the troopers and soldiers. Amaethon had been slowly gathering energy for the past several hours. He took energy from the trees, from the water, from the sun, and from the soldiers and troopers themselves so they'd be weakened once the dragon attacked.

"I'll need to be concentrating on the dragon, so I won't be able to defend myself or react if anyone sees us," he had told Belenus and Arawn earlier in the day. "One of you will need to lead me and the horse across the open ground and the river when we get there."

"I'll take care of that," Belenus said. "Arawn, you'll need to take care of any troopers or soldiers who see us."

Arawn nodded. "How do we know the dragon won't accidently attack us?"

'It's not a real dragon, Arawn," Amaethon said, smiling. "It's going to be an illusion, but the fire will be quite real and will only go where I send it."

Arawn looked doubtful but understood that this was their only choice if they wanted to get across the river.

Amaethon got on his horse and used his sword belt to tie himself to his saddle so he wouldn't fall off. Then he began concentrating.

For the next thirty minutes, no one said a word. Arawn stood guard while Belenus looked from Amaethon to the peak on the Mountain of Elohim where he knew the dragon would first appear. He saw something begin to take shape on an outcropping of rock, and as he kept looking, the shape slowly became a dragon.

Belenus was impressed. Given that no human on Alastríona had ever seen a dragon before, this illusion was almost perfect. It was considerably larger than a real dragon, but that wouldn't matter to the troopers and soldiers along the river.

A few minutes later, Belenus and Arawn heard the bellowing cry of the dragon, which was the signal that they needed to get ready to head for the river. Both men mounted their horses, and Arawn readied his bow.

The troopers and soldiers heard the sound and looked for the source. When the dragon spread its wings and bellowed again, every trooper and soldier saw it and was instantly terrified. The dragon began beating its wings and was soon airborne. It flew west along the southern face of the Mountain of Elohim and circled the summit. It circled the mountain a second time and flew east before turning around and heading for the troopers and soldiers along the banks of the river. It flew low over the ground, and Belenus and Arawn felt the wind from its wings, felt the heat of its breath, and even smelled it as the dragon passed overhead. The dragon bellowed again and flew in a circle to make another pass over the frightened troopers and soldiers.

Arawn started riding for the river, with the others following close behind. Belenus had the reins of Amaethon's horse in his hand, and he looked back often to make sure the young sorcerer was all right. The troopers and soldiers were so distracted by the dragon that they didn't notice the three riders approaching the ford.

The dragon flew overhead several more times, bellowing and using its wings to knock the troopers and soldiers to the ground. Archers fired their arrows into the air, but the dragon didn't seem to notice. In the low light, the archers couldn't see their arrows pass harmlessly through the illusion.

When the trio reached the halfway point between the forest and the river, one of the troopers guarding the ford noticed them and raised the alarm. "They've seen us," Arawn shouted, coaxing his horse to move faster.

Arawn saw archers moving into position to fire. "Amaethon, can you do something about the archers?" he shouted.

Amaethon didn't seem to hear Arawn, but the dragon changed direction and flew toward the troopers. Just as the archers released their arrows at the trio, the dragon opened its mouth and fire flew out, vaporizing the arrows and hitting the archers and the troopers along the near bank of the river. The troopers panicked. Several threw themselves into the river to put out the fire on their clothing, but the fire seemed impervious to water, and the troopers were unable to put out the flames.

The dragon unleashed its fire on the soldiers on the far bank of the river before flying on to the west. Arawn saw several of the longboats on the river burst into flames when the dragon attacked. The dragon turned around and flew straight at the troopers who were still standing between the river and the trio. The dragon bellowed once again before releasing its fire, lighting the landscape as the sun set behind the foothills to the west.

The troopers along the bank were in a state of complete panic. Some stood their ground, but over half were dead from the fire, and the rest were looking for shelter from the flames. The dragon attacked the soldiers along the far bank again, and Arawn shot several arrows at troopers who had escaped the fire and were still blocking the way across the river.

The dragon flew at the troopers again, and soon Arawn, Belenus and Amaethon were crossing the river. The horses kept their footing as they crossed at the ford, but Arawn, Belenus, and Amaethon's legs were soaked by the time they reached the other side.

The dragon attacked the soldiers again and again, since they were the larger force, and flew off to take care of three new longboats moving in from the east. By the time the riders had crossed the river, the longboats were burning and few of the soldiers were alive. The remaining soldiers broke and ran off to the east, and the few surviving troopers took refuge inside the forest. No longboats survived, and no sailors were on the water or on either shore.

The dragon hovered over the ford and let out a cry of triumph that was heard for miles. It flew off toward the west, circled the summit of the Mountain of Elohim two more times, and returned to the peak where it had first appeared. Then it slowly faded out of existence until there was nothing left but the memory, the dead, and the fires that burned along both banks of the river.

Belenus looked back at Amaethon, who swayed somewhat in his saddle. Belenus pulled Amaethon's horse alongside his own and held onto the fainting sorcerer as the two rode after Arawn.

They rode for almost two hours in the moonlight until they reached a grove of trees at the base of the foothills that surrounded the Mountain of Elohim. Arawn dismounted and helped Belenus gently lift Amaethon off the back of his horse and onto the ground. Arawn took up position to guard the camp while Belenus tended to Amaethon.

Arawn had never seen magic like the dragon before. Amaethon had demonstrated a few things that he had learned from Nemausus, and Arawn had seen Amaethon erase their tracks as they traveled from the farm, but the dragon and the fire were different. Arawn was in awe of his newfound brother, and as he stood watch while Belenus tended to Amaethon, he hoped that Amaethon would be all right.

Belenus couldn't imagine how much energy it had taken to create the dragon and inflict the damage that had been done, and he hoped Amaethon hadn't used too much of his own life-energy. He focused his mind toward Nemausus and told his old friend what had happened.

"Place your hands on his forehead and his heart and let me feel what you feel," Nemausus asked. Through the connection with Belenus, Nemausus was able to read Amaethon's thoughts and feel his life-energy. After a moment, he spoke again.

"He's fine, just exhausted. He learned his lesson well about not using his own life-energy unless there was no choice. The energy he gathered from all around was more than enough for the dragon and the fire, but the amount of concentration required was more than he had anticipated. He'll be fine in the morning, and he'll be very hungry. Make sure he drinks lots of water every time he wakes tonight. You might want to take it easy tomorrow if you can. It'll be a day or two before he's back to normal."

"Thank you, old friend," Belenus said, feeling relieved that Amaethon was going to be fine.

Belenus sent his thoughts toward Tridamus and brought the blacksmith up to speed on what had happened.

"I wondered why there was a dragon circling the mountain," Tridamus said. *"When will you get here?"*

"At least four days," Belenus replied. *"We need to make sure that we're not followed, and our young sorcerer needs time to recover from creating the dragon."*

"There have been soldiers coming and going around here for the last week," Tridamus commented. *"It's a good thing that no one ever bothers a blacksmith, or I'd be worried."*

"Be safe, and let me know if anything happens," Belenus said, breaking the connection with Tridamus. Then he contacted Alaunus. *"Did you see?"*

"Yes," she replied. *"Amaethon did well. However, Mider's actions concern me. You must be careful. We may have to confront him separately."*

"Isn't that dangerous?" Belenus asked.

"Dangerous or not, it may prove necessary. The choice must be made, and it must be made in the appointed place at the appointed time. If Mider understood that, he wouldn't fight it so. We will see, and we'll

do what must be done."

The trio travelled northeast into the eastern foothills of the Mountain of Elohim. Arawn kept a close watch but didn't see or feel anyone following them. Amaethon was better the next morning, and by the second day, he was his old self again.

Amaethon was staggered by the size of the Mountain of Elohim as they rode around its southeastern face. Grasses and trees went up the slopes of the mountain almost a third of the way to the top. Above that, the gray-white rock jutted up until it reached the snow that covered the peaks all year long. He saw the details of the cliffs and the sheer faces of the rock that formed the center of the mountain, and he wondered if it were possible to climb to the top. He knew that there was supposed to be a temple built by Airmid near the summit, but he could only assume that the way to get there was from the other side of the mountain. The summit of the mountain looked unreachable from the side they were riding past.

Around noon on the fifth day after crossing the river, the trio descended into a valley at the base of the mountain. There, nestled next to a grove of trees and a stream between two foothills on the eastern face of the mountain, stood the smithy.

Arawn, Amaethon, and Belenus Cross the Ford While the Dragon Attacks.

CHAPTER 30

moke rose from the chimney of the forge, and the clanging of a hammer on an anvil echoed around the two foothills. Belenus led the trio into the courtyard and dismounted, tethering his horse to one of the large iron rings on the side of the workshop. He gestured for Arawn and Amaethon to do the same.

"Tridamus!" Belenus shouted.

The blacksmith turned around at the sound of his name, and when he saw Belenus standing there, his face broke out into a look of joy.

"Belenus! You finally made it!"

The blacksmith put down his hammer and took off his leather apron as he rushed across the workshop. He reached Belenus and lifted him into the air with his two huge arms. "It's good to see you again, old friend," he said with a great smile.

Arawn watched the blacksmith and Belenus greet each other. He noticed another person, standing near the forge, who had stopped working to see what was going on. Arawn realized that the other person was a girl.

A girl as a blacksmith? I've never seen one before. I wonder if it's normal for women around here to take up a craft like this. I never saw the women on the farm do this kind of work!

Leaning over to Amaethon, Arawn whispered, "Do you think she's the other orphan?"

"Could be," Amaethon whispered back. "Nemausus said the other orphan was hiding in the open because no one would ever suspect who it was. I guess a girl working as a blacksmith is about as unexpected as you can get."

"Did you know the other orphan was a girl?" Arawn asked.

Amaethon shook his head. "I never even considered the possibility. It didn't occur to me that a girl might become the Ruler of the World."

"Me either."

The girl put down her hammer and took off her gloves and apron. As she moved toward Tridamus, she removed the leather strap that had been holding her light red hair back and let it fall down around her shoulders. Her leather halter revealed her exposed back. Arawn took a long look at her and felt a jolt like lightning go through him from his head to his feet. She was the most beautiful person he had ever seen. Next to her, Siena was plain. This girl was amazing! He found he couldn't take his eyes off her.

"Ah, Cerridwen, come here," Tridamus said as he put Belenus back down. He held out his hand and placed it on her shoulder. "Belenus, allow me to present Cerridwen, my apprentice. Cerridwen, this is Belenus, one of my oldest and dearest friends."

Cerridwen nodded to Belenus and said, "I'm pleased to meet you, Belenus. Tridamus has been telling me about you." Turning to Arawn and Amaethon, she said, "And these must be the others that I've been hearing about."

"Yes," Belenus said. "Allow me to present Amaethon, the student of the sorcerer Nemausus, and Arawn, who has been in my care for most of the last eighteen years."

The orphans exchanged greetings, and Tridamus greeted Belenus' companions. "Good to see you, boys," he said, hugging both of them in his strong arms. "It's hard to believe that the time is finally here when the three of you are all together. From what I've gathered, you've all been preparing for what lies ahead as the prophecy predicted, but now it's time to see if you can fulfill your tasks and put the universe back on track. No small feat, but then again you three are exceptional in your own ways."

Releasing the two young men and reaching for Cerridwen to join him, he added, "But you three need to get to know each other better, and Belenus and I have some things to discuss. I'll call you when it's time to eat."

Tridamus spun around, took Belenus by the shoulder, and walked past the horses toward the stream down the hill from the smithy. The three orphans were left alone.

Cerridwen looked at the two young men who had arrived with Belenus. Amaethon was tall and sandy-haired, which gave him a boyish look that Cerridwen thought was handsome. Arawn had longer dark hair and wasn't as tall as Amaethon. She knew that Arawn grew up on a farm, but he had the rugged look of someone who had been in many skirmishes. She also felt a jolt like lightning go through her that went straight from her ears to her toes when she first looked at him. She had never felt that before, and she wanted to get to know Arawn better so she could understand what had happened.

"So I guess we're going to save the world," she said with a smile to break the silence.

"Something like that," Amaethon said as the three laughed. "I understand that we were all born on the same day."

"That's what I was told," Arawn said, still unable to take his eyes off Cerridwen.

"Then we all have a birthday coming up, don't we?" Cerridwen asked.

Arawn nodded. "I see you're a blacksmith. What do you make here?" he asked.

"Everything from jewelry to armor to swords and daggers," she said, motioning for them to follow her into the workshop. She walked over to her work table where she had been creating some new jewelry for the next fair that was fast approaching. She held up a necklace and showed Arawn and Amaethon the design of a dragon worked into the metal.

"This is beautiful," Amaethon said, looking at the necklace.

"We had one fly over us the other day," Cerridwen said, showing them some of the other pieces. "Tridamus says there aren't any in this part of Alastríona, but it flew over us four times right around sunset. Did you see it?"

Arawn laughed. "We're the reason it was here. Amaethon summoned it."

"Made it, actually," Amaethon said. "It was an illusion I created to distract the soldiers that were blocking a river we had to cross. The fire was real, but the rest wasn't."

"You're kidding!" Cerridwen exclaimed. "It was fake? But I heard it and even felt the wind from its wings. That's incredible!"

Amaethon blushed. "I had done it before, several years ago, but this one was much larger than a real dragon. Still, it did the job, and we got across the river with no problems."

Arawn walked over to where Cerridwen had several swords stacked in neat rows. "Did you make these, too?"

"Yes," she said, pointing to another rack of swords on the other side of the workshop. "Those are the ones that Tridamus made, and these are the ones that I made. Mine are a different design from his, but they work better with the way I fight."

"You swordfight?" Arawn asked.

Cerridwen nodded. "I haven't fought anyone who actually wanted to hurt me, but I know how to fight. Tridamus had me take lessons before he let me start making swords. He said you can't make something properly if you don't know how to use it properly. So I got trained how to fight, and I started making swords and armor. I still train every morning with some of the local soldiers."

She pointed to several pieces of armor behind the swords. "I made all of those pieces as well."

She walked over to the corner where she had three complete sets of armor on stands. "These are my newest design. Tridamus makes armor the traditional way with one large chest plate and back plate that connect to each other below the arms and over the shoulders. It's heavy and doesn't let you move freely when you're fighting. I came up with a design that uses smaller pieces to cover the kill zones. The metal pieces are layered together over leather to make something light that allows you to move freely and protects you in a fight. These are three commissions that Tridamus asked me to make, and I just finished them yesterday."

Arawn complimented her on the workmanship. "Thanks," Cerridwen said with a smile. "Tridamus sketched out the ornamentation, and I worked the metal to make it look like that." Looking closely at Arawn and Amaethon, she added, "It looks like the ones on the left would fit you two perfectly."

"And it looks like the one on the right was made for you," Arawn commented. "Was it made for a woman?"

"Yes. Tridamus said to use me as the pattern since the patron is roughly my size. I usually take the measurements myself so I can get everything right, but I had to go by what Tridamus gave me. I think they turned out well, but I'll know for sure when I see the patrons wearing them."

Cerridwen stared at the armor for a moment. "I think they're for *us*," she said, turning to face Amaethon and Arawn. "I don't know why I didn't think of that when Tridamus told me to use my own measurements for one of them. Why else would he have me make three identical sets of armor that clearly fit the three of us?"

"I'll bet you're right," Arawn said. "Since we're the orphans in the prophecy, it makes sense that we'd have matching armor."

Amaethon went back to look at the dragon jewelry again, leaving Cerridwen alone with Arawn. "You don't look much like a farmer, if you don't mind my saying," she said.

"I live on a farm, but I don't do any farming. We have raiders who attack the farm every now and then, and I lead the men who keep the farm and its people safe. I hunt, track, and fight most of the time, and when we're not fighting, we're getting ready for the next fight. For a

179

long time, I didn't understand why the raiders wanted to destroy us, until Belenus explained who I am and what happened when I was a baby. He thinks they're after me. They followed us as we traveled here. When we crossed the river, they tried to intercept us with the help of Mongán soldiers and Étaíne longboats. That's when Amaethon created the dragon."

Cerridwen nodded. "I think all three of us have stories about people trying to kill us when we were babies."

"And they're still trying to, although I've heard that you've been protected from all that."

"Yes, Tridamus told me that none of the four tribes working against us thought that any of the children in the prophecy would be a girl, and even if they did, they'd never believe she was a blacksmith. They think the prophecy is about a new king, and for them that means a man. It kept me safe, but now that we're together, I guess I won't be safe for long."

"It's a good thing you know how to use a sword," Arawn commented. "I think we're going to need them a lot from now on."

Amaethon walked back over to join them next to the armor. "Do either of you know what happens now?" he asked. "We've been focused on getting here and bringing the three of us together, but I don't know what comes next."

Cerridwen and Arawn looked at each other. "I was hoping one of you was going to tell me," she said.

"I guess that's a question for Belenus and Tridamus when we see them again," Arawn suggested.

The three orphans spent the afternoon together, talking and sharing stories about their childhoods. Cerridwen let Amaethon and Arawn try some of her swords, and soon the three of them were having fun sparring with one another. Amaethon demonstrated some of his magic, and Cerridwen showed the boys how she made jewelry and blades by working with different kinds of metal. By the time Tridamus called to them from the house, they felt they had known each other for years.

Amaethon walked ahead of Arawn and Cerridwen as they crossed the courtyard to the house. He had immediately noticed something pass between those two when they met. Nemausus referred to it as the "touch of destiny" or the "thunderbolt," and it was something that someone trained in the magical arts could sense when it happened. He saw it in Arawn's face and saw it again in Cerridwen's face. He smiled as he entered the house. Clearly there was more that was supposed to happen between Cerridwen and Arawn than the orphans had been told.

"I'm assuming you three got to know each other better this afternoon?" Tridamus said once everyone was seated and the food served.

The three orphans nodded.

"Good. Now that the three of you are together, I'm sure you're wondering what happens next. That's what we're going to tell you."

Belenus started. "First of all, I need to make sure that the three of you understand something clearly. The future of Alastríona lies with the three of you equally. You all have different skills and talents, but it's together that you'll either succeed or fail. You'll need to rely on each other, protect each other, and help each other in order for things to happen the way they need to happen."

"Cerridwen, do you remember when you were designing your new armor?" Tridamus asked.

Cerridwen nodded.

"Do you remember how you finally got the design right?"

"Yes, you made a suggestion and I reworked the design around it."

"Exactly! We both contributed to the final design and made the design better."

"Arawn," Belenus continued, "When the raiders attacked the farm, did you take them on by yourself?"

"No, sir. The men and I worked together to defend the compound."

"Right! Whether it's two of you, all three of you, or an army of ten thousand soldiers at your back, success comes from working together as one, taking your individual strengths and using them in a way that solves whatever problem you're facing. Remember this in the days ahead. Each of you is strong, but together you're stronger than anything that can oppose you. You three have a destiny, but you can't fulfill your destiny without each other. Alastríona cannot be saved unless you work together."

"There's something else we need to clear up before we explain anything else," Tridamus said as he stood up, took a scroll out of a long, ornate wooden box on the shelf closest to the table, and returned to his seat. He unrolled the scroll so the three orphans could see it. He cleared his throat and read the scroll.

"Behold, there will come a time when three orphans shall come forth into the world. Their births shall be heralded by a black sun at high noon, followed a fortnight later by the two moons rising in the color of blood and then appearing as one at their zenith.

"It is from these three orphans that the Ruler of the World shall be chosen and shall receive the Kingstone and the blessing of Elohim.

"The Ruler of the World shall end the game of the disobedient ones, who have pitted the tribes of man against each other for their own amusement. The sky will be filled with shooting stars lasting from sunset to sunrise on the day the disobedient ones are vanquished.

"The tribes of Alastríona shall then gather at the base of the Mountain of Elohim and await the coming of the Ruler of the World. At that gathering, the tribes shall be united as one people with one supreme god.

"Look to the skies and watch for the signs that the fulfilling of this prophecy is at hand, for on the day of the fulfilling of this prophecy, the fate of the world shall be decided."

"For years, the prophecy has been misunderstood by some of the kings and the gods who still oppose the will of Elohim," Tridamus said as he put the scroll back in the wooden box. "They say the prophecy speaks of a king who will rule Alastríona. But this is the original prophecy as it was written down when Airmid first spoke it aloud."

"The first original, or a copy of the original?" Amaethon asked.

"The first original," Tridamus replied. "If you look closely, you'll see that it refers to the 'Ruler of the World.' It doesn't say 'king,' and it doesn't say 'queen.' It says 'Ruler.'"

"We know this," Amaethon said. "One of us will become the Ruler of the World."

"Where does it say that only one of you will become Ruler?" Belenus asked.

The three orphans looked at each other.

"We're all three going to be the Ruler of the World?" Cerridwen asked finally.

"We don't know yet," Tridamus replied. "We know that it'll be from the three of you that the Ruler will be selected, but it could be just one of you, it could be two of you, or it could be all three of you. That's why we need you to remember about working together. You're stronger together than you are separately. When the time comes for Elohim to select the Ruler of the World, that's when we'll know for certain who it will be. But even if only one of you is chosen to be Ruler, the Ruler cannot succeed unless all three of you continue working together. You're not being brought together just to perform a quest and then move on. You three are joined together for the rest of your lives."

"Speaking of quests," Belenus interjected, "I guess it's time to let you in on what's going to happen next. There's something that's important to do, and there's something that absolutely must be done. It's important that we travel to Danann, Athramail, and Batavia so you can be introduced to the Kings of the Macruhan, Dunmaine, and Penarduun tribes. They need to know that the part of the prophecy concerning you three has been fulfilled and that the time for the final part of the prophecy is at hand. It's unfortunate that there's no time to introduce you to the general who commands the Army of the Followers of Elohim, but he already knows what he's supposed to do."

"And what's the thing that must be done?" Arawn asked.

"You'll need to find the Kingstone by the right moment in time or the prophecy will fail. There are forces who will try to stop you, and you'll have to overcome their attempts. Once you have the Kingstone, you must force the gods to choose whether or not they're going to obey Elohim and leave Alastríona. If we survive the choice, you'll need to bring the Kingstone to the place where the tribes will gather on the west side of the Mountain of Elohim; and it must arrive there by the appointed time. There will also be forces who will oppose you bringing it to the gathering place, and you'll have to overcome them as well. On this, everything depends."

"What exactly is the Kingstone?" Cerridwen asked, "And where is it hidden?"

"As for where the Kingstone is hidden," Tridamus answered, "We don't know. But there's someone who will be joining us soon who does know and will lead us to it."

"Nemausus?" Amaethon asked.

"No, someone you haven't met before," Belenus replied. "As for what the Kingstone is, let's just say that it's a jewel infused with the spirit of Elohim. The Kingstone is the catalyst to encourage the gods to leave Alastríona and create the other worlds that are part of Elohim's plan. Once you have the Kingstone, the gods will come because the Kingstone will summon them, and it's essential that all of the gods be there at the same time."

"I don't understand," Cerridwen said.

"I know it's a bit vague," Tridamus admitted, "but when it's right to know everything, you will. For now, I think you're going to have to take some things on faith. That's what Belenus, Nemausus, and I have been doing for a long time."

"So when do we get started?" Arawn asked.

"The day after tomorrow," Tridamus replied. "Tomorrow we need to get our supplies together and load the wagons. We're going to be traveling as a party of craftsmen heading to a fair. No one we encounter will think twice about that, and we need to be disguised since we'll be traveling along the rivers and through part of the Étaíne territory. That's the great thing about having a trade. When you travel, people tend to remember what you do, but they rarely remember specifics about who you are or where you're from.

"We'll travel from here to Danann first. After we leave there, we should be able to fall in with a caravan heading for the fair in the eastern pass of the Valdunass Mountains. That will make it harder for the Étaíne patrols to spot us. We'll stop at the fair for a few days so Cerridwen and I can deliver several commissions. It'll also help us keep up appearances; we'd be noticed if we left the fair too early. Once it's safe to leave the fair, we'll go to Athramail and then Batavia. After that, we'll retrieve the Kingstone. Once the gods have made their choice, assuming we survive the event, we'll head for the base of the Mountain of Elohim."

Tridamus took a drink. "One more thing," he added as he put down his tankard. "I saw Cerridwen showing the new armor that she just finished making. You may have noticed that they look like they were made for the three of you. That's because they *were* made for you, although I didn't tell Cerridwen that when I gave her the commission. They're designed for the Ruler of the World, and since we don't know which of you that will be, I had Cerridwen make three identical sets. But you're not to wear them until after the Kingstone has been found and the gods have made their choice. We don't want to call too much attention to you before then, understood?"

The orphans nodded.

The group talked for a while longer.

"Come on, old friend," Tridamus said to Belenus as he stood up. "I'll show you to your room." Turning to Cerridwen, he added, "Cerridwen, please show the boys where they'll be sleeping."

"Yes, Tridamus," she said. "Good night, Belenus," she added.

"Good night, my dear. Good night, boys."

"Good night," Arawn and Amaethon replied.

After Belenus and Tridamus had disappeared down the hallway, Amaethon stretched and yawned. "I think I'll turn in, too."

"Let me show you your room," Cerridwen said as Amaethon stood up.

"Thanks. Good night, Arawn."

"Good night, Amaethon," Arawn replied, standing. "I'll be along in a little while."

Cerridwen led Amaethon down the hallway to the guest room he and Arawn would be sharing, which was next to the one Belenus was using. She wished Amaethon a good night as he closed the door.

When Cerridwen returned to the kitchen to see what Arawn was doing, he wasn't there. Looking around, she noticed something moving outside and walked out into the courtyard to see what it was. She saw Arawn walking toward the stables to check on the horses. She leaned against the doorway to the house until he came out of the stables and saw her standing there.

"What are you doing?" she asked softly so she wouldn't disturb the others who had already gone to bed for the night.

"I do this every night," Arawn replied, walking over to where she was standing. "I always check on the horses and check on the perimeter of the compound before I can go to sleep. It's a force of habit, and I can't sleep until it's done."

"I'll come with you," she said, closing the door of the house behind her.

The two walked out of the courtyard and around the house. Cerridwen watched as Arawn looked at all of the approaches to the smithy and the way the compound was arranged. By the light of the moon, she saw the look of determination in his face and guessed that it came from years of having to defend Belenus' farmers from raiders. They walked around the stables and ended up just outside the workshop. Before they knew it, they were walking down by the stream below the workshop.

They said very little in case their voices carried. They were enjoying each other's company, and neither wanted to go back to the house yet. Cerridwen was happy to be with someone her own age for the first time in a long time.

As they walked along the stream, which was fed by a waterfall from the melting snow on the peaks of the Mountain of Elohim, Arawn took Cerridwen's hand to help her climb over a large boulder so they could stand near the base of the falls and watch the water in the moonlight.

As the moons moved lower in the sky, Arawn and Cerridwen turned back toward the smithy, walking in silence. Arawn checked the compound one more time before joining Cerridwen at the entrance to the house.

She showed him to the room he'd be sharing with Amaethon. "Good night," she whispered before disappearing into her room across the hall.

Arawn entered his room quietly, trying not to wake Amaethon. A small candle burned in the corner, lighting the way to the empty bed near the window. He undressed and climbed into the first bed he had slept in for nearly three weeks. As he drifted off to sleep, his thoughts were on Cerridwen.

rawn woke up well before dawn the next morning. Amaethon was still asleep, so Arawn got out of bed, dressed quietly, and crept into the hallway, closing the bedroom door behind him without a sound. He stood there listening for a moment to see if he could hear anyone else stirring in the house. Then he walked softly toward the kitchen.

His sword and bow were still next to the door where he had left them the previous afternoon. He grabbed them and stepped into the courtyard. Even though he was used to being up before dawn, the sights, sounds, and smells of the smithy were different from what he had known at the farm. Even in the pre-dawn darkness, he saw the sun already illuminating the peaks on the Mountain of Elohim towering overhead, which gave the world a strange and fascinating look.

He tightened the sword belt, checked his quiver, and walked across the courtyard to inspect the perimeter of the smithy. Now that all three of the orphans were together, he felt the need to be more cautious than ever before. If the soldiers or troopers who had been trying to intercept them had managed to follow them to the smithy, or if there were longboats on the great river where the mountain stream emptied, everyone could be in great danger.

He walked around the smithy as quietly as he could, trying to see if anyone were approaching. He felt like he was being watched, but saw no one. When he returned to the courtyard thirty minutes later, the sunlight reflecting off the mountain made it possible to see more clearly.

Out of the corner of his eye, he saw movement near the workshop. He drew an arrow, placed it against the bowstring, and crept closer to the workshop to see who it was. Peering around the corner, he relaxed when he saw it was Cerridwen. She was reaching for one of her swords from the rack that she had shown Arawn and Amaethon the night before.

Arawn assumed that she was getting ready for her morning sword practice, but when she turned around, she motioned for Arawn to remain quiet.

Arawn remained silent and still as she walked across the workshop and joined him. "Men outside," she whispered.

"It was me," Arawn whispered back. "I just finished checking the perimeter."

Cerridwen shook her head. "I know. You woke me up. They're hiding in the grove of trees down the hill. I saw them through the window after you passed by."

She held up her hand for a minute. "They're coming up the hill," she said.

Arawn glanced around the courtyard and made note of the defensive positions. There were few places where two people could hide, and Arawn knew that it would be better to attack if possible. He motioned for Cerridwen to follow him as he hugged the wall of the workshop as closely as he could.

When he reached the edge of the workshop at the end of the courtyard, he carefully peered around the corner and looked in the direction of the trees. He saw at least a dozen soldiers, wearing the same uniform he had seen at the river crossing, making their way toward the smithy.

"They're coming," he whispered back to Cerridwen who nodded. She crept back to the workshop, disappeared for a moment, and returned a minute later wearing a leather jerkin and carrying a second sword. She also had another jerkin, which she handed to Arawn.

Arawn quickly put on the jerkin. He took several arrows out of his quiver and stuck them into the ground within quick reach. He placed the notch of one of the arrows against the bowstring, drew the bowstring back, and waited until the soldiers drew their swords. *I'm not going to fire on the soldiers until I know for sure that they're here to do us harm.*

The soldiers were less than a hundred yards from the smithy when the leader drew his short sword and motioned for the others to do the same. Arawn took aim at the leader, steadied his breathing, and let the arrow fly.

By the time the first arrow had found its mark, Arawn had fired again. A moment later, seven soldiers were lying dead on the ground, but the rest continued approaching the smithy. Arawn thought that it was odd for a small force to continue approaching after losing half its strength, and he realized that there must be other soldiers approaching from a different direction.

The sound of men shouting from the other side of the stables told

Arawn that he was right. He saw movement coming from his right and turned to see another squad of soldiers approaching from around the house. He pushed Cerridwen back toward the workshop and, after firing the last of his arrows at the new soldiers, he retreated to the workshop entrance.

"There's a lot of them coming," he whispered, throwing down his bow and empty quiver and drawing his sword. "Are you ready?"

Cerridwen nodded with a fierce look on her face. She knew how to fight, but this would be her first real fight. She had never crossed swords with someone who wanted her dead, and she shuddered at the thought. She gripped the hilts of her swords tighter, steadying her nerves. *I've never killed anyone before, but I'm not going to let these soldiers come into my home and hurt anyone.*

In that moment, she guessed what it had been like for Arawn to defend his farm. She adjusted her grip on the two swords and tried to calm herself.

Arawn and Cerridwen hid just inside the workshop. Arawn hadn't seen any of the soldiers carrying bows, and he hoped there were no archers approaching from a different direction. As soon as the soldiers entered the courtyard, Arawn silently charged into the open.

Cerridwen leapt from her hiding place a moment later to join him. She approached the soldier closest to her and attacked the way she had been trained. Her flashing swords sliced through two of the soldiers before anyone knew that she was there. Arawn killed one of the soldiers and had just stabbed a second when the remaining soldiers yelled and ran into the courtyard.

Arawn had never fought so many soldiers on foot before, but he instinctively knew that these soldiers were used to fighting in groups and not against individuals. The techniques and skills required to fight against a group were completely different from those needed to fight an individual, and that gave Arawn and Cerridwen a small advantage. The Mongán short swords were also much smaller than the ones Arawn and Cerridwen were using, allowing them to keep the Mongáns from getting too close during the fight.

Out of the corner of his eye, Arawn saw Cerridwen using her two swords as both a weapon and a shield. Several soldiers lay at her feet, but she was quickly being surrounded. Arawn moved toward her, killing several soldiers in the process, until he stood at her back. The two of them continued fighting, and the soldiers who were still alive had difficulty getting through their defenses.

A soldier managed to cut Cerridwen near her right elbow, and she took his head off with one sword while continuing to fight with the soldier standing in front of her. Arawn received a wound on his left leg just below the jerkin, caused by a knife thrown at him from a wounded soldier who was crawling away from the carnage surrounding the two orphans.

Another squad of soldiers suddenly appeared at the entrance of the courtyard, and Cerridwen wasn't sure that she had enough strength left in her to fight that many more. Arawn saw archers appear along the rooftop of the stables and workshop, and he knew that he and Cerridwen were in real trouble.

The archers pulled back their bowstrings, aiming at Arawn and Cerridwen. However, a moment later, the archers flew off high into the air. Amaethon came charging out of the house, using magic to pick up the squad of soldiers at the courtyard entrance and hurl them out of the compound toward the river.

Arawn heard the soldiers and archers screaming in terror as they found themselves suddenly airborne, but the screams stopped as they hit the ground – killed by the impact. Arawn saw the surviving soldiers run out of the compound. He stuck his sword into the ground and bent over, trying to catch his breath. He was exhausted, and he was drenched in sweat and blood.

When he saw Amaethon lower his hands, he asked, "Are they all gone?"

Amaethon nodded. "Are you okay?" he asked, looking at the blood on Arawn's leg. The concern was obvious on his face.

Arawn looked down at his leg. The knife had cut him as it flew past, but other than some blood, it had done little damage. The jerkin had protected him from most of the injuries he would've sustained.

"I think I'm fine. Cerridwen, are you okay?"

When she didn't answer, Arawn looked around quickly. He saw her swords on the ground where she had been standing. "Where's Cerridwen?" he asked, suddenly worried.

"I saw her when I ran out of the house," Amaethon said, looking around. "But I lost sight of her when the soldiers ran off."

Tridamus and Belenus ran out of the house to see what was happening.

"Are you both all right?" Belenus asked, looking at the dead bodies all over the ground.

"We're fine," Arawn said. "But we can't find Cerridwen. I had just finished walking the perimeter when Cerridwen saw soldiers approaching from the grove down the hill. We were surrounded before

191

we knew what was happening. Cerridwen and I fought them until Amaethon joined us. The survivors ran off, but I think they took Cerridwen with them."

Belenus and Tridamus looked at each other. "You need to find her," Tridamus said to Arawn a moment later. "Both of you need to go and find her."

Arawn nodded. Turning to Amaethon, he said, "Go get your sword."

There was a barrel of rainwater next to the workshop, and Arawn stuck his head in it to cool down and wash away the blood and sweat. Tridamus brought him a towel so he could finish cleaning himself and his sword.

When Amaethon reappeared from the house, he was strapping on a sword belt. "I need some of the arrows from the archers you sent flying," Arawn said to him.

Amaethon closed his eyes for a moment, and several dozen arrows flew into the compound and landed in the ground a short distance from where Arawn stood.

Arawn gathered up the arrows, put them in his quiver, and picked up his bow. He motioned for Amaethon to follow him, and they ran to the stables to saddle the horses. Belenus and Tridamus brought food and water pouches for their saddlebags, and Arawn and Amaethon raced out of the compound after Cerridwen.

Chapter 33

hen Amaethon had attacked the archers with his magic, Cerridwen was momentarily distracted. One of the soldiers hit her in the head, and she fell unconscious. When the leader gave the signal to retreat, the soldier grabbed her and threw her over his shoulder.

The soldiers ran down to the stream and stopped to make sure no one from the smithy was following them. They bound Cerridwen's hands, gagged her, and knocked her unconscious before heading northeast toward the river, where a longboat waited for them. It was a long trek on foot to the river, and as the sun rose higher in the sky, they moved as quickly as they could.

Around mid-day, they were still several miles from the river. The leader estimated that it would be well after nightfall before they reached the waiting longboat and safety. He ordered the men to stop and rest in the shade of an orange grove.

Cerridwen was angry at the soldiers and at herself for getting captured. *Do they know that I'm one of the three orphans, or did they take me prisoner to serve as bait to capture and kill Arawn or Amaethon?* She was awake by the time the men reached the orange grove, but she pretended to still be unconscious. She listened to the soldiers closely and tried to overhear their plans. These were disciplined soldiers who knew better than to reveal their plans in front of a conscious prisoner, but believing she was unconscious, they talked too freely.

"Do you think they'll come after her?" she heard one of the soldiers ask.

"They'd better," another soldier answered. "The place we found for the ambush is perfect, and if they don't show up, all of this effort and the men we lost will have been wasted."

So they are using me as bait. If only I could warn Arawn and Amaethon.

A few minutes later, the leader ordered the soldiers to continue heading for the river. She was tossed over the shoulder of another soldier and carried as the soldiers left the shade of the orange grove.

"It looks like they're still heading northeast toward the river," Arawn said as he knelt down next to the tracks the soldiers left behind.

Arawn and Amaethon had been following the trail left by the surviving soldiers for about an hour. The soldiers were making no effort to conceal themselves, and this made them easy to follow.

"Do you think they have a boat waiting at the river?" Amaethon asked.

"Probably," Arawn responded.

"Should we keep following them, or do we try to get around them and intercept them before they get to the river?"

"I've been thinking about that," Arawn admitted. "If we assume that they're still heading northeast, we can go around them. But if they change direction, we'll miss them and never get Cerridwen back."

"What if we can do both?" Amaethon asked.

"How? I don't want to split up. We don't know if there are more soldiers out there."

Amaethon looked up in the sky for a minute until he saw what he was looking for. He sent his thoughts to the bird in the distance, and soon a beautiful hawk was perched on his outstretched arm. Amaethon looked at the bird and concentrated for a while. The hawk opened its wings and flew off to the northeast.

"Nemausus taught me how to do that once," he explained to Arawn. "The hawk will find them and see if Cerridwen's with them. If so, it'll follow them and let us know if they change direction. We can get around them and ambush them before they get to the boat."

"That's amazing!" Arawn said, in awe of his friend's abilities. He mounted his horse, and the two rode north at full speed to get around the Mongán soldiers.

The hawk caught up with the soldiers right where Amaethon thought they'd be. It circled them a couple of times until it saw Cerridwen being carried across the shoulder of one of the soldiers. It also saw the river in the distance and a longboat beached on the southern bank. The hawk followed the soldiers until they stopped for another rest, and it flew off to give Amaethon an update.

The hawk saw Arawn and Amaethon in the distance, and soon it was perched on Amaethon's arm again. The hawk relayed Cerridwen's position, and Amaethon gave it a small mouse as a reward for its efforts.

"If we turn east here, we should intercept them about three miles before they reach the river. The hawk saw a longboat waiting on the river, but it didn't see any sailors on board."

"Do you think they're waiting for us somewhere?" Arawn asked.

"An ambush? It's possible," Amaethon replied. "It would explain why there were no sailors visible on the longboat."

"We'll need to make sure that we don't get caught in a trap," Arawn noted.

"I agree. I'll have the hawk look for the sailors and find us the best way to approach the soldiers to save Cerridwen." Amaethon looked intently at the hawk, and the hawk flew off a moment later.

"I think we need to take care of that longboat as well," Arawn commented. "I don't want to be caught between two forces out here."

"No problem," Amaethon said. "I'm thinking that there will be a sudden thunderstorm on the river."

"Perfect," Arawn said, smiling. "I'll take care of the soldiers holding Cerridwen. You take care of the longboat and the sailors."

"Thanks," Amaethon said. "It might be a bit much for me to create a thunderstorm *and* handle the soldiers."

The hawk return a short while later and landed on Amaethon's outstretched arm. After a moment, Amaethon said, "The sailors are definitely waiting in the foothills to the south of the river, and the soldiers are taking Cerridwen right for them. If we hurry, we can reach the soldiers before they meet up with the sailors."

"Let's go," Arawn said.

Cerridwen could tell that it was getting later in the afternoon. The shadows of the soldiers around her were getting longer as the sun sank lower on the horizon. She learned nothing of value from the soldiers' conversations, and her bindings were tied too well for her to attempt any kind of escape. She hoped that Arawn was following her, but she didn't know if he had survived the attack at the smithy. She felt helpless for the first time in her life.

As the sky grew darker, she saw that they were approaching a large grove of trees. The leader ordered the soldiers to rest for a minute, and as she was dumped onto the ground, the last rays of the sun disappeared behind the Mountain of Elohim.

In the distance, she heard the rumble of thunder, which she thought was strange. There hadn't been any clouds in the sky all day, so she was surprised that a thunderstorm was suddenly approaching.

One of the soldiers removed her gag so she could take a drink from his water bag. He was about to put the gag back in place when Cerridwen heard a slight whistling sound. The soldier fell at her feet – an arrow sticking out of his throat.

Cerridwen wanted to shout for joy, but she knew it would alert the other soldiers, who didn't know that one of their companions was dead. She lay down flat and watched as several of the other soldiers fell. After the sixth soldier had been silently killed, the leader realized that his men were under attack.

Arawn took aim at the leader, and the arrow flew straight and true, killing the leader before he could shout to his men to take cover. The sound of the thunder getting closer kept his men from noticing the leader falling to the ground, and soon three more soldiers lay dead.

After a couple of minutes, only five of the soldiers were still alive, but one of them noticed that his companions were dead and shouted to the others to take cover. The soldiers crawled toward Cerridwen, and Arawn couldn't get a clear shot.

Arawn motioned to Amaethon. "Can you help me with the last five?" he asked. "I don't have a shot."

Amaethon nodded and raised his right hand. The five remaining soldiers suddenly found themselves hurled high into the air. Arawn saw their arms flailing as they attempted in vain to control what was happening to them.

The airborne soldiers saw the longboat on the river as they flew overhead, and they saw the lightning hit the longboat and burst it into flames. Suddenly, they began falling. The last thing they saw before they died was the ground approaching and the waiting longboat burning out of control.

"What about the sailors waiting for us up ahead?" Arawn asked.

"I haven't forgotten about them," Amaethon replied. He raised both hands, and ten sailors flew into the air from their hiding place. Arawn heard their screams as their flight ended in the same way as the soldiers.

Arawn ran forward and untied Cerridwen's hands while Amaethon brought up the horses. When Arawn helped her to her feet, Cerridwen threw her arms around Arawn.

"Thank you," she said.

"You're welcome," Arawn said. "Are you hurt or injured?"

"I don't think so, but my arms are sore."

"What about me?" Amaethon asked with his usual grin. "I helped, too!"

Cerridwen laughed and gave Amaethon a hug. "Thank you, Amaethon. I'm guessing you were the one teaching my captors how to fly?"

"Yes, but I didn't have time to teach them how to land," he replied with a chuckle.

Arawn mounted his horse and held out his hand so Cerridwen could climb up behind him. Amaethon got on his horse, and soon the hawk was perched on his arm again. Amaethon reached into his bag and pulled out another mouse that he had caught earlier in the day. He handed it to the hawk, who took it and flew off into the night.

"What was that all about?" Cerridwen asked.

"Long story," Arawn said, "but the hawk was helping us follow you."

"I think I like sorcerers," Cerridwen said with a sense of wonder in her voice.

"Me, too," Arawn said.

Arawn and Amaethon Rescue Cerridwen from the Soldiers.

CHAPTER 34

t was well after midnight when the trio arrived back at the smithy, and Belenus and Tridamus were waiting for them. The bodies of the soldiers killed that morning had already been removed, and apart from a few blood stains on the ground, the smithy looked like it had never been attacked.

Arawn stopped his horse in front of Tridamus, who reached up and helped Cerridwen dismount. Tridamus gave her a huge hug once she was on the ground. Arawn led the horses to the stables with Belenus while Amaethon followed Tridamus and Cerridwen into the house.

Belenus and Arawn unsaddled the horses. Arawn began brushing them while Belenus fetched water and feed.

"You did well today, Arawn," Belenus said as the horses began eating.

"I'm just glad I was awake and armed before they attacked," Arawn said, following Belenus out of the stables and across the courtyard. "If Cerridwen hadn't be there fighting with me, I don't think I would've survived. She's a remarkable girl."

Belenus smiled. "Yes, she is," he agreed.

They joined the others in the house. Tridamus was preparing food, and Amaethon and Cerridwen were sitting at the table. Belenus and Arawn sat down, and Tridamus brought them fresh tankards. Arawn thought Tridamus looked frustrated, but he couldn't be sure. Tridamus served supper and joined everyone at the table.

"I want to hear about what happened," he said as everyone started eating. "Tell me everything. Don't leave anything out."

The orphans took turns telling the two elders about what happened. "I think they flew fine," Amaethon said with a wry grin at the end of his part of the story. "It's the landing that gave them the most trouble."

Tridamus let out a laugh and leaned over to put his arm around Amaethon's shoulders. "I'm impressed with you two," he said to Amaethon and Arawn. "You did a great thing rescuing Cerridwen today, and I'm grateful to you."

"Me, too," Cerridwen said. "This morning when I saw the archers on the roof, I thought we were going to die. And when I woke up and realized that I was a prisoner, I didn't know if anyone survived the attack here. Then I discovered that I was bait to draw Arawn and Amaethon into an ambush. I never felt so alone and helpless before."

"Well, you're here, and you're safe," Tridamus said as he stood up to clear the dishes from the table.

"I've been meaning to ask you something about this morning," Arawn said to Cerridwen after Tridamus has taken his plate and refilled his tankard. "Where did you learn to fight with two blades?"

"It's just something I learned when I was training," she replied. "I couldn't think of any decent way to fight multiple opponents at the same time with just one sword, so I learned how to use two. I like it better than fighting with a shield in one hand."

"I've fought with two swords before, but I've used shields as well," Arawn said. "When I use a shield, I keep a dagger in my shield hand so I can cut with my shield arm."

"That's a good idea," Cerridwen said. "I should work that into my shield and armor designs."

Arawn watched Tridamus throughout the meal. The blacksmith seemed to enjoy hearing about Cerridwen's rescue, but there was something clearly bothering him.

Maybe he's just upset about Cerridwen getting captured. As he continued watching Tridamus, it seemed that something else was bothering the blacksmith.

"What's wrong, Tridamus?" he asked.

"They're getting bolder," Tridamus said, darkly. "They've violated one of the unwritten rules that the tribes have lived by for centuries. They attacked a blacksmith!"

"It's not done?" Arawn asked. He had never heard that rule before.

"It's understood," Tridamus explained. "We don't take sides, and we're necessary no matter what's going on in the world. Without us, there are no door hinges, no horseshoes, and no cooking pans, not to mention weapons. We're an important part of any society, and we're not supposed to be touched. Furthermore, Cerridwen is an apprentice blacksmith, as far as the world knows. By trying to take her life, they've shown they care nothing about the rules that everyone has consented to live by. It's inexcusable!"

"But if they know she's one of the three," Amaethon commented, "they weren't treating her like a blacksmith. They never touched the workshop, after all."

Tridamus thought about this and nodded slowly. "You're suggesting that they were here to prevent the prophecy from being fulfilled, and they attacked the smithy because they knew that one of the orphans was here?"

Amaethon nodded.

"And you're sure they're all dead?" he asked.

"Cerridwen and Arawn killed almost thirty between them this morning, I killed the archers, Arawn killed most of the soldiers that captured Cerridwen, I destroyed the longboat, and the rest didn't survive their first flying lessons."

Looking at Belenus, Tridamus said, "We'd better get out of here before more soldiers come looking to see why their men didn't return."

"How fast can we get everything loaded?" Belenus asked.

"Well, if I can borrow our young sorcerer here, we can get the heavy stuff loaded in no time," Tridamus said, looking more relaxed than Arawn had seen him all night.

"Good," Belenus said. "The horses need to rest, and so do we. Everyone get some sleep. Tridamus, you and Amaethon get the wagons loaded first thing in the morning with what we're taking from the workshop. I'll get Arawn and Cerridwen to help me put our supplies together and get the horses ready."

An hour after dawn, Tridamus and Belenus drove the wagon out of the courtyard, followed by Amaethon, Arawn, and Cerridwen on horseback. They had made good time getting the huge wagon loaded with the wares and equipment they were taking to the fair, thanks to Amaethon's magic. He was able to load both Tridamus' and Cerridwen's traveling forges, along with several steel bars, into the wagon in under a minute – something that took Tridamus and Cerridwen considerably longer to do using pulleys and a ramp because of the weight.

All of the swords, armor, and jewelry were loaded into the wagon, as were the tents and furniture that they'd need at the fair. The armor that Cerridwen had made for the three orphans was also loaded. By the time they were finished, all that remained in the workshop was the larger pieces of furniture, some of the tools that Tridamus and Cerridwen used, the large forge and bellows, a few steel bars, and some scrap pieces of metal and leather.

Very little was left in the house or the stables either. Most of the horses were part of the team pulling the wagon. Cerridwen had her own horse that she'd ride, Arawn and Amaethon rode their horses, and Thunder and Tridamus' horse were tethered to the back of the wagon so they could be taken on the journey.

As they rode northwest between the Mountain of Elohim and the river, Belenus saw Tridamus look back at the smithy one last time. "I'm going to miss it," he said, turning back to watch where the wagon was going.

"A place is just a place," Belenus said. "I'm going to miss the farm, and I'm sure Nemausus will miss his tower. But it's time to move on."

"It's just that I've been there so long that I'm used to it. It's comfortable. It's become like home."

"I'm sure it was that way with the others," Belenus said, "And that's part of the problem that needs to be resolved. When you fall in love with a place, you forget what you're supposed to be doing. The universe is love, and when we're surrounded by love and see it expressed in every living thing, how can we ever really be separated from that love?"

"We can't," Tridamus admitted.

"That's what we need to convince the others of," Belenus said.

"Not us," Tridamus said, gesturing to the three riders following the wagon. "Them."

Belenus nodded as the two rode in silence.

Shortly before dawn the next morning, several dozen Mongán soldiers, Étaíne sailors, and Chulainn troopers crept up the hill from the river toward the smithy. Their orders were to kill everyone and burn the smithy to the ground.

They entered the courtyard and checked the workshop and stables before searching the house. The place was empty, but there was no sign that the occupants had departed. The soldiers knew that the smithy had been watched continuously for days, and they couldn't understand how anyone could have left without being seen. It never occurred to them that Amaethon had created an illusion to keep anyone from seeing what they were doing and had erased the tracks made by the horses and the wagon when they left.

The leader ordered his men to set everything on fire. They needed to report that the occupants of the smithy were gone, but first they were going to make certain that no one ever used the smithy again.

They set a fire in the middle of the courtyard to light the torches. They threw the torches in all the buildings and on the roofs. Once the fires started burning, the leader whistled loudly, signaling that it was time to leave. But when he turned around, he couldn't see a way out of the courtyard. There was no opening; only a solid wood wall where the opening had been!

The leader ordered everyone to try to find a way out, but the fires were burning too intensely to attempt to leave through one of the buildings. The roofs were all on fire, making going over one of the buildings equally impossible.

The smoke grew thicker, and the leader and his men found it hard to breathe. The courtyard appeared to be getting smaller as the fire spread all around them. His men fell to the ground, overcome by smoke and heat. It was hard to see, and a moment later, the leader joined his men on the ground. The fires raged, and soon nothing remained of the smithy but ashes and the stone chimneys in the workshop and the house.

Several miles away, Amaethon looked over at Tridamus and nodded. Tridamus suspected that there might be another raid on the smithy, and at his request, Amaethon made sure that the attackers got a hostile reception.

The spell that Amaethon cast took whatever the raiders used and turned it against them. Once the raiders chose fire, the spell ensured that the fire would consume them as well. Amaethon knew when the spell began its work, and he sensed when it was all over. The smithy was gone, but then again so were the raiders.

Tridamus gave Amaethon a pained smile from across the fire and continued cooking breakfast for the others in silence. The morning light was already reflecting off the peaks above the campsite, which was miles away from the smithy, along the northeastern face of the Mountain of Elohim.

"How far is it from the smithy to Danann?" Amaethon asked after Tridamus served breakfast.

"Just over four hundred and fifty miles," Tridamus replied. "It should take at least three and a half weeks to get there because of the weight of the wagon."

"I'm looking forward to seeing Danann," Cerridwen said. "I haven't been there since I was born, and I don't remember anything about it. I just wish we didn't have to go past the fairgrounds where Tridamus found me. I'm not sure I want to see that place."

"I'm looking forward to seeing Athramail," Amaethon said. "That's where Nemausus rescued me from Athanaric. I've never been back there. In fact, I never traveled all that much with Nemausus. In the last two months, I've traveled more and been farther from home than I've been in my whole life."

"You're going to be traveling even more over the next several months," Belenus pointed out.

"I know," Amaethon said, nodding. "I wonder if I'll ever see Nemausus' tower again. Something tells me it'll never be my home again."

"I feel the same way about Belenus' farm," Arawn said. "For some reason I don't think I'll ever go back there to live once this is all over."

"At least you two have someplace to go back to," Cerridwen said with a note of sadness in her voice. "My home was just burned to the ground."

Amaethon looked guilty, but Cerridwen burst out laughing. "I'm not blaming you, Amaethon," she said. "But it'll force me to find a new place to live."

"If Belenus and Tridamus are right, the three of us are going to be together for the rest of our lives," Arawn commented. "I don't know where we'll end up, but I doubt we'll be living at a smithy, in a sorcerer's tower, or on a farm."

Once the group passed the northern edge of the Mountain of Elohim, they turned more toward the west and headed for Danann across the central plains, keeping just south of the river.

"All of the roads that'll get us to Danann are close to the river," Tridamus said over supper one evening. "We'll be visible to any longboats patrolling and watching for us."

"Do you think we'll see any longboats?" Belenus asked.

"I'm sure of it," Tridamus replied. "The disobedient ones know that the orphans are on the move. I think we can count on some interference by the Étaíne and the others."

"I can take care of any longboats we see," Amaethon offered.

"How?" Tridamus asked.

"He has a talent for fog," Belenus replied with a chuckle. "He's also not too bad with the occasional lightning storm."

Tridamus stared at Amaethon and smiled. "Very well. I'll leave the longboats to you, Amaethon. But we all need to be vigilant as we cross the plains. There are a few places along the way where we could run into an ambush."

It only took two days to spot the first longboat. Shortly after dawn, Arawn noticed something on the river and pointed it out to Belenus.

"That's a longboat," Belenus confirmed.

Amaethon concentrated for a few minutes, and soon the mist was rising off the river all around the longboat. Within ten minutes, the longboat was completely engulfed in a thick fog.

"You know," Amaethon noted as they broke camp, "eventually they're going to know they're close to us because they keep running into fogbanks that spring up suddenly."

"What do you suggest?" Tridamus asked.

"If we can't hide from them until after they pass us, I may need to start destroying them. I hate the thought of attacking a longboat that's not looking for us, but I don't want a trail of fog leading them right to us."

"Why don't you just punch a hole in their hulls?" Belenus asked. "They'll either sink and have to swim to shore, or they'll be forced onto one of the banks to make repairs. By the time they're back in the water we'll be long gone. If they manage to find us again, you'll know they're looking for us, and then you can destroy the longboat."

Amaethon nodded. "I like that idea. Do you want me to punch a hole in the longboat we just spotted?"

"I think it's a good idea," Arawn said. "You could make it look like they ran into something in the fog."

Amaethon closed his eyes. From inside the fog bank, they heard yelling and the sound of confusion. Amaethon opened his eyes and smiled. "That'll keep them busy for the next several hours."

They finished breaking camp and were soon heading west away from the damaged longboat.

The three orphans kept a close watch out for anyone who might be trying to find them. Arawn rode ahead of the travelers, watching for ambushes. Cerridwen rode in the rear and watched for anyone following them. Amaethon kept an eye on the river and took care of any longboats that appeared.

At least twice a day, Amaethon was forced to deal with a longboat on the river. At first, he opened holes in their hull so the longboats would start sinking. After a few days, the number of longboat patrols increased, and Amaethon knew he was going to have to start launching stronger attacks.

A week after they left the smithy, just after midday, Amaethon saw three longboats appear together, rowing east toward the travelers.

"I don't think it makes sense to open their hulls," he said. "They'll know it was sorcery the minute they realize all three longboats were damaged the same way."

Belenus looked up at the sky. There were no clouds that day. "Lightning has the same problem."

"I know," Amaethon said. He stared at the longboats for a minute. "As long as anything I do will look like sorcery was used, I might as well make sure those longboats can't follow us anymore."

Before Belenus could ask a question, the lead longboat burst into flames. A moment later, the other two were also on fire. Belenus watched the longboats burn and saw sailors jump into the water.

"Do you think they'll try to follow us on foot?" Belenus asked.

"It's a long walk to Danann," Amaethon noted. "Hopefully they'll stay where they are and wait for the next longboats to come by."

CHAPTER 35

s the travelers continued their journey to Danann, the three orphans took every opportunity to get to know each other better. They often stayed up well into the night, talking about their lives in the care of the elders who had rescued them from the assassins responsible for killing their parents.

As Arawn heard Amaethon and Cerridwen talk about the ways they had been raised and what they had learned, he couldn't help but notice that the three of them had very similar skills – despite having been raised by a farmer, a blacksmith, and a sorcerer. The more he thought about it, the more troubled he became.

It's like we were raised just so we could fulfill the prophecy. Who we are, what we can do… it was all decided by others.

Traveling across the central plains gave Arawn the opportunity to think about his life for the first time. He realized that he had spent most of his life reacting to what was happening around him. The farm was in danger, so he learned to fight. The farmers needed a leader, so he took charge. There was a prophecy that needed to be fulfilled, so he was expected to live his life in service to the prophecy. For the first time since Belenus told him about his parents, Arawn found himself thinking about how differently his life might have turned out if his parents were still alive.

I've never stopped to think about that before. If my parents had lived, I wouldn't be here. But they died, and I never really had a choice in the matter. Things needed to be done, and I was raised to get them done. My life was decided for me.

Arawn began to have doubts about how he and the other two orphans were supposed to fulfill the prophecy, but he decided that he wouldn't mention his concerns to Cerridwen or Amaethon. *This is something I need to figure out on my own. Maybe they know more than I do. Maybe their skills make them better prepared for whatever has to be done. After all, a sorcerer should be able to handle anything that we're going to face. That's why he'd make a better Ruler of the World than I would. Given how I was raised, maybe my part in all of this is to be his protector. Maybe I know all I need to know for that role.*

Early in the second week of their journey, Arawn woke from a troubled sleep several hours before dawn. He had been dreaming about driving a wagon filled with barrels and crates as part of a large caravan making its way across a huge prairie. An older man was sitting next to him, showing him how to keep the horses working as a team. The older man had just taken the reins from Arawn when a troop of horsemen rode up and ordered the wagon to stop. The horsemen approached, and as Arawn started frantically looking for his sword, he woke up and realized that it was just a dream.

Arawn looked around. One of the moons was still visible on the southern horizon. The peaks of the Mountain of Elohim glowed in the moonlight and appeared to be floating high above the ground. Arawn's mind immediately filled with the same questions and doubts that had been bothering him for several days, so he quietly got up and walked out of camp and down to the stream where the horses were tethered.

He was standing on the banks of the stream, watching the moon set in the distance, when he heard someone approaching from the direction of the camp. Turning, he saw Amaethon walking down the hill toward him.

"What are you doing up?" Amaethon asked when reached Arawn.

"Couldn't sleep," Arawn answered. "You?"

"Couldn't sleep either," Amaethon replied. "I was having strange dreams."

"So was I. I dreamed about my father and he was teaching me how to drive a wagon as part of a caravan."

"I was dreaming about my father teaching me how to work in a brewery," Amaethon said. "Interesting that we were both dreaming about our fathers."

"It's more than that," Arawn said. "I was dreaming about how my life would have been if I'd never been an orphan."

"So was I," a voice said softly from behind them. Arawn and Amaethon turned around and saw Cerridwen coming down the hill toward them. "I dreamed I was getting ready for my joining day and my mother was helping me."

"Couldn't sleep either?" Amaethon asked.

"No."

"It's strange," Arawn began. "I've never really thought too much about my life or what might have been if my parents hadn't been killed. Belenus found me and raised me, and I'm grateful for that, but he knew all along that I was one of the orphans in the prophecy. He's spent my entire life preparing me for a specific purpose – teaching me about leadership, making sure I was trained to fight like a soldier… It seemed so natural that I never questioned what was being done for me – what was being done *to* me. There was never a choice in the matter. I was raised to fulfil a destiny, but no one ever asked me what I wanted. It never even occurred to me to question that until I started thinking about how different my life could have been."

"I know what you mean," Cerridwen said. "Tridamus was a great teacher and I learned a lot from him, but in the last day or so I've been feeling the same way. All my life was about preparing me to do some great thing that we three were chosen to do centuries ago. I learned how to fight, which is unusual for a girl, and I never thought anything of it. It seemed natural at the time, but now I see clearly that my life was never about me. It was about the prophecy and how best to make sure that I could fulfill my part of it."

"I agree," Amaethon said. "Tridamus taught me sorcery, healing, and many other things, but I never thought to question it once. He made the choices for me. No one ever asked what I wanted. It was just expected that I'd fulfill my part of the prophecy because that's what I was born to do. I wonder what my life would be like if I'd never been orphaned, but more than that, I wonder what my life would be like if I'd been given a choice in the matter."

"Think about it," Arawn interjected. "We're just three eighteen-year-olds from different tribes who have been raised to find the Kingstone, use it to save creation, and get the tribes to quit fighting and unite under one of us. That's a lot to ask of someone who's thirty-eight, let alone someone who just turned eighteen. Belenus, Tridamus, and Nemausus never questioned our role in what's to come, but I have questions."

"Like what?" Cerridwen asked.

"Like how we're supposed to do any of it," Arawn answered. "How are we supposed to inspire confidence in our allies? How are we supposed to convince the gods to obey Elohim when they've been disobeying Elohim's will for centuries? How are we supposed to get the tribes to put aside their differences and become one people? Were either of you trained to do that? I know I wasn't."

"No," Cerridwen and Amaethon admitted.

Arawn threw up his hands in frustration.

"So what do we do?" Cerridwen asked.

"I don't know," Amaethon replied slowly. "Everything's already in motion. It's not like we can just stop now. Each of us was chosen by Elohim to fulfill our part of the prophecy. I guess we need to trust in our training to guide us through whatever it is we need to do... and we need to trust in each other."

"I know, I know," Arawn said. "I just wish that I had some kind of choice in the matter. All my life, I've been getting prepared for this. Belenus just assumed I'd be fine with it, and until now, I was. But just once I'd like to know it was my decision."

"I agree," Amaethon said. "We're going to be forcing the gods to make a choice, and if we survive that, we're going to be forcing the tribes to make a choice. It seems kind of strange that the whole point of the prophecy is about making the right choices when we've never been given a choice about our role in all of this."

"Life is all about making choices and the results of those choices," Arawn said. "Cerridwen chooses what she creates at the smithy, and the metals she uses and the way she works with them determine the quality of whatever she's making. I choose how to protect the farm, and the way I deploy the men on the farm and the weapons I use determines whether I'm prepared to fight off raiders. You choose to hide us with fog and fire, and the magic you use and where the energy comes from determines whether the magic will do what it needs to do. If our choices define our future, how can we hope to succeed with fulfilling the prophecy when we were never given a choice? Aren't our own choices just as important as the choices that the gods and the tribes have to make? How can one of us lead the people correctly when we've never been given the chance to make a choice for ourselves?"

The three stood silently in the darkness for several minutes. "What would you choose if you were given the chance, Arawn?" Cerridwen asked finally. "Would you walk away from your destiny, or would you embrace it and fulfill the prophecy? I know you weren't given a choice before Belenus started preparing you, but if you were offered the choice right now, what would you choose to do?"

Arawn thought about it for a while. He thought back to all that Belenus and the others on the farm had taught him – all that he'd been through to protect the farm from the raiders. His entire life had been in preparation for what was about to happen. He thought about the tribes and loss of life resulting from centuries of warfare. And he thought about his parents and how they had died because of him and his destiny. *I can't dishonor them. They died because of me, and I can't let anyone else die if I can help it.*

"I'd choose to go on and fulfill my destiny," Arawn answered finally. "Not because there's no choice in the matter, but because it's the right choice."

"So would I," Cerridwen said.

"And so would I," Amaethon agreed.

The three of them immediately felt a profound sense of peace for the first time in their lives. Arawn felt his frustration melt away. He looked back at the Mountain of Elohim and somehow knew that they *had* been given a choice, and they had chosen correctly. Smiling, he turned back toward the stream and stood with Amaethon and Cerridwen in the pre-dawn stillness, feeling closer to them that ever before.

"They've made their decision," Alaunus said, *"and they've chosen to embrace who they are destined to be."*

"I'm glad," Belenus said. *"I know I never gave Arawn a choice in the direction that his life took. There was too much to do to protect him and to prepare him for what he'd be facing. He never had a normal childhood. I hope he'll understand why I did what I did."*

"It was necessary to raise Arawn as an instrument of prophecy," Alaunus said, *"and you raised Arawn with love and compassion, not like a pawn in a god's game. He'll remember that. And he'll remember that he did have a choice. Arawn, Amaethon, and Cerridwen each have been given the right to choose their destiny, just as we were. And they have chosen."*

"Does this mean they're ready?" Tridamus asked.

"It's not a question of whether they're ready," Alaunus answered. *"It's a question of whether they're willing to try. Their training and skills give them self-confidence and the ability to handle some of what they'll face, but it's not through training and skills alone that they'll succeed. It's their choices that will determine if they'll succeed."*

"Do you think they'll succeed?" Nemausus asked.

"We'll find out soon enough," Alaunus replied.

As dawn approached, thick clouds moved in from the south and covered the central plains. For the most part, the weather had been cooperating for the travelers. However, it rained for the next three days straight, delaying their arrival at Danann.

Amaethon was able to use the rain to blanket the river in a thick fog. Whenever he heard the splash of oars in the water, the creaking of wooden masts, or the thumping of sails and rigging, indicating that a longboat was nearby, he used lightning to damage or destroy the longboat in a way that seemed completely natural to the sailors who were forced to jump into the river and swim for shore.

After the orphans had made their choice to embrace their destiny, something began to change between Arawn and Cerridwen. Most evenings, they were the last to go to sleep, preferring to stay by the fire after the others had turned in. They talked quietly so they wouldn't disturb anyone, and they found themselves enjoying each other's company more and more.

Two nights after the rains stopped, once everyone else was already asleep, Cerridwen stood up and held out her hand to Arawn, silently suggesting that they take a walk. Without any hesitation, Arawn stood, grabbed his bow and quiver, took her hand, and walked with her away from the campsite.

The moons were climbing toward their zeniths, making the way easier to see. Arawn and Cerridwen walked hand in hand for a while until they reached a hill that overlooked the campsite and had a view of the river beyond. They climbed to the summit and looked around.

Even in the moonlight, they could sense how vast the central plains truly were. Standing there on the top of that hill, they felt as if they were the only ones alive in that part of the world.

Cerridwen loosened her sword belt and sat down. Arawn did the same, put his bow and quiver with his sword, and sat next to her.

He put his arm around her shoulder and pulled her close, looking at the outline of her face in the moonlight. She turned and faced him, smiling. He leaned in, wanting to kiss her, but she leaned over and kissed him first. Arawn had never kissed a girl before. He felt his heart racing, and he was getting lightheaded. He didn't want the kiss to end.

He put his arms around her, and she leaned back with her arms around him so they were lying next to each other on the soft grass of the hilltop. Neither wanted to let go, and they stayed there until the moons were low in the sky.

It was Arawn who finally pulled away and sat up. He pointed toward the campsite. The fire was still visible, but it was smaller than it had been when they left several hours earlier. She nodded, and they both stood up and brushed off the grass and dirt from their clothing.

Arawn bent down and picked up their sword belts. He handed Cerridwen's to her and tightened his around his waist. He picked up his bow and quiver, and he slung the bow over his shoulder.

Cerridwen reached for his hand, but he put his arm around her waist. She put her arm around him, and the two of them walked down the hill and back to the campsite.

When they arrived, Arawn added some wood to the fire so it

wouldn't go out before dawn. When he looked up to see what Cerridwen was doing, he noticed that she had moved her blanket next to his near the wagon. He walked over, removed his weapons, and sat down on his blanket next to her. He put his arm around her and, lying back on the rolled up traveling cloak he used as a pillow, pulled her close to him. She put her arm across his chest and moved as close to him as she could. The two fell asleep in each other's arms.

Belenus and Tridamus woke up early the next morning and rose quickly to build up the fire and start cooking breakfast. Belenus looked over to where Arawn and Cerridwen were sleeping and nudged Tridamus to get his attention. He pointed to the young couple asleep by the wagon, and both of the elders smiled.

"*Things are going the way they're supposed to,*" Tridamus said to Belenus in his mind.

"*Yes they are,*" Belenus agreed. "*I was worried that they might not have feelings for each other, but I should have remembered that love always finds a way.*"

"*Do you think they're moving too fast?*" Tridamus asked.

"*You know as well as I do that time is never a factor when it comes to love. When something is right, time is not required to make it so. And when something isn't right, no amount of time will change that. They'll move at the speed they're supposed to move.*"

The two elders kept smiling as they prepared breakfast.

Arawn and Cerridwen Kissing in the Moonlight.

CHAPTER 36

he travelers were attacked the next night. After everyone else had gone to sleep, Arawn and Cerridwen took a walk. The moons rose late that night, so the two walked slowly to keep from tripping in the darkness. They walked up a small ridge just south of camp and sat down next to each other. Arawn kissed her, and Cerridwen put her arms around his neck and pulled him closer.

Broken clouds filled the night sky. When the moons began to rise, the light shown between the clouds and illuminated the area in a pale blue light. Arawn thought he heard a sound and pulled away from Cerridwen.

"What is it?" she whispered.

"I heard something," he whispered back.

He looked around and thought he saw movement to the east of the camp. He pointed, and Cerridwen nodded. She saw it, too. They reached for their sword belts and tightened them around their waists. Arawn picked up his bow and quiver, and the two started making their way down the ridge.

They saw about a dozen men in the moonlight, creeping toward the camp. Arawn couldn't see anyone moving inside the camp and assumed that Belenus, Tridamus, and Amaethon were still asleep – unaware of the danger approaching them. Arawn motioned toward the right and Cerridwen nodded. The two orphans began moving around to get behind the men.

The men were several hundred feet from the campsite. Arawn motioned for Cerridwen to stop. Looking around, he couldn't see any other men approaching the camp or hiding nearby. There was a flat boulder a few feet away, and Arawn motioned for Cerridwen to crouch down behind it.

Arawn unslung his bow and took an arrow from the quiver. He drew back the bowstring and aimed at the man farthest from the camp, hoping that his death wouldn't alert the other men. He held his breath and released the arrow.

He saw the man drop without a sound. The other men continued moving toward the camp, unaware that one of their comrades was dead. Arawn took another arrow and released it.

The second man fell, followed a moment later by a third and a fourth.

Arawn motioned for Cerridwen to follow him. They quietly moved closer to the camp. She drew her sword as Arawn aimed his bow at another one of the men. The arrow found its mark, and a fifth man went down.

Arawn and Cerridwen continued approaching the men from the rear. They stopped only when Arawn shot his bow.

The sixth man went down, but his sword hit a rock, making a sound. The leader of the men looked around and saw that half of his men were missing. He whistled, and he and his remaining men began running toward the camp.

Arawn and Cerridwen ran after them. Arawn continued firing, but hitting a running target at night was not easy, and he didn't want to risk hitting Belenus, Tridamus, or Amaethon with a stray shot.

He stopped running and aimed an arrow at the fire in the middle of the camp. He pulled back the bowstring and let it go. The arrow flew through the men running toward the camp and hit one of the logs in the fire. Sparks flew up in the air as the log broke and rolled out of the fire pit.

Arawn yelled, dropped his bow, and drew his sword. Cerridwen, who was already well ahead of Arawn, also yelled.

The leader of the men heard them yelling and spun around. Seeing Cerridwen running at him, he shouted for two of his men to deal with her.

The first man reached Cerridwen, but she thrust her sword into his stomach before he could block her attack. She pulled her sword free and ran for the second man.

The second man swung his sword at her head. Rather than ducking, Cerridwen rolled forward into a summersault. As she stood back up, she swung her sword and caught the second man in his ribs underneath his outstretched arm. She spun around and her sword caught the man across his throat. As he fell, she grabbed his sword and ran toward the camp.

Arawn caught up to her as she picked up the fallen man's sword, and the two raced after the remaining men, shouting so their friends in the camp would know something was happening.

The leader entered the camp and jumped over the fire pit. Arawn saw him raise his sword, but the man was thrown backwards and landed in the fire. Belenus stepped into the light of the campfire – his walking stick held in both hands.

The leader rolled out of the fire, screaming in pain. The dying campfire suddenly erupted into a bonfire, and Arawn saw Amaethon standing just behind Belenus.

The three remaining men stopped running and hesitated when they saw the bonfire. One started backing up, but the other two ran for Amaethon and Belenus.

Amaethon turned to face the two men. Arawn saw the men raise their swords, but the swords flew out of their hands and disappeared into the night. Suddenly unarmed, the men stopped in confusion. A moment later, they were sailing up into the air. Arawn heard their screams fade away into the distance. The leader, who was still on the ground in pain from his burns, and the fourth man soon followed their two comrades into the air and disappeared from sight.

When Cerridwen and Arawn reached the camp, there was no evidence that anything had happened.

"Are you two all right?" Belenus asked.

Arawn nodded.

"Where were you?" Tridamus asked.

"We went for a walk over to the ridge just south of here," Cerridwen said. "Arawn saw movement in the moonlight. We moved around behind them and Arawn shot six before they knew we were there. I took care of two more, and you finished the rest of them."

"Can you tell if there are any more out there?" Belenus asked Amaethon.

"I don't think so. I can't sense anyone but the five of us."

"What about the ones you just sent flying?" Cerridwen asked.

"They should have landed in the river by now," Amaethon said, grinning.

Arawn looked around and remembered that he had dropped his bow. "I need to find my bow," he said.

"Don't worry about it," Amaethon said. He closed his eyes, and the bow and quiver landed on the ground in front of Arawn. A moment later, Arawn's arrows landed in the ground next to the quiver.

"Thanks!" Arawn said, putting the arrows in the quiver.

"You're welcome. Thanks for getting our attention with the fire. One of the sparks landed on my arm and it woke me up. That's when I heard you and Cerridwen out there shouting. I woke up Tridamus and

217

Belenus just before the men reached the camp."

"What should we do about the bodies?" Tridamus asked.

"I already took care of that," Amaethon said. "They're with their comrades in the river."

Belenus nodded. "I think you three need to get some sleep. Tridamus and I will keep watch for the rest of the night in case anyone else decides to attack."

The three orphans nodded and walked over to their blankets. Soon they were sleeping soundly.

"Where do you think those men came from?" Tridamus asked silently after the orphans were asleep and the bonfire had returned to being a campfire.

"I don't know," Belenus replied. *"I didn't hear any horses nearby. I suppose they could have come from one of the longboats on the river."*

"We're only halfway to Danann. There's a lot of ground we still have to cover before we have the Macruhan army to protect us."

"We could get a detachment from the Army of the Followers of Elohim to give us an escort," Belenus suggested.

"Not without revealing the identity of the three orphans," Tridamus point out. *"Stealth and speed are what we need, not armed troops calling attention to us. It would be like announcing to the world that the orphans are here."*

Belenus nodded. *"You don't think this'll be the last attack, do you?"*

"No, I don't. Our orphans will have to be on their guard."

"Are you saying that we shouldn't protect them?" Belenus asked.

"This is their quest, not ours," Tridamus replied. *"They have to prove that they're worthy to receive the Kingstone, not us."*

"I understand," Belenus said, putting another piece of wood on the fire. *"It's just that old habits die hard."*

"I know, old friend. I know."

The two elders stared at the fire in silence.

wo days later, Arawn was riding ahead of the group and stopped on a small incline about a hundred yards away. He motioned for the wagon to stop moving. Tridamus reined in the horses and brought the wagon to a halt. Cerridwen and Amaethon rode up next to Arawn so they could see what was going on.

A large force on horseback rode across the plains in front of them, traveling south.

"Are they Chulainn troopers?" Cerridwen asked.

"No, they're regular soldiers on patrol in this area," Amaethon said. He pointed to the rider just behind the leader. "Look, you can see their flag. We had patrols stop by the tower all the time when I was growing up."

"What tribe uses that flag?" Arawn asked.

"It's not one of the tribes," Amaethon answered. "They're part of the army of the Followers of Elohim who live in this territory. The army was originally raised by Airmid to defend the people who refused to worship the disobedient gods."

"So they're part of the army we'll be fighting alongside if there's a war?" Arawn asked.

Amaethon nodded. Once the patrol disappeared in the distance, Arawn motioned for the wagon to move forward again.

They saw several more patrols as they travelled to Danann, but none of the soldiers bothered them.

The next day, the orphans talked together just behind the wagon.

"I haven't seen any longboats in a while,' Cerridwen commented. "Do you think they've stopped patrolling the river?"

"No, and it worries me," Arawn replied.

"Me, too," Amaethon added. "We're too close to the Étaíne territory to be seeing fewer longboats."

"Do you think they're waiting for us ahead?" Cerridwen asked.

"Yes, if they've figured out that we're heading for Danann," Arawn said. "It's what I'd do."

"If they can keep us from reaching Danann," Amaethon added, "they can kill us more easily. The Étaíne have never successfully invaded the Macruhan territory. If they're going to do something, it would have to be before we cross the border."

"What can we do to prepare ourselves?" Cerridwen asked.

"We need to keep a close watch all around us," Arawn suggested. "They only have to kill one of us for the prophecy to fail."

A few hours later, the travelers approached a part of the road that snaked between several tree-covered hills.

"What do you think, Arawn?" Amaethon asked.

"It's where I'd plan an ambush," Arawn replied. "You could hide a lot of men in those trees, and if they have archers, they could easily pick us off."

"What do we do?" Cerridwen asked.

"I can put a protective shield around us so their arrows can't touch us," Amaethon offered. "Then we can see what happens."

"Okay. What do you need from us?" Arawn asked.

"Give me a few minutes to gather the energy I need."

Tridamus slowed the wagon down to give Amaethon time to prepare. Once Amaethon had the energy he needed and built the protective shield, he told the others he was ready.

They rode between the first two hills, but no attack came. The road curved around the hill on the left, and the thick tree cover blocked the sunlight between the hills. Many of the branches from the trees on both sides of the road had intertwined over the years, creating a living canopy above the road.

As the travelers rounded the final curve and reached the end of the canopy-covered part of the road, Amaethon sat up in his saddle.

"We need to move faster!" he said urgently. "They're all around us!"

Tridamus shook the reins and the horses pulling the wagon began to canter. The orphans followed close behind.

The air around them filled with arrows as the archers hiding in the trees began firing. The arrows disintegrated when they hit Amaethon's protective shield, but the archers released barrage after barrage of arrows at the travelers.

Tridamus coaxed the horses into a gallop. Arawn glanced over his shoulder and saw dozens of soldiers racing down the hills to block their path from the rear. Looking to either side, he saw soldiers stepping out from the trees with their swords drawn. There were hundreds of soldiers waiting for them, and Arawn wondered what lay ahead.

"We're surrounded!" Arawn shouted.

"I'll take care of them," Amaethon shouted back.

As they approached the last curve, Arawn saw a barricade of overturned wagons blocking the road ahead. Soldiers stood behind the barricade and on the hilltops on either side.

Arawn smelled smoke as they approached the barricade without slowing down. He glanced back and saw fire in the treetops.

I hope Amaethon is doing that. They raced toward the barricade.

Amaethon held his hand out toward the barricade, and the two wagons in the middle of the barricade flew out of the way, creating an opening. The barricade erupted into flames as Tridamus' wagon reached the opening. The wagon and the three orphans passed through the barricade and rode out into the open expanse of the plains.

Arawn looked back and saw the barricade close behind them. The hills were on fire, and Arawn couldn't imagine how any of the soldiers would survive the inferno.

"Amaethon, what's wrong?" he heard Cerridwen ask.

Turning back, Arawn saw his friend swaying in his saddle. He reached out and grabbed Amaethon to keep him from falling from his horse.

"Belenus, something's wrong with Amaethon," he shouted.

Belenus turned and shouted, "Riders behind you!"

Arawn looked back. Troopers dressed like the ones who attacked the farm were riding from their hiding place behind one of the hills, which was now on fire.

"What do you want to do?" Tridamus shouted.

Arawn watched the riders for a moment. "They're going to catch up with us soon. Amaethon's unconscious, so he can't help. Unless we can go a lot faster, we have no choice but to stop and fight."

Tridamus pulled back on the reins, and the wagon came to a stop. Belenus jumped down and pulled Amaethon off his horse. He handed the unconscious sorcerer up to Tridamus, who had armed himself with one of his swords from the back of the wagon.

"Stay with him," Belenus said to Tridamus. "I'll help Arawn and Cerridwen."

Belenus untied Thunder from the back of the wagon and mounted the horse. Cerridwen took two of her swords from the back of the wagon and handed one to Arawn. Arawn had his bow unslung and was moving his quiver around so the arrows were in easy reach. He put the extra sword from Cerridwen through his sword belt and pressed his heels into the side of his horse.

The three rode for the approaching troopers while Tridamus stayed behind with the wagon and Amaethon. Arawn fired arrows at the troopers as fast as he could. When his quiver was empty, he slung the bow over his shoulder to protect his back and drew his sword and the sword Cerridwen had given him.

Cerridwen had her two swords drawn. "I'm not used to fighting on horseback," she shouted. "I don't know how to control my horse and fight at the same time."

"I can knock some of them off their horses with my walking stick," Belenus shouted back. "Do you think you can handle them once they're on the ground?"

"Yes," Cerridwen responded, grateful for Belenus' suggestion.

Arawn was in the lead as they reached the troopers. Arawn's two swords flashed in the sunlight has he fought two attackers at a time.

Belenus rode up and knocked one of Arawn's attackers onto the ground. Riding forward, he knocked several others down.

Cerridwen dismounted and slapped the rear of her horse so it would get out of her way. She ran up to the first trooper that Belenus had unhorsed, and she killed the trooper as he was trying to stand. She moved to attack the other troopers Belenus had knocked off their horses.

Arawn continued fighting the troopers on horseback, taking on two at a time. He had several small cuts on his leg and a nasty gash on his right forearm, but he kept fighting.

Belenus used his walking stick to keep the mounted and dismounted troopers from getting too close to him with their swords. More than a dozen had been unhorsed, and the ones not attacking Cerridwen were trying to get through Belenus' defenses.

Cerridwen's arms were covered in blood, but it wasn't her own. She was bleeding from a cut on her right hip, but apart from that, she was unharmed. The troopers were no match for her skills with two swords, but she was outnumbered and they were beginning to get around her.

Arawn saw the troopers moving behind Cerridwen and broke off the fight he was having with two mounted troopers. He wheeled his horse around and rode toward Cerridwen, jumping out of the saddle as soon as he reached her.

"I'm at your back," he shouted to her.

"Thanks!" she shouted back.

The rest of the troopers dismounted and rushed the two orphans. They quickly realized their mistake. Arawn and Cerridwen, standing back-to-back and each fighting with two swords, proved to be unbeatable. The troopers who rushed the two orphans soon fell back dead or dying.

Belenus, seeing an opportunity, rode around the two orphans, striking the troopers in the head with his walking stick and knocking them unconscious.

Soon, none of the troopers was still standing, and most of their horses had run away to the south. Arawn and Cerridwen's horses had gone back to the wagon to wait with Tridamus for their riders to return.

Arawn and Cerridwen looked around at the carnage all around them. They had the troopers' blood all over them, and they had open wounds that needed to be treated. They looked at each other for a moment, dropped their swords, and embraced each other.

They were still holding each other when Tridamus rode up. "Plenty of time for that later," he bellowed as he jumped down from the wagon. "We should get out of here before someone comes to investigate the fire."

Arawn had forgotten about the fire and the soldiers. He looked back at the hills. Thick black smoke was rising from the burning trees high into the air. Arawn knew it was visible for miles. He let go of Cerridwen and bent down to pick up his swords.

Belenus quickly bandaged Arawn's arm and Cerridwen's hip, promising to do a better job once they stopped for the day. "I need to clean the wounds properly, but we need to get out of here."

Amaethon was still unconscious, so Belenus rode with Cerridwen and Arawn behind the wagon. Soon the hills and burning trees disappeared behind them, but they could see the smoke until the sun set in the west.

It was late in the afternoon when Tridamus found a good place to stop for the day. There was a clear stream on one side, and flat, open plains all around.

"Get out of those clothes and wash yourselves in the stream," Belenus commanded. "I'll get clean clothes for you and meet you there to tend to your wounds."

Arawn and Cerridwen obeyed. They walked down to the stream and removed their boots. The clothes were hard to remove. Blood had hardened, making the clothes stiff. Blood and sweat had dried on the inside of the clothes, making them stick to the skin. Arawn finally jumped into the stream fully clothed, using the water to help get the clothes off his body. Cerridwen did the same.

They rinsed the clothing in the stream to get as much of the blood out of them as possible. They tossed the wet clothes onto the banks of the stream and started washing themselves.

Arawn tried not to look at Cerridwen bathing, but he couldn't avoid seeing her altogether. When Belenus arrived with fresh clothes and bandages for their wounds, he turned his back so Cerridwen could have her hip looked at first.

The water felt good, and soon Arawn felt completely clean again. He kept his back to Cerridwen until the farmer told him it was his turn to come out of the stream. When he turned around, Cerridwen was already dressed and walking back to camp with her wet clothes to check on Amaethon.

Belenus examined the gash on Arawn's forearm. "It's not as bad as I feared," he said softly. "It should heal with only a slight pucker for a scar." He wrapped the arm carefully and told Arawn to get dressed.

Arawn dressed quickly and retrieved his wet clothes before joining everyone else at the camp.

Amaethon was sitting up, but looking very weak when Arawn reached the wagon to hang his clothes out to dry.

"How are you?" he asked.

"Exhausted. I didn't know there were so many soldiers in the woods. It took more out of me than I anticipated."

"Drink this," Belenus said, bringing Amaethon a large cup of fresh water. Amaethon drank it, and Belenus went back to the stream to refill the cup.

"How far are we from the Macruhan border?" Arawn asked later as they were all eating supper.

"Another six or seven days, depending on weather and interference," Tridamus replied.

"They sent a lot of soldiers after us today," Cerridwen said. "I hope they don't have more waiting up ahead."

"There are no more good places where they can ambush us between here and the border," Tridamus noted. "If they try anything again, we'll know it long before it happens."

"I guess we should figure out who's going to keep watch over the camp tonight," Arawn said. "I can take the first watch."

"No, Arawn," Tridamus said. "You've had a hard day today. I'll stand watch tonight. Belenus can help me drive the wagon tomorrow if I get too tired on the road. You, Cerridwen, and Amaethon need to rest. We still have a long way to go."

Arawn didn't argue. As soon as they finished eating and washing the dishes in the stream, the three orphans grabbed their blankets and fell asleep immediately.

"They fought well today," Belenus said silently as the two elders built up the campfire and watched the sun setting in the west.

"Yes they did," Tridamus agreed. *"I was worried when Amaethon fainted, but I contacted Nemausus and he showed me what to do. Arawn and Cerridwen certainly stepped up when the troopers attacked, didn't they?"*

"Yes. All three of them did their part to get us through that trap."

"I'm proud of you for how you handled yourself with the troopers," Tridamus said. *"You didn't do anything to affect the outcome of the skirmish, but you did help even the odds for Arawn and Cerridwen."*

"You reminded me that this is their quest, nor ours," Belenus commented.

"That's right, I did. I just hope we've seen the last of the interference for a while."

"Me, too," Belenus said.

ongboats were visible on the river as the travelers rode toward the Macruhan border, but there were no more attacks. They crossed the border without incident a week after the ambush, but as they approached the edge of the Great Forest, they found themselves suddenly surrounded by armed riders who appeared from the trees without a sound. The riders wore Macruhan uniforms, and many of them had the same hair color and complexion as Cerridwen.

Arawn, Cerridwen, and Amaethon drew their swords and took positions to protect the wagon, but the leader of the riders held up his hand.

"There's no need for weapons," the officer said. "We've been waiting for you. King Esus commanded that we escort you to Danann where he awaits your pleasure. You are all most welcome to the land of the Macruhans."

"Put your swords away," Belenus said to the orphans. Turning to the officer, he said, "Thank you for meeting us and escorting us to your king."

"My pleasure, sir," the leader responded. "If you'll all follow me, we'll reach Danann soon."

As the armed riders took positions alongside and behind the wagon, Belenus said, "Arawn, why don't you, Cerridwen, and Amaethon ride in front with the officer."

Arawn nodded and rode around the wagon with the other two orphans. As the officer and the escort began moving forward, Amaethon was on the left side of the officer, and Arawn and Cerridwen were on his right.

As they rode toward the city, Arawn asked, "May I know who escorts us to the king?"

"Captain MacInnis of the Third Battalion, at your service," he replied. "Am I correct that you three are the ones spoken of in the prophecy?"

"Yes," Amaethon said simply.

Turning to Cerridwen, the Captain said, "From your looks, I would have thought you were a Macruhan."

"I am," Cerridwen said, "but I was raised on the other side of the Mountain of Elohim after my family was killed."

"Where were they killed, if you don't mind my asking?"

"At a fair near Danann eighteen years ago."

MacInnis nodded. It wasn't uncommon for there to be murders at fairs. He noticed the fairgrounds off in the distance and pointed. "Did you know the fairgrounds are over there?"

Cerridwen shook her head and turned to look where MacInnis pointed. She watched in silence as they passed the fairgrounds.

Arawn, worried about Cerridwen, reached over and touched her on the shoulder. He saw her smile, but she kept looking at the fairgrounds until they had ridden past.

They reached a swift-moving stream a few minutes later. MacInnis held up his hand and signaled for everyone to stop.

"We'll arrive at Danann soon, and you'll be escorted straight to the king. Would you like to freshen up and change out of your traveling clothes?"

"Thank you, Captain," Cerridwen answered. "I'd hate to meet your king smelling like a horse."

MacInnis ordered the escorts to turn around and face away from the travelers. Belenus threw towels to the orphans, who dismounted and began washing themselves in the stream. By the time they washed the dust and sweat off, Belenus had found more suitable clothes for them to wear. They changed quickly and mounted their horses, feeling better about their appearance for the meeting with the Macruhan king.

MacInnis shouted an order and the escorts closed in around the travelers again. Soon they were approaching the capital city of the Macruhan tribe.

The orphans looked at the city up ahead in complete awe. At first, it looked like a giant grove of trees, but as they got closer, they saw the beauty of the architecture that made the city look like part of the surroundings.

"Welcome to Danann," MacInnis said, "the most beautiful city in Alastríona!"

227

"It's breathtaking," Cerridwen said.

"I felt the same way the first time I saw it," MacInnis said. "And once you leave it, you never feel whole again."

As they passed through the ring of trees that formed the outer wall of the city, they saw the stone inner wall and the great stone archway forming a tunnel to the main gates of the city. Looking up, Arawn saw the sharpened timbers along the bottom of the portcullis at one end of the tunnel. The portcullis was a lattice gate raised and lowered by a system of chains and counterweights inside the walls. It was designed to keep an enemy from entering the city while providing openings for archers to shoot through.

As they passed through the tunnel, Arawn saw the city gates at the far end. He estimated that the gates were made of solid wood almost twenty inches thick and reinforced with large iron bands that held them on their hinges. There were old scars visible where the two parts of the gates came together.

"What caused those scars?" he asked MacInnis, pointing to the gates.

"During the last war, the Gallasians attacked the city," MacInnis said. "They got through the portcullis and tried to break open the gates with a battering ram, but the gates held, and our archers forced them back beyond the outer walls. You can't see them, but there are arrow slits all along the stone tunnel between the portcullis and the gates. Anyone caught in there doesn't last long."

As they rode through the city, Cerridwen was taken with how the architecture incorporated the shapes of animals into the ornamentation of each building. It made each building seem alive – like it was part of the Great Forest itself.

The horse hooves against the cobblestone streets sounded like the city itself was applauding the arrival of its guests as the travelers and their escorts rode through the city toward the large cluster of buildings in the city center.

As they entered the central square, MacInnis said, "This is the center of the city. The government offices are on those buildings on the left side, and principal families of our tribe live in those houses on the right."

Pointing to the far side of the square, he added, "And that's the palace over there. It's where our king performs his official functions, and he's waiting for you there."

They rode through the entrance of the palace's courtyard. MacInnis' men stopped and took positions around the square behind them. MacInnis motioned for the travelers to stop, and grooms ran out to take hold of the horses so everyone could dismount.

"I need each of you to disarm yourselves before entering the palace," MacInnis said. "You can leave your weapons in the wagon. My men will stay with the wagon until you leave the city. Your things will be safe."

Arawn, Cerridwen, and Amaethon removed their weapons and put them in the back of the wagon next to their clothes. MacInnis led them up the stairs to the main entrance of the palace.

The tall, arched doors opened, and the orphans saw a long hallway lined with well-dressed Macruhans on either side. The walls, floors, and ceiling of the hallway were made of dark wood. The hallway had vaulted ceilings, which gave one the impression of walking through the inside of an enormous tree. On the floor, running the full length of the hallway, was a deep green carpet trimmed in crimson. The people along the walls bowed and curtsied as the orphans, the two elders, and their escorts walked past.

Standing at the end of the hallway was King Esus of the Macruhan tribe, dressed in deep russet wool trousers, black knee-high boots, a black wool doublet, and a leather chest piece with the image of a great tree embossed in the center. He wore a narrow gold circlet around his head to denote his rank, but apart from that, he wore little that would identify him as the head of his tribe.

"My King," MacInnis said loudly once they reached the end of the hallway, "I have brought the guests as you commanded. Allow me to introduce to you Belenus and Tridamus, two of the three teachers who were foretold by Airmid, and Cerridwen, Arawn, and Amaethon, who are the three orphans foretold in the prophecy."

There were gasps from several of the people lining the sides of the hallway, but the king just smiled. "My friends," he said kindly, "I'm honored to be in your presence. Please, may we speak for a while before I present you to the court?"

The orphans and the elders nodded, and the king, accompanied by MacInnis, led them into a large room at the end of the hallway.

"Please forgive the formality of MacInnis' announcement out there," the king began, "since I already know who each of you are. It was more for the members of principal families that you passed on your way in. I don't get to surprise them often, and your arrival gave me a perfect excuse to create a little drama. If all goes well, I won't be king much longer, so, again, forgive me if I used you to have a bit of fun. I'm truly honored to be in your presence, and if there's anything that I or the Macruhan tribe can do to help you fulfill the prophecy, you have only to ask."

"Thank you, King Esus," Belenus said on behalf of everyone. "May I ask how you know who we are and that we were coming?"

"Alaunus told me," King Esus said.

"Alaunus?" Belenus asked, sounding surprised. "Is she here?"

Esus shook his head. "No, she left a week or so ago to visit Vellaunus and Arvernus so they'd know you were coming. She said she'd meet you at the fair and that Nemausus would meet you there as well."

Turning to the three orphans, King Esus said, "I'm overjoyed to meet the three of you at last. We've lived for so long under the promise of the prophecy that it's overwhelming to see its manifestation standing right in front of me. If you're successful in your task, it'll be my honor to surrender my tribe to the one of you who is destined to be the Ruler of the World. In the meantime, what service may I perform for you?"

"We need you to lead your army to the western face of the Mountain of Elohim," Belenus answered. "All of the tribes must be assembled there when the Kingstone arrives, and time is growing short. Our enemies are already on the move. Longboats have been seen east and south of the Mountain of Elohim, and Chulainn Troopers and Mongán Soldiers have raided deep into Airmid's territory without fear. You and the other allies must be there to meet the enemies' main forces in case war breaks out before this is over."

"I understand, Belenus," Esus said. "I'll do as you request."

He gave orders to MacInnis to alert the other Captains and prepare to march to the Mountain of Elohim as soon as possible.

Turning to Cerridwen, he said, "I understand you're a child of the Macruhan. I'm deeply sorry that your parents were lost so near the city, and yet it was necessary for you to become who you were destined to be. You remind me of my own daughters. You have many of the same features as they do, although I must say that you're considerably more beautiful than most of the young ladies at court."

Cerridwen blushed, and Amaethon and Arawn smiled.

King Esus talked with each of the orphans for a while. When a servant appeared and informed the king that the reception guests had assembled, he motioned for everyone to follow him into the great hall next door so he could make the formal introductions to the Macruhan nobility and military leaders.

The great hall was immense, and the three orphans had never been in a room that large before. The style was much like that of the hallway and the chamber they had just left, but there were banners and military implements lining the walls between each of the large windows. Chandeliers, filled with candles, hung from the ceiling to provide additional light, and the floor was made of a smooth, polished wood that reflected light like a mirror.

The room was full of people, and for the first time Arawn saw the similarities between Cerridwen and the women of Danann. Most had the same red hair and deep green eyes, but their skin was much paler than Cerridwen's.

The king made the formal introductions. He presented Belenus and Tridamus, followed by Amaethon, Cerridwen, and Arawn. Belenus spoke for the travelers while servants brought in food so everyone could eat and mingle, as was the custom in Macruhan when dignitaries arrived.

The young men of the court quickly moved in around Cerridwen, just as the young women cornered Arawn and Amaethon. Arawn found the whole experience amusing, but he made certain that he didn't show it so he wouldn't risk offending anyone. He looked over at Cerridwen several times, and when he noticed a distressed looked on her face, he excused himself from the women who were surrounding him and walked over to rescue her.

"Tridamus wants a word with us when you have a moment," he said as he walked up to her. "What should I tell him?"

Cerridwen flashed him a grateful smile. "Give me a moment, and I'll go with you," she said. She excused herself from the gathering of potential suitors. Cerridwen and Arawn walked toward Amaethon, who was fending off a pack of young ladies who wanted to explore joining with a sorcerer and child of the prophecy as a way to advance the prestige of their families.

"If you would excuse us for a moment," Cerridwen said as she took Amaethon by the arm, "the Dragon Lord is needed for a conference."

"The Dragon Lord?" the girls crooned as Amaethon followed Cerridwen and Arawn.

"Why did you call me the 'Dragon Lord'?" Amaethon asked once they were safe from the younger members of the court.

"Well, you've created two dragons in your life, and I like the way it sounds. It's how I think of you."

"I like it," Arawn said with a grin. "It gives you an air of mystery."

Amaethon closed his eyes for a moment, and Cerridwen and Arawn wondered if he were still recovering from the ambush. The lights around the room dimmed for a moment, and a greenish mist began to appear on his right shoulder. As the mist cleared, there – perched on his shoulder with its tail draped around his neck – was a small dragon. As Cerridwen

231

and Arawn watched, the dragon stretched, yawned, and crouched down so its head rested on Amaethon's shoulder.

"I guess if I'm going to be the Dragon Lord, I should at least look the part, don't you think?" Amaethon said, trying to keep from laughing aloud.

Cerridwen and Arawn couldn't contain their laughter. The dragon picked its head up and looked at the two laughing orphans before putting its head back on Amaethon's shoulder.

The king was fascinated by Amaethon's dragon, and at his host's request, Amaethon made the dragon fly around the room and light the candles on the wall sconces as the sun began to set. Once the last candle was lit, the dragon flew to the center of the room, let out a tiny roar, and disappeared in a green puff of smoke.

The king used that as the signal that the reception was concluded and led his guests out of the great hall. He showed them to their quarters so they could rest before leaving the next morning for the fair.

Cerridwen, Arawn, and Amaethon had adjoining rooms in a large suite in the guest wing of the palace, while Belenus and Tridamus were housed in a similar suite nearby. Someone had brought their clothes from the wagon, but not their weapons. The three orphans put their clothes away in their bedrooms. They sat in the suite's common sitting area in front of the fireplace and talked about the king and the reception.

"I honestly thought that one of those boys was going to ask for my hand in joining right then and there!" Cerridwen said at one point. "They were asking such personal questions that it seemed they were trying to decide if they wanted to buy a horse, rather than court a woman."

"If you two hadn't rescued me when you did," Amaethon said, "I'm quite sure one of those clever little girls would have found a way to trick me into promising myself to her. I'm glad the king placed guards around our rooms, or I'm sure some of them would try to sneak in here tonight."

"I found the whole thing amusing," Arawn said, smiling at his companion's discomfort. "I was raised on a farm as a nobody, but those girls were throwing themselves at me because of something I haven't even done yet. It makes no sense to me at all."

"Those girls were raised to do whatever they can to advance their family's reputation," Amaethon said. "I guess joining with one of us would do that."

Looking at Cerridwen, Arawn said, "Fortunately, I'm not interested in any of them."

"Me either," Cerridwen added.

"And on that note," Amaethon said, standing up and heading for his room, "I think I'll turn in."

"It's still early!" Arawn protested. "Stay here!"

Amaethon shook his head. "I'm tired from conjuring the dragon. Even a small one takes a lot of effort. Besides, I know what's going on between you two, and I want you to have some time to yourselves."

"What do you mean you know what's going on?" Cerridwen demanded.

"Oh, come on!" Amaethon exclaimed with a big grin. "I felt the jolt that hit you two when you first met. I've seen you by the campfire after everyone's gone to bed and taking walks together in the night. I think it's great that you two found each other, and I know that you're not going to have that much time alone together until we do whatever it is we're supposed to do. So enjoy your evening, and I'll see you in the morning."

Amaethon disappeared into his room and was asleep almost as soon as he crawled into bed.

Cerridwen stood up and crossed the room to sit down next to Arawn. "Did you feel a jolt the day we met?"

Arawn nodded. "You too?" he asked.

Cerridwen nodded. "Is that what love is supposed to feel like?"

"I don't know," Arawn responded. "I think it was something inside us recognizing the other and letting us know that we're supposed to be together. I think love is what I've been feeling since our first kiss."

"Me too," Cerridwen said, putting her head on Arawn's shoulder. "I love you, Arawn."

"I love you too, Cerridwen."

CHAPTER 39

maethon was up well before dawn. He dressed quickly, packed away his clothes from the night before, and walked out into the common room, only to find Cerridwen and Arawn sound asleep next to each other on the couch. He gently shook their shoulders to wake them, and said, "It's time to get ready to leave."

The two got up and went into their rooms to change and wash their faces before returning to the common room with their things. A chamberlain brought breakfast along with food and supplies for the next part of their journey. The three ate quickly and were about to go and find the two elders when there was a knock on the door.

Amaethon opened the door, and Belenus and Tridamus walked in carrying their supplies and traveling bags. "Good morning," Belenus said, helping himself to one of the pastries on the platter that the chamberlain had brought. "I trust you all slept well."

The three orphans nodded. Amaethon repeated what he had said the night before about being grateful for the guards in the hallway, and Tridamus laughed. "We should have warned you to watch out for the people your age. Each of you would make a fine catch for anyone looking to move up in society, and you'll find more of the same when we visit Athramail and Batavia."

As the party left the suite and entered the hallway, the guards formed up around them and led them through the palace to the courtyard where the wagon and their horses were waiting and ready. King Esus was also waiting there to see them off.

"My friends, I enjoyed our time together, and I wish you a safe journey," he said as he grasped each guest's arm in turn. "My army and I will be waiting for you when you arrive at the Mountain of Elohim, along with any members of the tribe who wish to make the journey with us."

As the members of the party mounted their horses or climbed up onto the wagon, he added, "Thank you for giving me a wonderful way to end my stewardship over my tribe. I see in you more than just the people selected to fulfill the prophecy; I see the people who are ready and capable of fulfilling the prophecy and everything that comes after. I look forward to helping you unite all the tribes together."

"Thank you, King Esus," Arawn said. "We appreciate your hospitality and your willingness to take on faith what hasn't yet happened."

"My friend," Esus said with a wise smile, "in the end, faith is all we truly have."

MacInnis was there to lead the orphans and the elders away from the palace, and his escort formed up around them as they entered the square and rode toward the city gates. MacInnis and his men escorted them all the way past the border to the ferry at the great river, and they would've escorted them to the fair if Belenus hadn't insisted that it would call too much attention to their presence.

"Very well, then," MacInnis finally conceded. "If you insist, we'll turn back here. But we'll see you again soon."

"We look forward to that," Amaethon said.

"As do we, Dragon Lord."

Amaethon shot a pained look at Cerridwen, who burst out laughing. The members of the party continued laughing as they crossed the river on the ferry. MacInnis and his men remained on the riverbank until the party arrived on the far bank. McInnis raised his hand and signaled his men to follow him back to Danann.

There were two passes through the Valdunass Mountains. The first one was within the Étaíne territory where their capital city, Ardagh, was located. The second one was farther east where the Étaíne, Dunmaine, and Penarduun territories bordered the central plains. Situated in this pass, just over two hundred miles from Danann, was the fairgrounds where the party was heading.

The air grew chilly as they traveled north, but the weather was quite pleasant apart from that. They fell in with a caravan of other artisans and vendors heading for the fair, and this allowed them to remain unnoticed by the frequent patrols they saw along the road.

By the time they arrived at the fairgrounds a week later, Tridamus was anxious to sell out his inventory and deliver a number of commissions that he had taken at the last fair he attended. They checked in with the fair organizers, found their place, and set up the tent and forges. They unloaded everything from the wagon except for the orphans' new armor, which Tridamus said was to stay hidden.

The three orphans took care of the horses while Tridamus set up the workshop and display areas. Once Tridamus was finished, he and Belenus went to get enough wood, charcoal, horse feed, and water to last the next several days. The fair was supposed to last only one week, and Cerridwen knew it would be a busy time. As soon as they returned to the tents, Cerridwen and Tridamus built up the fires in their forges, leaving Belenus, Arawn, and Amaethon with little to do but sit in the tent and relax.

The next morning, Cerridwen rose early and started working on something next to her forge. After several hours, she still wouldn't let anyone see what she was making – including Tridamus. The third time that Arawn tried to look over her shoulder to see what was taking so much of her concentration, she sent him away to find her a walking staff like the one that Belenus sometimes carried.

Arawn found her a long walking staff and brought it back within an hour. Cerridwen covered what she was working on with a large canvas cloth, stood up, and took the walking staff from Arawn, giving him a kiss on the cheek as his reward. She pointed at the tents, letting him know that he needed to leave so she could finish her work.

Cerridwen kept working for the rest of the day and well into the night. The next morning she rose early again and started working. Tridamus had to handle selling her jewelry, blades, and armor, in addition to his own, to the patrons who came by their area.

It was close to midday when she finally stood up and asked Arawn and Amaethon to join her. She was standing next to her traveling forge, and Arawn saw that she was holding the walking staff behind her back to keep the top of the staff hidden. She walked up to Amaethon and handed him the staff, which was roughly as tall as he was. She stepped back to watch the expression on his face.

Fashioned out of copper and bronze was a metal dragon, roughly the size of the one Amaethon had conjured at Danann, grasping the top of the staff and peering over the top. It looked like a real dragon, except for the fact that it was made of burnished metal. Cerridwen smiled as she watched Amaethon's reaction to her gift.

Amaethon was stunned by the workmanship and the level of detail on the dragon. He turned the staff around so he could see the dragon from all sides. He was impressed at how Cerridwen had attached the dragon to the wood; it looked like the dragon's talons were holding it in place. He looked at Cerridwen with a sense of awe.

"This is beautiful," he said finally. "Why did you make this?"

"I thought the Dragon Lord should have a staff befitting his title," she replied with a twinkle in her eyes.

"This is for me?" Amaethon asked, surprised at the gift.

"Of course!" Cerridwen replied. "All I ask is that you let me display it near my dragon jewelry until we leave the fair."

Amaethon nodded. "That's fine with me. Thank you, Cerridwen. I'm touched. I might even grow to like being called Dragon Lord if I have this to walk around with."

Arawn laughed, and Amaethon gave Cerridwen a hug. Belenus and Tridamus came over to see what was going on, and both complimented Cerridwen on her dragon.

"And you did this in only two days?" Tridamus asked.

"It took several days to work it out in my head, but less than two days to actually make it and attach it to the staff."

Tridamus gave her a hug. "I always knew you were my best student, but I'm starting to think I have more to learn from you than you do from me."

Cerridwen quickly wiped away a tear so no one would see it. She was about to say something when a patron walked up to look at her dragon jewelry. She excused herself and walked over to the patron.

As expected, Cerridwen's new jewelry design was very popular and sold out by the next day. At Tridamus' suggestion, Cerridwen declined all commission requests and didn't make any more jewelry to replenish her inventory. Tridamus wanted to sell everything quickly and then leave for Athramail as soon as possible.

Tridamus' inventory sold well, and by the end of the fourth day, he had few items left. Cerridwen's inventory of armor and swords sold out by noon on the third day, leaving her with free time on her hands.

The three orphans decided to explore the fair that afternoon since Tridamus was talking about leaving sometime the next day. Belenus warned them to be careful, and he stayed with Tridamus to wait for Nemausus and Alaunus, who were supposed to arrive shortly.

Cerridwen, Arawn, and Amaethon strolled through the crowds and looked at everything that was for sale at the fair. Most of the items were overpriced and of poor quality, but several artisans were selling beautiful pieces that were well-made. There was one rug weaver in particular who managed to create some amazingly intricate designs by using different colored threads on his loom.

Amaethon was so caught up in watching the rug weaver that he didn't notice Cerridwen and Arawn moving away into the crowd. By the time he finally looked away from the loom, the others had disappeared.

Arawn and Cerridwen were holding hands as they walked. At first, Arawn felt something bothering him slightly, and after a while, he realized that it felt like someone was following them.

""What's wrong?" Cerridwen asked, seeing the concerned look on his face.

"I feel like someone's watching us," Arawn replied.

"I've been feeling it, too, but I figured it was just the crowd." Looking around, she added, "Where's Amaethon?"

Arawn looked around quickly. "I don't see him anywhere. When did you last see him?"

"At the rug weaver."

"Let's go back there and see if we can find him," Arawn suggested.

Cerridwen nodded, and they turned around and headed back to the rug weaver's booth to see if Amaethon were still there.

Arawn scanned the crowd as they walked, looking for Amaethon. At the end of one of the streets near one of the soap makers, he saw a woman with long raven-colored hair talking to two men dressed in black leather. *That looks like Siena, but there's no way she could be here.* He smiled at the thought.

A moment later, she turned around. Arawn's smile changed into a look of surprise and he stopped in his tracks. It was Siena!

"Siena?" he called out.

The woman disappeared into the crowd. "Did you see her?" Arawn asked Cerridwen as he started walking quickly down the street.

"Did I see who?" Cerridwen asked, not knowing what Siena looked like.

"Siena. She's that dancer I told you about who came to Belenus' farm just before we left to find you and Tridamus. She wanted to come with us, but we made her stay on the farm. She disappeared the next day. I think I just saw her in the crowd up ahead."

"Why would she be here? Is she following us?"

"I don't know," Arawn replied. "But I'd like to find out."

Cerridwen tried to keep up with Arawn as he searched the crowd for this mystery woman. They passed several vendors and looked down at least a dozen of the side streets without finding any trace of her. Arawn finally caught sight of her up ahead and started walking even faster.

Arawn had told Cerridwen about Siena on their journey from Tridamus' smithy, and Cerridwen felt a pang of jealousy that Arawn was so intent on finding her. Cerridwen had fallen in love with Arawn, and she knew that Arawn felt the same way, but she wasn't sure she wanted to meet Siena after hearing about the way she acted around Arawn and Amaethon at Belenus' farm.

The crowds were thick that afternoon, and Arawn lost sight of Siena several times. Arawn was so intent on catching up to her that he didn't keep a close watch on where they were and who was around them. He soon realized that he had no idea where they were. After about twenty minutes, Arawn thought he saw Siena turn down one of the streets of vendors on the opposite side of the fairgrounds from where Tridamus' tent was set up. He and Cerridwen followed her.

As they rounded the corner into an alley behind a row of vendors, there was Siena waiting for them.

iena wore the same clothes she had on the day that Arawn and his men rescued her. Her lips were curled into a seductive smile, but the expression on her face was a mixture of contempt and triumph. She pulled back her traveling cloak, showing off her dancer's body and her daggers, which were plainly visible in her vest and gauntlets.

"Siena, what are you doing here?" Arawn asked when he saw her.

"Waiting for you, Arawn," she replied with a sneer. "Who's the redhead?"

Cerridwen felt an immediate dislike for Siena, not just because there was a history there with Arawn, but because Cerridwen instinctively didn't trust the raven-haired woman. She felt uneasy, and she wished that they were back at Tridamus' tent.

"This is Cerridwen," Arawn said, introducing her to Siena.

"Oh, so you're the blacksmith," Siena purred. She looked like a cat that had just cornered a mouse. "Pleased to meet you at last."

"How do you know I'm a blacksmith?" Cerridwen asked, puzzled that Siena would know anything about her at all.

"Oh, I know about all three of you," Siena replied with a tone of superiority in her voice. "I've been following you for weeks. It was nice of you to follow me for a change. And you both ended up right where I wanted you."

Before Cerridwen could respond, several sets of strong arms seized her and Arawn from behind. She struggled, but a blow to the back of her neck knocked her to the ground next to Arawn.

"Tie them up and gag them," she heard Siena command. "And make sure that they're disarmed."

Cerridwen felt her sword belt being loosened and removed as she lost consciousness.

Amaethon pushed his way through the crowds to find Cerridwen and Arawn. After searching for them for a while, he saw them following a dark-haired girl that looked like Siena.

If that's Siena, I need to let Belenus and Tridamus know. But I don't know where they're going. I'd better follow Arawn and Cerridwen in case I can't find them again.

Several minutes later, he turned the same corner as Cerridwen and Arawn had, and he saw Siena standing over the bodies of his two companions. Siena looked up and smiled when she saw Amaethon.

"Glad you could join us," she said softly, looking up at him with wide eyes. "It wouldn't be a party without the Dragon Lord."

Amaethon felt something behind him and turned around quickly. Standing there with a large scar on his face, snarling, was Athanaric.

Realizing that he had walked into a trap, he said, "I see you finally landed, Athanaric."

"No thanks to you, Amaethon," Athanaric said darkly. "I'm surprised you lived through our last encounter. That much energy must have drained you terribly."

"And yet, here I am."

"Yes, here you are… caught in a trap so easily."

"I'm not caught yet," Amaethon said, focusing his mind to draw energy from his surroundings.

"Yes, you are," Athanaric said with a look of satisfaction on his face.

Amaethon felt a blow on the back of his head and his world turned dark. He never felt himself hit the ground.

"Take them to the longboat," Siena ordered once Amaethon was disarmed and bound like the others.

The Étaíne sailors, who had been standing in the shadows, stepped forward and grabbed the three unconscious orphans. The sailors left the orphans' weapons behind and carried the prisoners to a nearby wagon.

The wagon carried Siena, Athanaric, and the three orphans to the river that formed the boundary between the Étaíne and Dunmaine territories. When they reached the river, the prisoners were carried onboard a longboat that waited to take the prisoners and their captors to Ardagh where King Taranus was waiting.

Several hours later, Belenus walked out of the tent and looked around. "Are they back yet?" he asked Tridamus, who was putting his tools and remaining inventory away for the night.

241

"No," Tridamus replied. "I thought they might have gotten lost in the crowd, but there's no crowd left."

"They wouldn't be gone this long unless something happened," Belenus said.

Tridamus nodded. "Perhaps we'd better go looking for them."

The two elders walked in the direction where the three orphans had gone when they first left the tent. Belenus and Tridamus searched the entire fairgrounds quickly, but there was no sign of the orphans.

"Where could they have gone?" Belenus asked.

Tridamus shook his head. "I have no idea," he said, looking down one of the alleyways behind a row of tents.

Tridamus saw three sword belts and two daggers lying on the ground. He ran forward and picked up one of the sword belts, recognizing the design immediately. "This is Cerridwen's scabbard. There's no way they'd go anywhere without their weapons."

"Could they have been carried off?"

"Yes, but where?"

Suddenly, Belenus and Tridamus heard a voice in their minds. *"Where is everyone?"* It was the voice of Nemausus.

"Cerridwen, Arawn, and Amaethon are missing," Belenus said. *"Are you here at the fair?"*

"Yes, we're both here at your tents."

"We'll be right there," Tridamus said, picking up the sword belts and daggers.

When they got back to the tents, Tridamus and Belenus saw Nemausus and Alaunus waiting for them. They went inside the main tent to talk.

"They went exploring and never came back," Tridamus said. "We searched everywhere, but we couldn't find them. We had just found their weapons on the ground when you called to us."

"Take my hand," Alaunus said.

The four joined hands, and Alaunus began concentrating intently. No one spoke. Alaunus looked up and said, "They've been taken by Étaínes."

"I knew Mider was up to something," Nemausus said angrily. "What do we do?"

"There's nothing we can do, directly," Alaunus said. "If we enter Étaíne territory, Mider will know instantly, and it'll force him into doing things he must not do. This is one of the tasks appointed to the three to prove their worthiness. But we can watch, and we can listen. There may even come a moment when we must speak, but we cannot act without changing the way things need to play out."

Arawn woke up to the sound of a drum beating. At first, he thought it was the pounding in his head. But when he opened his eyes, he saw a large man sitting at the far end of the deck, beating a drum to keep the rhythm of the rowers. The man's long blonde hair and mustache identified him as an Étaíne.

We must be on an Étaíne longboat.

He tried to move, but someone had tied his arms behind his back with ropes. He could taste the gag in his mouth. He swung his legs forward and rolled into a sitting position to look around.

The longboat was quite large. It had a raised deck in the center that went the entire length of the vessel, and an exposed lower deck along the sides of the longboat where the rowers sat. There was a mast with a furled sail in the center of the raised deck. There were intricate carvings of a bear snarling in the wind on both the prow and the stern of the longboat.

From the shape of the longboat, Arawn assumed that it could travel forward or backwards equally well. Arawn could tell that they were heading into the wind, which would make the sail useless. He looked to the north and saw nothing but plains. He guessed it must be part of the Dunmaine tribe's territory.

Looking south alongside the riverbank, he saw the Valdunass Mountains rising like great teeth into the clouds. The size of the mountain range was mesmerizing. He stared at them for a minute until he remembered where he was. He looked around for his companions.

Cerridwen lay unconscious next to him, but she didn't seem to be hurt. Amaethon lay on the deck behind Arawn but was facing away. Looking toward the rear of the longboat, Arawn saw Siena talking to a tall figure dressed in black with a huge scar on his face. She saw that Arawn was awake, and she motioned for the other man to follow her.

"I see you're awake. Good," she said, removing his gag. "We'll be arriving soon enough, and I want you to enjoy your first, and last, view of Étaíne territory."

"You're taking us to Ardagh?" Arawn asked, moving his jaw around to relieve some of the stiffness caused by the gag.

Siena nodded. "King Taranus wants to see you, and so does Mider."

Arawn stared at her for a moment. "So I'm guessing it was part of your plan for me to find you in the forest and bring you to Belenus' farm."

"Very good, Arawn. You're not as dumb as you look. Yes, I made sure that you found me. I was there to get close to you. After those stupid Chulainns kept messing everything up, Taranus decided that a more subtle approach was needed to get to you. Amaethon's arrival made it all the sweeter until you decided to leave without me. That's when things went from bad to worse."

Siena shook her head and looked angry. "I finally caught up to you in time to watch that dragon kill most of our forces. The raid on the smithy turned out to be a complete disaster. Our ships kept sinking on the river after you left the smithy. And we won't even discuss the ambush on the road to Danann. It took a while to discover that you'd be at the fair, but once we did, I sent for Athanaric here, and that's where we set our little trap. It worked rather well, don't you think?"

Arawn just glared at her.

"Now don't be upset," she said, leaning forward with a wicked look in her eyes. "You should feel honored that anyone cares about you enough to go to such lengths to find you and keep you from getting any older. Frankly, I'd be flattered if I were you."

"Forgive me if I don't feel the same way," Arawn said with as much contempt as he could put into his voice.

"It doesn't really matter anyway," she said, getting to her feet. "You never had any chance of succeeding. Our armies can't be defeated. Even if you had the Kingstone, we'd still destroy your forces. Mider will be the god of Alastríona. You'll never become king, and neither will your friend over there," she said, pointing to Amaethon.

Arawn looked back at Amaethon and saw him move slightly. Arawn heard the man Siena called Athanaric speaking.

"Don't try it, Amaethon. I can sense you every time you try something. If you make any attempts to use magic of any kind, you'll be killed immediately. Understand?"

Amaethon nodded.

"Good. I think I'll keep your gag in place, just in case."

Arawn watched as Athanaric walked to the rear of the longboat. As he looked back at Siena, she was leaning over Cerridwen, removing her gag.

"Who would have ever thought that one of the orphans was a girl... and a blacksmith?" she said. Standing up, she looked at Arawn and said, "And who'd have thought that you two would have gotten so close so quickly? Pity, really. Like you, she has to die, and I'm sure Taranus will make it very unpleasant for her before he finally gives the order to kill her. I think I'll ask him to let me do it."

Siena walked back to stand next to Athanaric, and Arawn felt rage boiling up inside of him. A moment later, he heard a voice inside his head. It was Belenus!

"Arawn, can you hear me?"

"Yes, sir. But how?" he answered in his mind.

"That's not important right now. Where are you? Is anyone injured?"

"We're tied up on a longboat heading for Ardagh, but I'm fine and I think Amaethon is, too. Cerridwen is still unconscious, though."

"What do they want with you?"

"King Taranus and Mider want to see us, and then we're to be killed," Arawn said silently in his mind.

"That's what we feared," Belenus said. *"There may be a moment when you're in the presence of Mider when something strange will happen."*

"What?"

"There's someone who will need to say something directly to Mider and will do it through you. Just relax and let it happen. It'll be your voice, but someone else's words. I wanted to let you know so you wouldn't be shocked when it happened."

"Whose words will they be?" Arawn asked.

"Airmid's."

Siena Captures Arawn and Cerridwen at the Fair

CHAPTER 41

erridwen woke up feeling disoriented. The back of her neck hurt, and she couldn't move. She opened her eyes and saw Arawn nearby. She noticed his hands tied behind his back like hers were, but he seemed to be uninjured. He had a strange look on his face, and Cerridwen wondered what was going on.

After a couple of minutes, she saw Arawn shake his head and look at her. She managed a weak smile, and Arawn smiled back and moved closer to her.

"Are you hurt?" he whispered.

"Not too badly. Getting captured and tied up is starting to become a habit, though. What happened?"

"We were ambushed by Étaíne sailors. We're on one of their longboats heading for Ardagh."

He motioned with his head toward Amaethon and continued. "They're watching Amaethon closely to see if he tries to use magic. They say they'll kill him the instant he does."

"How will they know?"

"See that tall guy dressed in black at the back of the boat? His name is Athanaric, and he's a sorcerer, too. Amaethon told me about him. He killed Amaethon's parents and has been watching Amaethon for years. Amaethon told me that Athanaric tried to kill him just before he and Nemausus came to Belenus' farm."

"Arawn, what's going to happen to us?"

"They're taking us to see King Taranus and Mider. After that, we're supposed to be killed so Mider can be the god of Alastríona."

Arawn heard Cerridwen gasp. He leaned closer to her and whispered in her ear, telling her about his conversation with Belenus. When he was done, she looked at him.

"Airmid is going to speak to Mider through you?"

Arawn nodded.

"Then they're trying to help us?"

"I think so, but I don't really understand it. I still don't know how it's possible. All I know is that we need to keep a close watch for any chance to escape. I think the meeting with Mider has to happen, but after that we need to try to get away."

Cerridwen nodded. She looked toward the rear of the boat and saw Siena. Arawn had talked about her, but seeing her helped Cerridwen understand what he had been describing. She was beautiful and moved like she was dancing all the time, but Cerridwen could tell that she was dangerous and would be a fierce opponent in a fight.

Amaethon, who was watching Athanaric closely, hoped that the older sorcerer wouldn't detect that he was drawing energy from all around. He took a little at a time from the sailors, from the wind, from the water, and from anything else he could without being noticed. He knew that he'd need a tremendous amount of energy if he were going to help the others escape from Taranus and Mider.

While Siena was talking to Arawn, Amaethon heard Nemausus speaking to him in his mind. They talked for several minutes until Athanaric walked over to warn him. It made him feel better knowing that his master was still watching over him and the others.

Cerridwen had just managed to sit up when she heard Tridamus' voice inside her head. *"Cerridwen, it's Tridamus. Don't try to speak; just listen. Whatever happens when you're in the presence of Mider, follow Arawn's lead. He knows what to do. After that, look for any opportunity to escape. We'll be waiting at the ferry across the river from Athramail."*

Cerridwen felt less afraid, knowing that Arawn was with her and was part of something that Tridamus and Belenus had planned. She whispered to him what Tridamus had told her. After that, the two sat in silence as the longboat continued its voyage to Ardagh.

The longboat approached a fork in the river and turned south onto a branch that flowed through the western pass of the Valdunass Mountains before emptying into a large lake. Nestled at the base of the mountains on the eastern banks of the lake was the city of Ardagh.

The longboat approached the city three days after the trio had been captured. Arawn saw a large fleet of ships beached along the shore or tied up on docks that jutted out from the shore into the lake. Some of the ships were the size of the longboat that had brought the captives from the fair, but some were much larger.

Arawn saw several warehouses along the wharf and remembered that the Étaínes were explorers who transported goods across the various rivers and waterways that crisscrossed the territories of the tribes.

The longboat approached one of the docks near the center of the wharf. When it was almost to the dock, the rowers lifted their oars out of the water and pulled them in so they wouldn't hit the timbers of the dock. The longboat coasted into position next to the dock, and sailors at both ends of the longboat tossed ropes to the men waiting on the dock to tie the boat into position.

Some of the sailors came up on the deck and grabbed Arawn, Cerridwen, and Amaethon roughly. The sailors took the orphans off the boat and marched them along the dock under heavy guard. At the end of the dock, a wagon with a large iron cage was waiting. The sailors pushed the orphans into the cage and locked the cage door. The wagon drove through the streets of Ardagh toward the palace.

The city of Ardagh jutted out from the mountain toward the lake. The palace sat in the center of the city against the side of the mountain and next to the temple of Mider.

The city had none of the beauty of Danann. It was a dark and plain city with little architectural style. It looked more like a military garrison than a capital city, and it was evident that the Étaíne tribesmen preferred their ships to the land.

The residents of the city stared out their windows at the prisoners. Bringing captives through the city in a cage was the Étaíne way of inflicting the maximum humiliation on prisoners. The purpose was to make prisoners feel like caged animals.

The wagon passed through a number of gates on its way to the palace, and Arawn found the layout of the city fascinating. He had never heard of a city that used giant gates to separate the sections of the city, and he was equally surprised to see so many soldiers guarding each of the gates. He couldn't tell whether King Taranus was taking these precautions because the prisoners were the orphans of the prophecy, if the city were preparing for war, or if this were normal for the Étaíne capital.

After a while, the wagon finally reached the palace. The wagon stopped, and soldiers opened the cage and ordered the prisoners to climb down one at a time. This wasn't easy to do with their hands tied behind their backs, and Cerridwen fell to the ground when it was her turn. Someone picked her up roughly, and soldiers carrying large spears prodded the three orphans up the stairs to the palace.

The soldiers led the orphans around the outer ring of the palace to a heavily guarded hallway. The bonds around their hands were untied, and

Arawn, Cerridwen, and Amaethon were taken to separate rooms that locked from the outside. They heard the guards outside and knew that they weren't going anywhere anytime soon. The rooms had no windows and only the one door, so there was no way to escape.

Amaethon thought about using magic to blow open his door, but he knew that something was supposed to happen with Arawn in the presence of Mider, so he decided to wait. There was always time to use magic later when the opportunity presented itself.

The next day, guards came to take them to see the king. The guards tied their hands and led them through many corridors before reaching a large chamber. The guards pushed them through the entrance of the chamber and led them to the center of the room. At the far end, sitting on an oversized chair on the dais, was King Taranus.

CHAPTER 42

aranus was tall like most men of his tribe. He had long blonde hair and an equally long mustache and beard – braided on the ends to keep it in place. He was dressed like a sailor, but he wore an armor chest piece and an ornate crown with fish worked into the design. He wore black trousers and boots, and he wore a short cape of deep blue attached to the armor at the shoulders.

"You took your time getting here," he taunted the prisoners as they entered the chamber.

"Then next time send stronger men and a faster boat," Arawn countered. He was angry at the man on the throne for trying to interfere with the fulfillment of the prophecy and for the way he, Cerridwen, and Amaethon had been treated since being taken prisoner.

King Taranus turned red in the face and slammed his hands on the arms of his throne as he jumped to his feet. "Who do you think you are, you pathetic little farmhand?" he shouted.

"I know I'm one of the three orphans that the Ruler of the World will be selected from according to the prophecy. Just who do you think *you* are? You look like an overdressed fisherman to me."

Arawn noticed that the faces of the soldiers in the great hall were turning either pale or red. Even Siena and Athanaric looked visibly shocked. Evidently, they had never heard someone dare to speak to their king in that way before. King Taranus, however, looked like someone was strangling him. He could barely speak, and his eyes were bugging out from the insult Arawn had just given him.

Both Cerridwen and Amaethon were surprised at how Arawn was behaving. Normally, he was polite to people. But for some reason, he was acting out of character, and they wondered how the king would continue to react.

Arawn was equally surprised at his own behavior. He had been raised to treat all people with respect, but he viewed Taranus as an enemy, and he knew taunting was often an effective way to get the enemy to expose his weaknesses. Apparently, Taranus' weakness was pride, which Arawn had wounded by not acknowledging the king's superiority or acting afraid.

"Do you know how easy it would be for me to kill you?" Taranus managed to ask once he finally got the words out.

"Then get on with it," Arawn countered, "but stop wasting my time. We have work to do. Either let us go or end it. But stop your ridiculous babbling as if I'm supposed to be impressed. I'm not frightened of you or your god."

The large iron doors that separated the great hall from the temple of Mider banged open, and the sound caused everyone in the chamber to jump. A glowing figure, twice the height of a man, strode into the room, and Arawn realized he was in the presence of one of the gods.

"So you're not afraid of me?" Mider's voice boomed, causing the floor to shake and the lights suspended from the ceiling to sway.

"Why should I fear one of the disobedient ones?" Arawn shouted. "It's you who should be afraid."

"And yet you're my prisoner," Mider said with a dangerous smile.

"For now, but your attempts to stop us will fail. The prophecy doesn't say what *may* happen, it says what *will* happen. You can't stop it."

"And if I kill you now, what happens to your precious prophecy then?" Mider said, taking a step forward.

What happened next was something that Cerridwen would never forget. Mider approached Arawn with his fists clenched to crush Arawn and kill him, but suddenly Arawn began to glow with a white light that filled the chamber. Arawn looked like he was in a trance, but a voice as booming as Mider's was coming from his mouth.

"So this is how 'Mider the Terrible' shows his followers that he's omnipotent? By adding murder to disobedience? You shall not kill this human, Mider. He and his companions are under my protection."

"Airmid? How dare you speak to me!"

"I'll dare to do a lot more than this before the end, Mider."

"This is my domain, Airmid. I do as I will here, and you can't stop me."

"And what does this teach your followers, Mider? That the gods will destroy anyone who opposes them? That you can destroy what was never intended to be destroyed regardless of the consequences? That you'll continue to try to control and manipulate what was never yours to possess in the first place? To what end, Mider? The destruction of everything we created? You're a fool, Mider, and the only one who can't see that is you."

"Tell your followers to prepare for battle, Airmid. My forces will wipe the field with you, and I'll rule here long after man has forgotten all about you. You can't win this war."

"They're not my followers, Mider. They follow Elohim, and so should you. Elohim created you, but not so you could stay here on Alastríona and be the most high god. You have a task to perform, and it's time you started doing it again. Is war what you honestly think the prophecy is all about? It's not about winning a war; it's about saving creation. If you ever bothered to try to understand the nature of the universe, you'd understand the extent of your crime. But you're too stubborn, too blind, and too foolish to know that what hangs in the balance isn't who wins and who loses, but whether the universe itself survives the choice that you have to make."

"The prophecy will fail, Airmid. The orphans will die, and all your plotting and interference will have been for nothing."

"If the prophecy fails, so will you, Mider. Elohim has told you, even though you don't listen. If you don't learn to be obedient, you condemn everything you hold dear."

"It won't come to that, Airmid. Elohim will never let it come to that."

"Elohim will do as Elohim has promised, Mider. If the plan fails, so does creation, and Elohim will just start over. If that happens, do you actually think Elohim will keep you, knowing that you're nothing more than an ungrateful, disobedient child? Everything you love will be gone and so will you."

"That means you'll be gone too, Airmid."

"I know that, Mider. I know the price and the consequence of my failure. Do you know the price and the consequence of your success? When we meet at the place where the Kingstone is hidden, as was foretold, the twelve of us will have a choice to make. The meeting won't be a battle between our armies, but between us. We must choose to obey Elohim and leave this world. The universe hangs in the balance – trapped between your obedience and your arrogance. Be prepared to make your choice, Mider, but make sure it's the right choice. Either way, it's Elohim who will win, not you."

The light faded from around Arawn. Airmid was gone, but the effect that the confrontation had on the Étaíne soldiers in the room and their king lasted much longer.

Arawn stood in front of Mider without fear. He had felt the presence of Airmid inside of him, and he knew that Airmid's protection remained around him and his companions.

Mider stared at Arawn for several minutes, lost in thought. Then he vanished from sight as he left the Étaíne capital to confer with the other disobedient gods about what just happened.

King Taranus, jolted by the sudden disappearance of his god, looked around the room at his soldiers. "Take the prisoners to the dungeon," he shouted, returning to his seat on the throne.

As the prisoners were ushered from the chamber, the king turned to Athanaric and Siena and said, "Unless Mider says otherwise, kill them at dawn."

CHAPTER 43

he three orphans were taken deep into the mountain to the dungeons where the king's prisoners were locked away. Cerridwen's hands were untied as they reached the first empty cell. One of the guards pushed her in and locked the door behind her. Two of the guards returned to the palace, and five continued on with Arawn and Amaethon.

The guards untied Amaethon's hands and locked him in the second empty cell they reached after they rounded a corner. Two more guards returned to the palace, leaving three to guard Arawn and take him to his cell.

Arawn and the remaining guards walked to the far end of the hallway to the third empty cell. His guards seemed to be having a hard time untying his hands. They were clearly terrified of Arawn after what had happened in the great hall, and they were nervous to be anywhere near him.

Arawn studied his guards carefully. Two of the guards carried spears, but they were standing several feet away. The third had leaned his spear against the wall next to the cell door and used a long dagger to saw through the bindings around Arawn's hands.

Arawn felt the bindings fall from his hands, and in a quick motion, he twisted, grabbed the dagger from the guard's hands, and spun the guard around so he stood between Arawn and the other two guards.

"Drop your spears," he ordered, holding the dagger against the throat of the guard with one hand while reaching for the spear against the wall with his other hand.

The other two guards hesitated, and Arawn threw the spear at the guard on the left, piercing his heart and killing him instantly.

"Drop it," he said to the guard on the right.

The guard dropped his spear and held out his hands as a sign of surrender. Arawn motioned for the guard to get into the open cell. Arawn pushed the other guard into the cell and quickly closed the door on them both. The keys were in the cell door, and he locked the two guards in. He bent down to pick up the spear that the guard left on the floor and the dagger that the dead guard was wearing, took the keys from the lock, and ran back to free Cerridwen and Amaethon.

Amaethon stood in the center of his cell and tried to keep control of the energy that he had been gathering for the past several days. Being in the presence of a god gave him the chance to draw energy directly from Mider, and Amaethon was glad that Airmid had kept Mider and Athanaric distracted enough not to notice.

Amaethon focused his mind on the lock of his cell door. He heard someone approaching, and from the sound of keys jingling, he assumed it was the guards coming back from Arawn's cell. He pushed with his mind to unlock the cell door, but he couldn't control the energy, and the entire door blew off the hinges and crashed into the wall on the other side of the corridor, bursting into pieces and cracking the stone walls.

When the dust settled, he saw Arawn standing there holding the keys to the cells.

"What was that?" Arawn demanded in a state of shock. The door had missed his head by inches.

"Sorry. I overdid it."

"Really? That's your excuse? You overdid it?"

"Do you want to rescue Cerridwen, or do you want to yell at me some more?" Amaethon asked, stepping out of the cell into the corridor.

"Let's rescue Cerridwen," Arawn said, coming to his senses. "We can yell later."

As they crept toward Cerridwen's cell, Amaethon explained the trouble he was having. "I've absorbed enough energy to bring down the mountain on the whole city. It's a little hard to control right now."

Arawn put his hand on Amaethon's shoulder and nodded but said nothing. They reached the turn that led to Cerridwen's cell, and Arawn peered carefully around the corner to make sure that there were no guards nearby. Seeing none, he ran forward and stopped at Cerridwen's cell door.

"Cerridwen," he whispered. "Are you in there?"

"Arawn? Yes I'm here," she answered.

Arawn unlocked the door and swung it open. Cerridwen ran out and hugged him around his neck, giving him several kisses on his cheek.

Arawn handed Cerridwen the dagger but kept the spear. "We need to find some weapons and a way out. And we need to find some horses."

Arawn led the way back to the palace. When they reached the large door that separated the palace from the cells, Arawn heard the voices of guards on the other side. He was about to unlock the door when Amaethon grabbed his shoulder and motioned for him to take Cerridwen and get behind him.

Amaethon focused his energy on the door, and a moment later, it blew off its hinges, falling on top of the guards in the next room. Arawn ran into the room, but the guards were all either dead or knocked senseless. He unfastened the sword belts of three of them and handed two of the weapons to Amaethon and Cerridwen. The three tightened their captured sword belts and continued walking carefully through the palace's maze of corridors, grateful to be armed. Arawn still held the spear, but Cerridwen had drawn her sword so she now had a blade in each hand.

They reached a point where two corridors crossed each other. Arawn looked down the corridor to the left and saw no one. He looked to the right and found himself face-to-face with a squad of six guards who were on patrol.

It took the guards a moment to realize who they were seeing, but before they could react, Arawn thrust his spear into the first guard and drew his sword to attack the second one. Cerridwen, seeing Arawn draw his sword, pushed Amaethon against the wall and motioned for him to stay where he was. She ran forward with her sword and dagger raised for attack.

The guards fell back and tried to regroup and defend themselves, but Arawn and Cerridwen had caught them unprepared. Soon the six guards were lying on the floor in a growing pool of blood. Arawn and Cerridwen wiped off their sword blades on two of the guards' tunics. Arawn retrieved his spear as Cerridwen motioned for Amaethon to follow. The three orphans moved on, looking for a way out of the palace.

There were two more skirmishes as the trio crossed paths with some of the palace guards, but these were over quickly. The guards were still frightened of Arawn after the incident with Mider in the great hall, and seeing him charging them with a spear made them want to run away in terror. Cerridwen helped make sure that none escaped to raise the alarm.

Arawn and Cerridwen had just finished wiping down their blades from the last skirmish when they heard more guards approaching.

Cerridwen grabbed Amaethon, and the trio started running in the opposite direction. The sound behind them faded, but when they approached a bend in the corridor, Arawn heard more voices in front of them.

He motioned for the others to be quiet and move against the wall. He carefully peered around the corner. There were fifteen guards lining the corridor that led into the great hall. He pulled back and told the others what he had seen.

"What do we do?" Cerridwen asked. "I'm not sure that we can get past fifteen guards."

"And we can't go back the way we came," Arawn pointed out. "This palace is like a maze. We could get lost here for weeks if we can't find a way out. We need to get to the great hall somehow."

"I'll take care of it," Amaethon said.

"Are you sure?" Cerridwen asked.

Amaethon nodded. "It might be loud though. I'll try to be quiet, but I'm still having problems controlling things right now."

Cerridwen nodded. Amaethon focused the energy and stepped into the corridor. Before the guards saw him, an unseen force hurled them back against the wall. Hitting the wall knocked most of the guards unconscious, but the necks of some of the guards were snapped on impact. The guards dropped their spears with a loud clatter that echoed through the hallway.

The trio didn't wait to see if anyone heard the sound. They ran past the fallen guards to the doors of the great hall.

Arawn stopped just outside the doors and cracked one of the doors open just enough to peer inside. He saw there were still guards in the room, even though King Taranus and Mider had long since left. Some of the guards had heard the noise in the corridor and were coming closer to investigate.

"Guards coming," Arawn whispered as he stepped back away from the door to keep the approaching guards from seeing him.

"What do we do?" Cerridwen asked.

Arawn drew his sword. "We fight our way out of here."

Cerridwen looked at Amaethon. "Can you fight?"

"I don't know. I'm worried that I might lose control and bring the palace down on top of us."

"Stay against the walls then," Arawn said. "We'll take care of the guards. Try to keep the energy under control until you know you need to use it."

Amaethon nodded, grateful that his companions understood.

Cerridwen tucked the dagger into her belt and ran over to the closest of the guards that Amaethon had slammed against the wall. She bent down and grabbed the guard's sword before rejoining her companions. Arawn looked over at her, and she nodded to him. She was ready for a fight.

Just as the guards reached the doorway, Arawn and Cerridwen kicked the doors open and ran inside.

CHAPTER 44

The guards were startled at the sound and even more startled to see Arawn and Cerridwen charging at them through the doors. Several fell quickly, and the rest moved back and held their spears at the ready. When the other guards around the room saw what was happening, they ran toward the trio. Arawn knew that getting through the great hall wouldn't be easy.

Arawn threw his spear at the guard closest to him and attacked the guards approaching from his right. Cerridwen ran for the guards approaching her, which gave Amaethon time to move to the wall and start edging around the room to the left. Amaethon frequently glanced toward Arawn and Cerridwen to see if they needed any help while he looked for a way that they could escape the great hall.

The guards, unable to gain the advantage against Arawn and Cerridwen, threw down their spears and drew their swords. Arawn killed the first two guards with little effort, but four more guards tried to surround him. He kept moving around to the right to keep them from getting behind him as he fought as hard as he could.

Cerridwen killed three guards quickly, forcing the other guards to fall back and try to move around her. Seeing one guard approaching her blind side, she dropped one of her swords, drew the dagger from her belt, and threw it at him. She quickly reached down and retrieved her other sword as the guard fell forward – the dagger sticking out of his chest. She heard the dagger hilt hit the floor and knew that the impact had driven the blade even deeper into the dying guard.

She changed her stance, crouching slightly so she could react to the next attack. "Who's next?" she taunted.

Two guards attacked her from opposite directions, but she fought them off. She killed one of them and spun around to attack the second one, catching him by surprise. A moment later, the second guard lay dead at her feet. Another squad of guards rushed her, but they soon realized that they were losing too many men trying to disarm her.

The squad leader reached down and picked up one of the fallen spears. When she was distracted by one of the other guards, he threw it at her exposed back.

"Cerridwen, drop!" Amaethon shouted when he saw the spear flying toward her. He dared not try to use magic to deflect it in case he accidently threw Cerridwen across the room with it.

Cerridwen heard Amaethon's warning and immediately dropped to the floor. The spear flew over her head and clattered against the floor across the great hall. She leapt to her feet, spun around, and threw one of her swords at the squad leader. It hit him in the stomach, and he fell back, looking shocked at the blood pouring from his wound. A moment later, he was on the floor, dying slowly as the blood pooled all around him.

Cerridwen picked up another sword from a fallen guard and turned to face the remaining guards in the squad. She rushed the survivors but saw a dagger flash past her face, narrowly missing her. Turning, she saw Siena entering the great hall with an escort of soldiers. The raven-haired killer was pulling her daggers out from her vest and gauntlets. The soldiers moved toward Amaethon, and Cerridwen moved to put herself between them and her friend.

Arawn saw Siena enter the room with the soldiers and watched Cerridwen move to protect Amaethon. Another escort of soldiers entered the great hall from behind the dais, and Arawn turned to deal with this latest threat, leaving Cerridwen and Amaethon to handle Siena and the other soldiers.

Before Cerridwen reached Amaethon, Siena threw several of her daggers in quick succession. Cerridwen dropped and rolled out of the way as the daggers flew harmlessly past her. Siena, frustrated at missing her foe, moved closer and threw several more. Cerridwen dove out of the way of those as well. She did a summersault when she landed and sprung back to her feet with both swords at the ready.

Siena nodded in appreciation of the maneuver. She stepped forward and took two swords from the guards that Cerridwen had already killed. She straightened up, facing Cerridwen. She gave Cerridwen a salute with the swords, and in the flash of an eye, she attacked.

Siena's movements as she attacked looked more like a dance than any traditional fighting style. She whirled around in circles, and her blades flashed past Cerridwen at blinding speeds.

Cerridwen watched her opponent, trying to learn her weaknesses. After a moment, she thought of a way to neutralize Siena's movements. She counter-attacked, and soon the two women were fighting as equals across the floor of the great hall.

Siena was surprised at how well Cerridwen fought. She didn't know many people who fought with two swords, and none of them were women. After a couple of minutes, she wondered if she had made the right decision by attacking her alone. She slashed at Cerridwen and tried to stab her several times, but Cerridwen managed to move out of the way each time. Cerridwen cut Siena near her left shoulder, sending the raven-haired assassin into a rage.

"What makes you think you can beat me?" Siena snarled as she spun around and aimed her sword at Cerridwen's head.

"Because I'm better than you," Cerridwen answered as she parried Siena's stroke and cut the raven-haired dancer's upper thigh with her other sword.

Siena was no longer fighting like a dancer. Her shoulder and leg were bleeding, but it was her pride that was injured the most. She fought like a wild animal, snarling with each failed thrust or parried cut.

Cerridwen knew from her teachers never to get angry while fighting. "It blinds you to opportunity," William had said. Cerridwen kept herself calm as she and Siena continued fighting around the room.

"You can't win," Siena spat at Cerridwen, wondering if she believed the words coming out of her own mouth.

"Yes, I can," Cerridwen replied coldly.

"What makes you think that?"

"Because, unlike you, I have something worth fighting for."

"What, Arawn?" Siena sneered. "He's just a foolish little boy."

"You're wrong, but he's not the only thing that keeps me going," Cerridwen answered.

"Amaethon, too," Siena asked. "My, you have been busy, haven't you?"

"No, not Amaethon."

"What else could you have to keep you going?"

"Alastríona."

"Ha!" Siena shouted as she renewed her attack.

Cerridwen fought well, but after a while she began to tire. Siena was an accomplished swordsman, and Cerridwen couldn't find the opening she needed to gain the advantage. They were getting closer to the guard that Arawn killed with his spear, and Cerridwen made a quick decision. She pressed Siena back, getting closer to the spear sticking out the fallen guard's chest.

When Siena's foot caught the edge of the spear, Cerridwen saw her chance. Using both of her swords, she forced Siena's swords upward, leaving Siena's chest exposed. Using one sword to keep Siena's swords out of the way, she thrust with her other sword, running Siena through her chest. She watched Siena collapse on the floor with a look of complete surprise on her face.

"Yes, I can," Cerridwen said to Siena as she pulled the sword from the raven-haired assassin's chest.

Cerridwen was breathing heavily as she watched Siena die, but the sound of metal clashing made her forget how tired she was. She felt the floor lurch slightly, and she glanced over at Amaethon. She heard a loud crack as he obliterated the last of the soldiers that had come into the great hall with Siena. Looking around, she saw Arawn fighting three soldiers carrying battle-axes, and she saw more soldiers racing to get behind him. She looked back at Amaethon to make sure he was okay, and he motioned for her to help Arawn. She nodded and ran forward, taking her place at his back as the other soldiers attacked.

The two were surrounded, but that didn't give the soldiers an advantage. Cerridwen and Arawn had fought back-to-back before, and soon the number of attacking soldiers had decreased substantially.

Amaethon had almost reached the main entrance of the great hall when the doors flew open. Athanaric strode into the chamber and looked around. He saw Amaethon and faced him with an evil smile on his face.

Amaethon stopped and stared at Athanaric. The energy that Amaethon had been storing was getting harder to control because of the soldiers he had just fought. He was worried that he might destroy the entire city if he had to fight a well-trained sorcerer like Athanaric.

"Let's end this game," Athanaric said to Amaethon as he unleashed his opening attack. The glass windows behind Amaethon shattered, and the shards few directly at the young sorcerer.

Amaethon released some of the energy that he had been storing, and the shards vaporized before they hit. But Amaethon released too much energy and parts of the walls of the great hall vaporized as well.

Athanaric looked stunned as the walls and the doors around the entrance vanished from sight. Mider had been his teacher, but he had never seen so much power released so casually before. For the first time, he actually felt afraid of the young sorcerer standing in front of him.

He attacked again, and in a moment, Amaethon was engulfed in fire. Athanaric smiled, but the smile faded when the fire grew dark. A moment later, fire flew out of Amaethon in all directions, catching the remaining walls of the great hall on fire, along with the ceiling, the dais, and parts of the floor.

The four surviving soldiers attacking Arawn and Cerridwen fled from the chamber when they saw the fire. Amaethon moved between his companions and Athanaric, and attacked. Unable to keep the energy under control, Amaethon released more energy into the attack than he planned.

Athanaric was hurled up in an arc through the burning ceiling, through the roof of the palace, and through the rock face of the mountains, coming to a stop almost two thirds of the way to the other side of the mountain peak overlooking the palace. The sudden release of energy as his body moved through the rock caused the tunnel he made to collapse, crushing Athanaric to death and triggering an earthquake that shook the city down to its foundations. As he fought to keep his balance on the buckling chamber floor, Amaethon felt Athanaric's life force extinguish and knew that he was dead.

Arawn grabbed Cerridwen by the arm and started running toward Amaethon, who was clearly tired. The trio ran out of the burning hall and through the long corridors to the palace entrance. When they reached the entrance, mounted guards were at the base of the stairs waiting for them.

Arawn leaped down the stairs and pulled one of the guards to the ground. He stabbed the guard and swung himself up onto the back of the horse. He attacked the other guards ferociously, taking them completely by surprise.

Cerridwen ran down the stairs and joined in the attack. Soon the guards were dead. Arawn and Cerridwen helped Amaethon mount one of the horses. Arawn secured two more horses, and soon the trio was riding away from the palace.

The sound of the energy that Amaethon released when he pushed Athanaric into the mountain echoed throughout the city. Guards from all around rushed to close all of the city gates so no one could escape.

As the trio approached the first closed gate, Amaethon focused his energy. The gate and the stone arch around it were instantly obliterated, killing or wounding most of the guards nearby. The trio rode through the debris and continued making their way through the city. Amaethon did the same with each of the gates they encountered, destroying them and sending the guards running for cover as the debris flew in all directions.

When the trio reached the main gates, Amaethon released enough energy to take out the gates and the two watchtowers on either side, leaving a huge hole in the outer wall of the city.

As the trio exited the city and rode toward the wharf, Amaethon released a tremendous amount of energy aimed at the fleet anchored in front of them. He turned back to face the city as the docks and the ships on the water disintegrated and disappeared below the surface of the lake. He then released the rest of his pent-up energy and directed it toward the palace and the temple of Mider. The mountain shook, and one entire face of the mountain broke free and slid down the slope toward the palace.

The trio turned the horses northward toward Athramail to escape alongside the banks of the river that their captors had used to bring them to Ardagh. The trio circled the lake, heading for the river beyond as the landslide struck the palace and buried it under tons of rock and dirt.

CHAPTER 45

I t was a long and difficult journey traveling away from the ruins of Ardagh. Arawn, Cerridwen, and Amaethon's trek to the ferry across from Athramail would take them through the mountain pass leading north from Ardagh to the river fork, and then east along the southern bank of the river to the ferry where Belenus, Tridamus, Nemausus, and Alaunus were waiting for them.

Amaethon, exhausted from controlling and releasing the energy he had been storing, could barely remain conscious as the trio galloped away from the Étaínes' capital city. They had to stop shortly after leaving the city because Amaethon fell off his horse. Cerridwen and Arawn looped their sword belts underneath Amaethon's saddle, and after helping him mount the horse, they cinched the belts around his upper legs to hold him in place so he wouldn't fall off again.

They left the city without any food, supplies, or traveling clothes. The air was chilly during the day and cold at night as the winds howled through the mountain pass and blew snow off the peaks above.

On the second day of their journey, they came upon a squad of horsemen who were protecting the pass. Arawn knew that they couldn't have heard about the destruction of the palace yet, so he decided to take a more subtle approach.

"Follow my lead," he whispered to Cerridwen as they approached the horsemen.

"State your business," the leader of the horsemen said when the trio stopped in front of him.

"We need your help," Arawn said. "We're heading to the river fork to get passage on one of the boats beached up there, but we ran out of our supplies too quickly. We were traveling to Sétanta, the capital of the Chulainn territory, but my friend has taken ill. I don't think he'll make it to the river fork, let alone to Sétanta, if we don't get some supplies and some blankets to keep him warm. Is there anything you can do to help us?"

The leader of the horsemen looked at Amaethon and could see that the young man was unwell. Having no reason to doubt Arawn's story, he said, "Of course. We have several blankets we can spare, and we can let you have enough supplies to get you to the river fork. You shouldn't have a long wait there for a boat that can take you to Sétanta."

"Thank you, sir," Arawn said. "You've probably saved my friend's life."

"Don't mention it," the leader of the horsemen said as his men gave the trio the needed supplies and nine spare blankets. "Do you need an escort?"

Arawn shook his head. "Thank you for the offer, but you've been more than helpful already. We don't wish to inconvenience you any further."

"Very well," the leader said. "I hope your friend recovers soon. May your journey be safe!"

The trio rode north, leaving the horsemen behind them. When they stopped for the night, Cerridwen cut a slit in the center of three of the blankets so the trio could pull them over their heads and wear them over their shoulders. They'd use the rest of the blankets as bedrolls.

It took another day before Amaethon was able to travel without using his sword belt to keep him on his saddle. The supplies and the blankets helped him get his strength back, and soon he seemed normal again.

Around noon the next day, the trio heard horses approaching from the direction of Ardagh and quickly hid behind one of the rock outcroppings that lined the mountain pass. They were almost through the pass, but Arawn decided not to try to run for it in case there were ships waiting at the fork in the river.

The same squad of horsemen that had helped them rode past their hiding place. Amaethon had been erasing the evidence of their path, so the horsemen had no way of telling where the trio was hiding. Arawn guessed that they had heard about the attack on Ardagh and the identity of the three strangers they had helped. The trio waited for almost an hour before leaving their hiding place and continuing their journey.

"What do we do if they're waiting for us at the fork in the river?" Cerridwen asked as she saw the end of the pass coming into view in front of them.

"I'll take care of that," Amaethon said.

"Are you sure?" Cerridwen asked, concerned for her friend.

He nodded. "I'm fine, and this is something I know how to do easily. Don't worry."

They camped just inside the pass behind another outcropping of rock, but they lit no fire. The next morning, Amaethon blanketed the area with a thick fog. They turned east, and by afternoon, they were out of the fog and far away from the horsemen waiting at the fork in the river.

They saw no more horsemen or soldiers of any kind after that, and there were no longboats patrolling the river, either. They were able to continue to the ferry quickly and easily.

Shortly after noon on the ninth day after they left Ardagh, the trio approached the ferry across from Athramail. As they got closer, they saw four people waiting for them, along with the wagon and their horses. They sped up, and when they reached the ferry, they dismounted and allowed the Étaíne horses to return home.

Tridamus ran forward and hugged Cerridwen in his large arms. Belenus hugged Arawn, and Nemausus hugged Amaethon. Belenus introduced the trio to Alaunus.

"I'm very pleased to meet you all," she said.

She looked at each of the orphans, but when she looked at Arawn, he felt he knew her from somewhere. He couldn't put his finger on it, but there was something familiar about her.

Alaunus was a beautiful woman with long white hair and a face that had no blemishes from age. Based on her hair color, Arawn assumed that she was old, but her face, voice, and stature gave no evidence of it. She smiled broadly as the trio was introduced to her.

Once they were onboard the ferry, Alaunus asked the trio to tell their story about what happened. They all told their parts, leaving nothing out. Belenus was sad to hear that Siena had to be killed, but Nemausus wasn't sad that Athanaric was dead. "He was a threat to us," he said.

Alaunus seemed particularly interested in the confrontation between Airmid and Mider, and Nemausus wanted to hear about how Amaethon brought the mountain down on the palace and obliterated the Étaíne fleet. "That should keep Taranus from sending too much of his army to meet us," he commented.

"He'll be there with as many soldiers as are needed," Alaunus said. "Just like all of the kings. I think this just means that Taranus will have to walk there instead of sailing there."

Everyone laughed, and Alaunus just smiled.

Ten minutes later, the ferry arrived on the north bank of the river, and in front of them was Athramail, the capital of the Dunmaine tribe and the city where Nemausus rescued Amaethon from Athanaric eighteen years earlier.

Amaethon, Arawn, and Cerridwen meet Tridamus, Nemausus, Belenus, and Alaunus at the Ferry Crossing across the River from Athramail.

Athramail hadn't changed at all since Nemausus had rescued Amaethon. The colors of the paint on the buildings hadn't faded, there was no weathering of the masonry, and the timbers looked just as new as they had eighteen years earlier. It was as if time stood still in the capital city of the Dunmaine, and Nemausus knew that was just the way the inhabitants wanted it.

There was an escort waiting for them at the city gates, and soon the party was making its way through the city to the palace. The city sat alongside the river, so part of the city was on the slope of the north bank of the river, and the rest of the city was on the plains above.

Arawn was amused by the way the streets of the city were laid out. Danann streets curved and twisted like mountain paths, but the streets of Athramail were perfectly straight. Only the part of the city on the riverbanks was slightly different because the streets were on a slope.

Amaethon felt strange being back in the city for the first time since Nemausus had rescued him. He had no memories of the city, and after living in a circular tower with Nemausus for almost eighteen years, he found the grid-like layout of the city to be quite strange. However, as they approached the part of the city where the bakeries were located, he realized that he didn't mind the layout of the city as long as he could smell those smells every day.

The escort led them up to the palace where King Vellaunus waited for them. As soon as they had dismounted, the king ran down the stairs to greet them warmly and welcome them to the city.

King Vellaunus was a young man in his twenties. He was a good leader and an excellent soldier, which is why he had been chosen to be king, but he was unaccustomed to the pageantry and ceremony that accompanied his position. He didn't like visitors being led through the palace to get to him. He preferred to greet his visitors as soon as they arrived, to make them feel welcome.

When he greeted the four elder members of the party, he was very polite. He evidently knew Alaunus quite well because he gave her a hug as soon as she stepped down from the wagon.

She introduced the three orphans to the king, and he was clearly quite pleased to meet them. "I've heard so much about you," he said, speaking quickly as people often do when they're nervous or excited. "Mostly, I've heard that I don't have to be king anymore once you're successful. I can't tell you how much I'm looking forward to that!"

"Why is that?" Cerridwen asked.

"Because I'm a soldier from a long line of bakers," Vellaunus replied. "I was chosen to be king because the Council knew that the prophecy was about to be fulfilled and our tribe would need to go to war one more time. They wanted a soldier to be our last king, and I was the only one from a family that had a seat on the Council. My father passed away three years ago, and I took his place on the Council. Since the king must be selected from the Council members, I was elected."

"And I hate it," he added with a grin. "All this pomp and ceremony... I can't tell people what I really think or how I really feel. Everything I do must represent the Council and the tribe. But when you three are successful, we won't need a king anymore, and I can be myself again without having to worry about what people think."

He led them into the palace, where the Council was waiting. He introduced each member of the party to the Council members before leading everyone to the Council chambers where dinner had been prepared.

Unlike the Macruhan, where the prominent members of the city were invited to the reception for the travelers, only members of the Dunmaine Council were invited to this gathering. Each member of the Council stood and gave a well-rehearsed speech about the greatness of his tribe and his pleasure at meeting the instruments of the prophecy, but the speeches all sounded the same and were boring. Arawn knew that they did it as a sign of respect, but he found it difficult to remain awake after the fifth speech.

Once the Council members had ended their speeches, Belenus stood and thanked everyone for their kind words. He told them of the need to take their army and meet up with the Macruhan army on the western face of the Mountain of Elohim as quickly as possible.

"Things have been set in motion that require immediate action," he told the assembled Council members. "Everyone must be there when the Kingstone arrives."

"I'll lead our armies as you have requested, Belenus," the king promised. "I'll have riders dispatched immediately to begin gathering our forces."

"I think that is something the Council needs to discuss first, King Vellaunus," one of the Council members said politely, but with an expression that looked anything but polite.

"No, it's not," Vellaunus replied sternly. "According to the Dunmaine charter, the king requires approval of the Council in all matters except for the military. In that, the king has supreme command and the full authority in all matters of defense and war. Since the fulfilling of prophecy is the culmination of generations of war with our neighbors, our presence with the other armies of the Followers of Elohim is a matter of military necessity and a demonstration of our faith and obedience to Elohim. However, since you obviously believe that the Council needs to be part of this decision, the Council shall accompany the army so you may continue to advise me."

"But who will see to the city's defense or the welfare of the tribe if we are gone?" another Council member said, sounding shocked at the idea of making the journey to the Mountain of Elohim with the army.

"If you're so worried about the tribe, then let's bring them with us," the king said, irritated at cowardice of the Council members. "I understand that many of the Macruhans will be in attendance, and it might do everyone good to mingle a bit with our fellow man somewhere outside our own borders. As for the defense of the city, all of the armies of man will be assembled near the Mountain of Elohim, so there won't be anyone around to threaten the city."

"But, My King..." one of the other Council members began, but he was quickly silenced by the king.

"Enough!" the king shouted, rising to his feet. "This is a military decision, and as supreme head of the military, this is my order. These three," he said, motioning to the orphans, "are the orphans who are mentioned in the prophecy. The prophecy states that it's from these three that the Ruler of the World will be chosen. When that happens, my position as king and your positions as members of this Council will be abolished. Our tribe will no longer have the need for a separate governing body. The tribes will be united, and our timid isolation from the others will end once and for all. You may not like it, but you can't prevent it. It's happening right now. If you want to come with the army to see it happen, you're welcome to. Otherwise, you may consider you and your families no longer part of the Council and no longer one of the prominent families of this city. Do I make myself clear?"

"But, but, My King, you can't..."

"Can't I? The Dunmaine charter clearly states that any member of the Council who refuses to come to the aid of the king when requested shall be removed from the Council along with his family forever. I have requested that you accompany the army and me. If you refuse, you'll no longer be on the Council and neither can any member of your family for as long as the Council exists, which won't be much longer. Honestly, do any of you ever read the Dunmaine charter?"

The king looked around the room at the ashen faces of his Council members as they realized that they could no longer control the king. He hid a smile of satisfaction at their discomfort. He knew that he had been chosen to be king because he was young and inexperienced, and he'd have to rely on the Council heavily. But this was a military matter, which he understood perfectly without the Council's help. He was tired of being bullied by these old men who hid behind the city walls and had completely lost touch with much of the tribe and the rest of Alastríona.

As he sat down, he admitted to himself that this was the best day of his reign as King of the Dunmaine.

"We will accompany you and the army, My King," the first Council member stated.

"Good!" Vellaunus said with a smile. Turning to a servant, he said, "Tell the Captain of the Guard I need to see him at once. Tell him to speak to no one other than myself. He isn't to speak to any member of the Council at any time for any reason. Understand?"

The servant nodded and left the chamber immediately.

After the Council members gave their farewell speeches and filed out of the chamber, the king was left alone with the elders and the orphans.

"I'm sorry you had to witness that," he said. "The Council has grown old, fat, and complacent. I don't think that they've had an original idea between them for at least three generations."

"You did very well making them come around, Vellaunus," Alaunus said with a look of pride in her eyes. "They may have chosen you for the wrong reasons, but they chose well when they made you king."

Vellaunus blushed. Turning to Arawn, Cerridwen, and Amaethon, he asked, "So what happens now?"

"You take your army and your tribe to meet up with the Macruhan army," Arawn answered.

"And then what?"

"I'm not completely sure how everything will play out," Arawn admitted, "but if the last couple of months are any indication, we'll be shown what we need to do when we need to do it. I'm starting to think the universe doesn't want to burden us with too much information all at once."

"I feel exactly the same way every day of my life," Vellaunus said, laughing.

They spoke for a while longer until the Captain of the Guard was escorted into the chamber. It was clear from the look on his face that he had already heard about how the king had put the Council in its place.

"How may I serve My King?" the captain asked, the respect for his supreme commander evident in his voice.

"Send riders to all our troops, Captain. We're taking the army to the Mountain of Elohim to join with our allies for the fulfilling of the prophecy. Any members of the tribe who want to make the journey may come as well. Oh, and the Council is going, too."

"When do we leave, My King?"

"Two days."

"What about when we cross the rivers, My King? There are two we must cross, and the Étaíne longboats patrol both."

"I wouldn't worry too much about the longboats," Arawn said. "Most of their fleet was destroyed nine days ago, and they'll need the rest just to get their own troops to the gathering place."

"Destroyed? How?" the king asked.

"Let's just say that it's never a good idea to anger a sorcerer."

The king's eyes opened wide. "Which one of you did it?"

"I did," Amaethon said.

"I want to hear all about it!" Turning to the captain, the king said, "Send out the riders and prepare the army, Captain."

"Yes, My King," the Captain said. He turned and left the chamber.

Amaethon told the king about their journey and their unexpected visit to Ardagh. Despite the Dunmaine reputation for not liking anything to do with magic, the king listened to every word with great interest.

"I visited there once when I was younger," the king said after Amaethon was finished with his tale. "Dreadful place. I can't imagine that you made it looks much worse than it already was."

"I think you'd be surprised," Arawn said, smiling.

They talked for a while longer.

"My friends, I can't remember a night I enjoyed more than this one," the king said. "When do you have to leave?"

"At first light," Belenus said.

"Then I won't keep you. Let me show you to your rooms."

He led them to the guest wing of the palace, which was arranged similarly to the guest wing of Danann's palace. The four elders were in one suite, while the three orphans were in another suite down the hallway. The king wished them all good night and told them that he'd be there when they left.

"I can't wait to sleep in a real bed again," Amaethon said as he disappeared into his room and closed the door. He fell asleep immediately, and Arawn and Cerridwen heard him snoring softly.

Arawn looked around the small common room and was about to suggest that they get some sleep when Cerridwen put her arms around him.

"We need to get some sleep," he said softly, enjoying the feeling of her next to him.

"I know. I just don't want to be separated from you anymore. Not even for one night."

"Cerridwen…"

"Stay with me, Arawn? Please?"

Arawn nodded. He followed Cerridwen into her room, which was across the common room from where Amaethon was sleeping, and she closed the door behind them.

Down the hallway, Alaunus was sitting in front of the fireplace when Belenus stuck his head out of his room. Seeing her, he walked over and sat down next to her.

"Are they together?"

Alaunus nodded with a smile.

"Are they ready?"

"Almost," she replied. "They have all fulfilled their tasks well. Only three tasks remain, but I can't see how the final tasks will turn out. It's out of our hands now."

"I'm ready. Are you?"

"I think so," Alaunus said, sounding tired. "I'm ready to move on. There's so much to do."

"If we win," Belenus reminded her.

"Even if we don't, remember that eternity isn't the presence of infinite time, it's the absence of time. In a universe where time has no real meaning, imagine how much you can get done in that instant before the end comes."

"Only to see it all go to waste?"

"Perhaps, but was that ever the issue to begin with? It's not what happens after you create something, it's the act of creation itself. Once it's created, it has a life of its own, and you no longer have any control over it. But at the moment when the creation happens, you are one with the creation, and in that instant there is eternity. It's why we exist."

Belenus nodded and sat next to his old friend in silence, watching the fire die down.

Arawn woke up early the next morning. He lay there listening carefully but didn't hear anyone stirring. It was still dark outside, and Arawn wondered how long it would be before dawn. He felt Cerridwen's arm across his chest and smelled her scent all around him. He turned carefully so he could face her and watch her sleeping. Even asleep with her hair covering part of her face, she was beautiful, and Arawn felt like the luckiest man alive to have her in his life. He leaned forward and kissed her gently on her forehead.

Cerridwen moved slightly and opened her eyes. She saw Arawn next to her and smiled. "What are you doing?" she asked sleepily.

"Watching you sleep," he whispered softly.

"That's weird."

"Really? What do you call it when you watch me sleeping?"

"I don't watch you sleeping."

"I've seen you."

"You must be mistaken. I never…"

Arawn kissed her, moving his arms around her and pulling her closer. She kissed him back, enjoying the feeling of having him next to her. They lay next to each other for a while before drifting back to sleep.

The noise caused by the changing of the guards in the hallway an hour later caused Arawn to wake up again. He gave Cerridwen a nudge to wake her, gently lifted her arm off his chest, and got out of bed. He washed his face quickly and put on his traveling clothes. Cerridwen did the same, and the two walked into the common room just as Amaethon was coming out of his room.

"No matter what happens," Amaethon said after the couple had greeted him, "I want a bed like that one to sleep in for the rest of my life!"

"It was that comfortable?" Cerridwen asked.

"Perfect," Amaethon replied. "This is the most rested I've felt in a long time."

"How far is it to Batavia?" Cerridwen asked.

"About three hundred miles, if I remember the maps correctly,"

Amaethon responded.

"So about two and a half weeks?" Arawn estimated.

Amaethon nodded. "Less if we didn't have the wagon."

"And how far is it from Batavia back to the Mountain of Elohim?" Cerridwen asked.

Amaethon closed his eyes and thought about it for a moment. "About four hundred and fifty miles," he said, finally.

"So about three and a half weeks?" Arawn asked.

Again, Amaethon nodded.

"Six weeks total," Arawn noted.

"Don't forget we have to retrieve the Kingstone, wherever it is," Cerridwen pointed out. "So it could be anywhere between six weeks and ten weeks before we have a chance to sleep in one of these beds again. Do you think King Vellaunus will let us take a couple with us? We might be able to get them into the wagon."

The three laughed. They were certain that the king would give them the beds willingly, but they knew the extra weight would just slow them down. All three were feeling strongly that they had to be back to the Mountain of Elohim within ten weeks, but they weren't certain why.

There was a knock on the door, and King Vellaunus came into the common room. "Your companions are already outside and waiting for you. There are fresh supplies in the wagon, and the boat is waiting."

"What boat?" Cerridwen asked.

"Oh, I guess I forgot to mention it. Étaínes aren't the only ones who understand boats. We have a few ourselves. Batavia is on a lake, and it's quicker to get there by water, so we have some of our own boats that go back and forth between the two capitals since we're allies. Alaunus asked me to make one available to you when she was here last time. It'll cut two weeks off the journey."

"Thank you, King Vellaunus, for your hospitality," Cerridwen said, giving the young king a kiss on the cheek. He blushed and quickly turned to lead them to their companions, who were waiting outside in the wagon. Once outside, everyone mounted up, and the king led the party through the city to the dock where the ferry had brought them the day before.

Tied to the dock was a large barge that had none of the sleek beauty of the Étaíne ships, and it was clearly designed to carry heavy cargo in shallow water. It appeared to Arawn to be a well-designed ship, and he looked forward to watching the crew operate it.

There was a ramp running from the dock to the barge so the horses and the wagon could be loaded. Sailors were busy loading cargo onboard as the elders and the orphans dismounted. King Vellaunus dismounted as well, and he wished every member of the party a safe journey.

"I'll see each of you at the gathering place when you get there," he said as they made ready to follow their horses and the wagon onboard.

"Make sure that your soldiers don't do anything to provoke the opposition," Alaunus cautioned. "That many soldiers in one place invites conflict, and with so many civilians around it could quickly become a tragedy."

"I will, my Lady," the king replied, bowing.

They boarded the barge, and the sailors pulled the ramp onboard after them. Several sailors untied the ropes that were keeping the barge alongside the dock. They jumped back onboard and coiled the ropes before putting them away for the voyage. The elders and the orphans waved to the king as the boat began moving toward Batavia. The king mounted his horse and rode back up the hill toward the palace with his escort following close behind.

"There goes a remarkably sensible young man," Alaunus said as she watched the king disappear into the city.

CHAPTER 47

nce the barge picked up speed along the river, Alaunus motioned for everyone to join her by the wagon, which had been lashed to the deck to keep it from moving while the barge sailed to Batavia. The sailors tethered the horses along both sides of the barge to keep the weight evenly distributed, and Arawn thought that the Dunmaine sailors were handling the barge well.

Unlike the Étaíne longboats, Dunmaine barges had no rowers. They used wind and the river's current to move downriver toward Batavia. Arawn had no idea how they moved the barge upriver, but hoped he'd get to see it before the journey was over. He noticed that there were three masts on the barge and wondered if the additional sails they carried would make it possible to do what the single sail on the longboats couldn't do – sail into the wind. Ropes, which Arawn learned were "rigging" on ships, were everywhere, and Arawn watched as the sailors used the rigging to change the positions of the sails to make the best use of the available wind. In spite of the size of the barge, they were moving at great speed, and Arawn wished that he had time to learn more about how this ship worked.

When he joined Alaunus and the others, she handed everyone some of the food that King Vellaunus had provided. "I wanted to talk to you all here because no one will overhear what I have to say," she began. "We're beginning the last leg of this journey, but we still have a long way to go and not much time."

"Is it time to retrieve the Kingstone?" Arawn asked.

Alaunus nodded. "Once we make an appearance at Batavia and tell King Arvernus what we need him to do with his army, we have to retrieve the Kingstone from its hiding place. It'll be a dangerous journey, and we have little time left to complete it. That's why I asked Vellaunus to lend us his barge. We need all the speed we can get if we're to be where we're supposed to be at the right time."

"Where is the Kingstone?" Cerridwen asked.

"In a cave on the northernmost peak of the Merthyr Mountains," Alaunus replied.

"It's in Chulainn territory?" Amaethon asked.

"Can you think of a better place to hide it?" Alaunus asked. "Who'd ever think to look for it there? The area isn't inhabited, and Morrigan would never guess that Airmid hid it inside the Chulainn borders, since Morrigan is an enemy of Airmid."

"How do we get to it?" Arawn asked.

"We travel northeast from Batavia along the river until just before we reach the inlet that leads to the Ceres Sea. Then we cross the river into Chulainn and head northeast as far as we can. After that, we climb to the cave and retrieve the Kingstone. But only the Ruler of the World can enter the cave and retrieve the Kingstone. That's when we'll know who among the three of you has been chosen."

"What if we run into Chulainn soldiers?" Arawn asked.

"We'll be taking an escort of Penarduun cavalry with us," Belenus replied, "but I'm going to tell King Arvernus to send the bulk of his army to the Chulainn border and make King Grannus think that the Penarduuns are planning an invasion. He'll concentrate his forces to protect Sétanta, and that'll open up the way for us. If you remember the prophecy, there will be shooting stars in the night sky once the Ruler of the World is chosen and has the Kingstone. That'll be the signal for Arvernus to move his army and join the others at the Mountain of Elohim. The Penarduun escort will stay with us until we arrive at the gathering place."

The three orphans were silent for a while, absorbing what Alaunus had told them. Alaunus watched them and suddenly felt great compassion for these young people. *They were born into a destiny that was chosen for them, they've endured great sacrifices, and yet they've performed their tasks to the best of their ability and without complaining. I know that the upcoming tasks will test every ounce of their resolve. I wish that there was something I could do to reassure them about the final outcome. But the future isn't written yet. They'll be its authors, and it's the rest of us who must wait in anticipation of their success or failure.*

It only took three days to reach the lake on the border of Penarduun and Chulainn territories where Batavia was located. An hour after sunrise on the fourth day, the barge pulled up to the docks of Batavia and furled its sails. Thirty minutes later, the sailors finished offloading the horses and the wagon. An escort of Penarduun cavalry met them as they left the docks. The horsemen formed up around them as the elders and the orphans rode to the palace.

Arawn was surprised as they entered the capital city. It was the first city he had seen that didn't have any walls or any other visible defenses. The city had wide streets, and all of the buildings were between one and two stories high with thick thatched roofs. The lower halves of the buildings were made of dark timbers, but the upper halves were made of a whitish material with diagonal beams that crisscrossed between the timbers and the roofs.

"Are there no walls or other defenses for the city?" Arawn asked one of the horsemen.

"The Penarduun cavalry protects the city," the horseman replied with a superior tone. "We have no need for walls or other defenses."

The tenor of the escort's voice told Arawn that the people of Penarduun were proud of their cavalry.

Belenus had told Arawn about the Penarduun people. They were considered the finest cooks in all of Alastríona and were also expert winemakers. They enjoyed fine foods and fine drink in equal measure, and they were generally a happy people unless they felt insulted. The smallest of insults could trigger an all-out war, and the Chulainn had learned the hard way to never attack the Penarduun or cross the border into their territory. Even the Dunmaine, who were their allies, knew better than to approach the Penarduun territory uninvited.

The palace wasn't as grand as the other palaces Arawn had seen, but it was quite large. The party dismounted and entered the outer chamber of the palace, where they were able to wash their faces and hands before continuing toward the Council chamber where King Arvernus was waiting.

Arawn's first impression of King Arvernus was as a man who had led his people well for many years. He had piercing dark blue eyes, gray hair, and his beard was white with the occasional streak of black. His well-weathered skin gave him the look of someone who had spent most of his life in the saddle, and the sword he wore looked well-used.

"My good friends, welcome to Penarduun," he said with a voice that sounded like it could still command a large force. He gave each of the elders a kiss on each cheek, but when he came to the three orphans, tears welled up in his eyes.

"I wasn't sure I'd get to see the three of you in my lifetime," he said with genuine emotion, "but here you are in my home. I'm so happy to meet you. I had begun to doubt the prophecy until I saw the red moons eighteen years ago. That's when I knew that the world was about to change, and I'd probably be the last king of this tribe. It's time, and I have no regrets. I did the best I could, but now you're here and the task of leading the people will fall to you. My sword is yours to command, My Lords. Whatever you ask, I will do."

"Thank you, King Arvernus," Arawn said. "I hope we live up to the trust you've placed in us. As far as commanding you goes, let's just say that we're in need of a very large favor."

"Name it," Arvernus said, ushering them to a large table surrounded by several chairs. In the center of the table was an oversized map showing the borders of the Penarduun territory and topographical details about the neighboring territories.

Once they were seated, Arawn motioned for Belenus to share with King Arvernus what they needed.

"We need a cavalry escort to go with us on a secret mission," Belenus began, "and we need a diversion so the Chulainn won't know what we're doing."

"That's easy enough to do. What are the details?"

"We need you to move your remaining forces along the Chulainn border so it looks like you're planning to attack Sétanta."

"How much of my forces?"

"All of them," Belenus replied. "We need the Chulainn so distracted by what you're doing that they won't notice what we're doing. We need the Chulainn to bring all their forces south, but we don't want war to break out between you. Once you see the shooting stars in the sky, you'll know that we've succeeded. You can withdraw your army and head south to the gathering place on the western face of the Mountain of Elohim to join with the rest of our allies. We'll bring the cavalry escort with us and arrive shortly after you do."

King Arvernus looked at his map and thought about Belenus' request. Looking up at Belenus, he said, "It sounds to me like you're planning an incursion into the northern Chulainn territory. Otherwise you wouldn't be asking me for such a large show of force to the south that's only to be used as a diversion, am I right?"

Belenus nodded silently.

"The Chulainn forces are no match for ours and they know it," Arvernus said, still staring at the map. "You realize, though, that the Chulainn might decide to attack out of desperation? If that happens, I could lose much of my cavalry, and we wouldn't be able to reach the gathering place with any significant force to help if war breaks out."

"That's why it's important to avoid any engagement with the Chulainn," Belenus said. "Your forces need to stay on your side of the border. You're meant to scare them, but not enough for them to cross the border into your territory."

Arvernus nodded. "Very well, I'll do as you ask. When do you want me to start the diversion?"

"Immediately," Belenus said. "It will take us almost two weeks to get to the ford where we're crossing the river into their territory. We'll be there for no more than a week, and then it's another two weeks back. By the time we get to the crossing, you need to have the Chulainn terrified that you're about to pour across the border and wipe them all out."

"Won't Morrigan interfere?" King Arvernus asked.

"Possibly, although after what happened with Mider in Ardagh a few weeks ago, I don't think Morrigan will be too much of a problem."

"What happened with Mider at Ardagh?" the king asked.

Arawn told the story of their capture and eventual escape from Ardagh, and Cerridwen told how Airmid spoke to Mider through Arawn. King Arvernus laughed when Arawn told him how Amaethon brought down the mountain on top of the palace and destroyed the Étaíne fleet.

"It's about time someone taught those fish-heads a lesson," he said happily. "They charge a fortune to transport our goods, and they keep half of what they're supposed to be transporting for us. It may make trade a little harder, but they need to learn humility if all the tribes are going to be united soon. Besides, the Penarduun barges are more practical for commerce than the Étaíne longboats any day."

The king passed the word for his captains to join the meeting, and when they arrived, he filled them in on what they needed to do. An experienced captain named Monteria was assigned to escort the orphans and their companions on the secret mission. Once the captains had their orders, the king gestured to a servant that it was time to serve the food.

"A little something to tide you over until this evening," the king said as heaping platters of food were brought in and placed around the table. "I must present you to the court this evening, which is really just an excuse for the noble families to empty my wine reserves. However, I need to know if any of you are spoken for at the moment."

"I am," Cerridwen said, looking over at Arawn.

"So am I," Arawn said, smiling at Cerridwen.

"Ah," the king said with a smile. Looking at Amaethon, he asked, "And are you spoken for?"

Amaethon thought about it for a moment. "I have no idea what's going to happen between now and when we reach the gathering place," he answered finally. "Ask me again once all this is over."

The king nodded. "I understand. I'll inform the court that there will be no opportunities for suitors this evening. The youth of this city will be crushed, but there's always hope for the future, yes?" he added, looking at Amaethon, who blushed and said nothing.

CHAPTER 48

O nce they finished eating and the serving platters were removed, the king had servants show the orphans and their companions to the guest quarters so they could rest before the reception that evening. Rather than guest suites like the palaces at Danann and Athramail, there were separate quarters for each member of the party.

Arawn and Cerridwen chose to stay in the same quarters together, and the servants moved them into one of the larger rooms out of respect. They had just put their things away when there was a knock on the door.

Arawn opened the door, and Belenus, Tridamus, and Alaunus walked in.

"Forgive the intrusion," Alaunus said, "but we felt that we needed to speak with you regarding your decision."

"Which decision is that?" Cerridwen asked.

Alaunus gestured around the room. "To be together like a couple who has been joined."

"It's customary to understand the intentions of two people who are clearly in love and are choosing to reflect that love in their living arrangements," Belenus added.

"And it's important for the two people to understand their families' position on the subject," Tridamus said.

"You told the king that you are both spoken for," Alaunus continued. "Have you made a decision to pledge yourselves to each other, or was that just a ploy to keep from enduring potential suitors this evening?"

Arawn looked at Cerridwen and answered for both of them. "It was no ploy. We're committed to each other."

"I thought as much," Alaunus said with a smile. "Though you are both orphans, Belenus and Tridamus have served as your families for the past eighteen years, and it seems only proper to include them in any sort of decision regarding your commitment, don't you think?"

Cerridwen and Arawn nodded.

"Do you wish to be joined?" Alaunus asked.

"Can we discuss it for a moment?" Cerridwen asked. Neither she nor Arawn had really discussed their future plans due to the uncertainty about upcoming events.

Alaunus nodded. Arawn took Cerridwen to the far corner of the room and turned to face her.

"We've never really talked about the future," he whispered. "We've been too busy living in the moment ever since we met. I know I want to join with you, but do you know me well enough to make a decision like this? I know we love each other, but are you ready to decide if you want to spend the rest of your life with me? After all, we might not even live through whatever is ahead of us."

Cerridwen looked at Arawn and took his hands in hers. "I do love you Arawn," she whispered, "and I can't imagine not being with you for the rest of my life. We may die tomorrow or a hundred years from now, but even if we only have an hour to live, I want to spend it with you. I knew you the minute we met, and everything I've seen since then convinces me more that you're the only one I'll ever want to be with. All that I am and all that I'll ever be, I give to you if you want me."

"And all that I am and all that I'll ever be, I give to you if you'll take me," Arawn said seriously. "I want you in my life forever, but not as just my wife. I want you as my equal, my partner in all things. We've already proven that we're better when we're together, and I want you by my side or standing back-to-back no matter what we have to go through."

"So it's decided?" Cerridwen asked with a smile.

Arawn nodded. Turing back toward Alaunus, he said, "We wish to be joined."

"I have no objections to a union between these two young people," Belenus said.

"And I have no objections, either," Tridamus stated.

"Now that your families have given their blessing, when do you want the joining to take place?" Alaunus asked

Arawn looked at Cerridwen. "Do you want to wait, or do you want to go ahead and be joined now?"

"I can't think of any reason to wait," Cerridwen replied. "Besides, we don't know what's going to happen in the future, so it seems pointless to put it off until later.

"I agree," Arawn said. Turning to Alaunus, he said, "We wish to be joined immediately."

"You mean right now?" Alaunus asked, sounding astonished.

"Yes, now," Cerridwen said.

Alaunus looked at Belenus and Tridamus, who were also looking rather surprised. Finally, Alaunus nodded. "Very well. We'll have the joining now. Belenus, would you go get Nemausus and Amaethon? They should be here for this."

Belenus nodded and left the room. He returned a few minutes later with Amaethon and Nemausus.

Alaunus looked at Cerridwen and Arawn. "The two of you have asked to be joined, and your families have given their blessings. Now I need to know who shall be the head of your house?"

It was common for there to be someone designated as the head of the house. This person would be the dominant partner in the relationship. By tradition, the male was the head of the house, but there were examples in the past where the female was the head of the house.

"Neither of us," Arawn replied. "We are equals in all things and partners in all things. Neither one of us will be above the other."

"And do you consent to this, Cerridwen?" Alaunus asked, sounding even more astonished than before.

Cerridwen nodded. "I know it's unusual for the woman to be an equal partner in most relationships, but we're an unusual couple. If we're going to be part of uniting the tribes, one of the first things that needs to be changed is the notion that women are inferior to men. How can I refuse the chance to be in a relationship where no one is inferior to the other?"

Alaunus' expression was replaced with a look of deep satisfaction as if she were remembering something from long ago. "It is as it was foretold, but in an unexpected way," she said softly. "As you have pledged, so be it. I join you together as equals for the rest of your lives. The covenant that has been made this day must be nurtured and protected so that it is never broken."

Tridamus handed Alaunus a small box, which she handed to Arawn. Inside, were two rings made from two different colored metals that were knotted together. Arawn and Cerridwen placed a ring on each other's finger to symbolize their pledge.

"It is done," Alaunus said. "May your life be long and filled with love and joy, but when there is strife, discord, pain, or storm, remember that it's by working together that you'll find the answers."

Everyone came forward and hugged the couple. Nemausus offered his congratulations, and Amaethon congratulated the couple and gave Cerridwen a kiss. Amaethon and the four elders returned to their own chambers, leaving the young couple alone.

"Is that how joining ceremonies work?" Cerridwen asked after they were alone. "I've made joining rings before, but I've never been to a ceremony."

"I've seen two ceremonies, and they're similar, but they asked different questions," Arawn said. "I guess it depends on the circumstances."

Cerridwen looked at Arawn and giggled. "You're my husband!"

"And you're my wife." Arawn kissed Cerridwen, and she started giggling again.

Everyone met outside Arawn and Cerridwen's room to go to the reception.

Amaethon pulled a small ingot of gold from his pocket that he had gotten from Tridamus earlier. He concentrated for a moment, and the ingot transformed into a necklace made of interlocking links and a pendent that had the most intricate knotwork design Cerridwen had ever seen before. In the center of the pendent were two interlocking crowns that were visible when the light caught it just right.

"Amaethon, it's beautiful!" she said as he helped her put on the necklace. "I can't thank you enough."

"It's the least I could do for the one who made the Dragon Lord's staff," he said with a chuckle.

Turning to Arawn, he said, "It wasn't as easy to come up with a joining present for you, but I hope you like it."

He took out a piece of leather from another pocket that had a piece of steel wrapped inside. Amaethon concentrated on the steel, and Arawn watched it transform into a beautiful dagger. There was a subtle knotwork design along the thick part of the blade. The hilt was also made of steel, but a piece of the leather wrapped itself around the grip while a steel wire wove itself around the leather to hold it in place. The hand guard of the dagger had a knotwork design on it as well, and the pommel had the design of the two interlocking crowns.

The rest of the leather wrapped itself around the knife blade and stitched itself into a beautiful scabbard that had both the knotwork design and the interlocking crowns on both sides. Amaethon handed Arawn the scabbard and knife with a short bow.

"Thank you, my friend," Arawn said, gripping Amaethon by the forearm. "This is a priceless gift!"

He tucked the scabbard into his belt as the chamberlain came to escort the group to the reception.

Arawn and Cerridwen discovered that Alaunus had informed King Arvernus of the joining when he announced it to the court as he was making the introductions. The group mingled with the members of the court, and Cerridwen and Arawn never left each other's side. After a while, they understood what King Arvernus had meant when he called the reception an excuse for the noble families to drink all of his wine. The spirits were flowing rather freely, and after an hour, most of the members of the court were drunk.

Belenus reminded the king that the companions needed to get an early start the next morning, and the king made the announcement to the members of the court that the guests of honor were retiring for the evening. The chamberlain led the companions back to their rooms, and Arawn heard the party continuing for several hours.

Arawn put out all of the candles in the room except for one small one on the far side. When he turned, He discovered that Cerridwen had undressed and changed into a blouse that she found in the wardrobe in the far corner or the room. The blouse was open at the top, and only covered down to her upper thigh, leaving her legs fully exposed. Apart from the joining ring, the blouse was all she was wearing.

Arawn quickly undressed down to the short britches he wore under his clothing. Cerridwen walked toward him and put her arms around his neck. In the candlelight, he thought she looked like what the gods must look like in their true form. She kissed him, and Arawn, twisting slightly, reached down and picked her up in his arms. He carried her to the bed, gently set her down, and lay down next to her on the bed.

He kissed her passionately and soon let his hands begin exploring her body, making note of the places that made her gasp from the sensation of his touch. She did the same, and soon the blouse and britches were on the floor as they explored everything the other partner's body had to offer.

It was several hours later when they finally reached the point of complete satisfaction and exhaustion. Arawn got out of bed and brought back two towels from the cabinet underneath the basin of water near the door. Both Arawn and Cerridwen were bathed in sweat, and Arawn slowly and carefully dried Cerridwen with the towel before she did the same for him.

Arawn pulled up the covers, and Cerridwen nestled next to him with her arm across his chest and one leg intertwined with his. They lay there for a while, simply enjoying the sensation of being next to the other and knowing that this would be the last bed they'd slept in until after they had fulfilled the prophecy. The next several weeks would provide little opportunity for acts of tenderness or lovemaking as they raced to retrieve the Kingstone and reach the gathering place by the appointed time.

"Again?" Arawn whispered in her ear.

"You've got to be kidding me," she replied, amused.

"Who knows when or if we'll ever get the chance to do this again?" he said, turning to face her.

"Good point," she conceded. "Who needs sleep anyway?"

Arawn pushed the covers down and pulled Cerridwen on top of him. "Plenty of time to sleep when this is all over," he said softly. "Right now, all I need is you."

Cerridwen kissed him. "All I need is you, too."

CHAPTER 49

rawn woke to the sound of a faint knocking at the door. He carefully separated himself from Cerridwen so she wouldn't wake up, wrapped himself in one of the towels that was on the floor next to the bed, and crept across the room. When he cracked the door open, he saw Belenus standing there.

"Sorry to wake you this early, Arawn," Belenus said, "but I figured you two might need a little extra time to get ready this morning."

"What time is it?" Arawn asked.

"Less than two hours before dawn," Belenus replied. "We need to get our supplies together and be out of the city before sunrise."

"Thank you, Belenus. We'll be ready."

Belenus turned to walk back to his own room as Arawn closed the door. Arawn crossed the room to the one candle that was still lit and used it to light the other candles. He walked over to the bed and gently rubbed Cerridwen's shoulder.

The covers were still pushed down past Cerridwen's waist, and Arawn looked at her perfect body as she was waking. The memories of the previous evening rushed into his mind, and when she opened her eyes and looked at him, he was grinning unconsciously.

"What time is it?" she asked sleepily.

"Less than two hours before dawn. We need to be away from the city before sunup."

Looking at her husband standing over her, she reached for the towel he was still wearing, pulled it loose, and let it fall to the floor. "Then we have no time to waste," she said.

Arawn agreed and joined her quickly.

Captain Monteria was waiting with his escort of twenty men at the main entrance when Arawn and the others walked out of the palace an hour and a half later. The supplies for the journey were loaded into Tridamus' wagon, but there were enough horses saddled for everyone to ride.

"We'll take the wagon for our supplies, but it'll be one of the Penarduuns driving it," Alaunus had told them as they were leaving the guest rooms. "We'll leave it at the river crossing since it can't go with us into Chulainn territory. After we return from Chulainn, we'll be in too much of a hurry, and it'll just slow us down. We'll restock our supplies and leave the wagon behind. We'll return here, take the barge to the eastern pass through the Valdunass Mountains, and from there we'll head straight for the gathering place."

They mounted their horses, and the escorts closed in around the orphans and their companions. With Captain Monteria in the lead, they left the palace and headed north out of the city. By the time the sun had risen over the Merthyr Mountains, they were several miles away heading northeast as fast as the horses could carry them.

King Arvernus watched them leave the palace from the room where he had met with them the day before. He was dressed in the uniform of a cavalry Field Marshall, and he was making a final adjustment to the shoulder strap that held his chest armor in place. Once the riders were out of sight, he turned and faced the cavalry officers assembled behind him.

"Are the troops ready?" he asked his senior captain.

"Yes, My King."

"Then let's ride," he said as he strode across the room and out the door. The officers turned and followed him out of the room to the parade grounds on the opposite side of the palace.

When King Arvernus stepped out of the palace, he saw over a thousand of his horsemen waiting. They saluted their king as he took his horse from the groom and mounted it. These were the troops of the regiment that guarded the capital, and there were over a dozen more regiments plus auxiliary troops already heading for the Chulainn border.

"You know what we must do," he said to his men as the officers mounted their horses. "We are a diversion, but it must appear real. The mission we're protecting is the single most important mission of our age, and it's up to us to ensure its success. Will you follow me?"

The horsemen shouted "Aye!" The king's question and the horsemen's response was the tradition of the Penarduun cavalry, and the king felt a surge of pride when he heard his men shout their loyalty to him. He knew that this would be one of the last times the men would follow him, but today he was still the master of the finest cavalry in Alastríona. He adjusted his grip on the reins, and his horse obeyed its rider and galloped toward the entrance of the parade grounds. The horsemen, in perfect precision, followed their king and formed their ranks, riding four abreast through the streets of the city with their lances pointing toward the sky.

The journey to the ford where the orphans and their companions planned to cross the river into Chulainn territory was relatively uneventful. Scouts sent to ride along the river reported that Chulainn troops were moving south, evidently in response to the appearance of the Penarduun cavalry massing on their border. The diversionary plan seemed to be working.

Cerridwen and Arawn rode together most of the time. Cerridwen didn't feel tired the morning they left Batavia. If anything, she felt more alert and relaxed than she could remember. Arawn was tired at the beginning, but once the sun rose and the excitement of the journey set in, all fatigue vanished.

Amaethon was happy for his friends, but he kept thinking about something that Nemausus had told him the previous afternoon when he learned about the joining.

"I believe it was always part of the plan that Cerridwen and Arawn should be joined at some point," Nemausus said, "but there was something special about when and how the joining took place. I don't know if a new element has been introduced into future events, and I don't know if it'll help things turn out for better or worse."

"What was so special about the joining?"

"Arawn and Cerridwen joined each other as equals, and they were joined before the Kingstone was retrieved," Nemausus replied. "By tradition, and don't ask me where the tradition started because it certainly isn't what Airmid or Elohim had in mind, one person in the joining is considered to be the head of the house and takes on a superior role in the relationship. Why women typically become the subordinate ones, I have no idea because, in many ways, women have more strength and cunning than men could ever dream."

"Really?" Amaethon asked.

"Have you ever seen a mother bear when her cubs are attacked?"

Amaethon nodded.

"Have you ever seen a male bear fight like that?"

Amaethon thought about it for a moment and shook his head. Nemausus was right that females were more ferocious when defending their families.

"It's the same with humans. Women don't fight as freely as men do since they tend to be less aggressive, generally speaking. But threaten someone they love, and no army or mountain or ocean will stop them from their defending what's theirs."

"Anyway," Nemausus continued, "Arawn and Cerridwen chose to join as equals in all things. That means the fate of one is now intertwined in the fate of the other."

"They're stronger together," Amaethon commented, "so maybe the outcomes will turn out better."

"Possibly," Nemausus said, nodding. "I just don't like not knowing, especially so close to the moment that the prophecy will be decided."

Amaethon glanced over at his two friends, who were riding next to him with the Penarduun escort, and he wondered if the joining would set in motion something that could change the fate of Alastríona.

Even though they were on the equivalent of a military campaign to retrieve the Kingstone, Arawn still found time to show Cerridwen how grateful he was that she agreed to join with him. He always selected a place around camp where there were no rocks to hurt her back at night, and on the rare occasions that they passed any on their journey north, he presented her with flowers.

Cerridwen appreciated the attention that Arawn paid to the details, and she loved him even more for it.

One evening, while Arawn helped the horsemen get the campsite set up for the night, Tridamus asked Cerridwen to take a walk with him.

"I haven't had the chance to ask this yet," Tridamus began as they were away from the others, "but how is being joined with Arawn?"

"I've never been happier, Tridamus," she replied with a genuine smile that told Tridamus all he needed to know about how she was feeling.

Tridamus kissed her forehead. "Good," he said. "I'm happy for you both."

Cerridwen smiled, and she and Tridamus continued walking in silence.

A short while later, Alaunus, Tridamus, Belenus, and Nemausus were talking. "Do you have any more insight into how things will change now that Arawn and Cerridwen have joined as equals?" Belenus asked.

"No," Alaunus replied. "For all I know, nothing will change. I trust that Elohim's plan can handle this and events will unfold as they need to."

The others nodded.

Twelve days after they left Batavia, they arrived at the river crossing. Horsemen were sent to scout the other side of the river, and they came back an hour later reporting that the region seemed deserted.

Leaving the wagon behind, they crossed the river and followed it for two more days until they reached the place where the mountains and the river touched. Once they arrived, the horsemen quickly set up camp at the base of the mountain.

Alaunus told the other elders and the orphans to put on the heavy cloaks that they had brought with them. She led them up a narrow trail into the mountains. Arawn and Amaethon had to pull their heavy traveling cloaks tighter as the wind whipped past them on the trail. Gusts of wind loosened some of the snow on the summit, causing it to blow into their faces as they climbed.

Cerridwen wrapped herself tightly in her cloak and pulled the hood farther down around her face. She wished that the trail were wide enough for her to walk next to Arawn so he could help keep her warm.

The higher they climbed, the harder it was to see where they were going. Amaethon looked down once or twice and saw that they were walking along the edge of a sheer cliff that disappeared into the mist far below. The blowing snow was so thick that neither the summit nor the base of the mountain were visible. They couldn't see anything except the path right in front of them, and it was as if the mountain itself were trying to keep them from going any farther.

At the top of the trail, just below the snow line near the summit, there was a ledge shielded from the wind by an outcropping of rock. The ledge was invisible to anyone at the base of the mountain. At the far end of the ledge, cut into the rock, was a cave. The entrance to the cave looked blurry for some reason, and what lay beyond the entrance was as black as night. Arawn thought that he saw a faint blue light deep inside the cave, but he couldn't be sure.

Alaunus had them stand in a circle so she could speak to them without having to shout over the wind. "This is the cave where Airmid hid the Kingstone. Only the Ruler of the World may enter and retrieve it, although once it has been successfully retrieved, we all may enter."

"Who is the Ruler of the World?" Arawn asked.

"That remains to be seen," Alaunus said. "The Ruler was foretold to be from among the three of you. You must all try to enter together, but only the Ruler will be allowed inside."

"You must hurry, though," Alaunus added. "The moment for the fulfilling of the prophecy is almost at hand."

Arawn looked at Cerridwen and Amaethon. He wondered which of them was the Ruler and what would happen as soon as he or she entered the cave. Knowing that time was growing short, he motioned for the others to walk to the mouth of the cave.

Arawn stood in the middle with Cerridwen on his right and Amaethon on his left. They stared at the entrance to the cave for a moment, and all three saw that the mouth of the cave was still blurry from whatever was there to keep anyone but the Ruler from entering. Finally, Arawn said, "Let's go."

They stepped forward and immediately felt a tingling sensation all around. They pushed forward, and the tingling grew stronger. They heard a sound building up around them, and as they continued to push, the sound grew louder until it became a shrieking in their minds.

Arawn and Cerridwen continued forward, but Amaethon felt something blocking his path. No matter how hard he pushed, he couldn't go any farther. He looked over to Arawn and Cerridwen, and he saw that they were still moving toward the entrance of the cave. A moment later, he watched them both pass through the barrier and into the blackness of the cave, disappearing from sight.

Arawn and Cerridwen are both the Ruler of the World! Amaethon felt happy for his friends, and to his surprise, it didn't bother him at all that Elohim hadn't chosen him. He smiled, stepped back from the cave entrance, and turned to face the others.

"It was both of them," Belenus exclaimed softly.

Tridamus nodded. "This must be part of what their joining has set in motion."

"I'm not so sure," Alaunus said.

"What do you mean?" Tridamus asked. "Are you saying that you believe things are happening the way they were meant to happen all along?"

"No, I'm just suggesting that Elohim knew that they'd join as equals, and whatever is going to happen to both of them is already part of the plan."

Amaethon and the four elders stared at the cave entrance in silence, wondering what was going on inside.

s soon as Arawn stepped through the barrier into the cave, the shrieking in his head stopped immediately. The sudden silence was startling. Arawn noticed that Cerridwen was standing next to him, and he thought it was strange that both of them would be able to pass through the barrier. Looking around, he saw Amaethon still standing outside the cave with the four elders.

In spite of the wind and cold on the ledge, the cave was quite warm. Both Arawn and Cerridwen loosened and pulled back their traveling cloaks. Arawn took Cerridwen's hand in his. There was still the Kingstone to retrieve, and he knew that it lay deeper inside the cave.

To Arawn, the cave was completely dark except for a faint blue light coming from somewhere farther ahead. *I wonder if that's the same light that I thought I saw from the ledge.*

He reached out to touch the cave wall, and found that it was smoother than he expected. He kept one hand on the wall to guide him as they carefully walked forward. The blue light was enough to show them where to walk, but it didn't let them see the features of the cave or what obstacles there might be along the floor. Looking back, Arawn could no longer see the cave's entrance. They were surrounded by darkness except for the blue light beckoning them deeper into the mountain.

After several minutes of walking, they reached a place where the cave opened into a vast circular chamber on their right. The blue light was very bright as they entered the chamber, and Arawn and Cerridwen saw the features of this part of the cave perfectly.

The chamber walls were a bit rough, but the floor was as smooth as polished stone. The center of the chamber was lower than the ledge that Arawn and Cerridwen were standing on, but there were three steps leading down to the center. In the middle of the chamber was something that looked like a well carved out of the mountain.

The well was almost completely white. There was a perfectly round basin that rose up from the floor waist-high. It had four columns equally spaced around the outer edge of the basin, each about four feet high and intricately carved at the top. Resting on top of the columns was a mirror image of the basin below. It descended from the roof of the cave and had strange letters carved around the top. Floating between the two basins, in the center of the columns, was the source of the blue light: the Kingstone.

The Kingstone was an oval jewel that was larger than Arawn's fist. It was brilliant blue, and near the top was a golden crown attached to the stone. The Kingstone was glowing brightly, and Cerridwen thought that she saw it pulsing, as if it had been waiting a long time for something to happen and was now excited that the time had finally come.

Arawn walked to the center of the chamber to get a better look at the Kingstone. He reached for it, but felt a jolt of energy pushing him back as he tried to move his hand through the columns.

"Ouch!" he cried out, pulling his hand back quickly.

"What happened?" Cerridwen asked.

"It won't let me reach the stone," he said, turning to Cerridwen. "I guess you're the one who's supposed to retrieve it."

She stood next to him and stared at the Kingstone for a moment, watching it pulsing in anticipation. She reached for the stone. As soon as her hand reached the columns, she felt the same jolt of energy pushing her back that Arawn had felt.

"Ouch!" she said, shaking her hand to stop the tingling. She tried a second time, but felt the same jolt as before. The Kingstone continued pulsing, and Cerridwen wondered if it were laughing at them.

"How are we supposed to retrieve the Kingstone?" she asked.

"I thought we were supposed to reach in and take it," Arawn said. "Maybe we're supposed to use something to pull it through the barrier."

"What?" Cerridwen asked.

"I don't know. Look around and see if you can find something we can use."

Both Cerridwen and Arawn walked around the chamber, looking for something they could use to reach the Kingstone, but there was nothing inside the cave apart from the Kingstone, the well, and the two of them.

"What about a sword?" Cerridwen asked.

"It's worth a try," Arawn said. He drew his sword and extended it forward toward the Kingstone, but when the tip of the blade reached the columns, the sword was pushed back and flew out of Arawn's hand, landing with a loud clanging sound several feet away.

"I guess my sword won't work," he said as he retrieved his sword and put it back in the scabbard.

The Kingstone continued glowing and pulsing as if it were getting impatient with them.

"Should we go back out and ask Alaunus how to retrieve it?" Cerridwen asked.

"I think this is a test, and we need to solve it on our own if we're to prove ourselves worthy of receiving Elohim's blessing," Arawn commented.

Cerridwen nodded. "It has to be one of us, doesn't it?" she asked. "The prophecy says the Ruler of the World will retrieve the Kingstone. Alaunus said only the Ruler of the World could enter the cave. We're in the cave, so why can't we retrieve the Kingstone?"

Arawn thought about it for a moment, and an idea came to him. "Why are *we* here?" he asked.

"To retrieve the Kingstone," Cerridwen answered, sounding surprised that Arawn was asking such a basic question.

"No, I mean why are we *both* here? If the Ruler of the World is the only one who can enter the cave and retrieve the stone, why are there two of us here? Shouldn't there only be one person in the cave to retrieve the Kingstone?"

"I don't know," Cerridwen admitted. "Only one person can be the Ruler, right?"

"We're joined as equals, aren't we?" Arawn asked.

Cerridwen nodded. "Are you saying we're both the Ruler of the World?"

"If we're both here in the cave, then doesn't it make sense that we're both the Ruler of the World?"

"The prophecy didn't say anything about two Rulers, did it?"

Arawn shook his head. "No, but Tridamus mentioned that the Ruler could be one of us, two of us, or all three of us. Maybe it was originally supposed to be just one of us, but that changed when we were joined. Remember, we joined as equals in all things. So together, we are the one Ruler."

"So we have to retrieve the Kingstone together?"

"That's what I'm starting to think," Arawn replied.

Cerridwen looked at Arawn and her face lit up. "You're brilliant," she said. She gave him a kiss on the cheek.

She turned to face the Kingstone and extended her hand. Arawn did the same. They reached forward, and as their fingers reached the columns, there was no jolt of energy. Their hands passed between the columns easily.

Cerridwen looked at Arawn and smiled. They both leaned forward until they each had a hand on either side of the Kingstone. The Kingstone was pulsing rapidly by this time. They touched it at the same time, and suddenly the glow from the Kingstone burst into a bright blue-white light that lit up the chamber like the sun.

Arawn and Cerridwen froze with their hands on the Kingstone as it touched their minds with images and knowledge that they could scarcely comprehend. In an instant, they saw all of Alastríona and every living thing on it – not just the part of Alastríona where the tribes lived, but all of it, from the uninhabited islands and territories to the home of the dragons to the vast underwater habitats of fish and other sea creatures. They saw how all living things in the world linked together according to the plan of Elohim.

Arawn also saw something else. He saw himself standing in the middle of the chamber and holding the Kingstone. The gods were all standing around him, and they were debating what to do. Arawn kept holding up the Kingstone, but it was as if some of the gods were afraid to touch it.

The image jumped, and he was standing alone, facing Manannan, Mider, Morrigan and Artio, with Balor, Llyr, Camalus, Mebd, Branwen, Lugh and Airmid watching from a distance. He was shouting at the disobedient gods when he saw Mider approach him. Mider raised his fists, but Arawn couldn't see what happened after that.

Is Mider going to kill me? Do I have to die to save Alastríona? Suddenly he heard a voice in his mind. It was like no other voice he had ever heard. It was filled with love, and it made Arawn feel immediately at peace.

"Fear not, my son. You will face the gods, and through you they will learn what they must learn to make their choice. You won't be alone. I am always with you."

Arawn knew he had heard the voice of Elohim speaking to him. He continued holding onto the Kingstone, but the voice didn't say anything else.

Suddenly the light dimmed. Arawn and Cerridwen were no longer paralyzed by the knowledge that the Kingstone gave them. They pulled the Kingstone toward them, and when it passed through the columns, its light faded, and it seemed to become smaller in their hands. The chamber

301

grew dark, and sconces that were cut into the rock along the outer wall burst into flame.

Cerridwen and Arawn heard someone approaching from the cave entrance, and when they turned to look, they saw Amaethon coming toward them. But rather than Alaunus, Belenus, Tridamus, and Nemausus following him, they saw four luminous beings shining from their own radiance. They both realized that they were in the presence of four of the gods, and they instantly knew which ones. Still holding the Kingstone, they each went down on one knee and bowed their heads.

"Airmid, Llyr, Balor, Camalus, it is an honor to be in your presence," they said in unison.

"What are you talking about?" Amaethon asked, looking confused. He still saw Alaunus, Belenus, Tridamus, and Nemausus standing next to him, not four of the gods.

The woman he knew as Alaunus put her hand on his arm. "They have touched the Kingstone and now see us for who we truly are. Nothing remains hidden from them any longer. The one you knew as Nemausus is Camalus, the creator of the sky above us. Belenus is Llyr, the creator of the waters of the world. Tridamus is Balor, the creator of the ground beneath our feet."

Amaethon looked at her and at the others, including his Master. Looking back at Alaunus, he asked, "Then you're Airmid, the creator of man?"

"I am," she replied.

Amaethon immediately went down on one knee and bowed his head.

"Get up, my children," she said. "We have never desired worship or the homage that the other gods seem to crave. We obey Elohim and worship no other."

"What happens now?" Cerridwen asked and the three orphans rose to their feet.

The Kingstone suddenly seemed to come alive. It began glowing bright blue. Arawn and Cerridwen managed to keep holding it, but soon it was so bright that the orphans had to close their eyes. They heard a loud sound like the striking of a gong.

"It is time for the gods to meet and decide once and for all the fate of Alastríona and the rest of creation," Airmid stated.

CHAPTER 51

or a moment, the world seemed to stand still. There was no sound heard by anyone in the cave, except for the sound of the beating of his or her own heart. It was as if all movement in the universe had paused, waiting in anticipation of what was about to happen.

The first god to obey the summons was Cerrunos, the faithful god who moved on to create the other worlds as commanded by Elohim. He appeared in the form of a luminous being, and he bowed to Arawn and Cerridwen. Balor, Llyr, and Camalus soon stood next to Cerrunos and bowed to Arawn and Cerridwen.

The next to appear were Mebd, Branwen, and Lugh. These gods had originally opposed the will of Elohim but had yielded when they saw that the conflict caused by the gods was only serving to destroy, not enrich. They bowed to Arawn and Cerridwen and took their place in the circle around the Ruler of the World.

Manannan, Mider, Morrigan, and Artio, the disobedient gods, appeared and took their places in the circle, but didn't bow. They hadn't intended to obey the summons, but they were compelled by the Kingstone to appear anyway.

Last of all, Airmid bowed to Arawn and Cerridwen before completing the circle. Somehow, Arawn knew that the gods were standing just as they had stood when they created the world before they abandoned the will of Elohim.

Both Arawn and Cerridwen looked around the circle, wondering what was supposed to happen next. Suddenly the Kingstone touched their minds again, giving them the knowledge that they needed to perform their next task.

"The time has come for a choice to be made," Arawn began.

"Elohim created you to be the builders of worlds and creators of life on those worlds according to the plan for the universe. Many of you abandoned your purpose and disobeyed Elohim. The Father-Mother of the universe now commands that you leave Alastríona and return to the purpose for which you were created or be the cause of the unmaking of all creation."

"Elohim would never unmake the universe," Mider stated. "Elohim wouldn't cause everything to be unmade to punish us."

"You don't understand, Mider," Cerridwen said. "Elohim won't unmake *the universe* to punish you; Elohim will unmake *you and the rest of the gods* to punish you. The universe and all that you created in it will be unmade so Elohim can start over. Why allow something to exist when it was made by flawed builders who were proven to be unworthy of existence?"

"Elohim won't unmake the gods," Mider said. "We are the builders according to the plan, and Elohim needs us."

"What value does a disobedient builder add to Elohim's plan?" Arawn asked. "What have you built since you created Alastríona? From what I can see, all you've done since you created this one world is to pit people against each other for your own amusement. You no longer build; you destroy, and Elohim is going to destroy all of creation because of you unless you leave this world and start building again."

"Why do you claim that you're following Elohim's plan?" Cerridwen asked. "If you were the builders according to the plan of Elohim, you wouldn't be here now, and you wouldn't have taught your worshippers to make war on each other. The only thing you've done since you abandoned your purpose is to interfere with the plan of Elohim."

"The tribes of man will be united once again to follow the will of Elohim," Arawn continued. "The wars will end, and we'll no longer fight amongst ourselves for your amusement or to satisfy your lust for being worshipped. Elohim is the only god of Alastríona now. It's time for you to leave and create the other worlds that Elohim has designed. We will remember you, but we'll follow you no more."

"We won't leave our world to you," Morrigan said, speaking for the first time. "You aren't worthy of our world."

"It's not your world," Cerridwen replied, "and it's not your choice who will lead it. Elohim has made that choice. Who are you to go against the will of Elohim?"

"We are the creators of the world," Manannan said. "We made it, we nurtured it, and it is ours."

"But you created it according to Elohim's plan," Arawn said. "The world is Elohim's, not yours."

"This is our world, and we decide what happens to it," Artio said.

"And that's the real issue, isn't?" Arawn asked. "You want the world for yourselves. You think that it belongs to you because you were the builders. But what about the architect? Elohim made the design and told you what to build. The world doesn't exist for *your* purpose; it exists for *Elohim's* purpose. This world isn't yours; it never was. It's normal to love what you created, but there's so much left to create out there. Why stop at just one world? Aren't you capable of so much more than that? Or are you just afraid of moving on?"

"We are afraid of nothing, man-child," Mider roared, growing brighter in his rage.

"Not even of your own destruction?" Arawn asked.

"I am a god!" Mider shouted, causing the cavern to shake slightly from the force of his voice. "I cannot be destroyed!"

"Yes, you can, Mider," Arawn replied. "Your creator is ready to unmake you right now."

Mider roared and stamped his foot, causing the cavern to shake violently. Amaethon nearly lost his balance as Mider raged at Arawn and Cerridwen.

Arawn looked at Mider and realized that the god wasn't going to be easy to convince. Arawn also knew that there wasn't much time left for Mider to make his choice. He wondered what to say and glanced at the Kingstone, which was still pulsing in blue light.

"I am always with you," a voice suddenly said within his mind. *"Mider's pride has kept him from obeying me, and it is by hurting his pride that he may learn to listen."*

"How do I do that?" Arawn asked in his mind.

"By defying him," Elohim answered. *"Do not back down, no matter what he does."*

Arawn knew what he needed to do: fight fire with fire. He removed his hand from the Kingstone and stepped forward. Amaethon watched with alarm as Arawn approached Mider, but Cerridwen simply held the Kingstone in front of her and waited.

"What do you want, Mider?" Arawn asked. "What will it take to get you to do the right thing?"

"Who are you to decide what is right for a god?" Mider demanded.

"I don't decide, Mider. Elohim decided. I'm just the messenger."

"I reject your message, man-child. If Elohim has a message for me, let Elohim deliver it."

"You fool!" Arawn shouted. "Elohim has spent centuries trying to tell you what's right, and you've ignored every attempt to show you what you needed to do. I'm the last messenger being sent to you, and the message I'm here to deliver is this: leave Alastríona and fulfill your purpose, or be destroyed now, here in this place."

Mider stepped forward and lifted his hands in the air. "Who are you to talk to me like this, man-child? You think you can command me? I don't obey your orders!"

"Evidently, you don't obey Elohim anymore either. I'm surprised the universe can contain your arrogance!" Arawn knew that he was provoking the god, but he knew that he had to break through Mider's resistance before the god could make the right choice.

Mider swung his arm at Arawn, but Arawn ducked and the arm swung harmlessly over his head. Arawn straightened up and stared at Mider with a look of contempt. Mider swung his arm again, and again Arawn ducked out of the way. Mider raised his fist and brought it down quickly, aiming for Arawn's head. Arawn rolled out of the way and jumped back to his feet to face the god once again.

"What good will it do to kill me, Mider? Do you think my death will prevent Elohim from destroying you and the rest of creation? It won't. You'll be destroyed the instant you kill me, and the rest of creation will be destroyed with you. Do you have so little regard for your own creations that you'd allow everything the other gods have made to be destroyed with you just to spite Elohim?"

Mider roared again and took a step closer to Arawn, raising his fist high in the air. "I will swat you out of existence, man-child."

"So you think you're stronger than Elohim? You think you can prevent the destruction of creation? You think you can prevent your own destruction? Then go ahead and kill me."

Mider hesitated for a moment, and Arawn took another step forward.

"What will my death accomplish, Mider?" Arawn shouted. "You kill me, and Elohim will destroy you, the other gods, all life on Alastríona, and the rest of the universe in an instant. The only way to prevent your own destruction is to stop defying your creator and leave."

"You will be silent!" Mider screamed.

"No, I won't, Mider. You will hear me, and you'll listen to what I have to say."

"I'll kill you and anyone else who defies me, man-child. No one speaks to me like this."

Mider's rage could no longer be contained. He reached for Arawn, but then he stopped, distracted by the person who had moved to stand next to

Arawn.

"I defy you, Mider," Cerridwen said, moving to stand shoulder to shoulder with her husband. She offered the Kingstone to Arawn, and he placed his hand on it next to hers. The Kingstone glowed brightly, confusing Mider for a moment.

Mider raised both fists above Arawn and Cerridwen's heads, but Amaethon stepped into the circle and stood next to Cerridwen. Mider shouted, and the cavern shook once again. He raised his fists and brought them down, aiming for the orphans standing in front of him, but the Kingstone suddenly flared in a brilliant light. Mider felt his fists hit an invisible barrier that seemed to be protecting the humans. He tried to hit the orphans again, but he couldn't break the barrier.

Confused, Mider lowered his fists and stepped back, looking at the three orphans standing unified in their defiance.

"What's wrong, Mider?" Cerridwen asked gently.

"You don't understand," Mider said. "You are unworthy and therefore incapable of understanding."

"We understand you perfectly well, Mider," Cerridwen said. "You've spent centuries convincing yourself that you know what's best for Alastríona, that you know better than the other gods, and that you even know better than Elohim, your own creator! But you're wrong. You have no idea what Elohim has planned for this world, so how can you even begin to know what's best for it?"

Mider stood in silence, staring at the Kingstone.

"What will help you make the right choice?" Cerridwen asked.

"How do you know what the right choice is?" Mider asked, feeling his rage dissipate into confusion.

"Because obedience to Elohim is always the right choice," Cerridwen replied.

Mider looked from Cerridwen to each of the other gods. He slowly stepped back to his place in the circle and stood in silence. His mind was filled with doubt for the first time since the creation of the world.

Arawn remembered what had happened when he and Cerridwen first touched the Kingstone. He wondered if the Kingstone would show the gods what the plan for the universe was in the same way it showed Cerridwen and him the plan for Alastríona.

Turning to Airmid, Arawn mentally asked the question. When Airmid nodded, Arawn said, "When Cerridwen and I first touched the Kingstone, it revealed Elohim's plans for Alastríona. It showed us the

307

entire world – even the parts that we haven't discovered yet. It showed us that there's so much more to this world than we've seen, and it helped us understand what we're supposed to do. I believe it will do the same for you. All of you, please come forward and touch the Kingstone. Let it show you Elohim's plan for the universe so you'll better understand your part. Maybe that will help you make the right choice."

None of the gods moved at first, but then, one by one, they stepped forward and touched the Kingstone. Mider was the last to step forward, and when he touched it, a brilliant blue-white light suddenly engulfed them all.

Arawn and Cerridwen were still holding the Kingstone and were able to see what the gods saw. The Kingstone revealed the interrelationship between all living things on all worlds around all of the stars in all of the galaxies in the universe. It was overwhelming to the two humans, but not to the gods.

A moment later, the light from the Kingstone faded. The gods returned to their places in the original circle, leaving Arawn, Cerridwen, and Amaethon alone in the middle.

Mider was the first to speak. "I understand now... I never knew... Elohim, forgive me. I was wrong, and I have made my choice. I will obey."

"So will I," Manannan, Morrigan, and Artio said.

"So will I," Mebd, Branwen, and Lugh said.

"So will I," Balor, Llyr, and Camalus said.

"So will I," Cerrunos said.

"And so will I," Airmid said.

Looking around the circle at the other gods, Airmid added, "The tribes of Alastríona will soon reach the gathering place, and the Ruler of the World has a task to perform there. Once that task is completed, we will say our good-byes to the people of this world. I have prepared the temple near the summit of the Mountain of Elohim for you. Please wait there until the Ruler of the World summons you one last time."

The gods bowed and disappeared, leaving only Airmid, Balor, Llyr, and Camalus in their human form with the orphans.

The orphans turned and faced the four gods.

Airmid stepped forward and hugged each of them. "You've done very well, my children," she said. "The gods have made the correct choice, thanks to you, and the universe is safe. Now you must begin the work of uniting the tribes as one people."

Turning to face Arawn and Cerridwen, she continued. "I was curious to see who Elohim would choose to be the Ruler of the World. It is as it should be. I created men and women to be equals – neither one greater nor lesser than the other. When both the masculine and feminine work together in unity as equal partners, they achieve true completeness. It was never my intention that men and women should be solitary creatures. I created masculine and feminine so the two could join together and become one as you have."

"The gods aren't masculine or feminine, right?" Amaethon asked Airmid.

"Correct. The gods have no gender. We often appear as men or women, but this is an illusion. Some men believe we have offspring with humans, but this isn't possible. I created all men equal and didn't allow for a separate race of half-gods to come into this world."

Looking at the Kingstone, Airmid said, "It was foretold to me that the Ruler of the World would wield the Kingstone. If the two of you are as one, then I wonder if the Kingstone is the same..."

She reached out with a finger and touched the Kingstone, which was still in Arawn and Cerridwen's hands. The Kingstone glowed briefly at the touch of its creator, and there was a slight popping sound. The Kingstone split into two equal halves from top to bottom. Cerridwen and Arawn each had one of the halves in their hand. They looked at the Kingstone and back at her in confusion.

Airmid waved her hand, and two chains appeared at the top of each half of the Kingstone. She took the Kingstone half from Arawn's hand and placed it around his neck. She did the same thing with Cerridwen's half.

Placing her hands on Cerridwen and Arawn's shoulders, she said, "Just as the Ruler of the World is two acting as one, the Kingstone is now two. There will be times when the Kingstone will be one again, but until that time, you are both its guardians. It's your birthright and your responsibility. Protect it with your lives."

"We will," they both promised.

"To both of you is given all of Alastríona," Airmid continued. "The uniting of the tribes and restoring the world to the plan of Elohim is your destiny. The Kingstone has shown you this plan, which was foretold as the blessing of Elohim. You are now the caretakers of the plan for this world."

Turning to Amaethon, Airmid added, "And you, Amaethon, have an active role in the work destined for the Ruler of the World. You have an important part to play in uniting the tribes and helping the Ruler of the World guide the people of Alastríona wisely."

Amaethon bowed his head.

Airmid led them all to the cave's entrance. "And now I think it's time we were rejoining our escort. There's also something for you to see outside."

The tunnel stretched no more than twenty-five feet from the chamber to the cave entrance, which surprised Arawn. It had seemed much longer when he and Cerridwen had walked though it in the dark. He saw light coming in from the cave entrance, but he couldn't feel or hear the wind at all. As he reached the cave entrance, he saw that the mist and blowing snow were both gone, and the sky was clear.

They stood on the ledge outside the cave as the sun was setting on the horizon. Looking up, they saw the sky filled with shooting stars. This was the sign foretold by the prophecy that would signal when the Ruler of the World had received the blessing of Elohim and had retrieved the Kingstone. All that remained to fulfill the prophecy was to join the tribes meeting at the gathering place and begin the work of uniting the people of Alastríona.

Arawn looked back at the cave, but all he saw was the solid rock face of the mountain. The cave had served its purpose and was now gone. Airmid walked toward the path that led to the base of the mountain, and Arawn followed Cerridwen and the others as they descended the mountain path to the campsite where their escorts were waiting.

The shooting stars filled the sky above them until long after the two moons had set, in celebration of the blessing of Elohim and as heralds of the coming of the Ruler of the World.

Arawn and Cerridwen retrieve the Kingstone.

CHAPTER 52

hen they reached the camp, Captain Monteria was the first to approach them; the rest of the escort remained at their posts. He gestured to the night sky. "I see you were successful. May I ask which of you is the Ruler of the World and has the Kingstone?"

Cerridwen and Arawn both held up their halves. "We both are, Captain," Arawn said.

"Both of you, My Lords?" Monteria asked, confused.

Cerridwen nodded. "Just as we are joined as equals, we are both the Ruler."

Monteria nodded and quickly saluted Cerridwen and Arawn. "What are your orders, My Lords?"

"We'll stay here for the night and return to Batavia as quickly as we can." Arawn replied.

"Very well," Monteria said, saluting again. Then he turned and presented the Ruler of the World to his men.

Arawn put his arm around Cerridwen's shoulder and pulled her close as the men cheered their new Ruler.

They woke up early the next morning, broke camp, and rode back toward the river crossing. They encountered no Chulainns as they traveled southwest along the river, and by the evening of the second day, they had reached the river and started across.

They made camp where they had left the wagon behind, and once everyone had eaten, Balor asked the three orphans to help him with something. He led them over to the wagon and climbed inside. He moved the supplies around until he reached three large bundles wrapped in canvas.

Balor handed the bundles to Amaethon, Arawn and Cerridwen

before jumping out of the wagon to stand next to them. He motioned for them to unwrap their bundles.

The orphans unwrapped the canvas, and inside each was the armor Cerridwen had made before they left the smithy. "Is it time to start wearing these?" Cerridwen asked.

Balor nodded. "Even though only two of you are the Ruler of the World, all three of you are tasked with uniting the tribes of Alastríona. It seemed proper that you all have matching armor to wear when you're seen by the tribes for the first time."

Arawn looked at the armor carefully, remembering when Cerridwen had first shown it to him. The main armor was a series of overlapping and interlocking metal plates that were attached to a leather jerkin, which held the plates in position and provided reinforcement to the kill zones. The chest plate lifted up so the jerkin could be put on. Once the chest plate was lowered, it was secured with straps that held it in place. Attached to the bottom of the jerkin were additional armor plates that covered the kill zones above the knee.

The jerkin covered the upper arms, and there were two armored wrist guards included in the bundle. Covering the wearer's neck was an armored collar attached to the jerkin.

The helmet was a short helmet designed to cover the forehead, the top of the head, and the back of the head down to the jerkin's collar. Two sidepieces protected the cheeks but left the ears uncovered. The helmet had visor that could be lowered to protect the mouth and the nose, but Arawn knew that most fighters kept the visor up to provide added protection to the forehead.

The chest plate had an intricate design on it that looked like laurels etched across the top, but in the center of the laurels was a flat oval that looked like it was the same size as the Kingstone. Feeling the Kingstone around his neck, Arawn realized that the stone would rest on that exact spot if he wore it over the armor.

The shield was an oval and was completely smooth. The sword, which was another of Cerridwen's unique designs, was leaf-shaped, meaning that it was straight but was wider in the center than it was at the tip and the hilt to improve its cutting abilities. Worked into the scabbard and sword belt was the familiar knotwork design that matched Cerridwen's jewelry.

"Just one more thing," Balor murmured. He held out his hands, and the interlocked crown design that Amaethon had put on his joining gifts to Arawn and Cerridwen appeared on the center of Arawn and Cerridwen's helmet visors and underneath the place where the Kingstone would rest on their chest plates. He held out his hands over their shields, and the smooth surface turned blue with a gold crown at the top, taking on the appearance of the Kingstone. Their sword belts and scabbards also had the interlocked crown design added, as did the sword hilts. Arawn and Cerridwen's sword belts, scabbards, and jerkins took on a deep blue color.

"Balor held his hands over Amaethon's armor. Instead of the interlocking crown design on the visor, a dragon appeared with its wings stretched wide. The dragon design also appeared in the center of his chest plate, replacing the oval where the Kingstone would rest on Cerridwen and Arawn's armor. Amaethon's shield turned a deep red, and instead of a crown at the top, the dragon design appeared. Amaethon's sword belt, scabbard, and jerkin took on a deep red color.

"It's beautiful, Tridamus... I mean Balor," Cerridwen said as a tear ran down her cheek. She hugged her former teacher and said, "Thank you."

"Oh, my child," Balor said, hugging her back, "you are most welcome. And thank you for the joy you've given me for the past eighteen years."

He hugged Amaethon and Arawn, who each thanked him for the armor as well. "Take care of our girl," Balor said as he hugged Arawn. "She's a precious jewel."

"I will," Arawn promised.

When Balor left them alone by the wagon, Arawn said, "I can't believe I'm getting to wear your armor! It's beautiful!"

"I guess we should start wearing them in the morning," Cerridwen suggested. "We're supposed to unite the tribes of Alastríona. We might as well look the part."

"I like the way you think," Amaethon said with a grin.

The three carried the bundles of armor over to their bedrolls before lying down to get some sleep. They still had a long way to go, and they needed all the rest they could get. Arawn gave Cerridwen a kiss as he put his arm around her. She kissed him as she put her arm across his chest. They fell asleep quickly, not even noticing that the Penarduun escorts had placed twice the usual number of guards around them so they'd be undisturbed all night.

The next morning, they woke early, and Cerridwen helped Arawn and Amaethon put on the armor. The boys had never worn armor before, so they weren't sure how it needed to fit, but after a few adjustments, they

314

were surprised at how comfortable it felt. Arawn helped Cerridwen put on her armor and placed her half of the Kingstone around her neck before putting on his own half. The Kingstone halves fit perfectly inside the design on the chest plate.

"I wondered why Tridamus, I mean Balor, wanted that open space in the design when he sketched it out for me, but he was insistent. Now I understand."

Arawn strapped on his sword belt and stuck the dagger Amaethon had made for him into the belt. He heard a sound behind him and saw one of the Penarduun sergeants approaching them with their horses saddled and ready to go.

"Allow me to mount your shields, My Lords," he said, bowing. Arawn handed him his shield, and the sergeant showed them how shields attached to the Penarduun saddles. Once all three shields were in place, the sergeant withdrew.

Arawn saw Amaethon walking toward the wagon. The young sorcerer climbed up into the wagon and started going through the supplies and other bundles, looking for something. After several minutes, he found what he was looking for. He straightened up and jumped off the wagon with his dragon staff in his hand. Walking up to Arawn, he said, "If the Ruler of the World can be wearing the Kingstone, I'm going to start carrying my staff. That way we can all look impressive!"

The three orphans laughed. Cerridwen was happy that Amaethon felt that way about the staff she had made for him.

They rolled up their bedding and shook out their traveling cloaks, which they had been using as pillows. Cerridwen showed Arawn and Amaethon how to attach the cloaks to the armor. They secured the bedrolls on their horses, put on their helmets, and walked over to the fire to greet everyone else.

Captain Monteria was the first to see them, and he bowed deeply. The other Penarduun escorts turned and bowed as well. "Good morning, My Lords," Monteria said. "May I compliment you on your change of attire? You look splendid!"

Looking at the armor closely, he added, "What design is this? I've never seen anything like it."

"I designed and made it, Captain," Cerridwen said.

"How does it work?" he asked.

Cerridwen explained the design, using Arawn to demonstrate how the pieces worked together. The Penarduun used the heavier, traditional armor, which worked well for mounted soldiers, but was less practical once dismounted. Several of the escorts moved in closer to listen to

Cerridwen's explanation, and she was flattered at their interest.

"It's an impressive design," Monteria said when Cerridwen was finished with the explanation. "It seems so logical, but it goes against all of the techniques that are in common use. I look forward to seeing how well it works in combat."

Cerridwen knew that this was a compliment and took it as such, but she was hoping that she wouldn't have to use it in combat anytime soon.

Captain Monteria gave the signal to break camp, and the escorts quickly jumped into action. They retrieved everything that they needed for the journey back to Batavia from the wagon. The wagon's driver would follow them to Batavia, but he wouldn't reach the city for at least three days after the Ruler of the World and their companions and escorts had already left for the gathering place.

Monteria gave the signal for everyone to mount up. Arawn and Cerridwen rode near the front with Amaethon and Monteria, and the escort formed up around them as they galloped toward the southwest along the river to Batavia.

Arawn, Cerridwen, and Amaethon in their New Armor.

CHAPTER 53

hey made excellent time back to the Penarduun capital since they weren't slowed down by the wagon. It took only ten days to reach the city, and they entered its wide streets just as night was falling. They rode straight for the docks where the barge was waiting for them.

The horses and supplies were loaded onto the barge all night, and by sunrise, the barge and its passengers were ready to head for the eastern pass through the Valdunass Mountains.

Arawn, Cerridwen, Amaethon, the four gods, and the escorts slept on the docks, rather than take the time to go back to the palace or the barracks for the night. Captain Monteria woke Arawn and Cerridwen shortly before dawn and allowed them the honor of boarding the ship first. Once everyone was aboard, the ship was untied from the dock and began moving across the lake to the river.

Arawn got his wish; he was able to watch how the barge sailed into the wind. A white-haired older man with leathery tanned skin shouted orders to the sailors who climbed and adjusted the rigging. Arawn stood next to him – watching and listening, but trying not to interfere with the man's work.

The older man realized that Arawn was standing next to him. "Good morning, My Lord," he said with a rough voice. "How may I be of service to you this morning?"

"I don't want to keep you from your work," Arawn replied, "but I'm fascinated by how this ship works. It's so different from the Étaíne longboats."

"You've been onboard a longboat?" the older man asked.

"Not voluntarily, but yes, I've been on one."

"I'm guessing that they were using the rowers to go against the wind," the older man commented.

Arawn nodded.

"Well, we don't have that problem with this ship."

"How is that possible?" Arawn asked.

"A longboat only has the one sail on a single mast. We have three masts, and three sails on each. If the wind is at our backs, we can sail forward just like the longboats can. But when the wind is cutting across us at an angle, we do two things. First, we turn the ship in a zigzag, which we call 'tacking', so we can catch as much of the wind in our sails as possible. Second, we angle the sails so the wind, the angle of the sails, and the direction of the ship all work together to make us go forward."

The older man pointed to additional sails being hoisted perpendicular to the masts. "If the wind is cutting across at a bad angle for us, we hoist those additional sails. The wind hits them and is deflected into the main sails. We just keep maneuvering in a zigzag, taking advantage of whatever direction the wind is blowing, until we reach our destination or until the wind changes direction. Fortunately, the river is widest between Batavia and Athramail, so there's enough room to maneuver back and forth. If the river were narrow, we wouldn't be able to sail unless the wind was more favorable."

"How did someone figure out how to do this?" Arawn asked.

"Trial and error, My Lord. We were faced with a problem, we knew what we wanted to accomplish and what stood in our way, and we tried everything we could think of until we came up with a way that worked consistently."

It was time for the ship to maneuver again, so Arawn thanked the older man for the information and stepped back so he could watch the crew change the direction of the ship.

It took two days for the barge to arrive at a point just north of the eastern pass of the Valdunass Mountains, which was amazing given the fact that they were sailing against the wind and the river's current. When they reached the place where they were to disembark from the ship, Arawn and Cerridwen saw a large number of mounted troops waiting for them.

Captain Monteria disembarked first and approached the troops. Three dismounted officers stepped forward, and Monteria joined them. He spoke with them for several minutes and returned to the barge.

"It looks like you're going to have a larger escort to go with you to the gathering place, My Lords," he said. "There's a company of escorts from Macruhan and Dunmaine waiting to join us, along with a company of soldiers from the army of the Followers of Elohim."

"I sent for them," Airmid said. "It seemed best that you be escorted by representatives of all of the faithful tribes."

Monteria nodded and gave the order to take the horses ashore. Arawn, Cerridwen, Amaethon, and the four gods walked across the ramp to shore and approached the officers.

"My Lords," the officers said in unison, bowing to Arawn and Cerridwen.

"Gentlemen," Arawn began, "I understand you'll be escorting us to the gathering place?"

"Yes, My Lords," the officers replied.

Cerridwen recognized the officer in the Macruhan uniform. "Captain MacInnis?" she said as the officer straightened up and faced her. "It's good to see you again."

"It's good to see you, too, My Lord," he replied, happy that she remembered him. "I see your journey was a success."

"More so than expected," she replied, letting MacInnis know about the joining.

"Congratulations to you both, My Lords," MacInnis said, grinning.

"Thank you, Captain," Arawn said. "Has anyone seen any of the opposition lately?"

"A large Étaíne force passed near our borders about a week ago," MacInnis said. "They were on foot, which was strange since they usually take their boats."

"They don't have many boats left," Amaethon interjected. "Their fleet suffered a great loss when their king tried to interfere with the prophecy."

"We saw the Gallasians heading for the gathering place about a week ago," the Captain of the Followers of Elohim said. "We know the Mongán have been sighted coming around the south side of the Mountain of Elohim, but there's no sign of the Chulainn yet. Your escort is the first we've seen of the Penarduun, but the Macruhans and Dunmaine are already at the gathering place along with our forces."

"We had the Penarduun send their cavalry to the Chulainn border to make the Chulainn think they were about to be invaded," Arawn said. "It was a diversion, but it worked. Once the shooting stars appeared in the sky, the Penarduun were to make for the gathering place immediately. I would imagine that the Chulainn are doing the same by now."

Once the sailors finished offloading the horses from the barge, everyone mounted and formed ranks.

"I'd like the four captains to ride up front with my companions and me," Arawn said.

"It would be our pleasure," Monteria and the other captains replied.

"I'd also like our escorts to look like a single unit, rather than four individual units riding together," Cerridwen commented.

"How do you want us to do that?" MacInnis asked.

"Mix your units together so they aren't grouped by tribe," Cerridwen replied. "The Ruler of the World is supposed to unite the people of Alastríona. It seems fitting that the escort bringing us to the gathering place be unified."

"I agree," Arawn said.

"Very well," MacInnis said.

The four captains gave orders for their men to break ranks and merge with the other tribes' escorts. The horsemen shifted positions, and soon the horsemen from each tribe were intermixed with the others.

Seeing that the escorts were ready, Arawn gave the order to ride south. Soon everyone was riding toward the eastern pass of the Valdunass Mountains.

The road they were following took them directly past the fairgrounds where Siena and Athanaric kidnapped the orphans and took them to see King Taranus and Mider. They reached the fairgrounds on the second day of their journey through the eastern pass. Cerridwen thought that the fairgrounds looked strange, now that the tents were gone. As they rode past the deserted fairgrounds, she remembered her encounter with Siena as if it had happened only a few days earlier.

They left the fairgrounds behind them and rode for several more hours before stopping for the night.

On the third day of their journey through the eastern pass of the Valdunass Mountains, they broke camp before dawn to get an early start. The plan was to ride through the foothills that marked the southern approach to the pass, reaching the great river just south of the pass late in the afternoon.

Arawn knew that it would be well into the night before the ferry finished taking the entire party across the river. They'd make camp on the south bank and ride for the gathering place the following morning.

As the sun rose higher in the morning sky, the escorts stopped at a mountain stream to water the horses. Arawn noticed that several of the captains looked uneasy.

"What's the problem?" he asked the Captain of the Followers of Elohim.

"There are too many places to hide in these hills," he replied, pointing to the foothills to the east and west. "If I wanted to make one last attempt to stop you, I'd set up an ambush there."

"Is there a way around that would work against an attacker?" Arawn asked.

"Not without adding several days to the journey," the captain replied.

Arawn thought about this for a minute. He wondered if the gods traveling with them could do anything about an ambush.

"No, Arawn," Airmid said from behind him. "This is your task. We cannot interfere."

Arawn turned to look at Airmid. "You can't help us at all?"

Airmid shook her head. "Not in the way you're wanting. You three have all the skills you need to complete your tasks, and you have a sizable escort at your command. I have every confidence that you'll meet whatever awaits, and you'll triumph."

Arawn nodded and went to find Cerridwen and Amaethon. "The captains are worried about an ambush up ahead, and the gods can't do anything to help us. We need to be ready for anything."

"I think we can handle an ambush," Amaethon said, "as long as the gods don't mind me drawing some energy from them."

"They said they couldn't help, but I guess taking something from them wouldn't be considered help, would it?"

"You and I are beginning to think very much alike," Amaethon said to Arawn with a grin.

They rode south for several hours, keeping a close watch on the foothills nearby.

"Can you sense anything?" Arawn shouted to Amaethon.

Amaethon shook his head, scanning the skies above.

"What are you doing?" Arawn asked.

"Looking for a hawk or another bird to be my eyes, but there aren't any around. It's like they've been scared off. Why don't you send scouts to see if anyone's hiding behind the foothills?"

"Good idea," Arawn replied. Turning to captain of the Followers of Elohim, he said, "Captain, send scouts to check out the left and right foothills. They can warn us if anyone's waiting to ambush us."

The captain nodded and selected several horsemen to act as scouts. The horsemen rode off, sending up a cloud of dust from the horses' hooves.

As they rode past the southernmost foothills, a shout went up from one of the scouts riding to the west. A moment later, another shout went up from one of the scouts riding to the east. The scouts raced back to join the escorts as troopers poured out of the foothills and rode after them.

"Make for the river!" Arawn shouted as he coaxed his horse to run faster.

Arawn, Cerridwen, their companions and the escorts raced past the foothills into the open ground along the northern bank of the river. Looking to the left and right, Arawn saw the troopers moving in alongside and behind the escorts.

"They're trying to force us to the river," MacInnis shouted to Arawn. "If we get surrounded there, we have no chance of escaping!"

Arawn saw the river up ahead and realized that the troopers had set a brilliant ambush. In less than twenty minutes, they'd be at the river – and trapped!

rawn looked around for some way to escape the trap that the troopers had set for them. The problem was that troopers were approaching from the rear and both sides, leaving the way to the river as the only way open. The river was getting closer as the orphans and the escorts raced to outrun their pursuers.

"We can't fight all of them at the same time," he shouted to Cerridwen and Amaethon. "There's too many. We need a way to reduce their advantage of numbers."

"Do you care how many die?" Amaethon asked.

"Yes," Arawn replied, realizing that even these troopers were his people as long as he and Cerridwen were both the Ruler of the World. "I don't want to kill them, but I don't want them to keep us from reaching the gathering place on time either."

Cerridwen looked at her husband and nodded. She was pleased that Arawn was already thinking about the people this way.

Amaethon looked at Arawn with surprise, but he understood why Arawn didn't want to shed any more blood than was absolutely necessary.

"Attack the force to the east," Amaethon said after a minute. "I have a couple of ideas that might work."

Arawn signaled for the captains to follow him and wheeled his horse to the left. The escorts followed and were soon bearing down on the surprised troopers approaching from the eastern foothills. Arawn and Cerridwen drew their swords, and the escorts did the same.

The troopers slowed their advance in confusion. It never occurred to them that they'd be the ones attacked.

The leader of the troopers saw Arawn and Cerridwen point their swords at him and lean forward in their saddles. He ordered his troopers to draw their swords and prepare to meet the attack. A moment later Arawn and Cerridwen's forces slammed into his troopers.

Even though the troopers quickly surrounded him, Arawn's armor prevented them from causing him any injury. Their blows deflected off the overlapping plates without even making a dent in the metal. The Kingstone on his and Cerridwen's chests began glowing brightly and pulsing, blinding the attacking troopers and forcing them to break off the attack.

Arawn and Cerridwen's forces broke through the troopers' formation and rode into the clear. There was very little loss of life and few injuries on either side of the skirmish.

The leader of the troopers was confused that Arawn and Cerridwen's forces didn't turn and fight, but he didn't give the order to pursue. Nothing was going according to plan. He didn't understand why, so he decided to wait for the troopers riding from the west to catch up to him.

Arawn looked over at Amaethon, who motioned for him to lead the escorts west around the rear of the troopers so the troopers and the escorts would be facing each other with the river to the south. Arawn didn't understand, but he did as Amaethon suggested and turned to the left to ride north and then west.

The leader of the troopers had no idea what Arawn and Cerridwen's forces were doing. *Are they just going to ride in circles around us?*" He felt more confused than before.

The troopers riding from the western foothills reached his position. He watched Arawn and Cerridwen's forces move around behind his men, but they made no attempt to head for the river or move north back into the pass. He ordered the troopers to reform their ranks and hold their position facing Arawn and Cerridwen's forces.

"Form two rows and trust me," Amaethon shouted.

Arawn ordered the captains to spread out the escorts into two equal rows facing the still-confused troopers, who outnumbered the escorts almost three-to-one.

"Are you surrendering?" the leader of the troopers shouted once the escorts were in position.

"To you? No!" Arawn shouted back.

"You're outnumbered, and there's no way you can cross the river before we cut you to pieces. If you surrender, only you and the other orphans have to die. We'll let the rest of your men live."

"That's not going to happen," Arawn shouted back.

"Then you leave us no choice," the leader of the troopers said.

He raised his sword, but his sword flew out of his hand and landed in the river. The swords and weapons of all the troopers flew into the air a moment later and landed in the river as well. The troopers looked at their empty hands with dismay.

"You're all unarmed," Amaethon shouted to the troopers. "Ride away, and we'll let you live. Interfere with us one more time, and the next thing to fly into the air will be all of you! I promise that you won't survive the landing."

The troopers didn't move. Amaethon closed his eyes for a moment. Suddenly the lead trooper's horse bolted and started running north toward the eastern pass of the Valdunass Mountains at full speed. The rest of the troopers' horses did the same, and soon the troopers disappeared in the distance.

"What did you do?" Arawn asked as the escort closed in around the three orphans and the four gods.

"I was going to translocate us to the other side of the river, but that would take too much energy, and the troopers would still be able to attack us once they crossed the river. So I told the horses to run as fast as they could for as long as they could. It'll take at least a day for the troopers to get back here, and even if they manage to cross the river and follow us, they'll still be unarmed."

The captains burst out laughing. The gods smiled. "You did well preserving their lives, Amaethon," Airmid said.

Amaethon grinned as they rode for the river.

It took until after midnight to ferry the escorts across the river to the southern bank. Arawn knew that they needed to rest the horses, but he was anxious to get started after the delay caused by the ferry.

Airmid assured him that they were right on schedule. "You'll arrive at the appointed time, my child," Airmid told him.

As soon as the sun rose the next morning, they mounted up and rode southeast directly toward the Mountain of Elohim.

"How long will it take to reach the gathering place?" Arawn asked the Captain of the Followers of Elohim.

"At least two days, My Lord," the captain replied, "assuming that there are no more attempts to delay us."

Arawn nodded. He looked at Cerridwen and said, "I'd like us to meet with the kings and captains of our allies before anything happens. They should know that our purpose is not to fight a battle but to begin uniting the tribes in peace."

"I agree," Cerridwen said. "But I'm worried about what we'll find when we get there. It's dangerous for there to be so many soldiers in one place at one time. A simple misunderstanding between two soldiers might end up dragging all of the tribes into a battle."

"You're right," Arawn conceded. "The Gallasians, Étaínes, Chulainns, and Mongáns are expecting a battle to decide the final winner of the war that the gods started centuries ago. They may get impatient and start it before we get there. Once it starts, it won't be easy to stop."

"We have to stop it," Cerridwen pointed out. "We're supposed to be uniting the tribes. The Macruhan, Dunmaine, Penarduun, and the Followers of Elohim know that the conflict has always been between the gods and not the tribes of man. We need to make the others see this as well."

Late on the second day after they crossed the river, Cerridwen was anxious about what was waiting for them at the gathering place. "Do you have a way to see what's going on?" Cerridwen asked Amaethon when they stopped and made camp for the night.

Amaethon looked up toward the sky without answering her. Cerridwen could tell that he was looking for something, and she stood quietly – waiting. After several minutes, Cerridwen saw Amaethon smile. She followed his gaze, and saw a hawk flying toward them. The hawk landed on Amaethon's outstretched arm and let out a cry that caused the entire camp to stop and look at what was happening.

Amaethon looked at the hawk for a minute, and Cerridwen wondered if they were communicating somehow. The hawk let out another cry and took to the skies, flying southeast toward the gathering place.

"In answer to your question," Amaethon said to Cerridwen when the hawk had disappeared in the distance, "no, I don't have a way to see what's going on in front of us. But my new friend does, and he'll let us know where the tribes and their armies are and what they're doing."

"Is that how you found me when I was captured at the smithy?" she asked.

Amaethon nodded. "Hawks have amazing eyesight and are friendly to those who speak to them politely. If you ask nicely in a way they can understand, they'll fly anywhere you want them to and tell you what they saw. You just need to feed them when they return so they know that you're a true friend."

"What do you feed them?" she asked.

"Mice are their favorite. Would you like to help me find a few?"

Cerridwen laughed and the two set off to find some mice while Arawn and the escorts finished setting up the camp and getting the evening meal prepared.

Three hours later, after the sun had set and the first moon was rising in the south, Amaethon heard the hawk's cry in the distance. He stood up and left the campfire area, knowing that the hawk would feel more comfortable landing away from where the escorts were sitting.

Twenty minutes later, he returned and sat down next to Cerridwen and Arawn. "It looks like most of the armies and tribes have arrived," he said. "The armies and tribes loyal to Elohim have their backs to the Mountain and are in a good position along the ridges and foothills at its base. The other armies are facing the mountain and are spreading out to surround those loyal to Elohim on three sides. Their armies are much larger, so they might be able to finish surrounding our allies before we arrive."

"What about the Chulainn and the Penarduun armies?" Arawn asked.

"The Chulainn army has arrived and started moving around to the north of the mountain before it got dark. The hawk saw part of the Penarduun cavalry, but nowhere near as many as I expected there to be."

"King Arvernus must be holding them in reserve somewhere to the northeast of the gathering place," Captain Monteria said. "If the enemy attacks, he can quickly bring the cavalry in from the rear and crush the enemy's advance."

Arawn nodded. "Can you ask the hawk to look for them in the morning?" he asked Amaethon.

"Yes. I'll also have him see where each tribe is located and what weapons they brought with them, so we'll know what kind of battle strategy Taranus, Ocelus, Latobius, and Grannus might be planning."

Just after dawn on third day after they crossed the river, the hawk returned. There had been little movement by the armies and tribes during the night, but the hawk told Amaethon about the number of vultures and other carrion birds that were congregating around the gathering place. Amaethon communicated with the hawk for several minutes before the hawk flew away to the southwest.

"The vultures are expecting there to be a battle today," Amaethon said when he returned to the campfire area. "I think we should prepare ourselves for the worst."

The escorts broke camp, and soon they were riding southeast toward the gathering place.

Shortly after mid-day, they approached a ridge on the western side of the Mountain of Elohim. They heard shouting and the clashing of metal in the distance. Fearing the worst, Arawn led them to the top of the ridge and looked at what was happening on the plains below them.

The armies of the disobedient gods were attacking the armies loyal to Elohim. The great battle between the tribes had begun.

CHAPTER 55

rawn looked at the scene below him with alarm. The armies loyal to Elohim had their backs to the western face of the Mountain of Elohim. Their tribes were behind the armies on top of the foothills at the base of the mountain. Farthest to the south was the army of the Macruhan. The army of the Followers of Elohim was in the center, and the Dunmaine army was to the north. There was a contingent of Penarduun cavalry on the north end of the Dunmaine forces, but the main body of the Penarduun forces had not arrived.

Facing the forces loyal to Elohim were the armies of the disobedient gods. The Mongán army was in position to the southwest of the Macruhan army. The armies of the Gallasians and the Étaíne were in the center, and the Chulainn army was northwest of the Dunmaine army.

The Gallasians and the Étaíne were attacking the army of the Followers of Elohim. Arawn saw the Étaíne soldiers with their great battle-axes running up the hill at the northern flank of the Followers of Elohim, trying to separate them from the Dunmaine army. The Gallasians archers were attacking the southern flank, trying to force the Followers of Elohim back and cut off the Macruhan army. The cavalry of the Followers of Elohim were attacking the northern flank of the Étaíne army, but were suffering terrible losses.

Arawn turned and looked at his companions. Amaethon and Cerridwen looked concerned. The four escort captains, realizing that the Ruler of the World was exposed, quickly redeployed the escorts to strengthen their position on the ridge in case someone might want to attack Arawn and Cerridwen.

"What can we do to stop this?" Cerridwen asked, looking at Airmid and the three other gods.

"I'm afraid this task is yours," Airmid said with a tone of deep sadness. "Those are your people down there, and you must bring this bloodshed to an end."

"We must bring the peace," Arawn said, remembering what Llyr/Belenus had taught him years earlier on the farm. "That's what a true leader does."

"Exactly," Llyr said, smiling.

"But how do we bring the peace when they're already fighting?" Cerridwen asked.

Before Arawn could answer, the hawk returned and landed on Amaethon's outstretched arm. Amaethon communicated with the hawk for a minute, gave the hawk a mouse, and turned to face his companions as the hawk flew away.

"The Penarduun cavalry is approaching from the east," Amaethon said. "King Arvernus is maneuvering to the west to flank the Chulainn and the Étaíne armies."

Arawn nodded. "We need to get to King Arvernus before he attacks," he said. "If we can hit the Chulainn and the Étaíne armies hard in just the right way, we might be able to force them to redeploy, giving us a chance to stop this before more lives are lost."

The four captains signaled for the escort to form up around the orphans and their companions, and soon they were riding east to intercept the Penarduun cavalry.

King Arvernus led his cavalry around the ridge that kept his forces hidden from the Chulainn and Étaíne armies. Riders had brought him the news as soon as the attack started, and now he was putting the plan into motion.

The kings of the Dunmaine and Macruhan, as well as the General of the Followers of Elohim, knew his swift-moving cavalry was hiding behind the ridges to the north, waiting to see what would happen. If the enemy launched an attack, the plan was for Arvernus to bring up his cavalry and attack the enemy from the rear. That's exactly what he was doing.

The cavalry approached the western edge of the ridge. It was preparing to turn south when a shout went up from one of King Arvernus' captains.

"Riders ahead!"

King Arvernus looked where the captain was pointing. Riding toward the cavalry along a ridge further to the west was a large company of mounted soldiers. Arvernus thought he recognized the uniforms of the Followers of Elohim, the Macruhan, the Dunmaine, and even the

Penarduun. When he recognized Captain Monteria in the front ranks of the soldiers, he knew who was approaching. He raised his hand and ordered the cavalry to halt.

Arawn saw the Penarduun cavalry ahead and ordered the escorts to slow down. He didn't want King Arvernus to accidently think the escorts were the enemy.

As they approached the cavalry, Arawn and Cerridwen saw King Arvernus and his captains ride forward. The king saluted Arawn and Cerridwen when he reached the escorts.

"Hail to the Ruler of the World!" he said as he brought his horse to a stop. Seeing that both Cerridwen and Arawn were wearing an identical blue jewel on their armor, he asked, "Are both of you the Ruler of the World?"

Cerridwen nodded. "Yes, we are, King Arvernus."

Arvernus smiled and saluted again. "What a fascinating thing that is," he murmured. "Do you know the deployment of the enemy?"

Arawn shared with King Arvernus what Amaethon had learned from the hawk. "We need to end the fighting with as little loss of life as possible," he added.

"You're concerned with the lives of the enemy?" Arvernus asked with a tone of surprise.

"They're our people too," Cerridwen replied. "We're supposed to unite the peoples of Alastríona, not begin our reign by causing or allowing the deaths of thousands."

King Arvernus stared at them for a minute and slowly nodded. "I had never thought of that before, My Lords. My apologies."

"You have nothing to apologize for," Arawn said. "You led your tribe during times when peace was hard-earned. True peace is a concept most people won't understand until they see it in action for a while. But it has to start now."

They talked for a few minutes about how King Arvernus planned to use his cavalry. The original plan was to attack the Chulainn and Étaíne armies from the rear and try to capture or kill their leaders, who would be directing the battle well away from the front lines. At Arawn's suggestion, King Arvernus changed the plan so that the cavalry would drive a wedge between the Chulainn and Étaíne armies, separating the two forces and allowing the Penarduun to join the Macruhan, Dunmaine, and the Followers of Elohim.

"I believe we need all of our forces united," Arawn explained.

"We could get surrounded," Arvernus pointed out. "With the Chulainn to the north, the Mongán to the south, and the mountain at our backs, we may have nowhere to run if things go badly."

"I know," Arawn conceded, "but the gathering of the people of Alastríona was never supposed to be a battle between the tribes. We need to stop the fighting long enough to make everyone understand that."

King Arvernus nodded. "As you command, My Lord."

Airmid reached out and put her hand on Arawn's shoulders.

"We cannot follow you into battle, my children," she said. "This task is yours, not ours. We will find you once the fighting stops."

Arawn nodded. The four gods waved to the orphans and vanished from sight.

Arawn, Cerridwen, and Amaethon rode with their escort at the front of the Penarduun cavalry. King Arvernus and his bodyguards rode with them. The Penarduun cavalry rode just behind them in four columns.

Ahead of them, Arawn saw the Étaíne army still attacking the army of the Followers of Elohim. They were having a hard time attacking uphill, but they continued their assault. Arawn wondered if King Taranus were venting his rage over the loss of his fleet on the army of the Followers of Elohim.

The Chulainn army was moving closer to that Dunmaine army's position, but the Dunmaine archers were keeping them back. Arawn saw a gap between the Étaíne and Chulainn armies, and he pointed it out to King Arvernus.

"That's where we'll attack," Arvernus confirmed. Turning in his saddle, he motioned to his captains to get ready. Looking back to Arawn and Cerridwen, he said, "Where you lead, I follow."

Arawn and Cerridwen drew their swords and raised them in the afternoon sunlight. "Forward!" they shouted.

Arawn and Cerridwen were in the lead. Amaethon and the four escort captains rode behind them with the rest of the escorts staying close to the Ruler of the World as they rode into battle.

King Arvernus rode just behind the escorts at the head of the four columns of cavalry. As the cavalry approached the rear of the Étaíne and Chulainn armies, the columns spread out to form a wedge.

Arawn was surprised that none of the Étaíne or Chulainn forces had seen the cavalry approaching, but he knew that would change soon. He looked over to Cerridwen, who had a look of grim determination on her face. He glanced back at Amaethon, who was holding his dragon staff rather than his sword. Arawn remembered that Amaethon didn't need a sword to protect himself, and he turned to face forward again.

King Taranus felt his frustration growing. His men had been attacking the center of Elohim's followers for hours but hadn't managed to break their lines. Wave after wave of Étaíne soldiers attacked and were repulsed – forced to retreat back down those accursed hills.

His captains had requested to withdraw and redeploy their soldiers, but Taranus refused. He wasn't going to let the armies of Elohim see his army pull back. He was yelling at his captains again when he heard something that sounded like thunder coming from behind him.

There shouldn't be thunder on a cloudless day. He stopped yelling and turned around.

An endless sea of horsemen was approaching the unprotected rear of his army, and he suddenly realized that the Penarduun cavalry had arrived.

Arawn and Cerridwen led their forces into the gap between the Étaíne and Chulainn armies. The lancers of the cavalry columns in their wedge formation slashed at the soldiers who tried to stop their advance.

The deeper they rode into the gap, the wider the wedge became. Étaíne and Chulainn soldiers closest to the gap tried to hold their position, but eventually broke and ran, causing order and discipline to crumble among the Étaíne and Chulainn forces.

The Étaíne soldiers attacking the Followers of Elohim, seeing the cavalry attacking the rear of their army, fell back and tried to move into a formation to stop the advance of the horsemen. They held their formation as the cavalry approached, but felt a tremendous force pushing them out of the way as the horses reached their position. Amaethon was doing his part to keep the loss of life at a minimum.

As Arawn and Cerridwen led the lead columns of the cavalry past the front lines of the Étaíne and Chulainn armies, a cheer went up from the army of the Followers of Elohim. Arawn and Cerridwen led three of the columns of cavalry to the south, and King Arvernus led the fourth column to the north.

Arawn and Cerridwen led their escort past the Macruhan army, which began to cheer wildly when the Ruler of the World rode past. Once the cavalry had deployed between the opposing forces, Arawn and Cerridwen led their escorts north so they could ride past the Dunmaine army. Both Arawn and Cerridwen knew it was important for their allies to see them to build up the spirits of their armies.

The Chulainn army fell back as soon as they saw the cavalry approaching, as did the Étaíne, Gallasian, and Mongán armies. The appearance of the cavalry broke the momentum of the attack, and the armies of the disobedient gods returned to their original lines to regroup and decide how to deal with the arrival of the Penarduun forces.

Archers from the armies of the disobedient gods attempted to shoot at the orphans and their escorts, but Amaethon sent their arrows flying harmlessly in other directions. After the fourth group of archers tried to attack, Amaethon decided he needed to do something about them.

He concentrated for a moment, and thousands of arrows flew into the air and over the backs of the armies of the disobedient gods. Amaethon had emptied the quivers of every archer in the Mongán, Gallasian, Étaíne, and Chulainn armies and sent them flying to the west. He knew the armies had more arrows in their supply wagons, but it would take hours to distribute them to the shocked archers.

"Nicely done," Arawn said as Amaethon chuckled to himself.

The orphans and their escorts eventually returned to the center of the allies' position and rode up the hill where the army of the Followers of Elohim held the ground.

General Thorsen, who commanded the army of the Followers of Elohim, stepped forward and greeted them. "Welcome, My Lords," he said. "I am honored to be in the presence of the Ruler of the World, and I pledge myself and my army to your service."

"Thank you, General Thorsen," Arawn said, dismounting and handing the reins of his horse to one of the escorts. Cerridwen and Amaethon also dismounted and joined Arawn.

"I'm Arawn and this is Cerridwen, my wife," Arawn said, gesturing to Cerridwen. Pointing to Amaethon, he added, "And this is Amaethon, the Dragon Lord."

"I'm delighted to meet all of you," Thorsen said, bowing to each of them.

Turning to look at the armies of the disobedient gods, Arawn asked, "Do you think they'll attempt another attack today?"

General Thorsen looked up at the sky and noted that there was less than two hours until sunset. "I doubt it, My Lord. Their archers don't seem to have any arrows for some reason, and the appearance of the Penarduun cavalry has unnerved them. If they're smart, they'll wait until nightfall and redeploy their armies to surround us. If they can coordinate their attack once the sun has risen, things could go very badly for us."

Arawn nodded. Turning to his escorts, he said, "Send riders to Kings Vellaunus, Arvernus, and Esus, and ask them to join us for a council meeting here as soon as they can. We need a plan for how we're going to end this."

CHAPTER 56

The council meeting began shortly before sunset. Kings Vellaunus of the Dunmaine and Esus of the Macruhan arrived quickly, but King Arvernus of the Penarduun couldn't come until his men had deployed in defensive positions on both flanks and between the armies loyal to Elohim.

Once all of the kings had arrived, they, along with General Thorsen immediately pledged command of their armies to the Ruler of the World. They were surprised that Arawn and Cerridwen both were the Ruler, but they didn't let this shake their loyalty. Elohim chose the Ruler, and as faithful followers of Elohim, they obeyed their god.

"What were our losses today?" Arawn asked once the council meeting began.

"Surprisingly light," General Thorsen replied. "My cavalry losses were high, but the rest of the army suffered only minor injuries and few deaths."

Kings Vellaunus and Esus gave similar reports. "Our worst injuries were from archers," Esus said, "but most of those injured by arrows will recover."

Arawn and Cerridwen were glad that their forces had suffered few losses, but the battle wasn't over yet. If they couldn't find a way to end the fighting soon, they knew that the losses would increase.

"How is the opposition redeploying for tomorrow?" Arawn asked.

"They're extending their lines to surround us," King Arvernus reported. "They've closed the gaps between their armies, and they're extending their flanks to cut off any escape to the north or the south."

"And our forces?" Arawn inquired.

"We're entrenched along the crests of the foothills," General Thorsen replied. We have good defensive positions, and it'll be hard to break through our lines."

"So what do you suggest we do once morning arrives?" Arawn asked.

Arawn listened carefully as each of the kings and General Thorsen expressed different opinions about what to do in the morning.

"If we attack both flanks," King Arvernus began, "we can allow the members of our tribes to escape and we can keep the enemy off-guard. If we try to attack the center, they could surround us and wipe us out."

"We saw how much difficulty they had coming up the hill to get to us today," General Thorsen countered. "If we maintain our defensive position here on the higher ground, they can only reach us by attacking up hill in the open. It'll be easy to keep pushing them back. Eventually, they'll either give up or grow weak enough for us to attack safely."

"But we'll grow weaker, too," King Esus reminded them. "We have supplies, but we have no way to get more. They do. They can afford to wait until we starve. We can't. We need to act quickly."

"What do you think, My Lords?" King Vellaunus asked.

"I think you're all correct," Arawn replied. "But I think you're all missing the point. Cerridwen and I are supposed to unite the tribes – *all* of the tribes. If we unite the tribes with the sword, then the defeated tribes will always resent us no matter what good we do afterwards. We must unite the tribes in peace, not war. We need to end this battle so we can convince the leaders of the other tribes that war isn't what Elohim wants. Man was never supposed to learn warfare, and this is where it must stop so man can begin to *unlearn* it."

They talked for several hours but were unable to reach a consensus. Arawn sensed that everyone was feeling frustrated.

"I suggest we take a break and get a few hours rest," he said. "We'll meet again an hour before dawn. Agreed?"

Everyone agreed, and soon the orphans were the only ones left around the fire.

"It's not going well," Amaethon commented softly.

"No, it's not," Cerridwen said. "These men are men of war, and we're trying to turn them into men of peace overnight. It's not something they can do so quickly."

"Quickly or not, it still must be done," a voice said from the darkness. A moment later, the four gods stepped into the light and sat down with the orphans.

The four gods had a look of deep sadness in their faces. "This must stop," Airmid continued. Looking at the three orphans, she added, "You must stop it."

"How?" Arawn asked. "I have no idea how to get the armies to stop fighting." Looking at Amaethon, he asked, "Do you have any ideas, Dragon Lord?"

Amaethon looked at Arawn and shook his head. "I don't have the power to stop an entire army, let alone four armies. I can help defend our forces here and there, but not long enough to prevent the loss of life we could be facing."

"What about their weapons?" Cerridwen asked. "Can you make their weapons fly away like you did at the river?"

"Yes, but what if the armies leave once they're disarmed?"

"The tribes are gathered here for a reason," Arawn said. "This is where the uniting is to begin. If they leave before we can start uniting them, we'll have failed."

Airmid nodded in agreement.

Amaethon chuckled sarcastically. "I could always conjure another dragon to get their attention, if you thought that would help."

Arawn sat up. "Do you think that might work?"

"I don't know. I suppose so. But what would you want it to do?"

"It would have to put up a barrier between the two forces, but it would also have to make the opposing armies remain here until we could arrange some sort of meeting to bring everyone together."

"That's a lot of work for an illusion," Amaethon said, trying to think of how he could accomplish what Arawn wanted.

Camalus spoke up for the first time. "I think a mere illusion is more than we can ask of Amaethon in this case. We need something a little different." He leaned over and whispered in Amaethon's ear, and Amaethon's eyes grew wide.

"You want me to do WHAT?" he asked incredulously. "I don't know how to do that!"

"Balor and I will show you, and we'll help you. Think about it. If you conjure the illusion of a dragon and the archers down there start shooting at it, the arrows will fly right through it and potentially kill a number of soldiers on the field. In addition, you and your skills may be needed elsewhere before the day is done, and you must not be exhausted when that time comes. We'll supply the energy to do what must be done and show you how to do it. It's better this way."

"Why can't *you* just do it?" Amaethon asked, still shocked by Camalus' suggestion and feeling too tired to think clearly.

"Because this is your task to complete, and you may need to know how it's done after we're gone," Balor replied, joining Camalus.

"What are you talking about?" Arawn asked.

"I'm not going to conjure the illusion of a dragon," Amaethon replied, sounding doubtful. "I'm going to summon a real one."

When the council met before dawn, Arawn told them what the orphans and the gods had discussed earlier. "I need you to deploy your forces to defend the members of your tribes. The top of this hill needs to be cleared, so have the escorts move down to the base of the hill. The horses may react wildly to what's going to happen."

The kings and the general didn't completely understand all of the plan, but they agreed to do as Arawn asked.

When the sun rose over the Mountain of Elohim an hour later, the orphans saw that the armies of the disobedient gods had been very busy overnight. The four armies were in one long continuous line that stretched from the northeast flank around to the southeast flank of the armies loyal to Elohim. There were no breaks or gaps in the line at all, and there was no way to escape past them without a tremendous loss of life on both sides. Arawn thought that the armies of the disobedient gods must be very confident of victory, because they hadn't even bothered to entrench or set up any defensive barriers at all.

On the summit of the hill in the center of the armies loyal to Elohim, the three orphans and the four gods stood alone.

"Are you ready?" Camalus asked.

Amaethon nodded and took Camalus and Balor by the hand.

Arawn and Cerridwen watched as Amaethon closed his eyes in deep concentration. For several minutes, Amaethon, Camalus, and Balor clutched each other's hands with their eyes closed. Arawn saw a look of contentment come over Camalus and Balor.

Amaethon was not sure what happened, but he felt like he had been flying through a tunnel at high speeds. He opened his eyes and looked around him. He felt Camalus and Balor holding his hands, but he couldn't see them anywhere. In the twilight, nothing looked familiar. He saw the sun setting in the distance and knew that he was no longer standing on the side of the Mountain of Elohim.

He was standing on a ledge overlooking a lake. There were three rocky peaks silhouetted in front of him. Caves dotted the peaks from top to bottom. A waterfall, fed by an unseen spring on the left peak, fed the lake below him.

Looking down at the lake, he saw dozens of large beasts drinking the water. Glancing back at the peaks, he saw movement around the caves that looked like more of the beasts moving in and out. He turned his head toward the sky and saw some of the beasts flying in circles – their giant wings glowing in the setting sun.

An unusual sound forced his attention back to the ledge. Three large dragons were sitting in front of him, looking at Amaethon calmly as if they expected to see him standing there.

"Welcome to the island of the dragons, Dragon Lord," one of the dragons said with a deep, booming voice.

"You know who I am?" Amaethon asked.

"Of course," the dragon replied. "We've been expecting you ever since we saw the blood red moons rising and the shooting stars in the sky. We obey Elohim, too, and we've been waiting for the coming of the Ruler of the World and the Dragon Lord for many centuries – ever since the two prophecies were first shared with us. And now you're here. How may we be of service to you?"

Questions filled Amaethon's mind, but he remembered why he was there and said, "The tribes of man are engaged in a battle on the slopes of the Mountain of Elohim. The Ruler of the World needs your help to end the battle so the tribes of man can be united as Elohim intended."

"It is as it was foretold," the dragon said. "We will answer the summons of the Ruler of the World and go with you."

"Thank you," Amaethon said. He felt Camalus and Balor squeezing his hands, and he felt himself flying through the tunnel that had brought him to the island of the dragons. But instead of being in the tunnel alone, three dragons were with him as he returned to the slopes of the Mountain of Elohim.

A moment later, Arawn and Cerridwen heard three loud popping sounds. Looking around, they saw three dragons staring directly at them.

Arawn heard the horses at the base of the hill whinnying in fear, but the escorts worked to keep them under control.

The three dragons stared at the three orphans and the four gods. Each bowed its head slowly.

"We answer the call of the Dragon Lord to help the Ruler of the World," the dragons intoned with deep, rumbling voices.

"You can speak?" Cerridwen asked, still recovering from the shock of seeing three real dragons up close.

"We speak when necessary," the dragons answered, "and this is one of those times. We are part of the world, and as you are the Ruler of the World, we are also your subjects. Command us."

Arawn recovered his composure and looked at Amaethon, who was looking as surprised as Cerridwen was. Arawn pointed to the armies on the plains below.

"I need to get their attention, I need to make sure that they don't attack, and I need to make sure that they don't leave until I've spoken to their leaders. I would prefer to do it with as little loss of life as possible. Can you help?"

"We can help," the dragons said. "We obey the Ruler of the World."

"This is where we leave you again," Airmid said. "We can only come to you one more time, and that's when you summon all twelve of us to say good-bye to this world."

"I understand," Arawn said.

The four gods vanished. Amaethon moved next to Cerridwen and Arawn, and the orphans stepped forward to stand in front of the dragons. Arawn raised his hand and the dragons roared, shaking the earth with the sound.

Everyone at the gathering place heard the roar. They immediately stopped what they were doing and turned toward the sound. On the hilltop, the Rulers of the World with the Kingstone halves glowing brightly on their chests, the Dragon Lord, and the three dragons were visible to all. Everyone watched as the dragons spread their great wings and lifted into the air. The dragons roared again and dove directly at the armies of the disobedient gods, who were moving forward to continue the battle.

"So those are real dragons?" Arawn asked. "They look just like the ones you conjured."

"Tell me again exactly what you did, Amaethon," Cerridwen asked.

"We translocated three dragons from the island of the dragons on the far side of Alastríona," he replied with a sense of wonder still evident in his voice. "I didn't even know it was possible, but we did it."

"Evidently I really am the Dragon Lord," Amaethon continued. "Camalus and Balor helped me send my thoughts to the dragons and ask them to come back with me. When my thoughts returned here, the dragons came back with me. Somehow, they knew this was supposed to happen and were ready to help. I'm starting to think that there's a lot more to the prophecy that we haven't been shown or was never written down. The dragons seem to know all about it."

The dragons flew across the space between the armies loyal to Elohim and the armies of the disobedient gods. Fire shot from the dragons' mouths to create a natural barrier between the two forces, driving back the armies of the disobedient gods. The dragons left one place in the center of the field free from fire; in fact, none of the dragons would even fly directly over that spot.

The dragons flew to the rear of the armies of the disobedient gods. Fire shot from their mouths again, destroying supply wagons and trapping the armies of the disobedient gods between two barriers of fire. The members of their tribes, who were camped well behind their armies, watched as the dragons' fire cut them off from the soldiers and their kings. They became fearful about what would happen next.

Once the armies of the disobedient gods had retreated from the fire, preventing the anticipated battle from starting, the three dragons hovered over the field and roared again. Then they flew back to the hillside where Arawn and Cerridwen were standing.

"It is as you requested, Ruler of the World," the dragons said and they landed next to the orphans. "We will remain here and watch what happens. If you need us, call and we will obey." The dragons folded their wings and bowed their heads. The great beasts were still visible to the people at the gathering place, and the presence of the three dragons took the desire to fight out of most of the soldiers and their leaders.

Motioning for the escorts to bring up the horses, Arawn shouted, "Mount up!"

CHAPTER 57

heir horses were brought up, and the orphans mounted quickly. Arawn signaled the escorts to follow him, and soon Arawn, Cerridwen, and Amaethon were riding forward to the place between the two forces where there was no fire. Apart from the crackling of the fire and the wind in their ears, there was silence across the plains around them.

When they reached the center of the field, Arawn felt something special about the place. He touched the Kingstone on his chest, and in his mind, he saw the twelve gods standing in a circle as they created the world. Arawn realized that they were on the same spot where that had happened.

"This is where it all began," he said to Cerridwen and Amaethon. "This is where the twelve stood to create Alastríona."

Turning to the escorts, Cerridwen said, "I need General Thorsen and the kings of all of the tribes brought here immediately so we can put an end to this battle. Tell them that the bloodshed must stop."

Escorts raced off in all directions to obey Cerridwen's wishes.

Kings Vellaunus, Arvernus, and Esus joined them as soon as each received the summons, as did General Thorsen. The general and all three kings immediately dismounted. The kings removed their crowns and handed them up to Cerridwen.

"We formally surrender our tribes to the Ruler of the World," Vellaunus, Arvernus, and Esus said.

"And I formally surrender the followers of Elohim to the Ruler of the World," General Thorsen stated.

Cerridwen handed the crowns to an escort who was holding a short lance. The escort placed the crowns on the lance and held it up for the armies to see. Cerridwen heard a cheer coming from the loyal armies and tribes when they saw the crowns on the lance. They knew that the uniting of the tribes had finally begun.

The escorts returned from delivering the summons to Kings Ocelus of the Mongán, Latobius of the Gallasians, Taranus of the Étaíne, and Grannus of the Chulainn.

"They refuse to meet with you, My Lords," the escorts reported. The escort who was sent to summon King Taranus added, "He said that you can come to him and give him homage, but he'll never submit to you."

Arawn looked back at the dragons. Turning to the riders, he said, "Tell Kings Ocelus, Latobius, Grannus, and Taranus that if they don't join us here in five minutes, I'll unleash the dragons and destroy them and their armies to the last man. Then I'll decide whether or not to unleash the dragons on their tribes."

"That's a bit ruthless, don't you think?" Amaethon said as the riders saluted and rode off to deliver their messages.

Arawn nodded. "I'm just hoping that it'll get their attention enough so I don't have to make good on the threat," he stated with a look of grim determination.

Cerridwen nudged her horse closer, and Arawn looked at her. "Do whatever you think needs to be done, Arawn," she said softly.

"You and I are equals in this, Cerridwen. If you see a better way or if you think I'm taking the wrong approach, say so."

"I will," she stated. "But you have my support, no matter where it takes us."

Arawn nodded. A few minutes later, they saw the riders returning with Kings Ocelus, Latobius, Grannus and Taranus. When the kings arrived, they remained on their horses, glaring at Arawn and Cerridwen.

King Taranus sneered at the three orphans. "Which one of you destroyed my palace?"

"I did," Amaethon replied coldly.

"You destroyed my home, you broke my city, and you obliterated my fleet. I'm not leaving here without your head."

"Be glad he let you live after what you did," Arawn countered. "You ordered the death of hundreds, if not thousands, of innocent children across all of Alastríona, you sent Athanaric to kill him, you sent Siena to kill me, you sent your longboats into other territories to intercept and kill us all, and then you captured us and locked us in your dungeons. If anyone's going to lose a head today, it's you, so shut up."

"How *dare* you speak to me that way?" Taranus sputtered.

"Are we really going to have this conversation again, or are you

345

going to be quiet and listen for once in your miserable life?" Arawn said, reaching for his sword.

Taranus kept his mouth closed, but it was clear he wasn't happy to be there.

"Very well. Now to the business at hand," Arawn said to the gathered leaders. "As was foretold in the prophecy, the Kingstone has been retrieved, and the Ruler of the World has received the blessing of Elohim. The twelve gods have chosen to be obedient to Elohim and will leave this world forever. Elohim is the one supreme god of Alastríona now and for all time."

The kings looked startled at the news that the gods were abandoning their tribes. Arawn waited for the information to sink in, and then continued. "The mission of the Ruler of the World now is to unite the tribes so that all Alastríonans can begin living as Elohim intended before some of the gods disobeyed Elohim's will."

"Where is the Kingstone, and who is the Ruler of the World?" King Ocelus demanded.

Arawn and Cerridwen held up their halves of the Kingstone. "This is the Kingstone, and *we* are the Ruler of the World," Cerridwen answered.

"A woman?" Ocelus asked with a laugh. "A woman can't be king. That's for men alone."

"What makes you think that?" Arawn asked.

"Because the gods are male, therefore the male is the dominant creature," Ocelus stated flatly.

"The gods aren't male," Arawn countered. "They aren't female either. Gender is a human condition, not a divine one."

"Look, you young upstart," Ocelus said. "I've seen gods before, and they're definitely male."

"What about Airmid and Branwen?" Cerridwen interjected. "The gods can take any form they want when they appear to us, but I've seen what they really look like, and they're neither male nor female."

"Then how do you explain their children?" King Latobius asked.

"The gods have no children," Cerridwen replied. "Airmid created humans but made certain that humans and gods could never breed and create a race of semi-divine creatures."

"Liar!" Latobius shouted. "My great-great grandmother was visited by a god who got her pregnant. That's how my family came to rule our tribe!"

"A god lay with your great-great grandmother?" Arawn asked. "Isn't it more likely that she found herself with child and told her father that it was a god who caused it, so she and her lover wouldn't get

346

punished? Isn't it more likely that her father, seeing an opportunity to advance the standing of his house, told everyone else so the child would become king when it was born? Her claim of a divine pregnancy isn't proof that you're descended from a god, but it does indicate that you're descended from a liar and an opportunist."

"How *dare* you insult my family?" Latobius exploded.

"How dare *you* insult our intelligence with such nonsense?" Arawn countered. "A god told me personally that humans and gods cannot breed. I'm more inclined to take the word of a god than I am to take the word of a man whose great-great grandmother lied to keep a secret safe."

"So no one is descended from the gods?" King Grannus asked, looking confused. "We've always believed that the ruling families had divine blood in their veins."

"It's never too late to stop believing a lie," Cerridwen said kindly. "All humans were created by Airmid, and that's as close to divine as any of us can ever be. Airmid created men and women to be equal, but over time, it was men who attempted to dominate and make women less important and subordinate. I was chosen to be the Ruler of the World along with my husband in order to restore the balance between the men and women of Alastríona. The prophecy never said anything about a king. That misinterpretation occurred centuries ago. The prophecy only speaks of a Ruler, and in this case, the Ruler is the two of us – equal in all ways."

"All my life, I thought I was superior," Grannus said softly. "I thought I was of a superior bloodline, I thought I was of a superior gender, and I thought my god was the superior god who would rule the world. Now you're telling me I've been mistaken for my whole life?"

"You're not buying into this nonsense, Grannus, are you?" Ocelus demanded angrily.

"The proof seems to be right in front of us," Grannus replied. "The gods are leaving us, these two have the Kingstone, and they've fulfilled the requirements of the prophecy. They've communed with Airmid, who created humans. Who would know better what man is capable of than the god who created man?"

"And what of your loyalty to Morrigan, the god of your tribe?" Ocelus demanded. "Just because he's leaving doesn't mean you're released from your bond to him."

"Morrigan disobeyed Elohim by staying here," Grannus replied. "We should never have started worshipping Morrigan, and our tribe should never have been separated from the rest of the peoples of Alastríona."

"What are you saying, Grannus?" Latobius asked.

"That it's time to do what my ancestors were too foolish or too arrogant to do. It's time to do the right thing." Grannus removed his crown and handed it to Cerridwen. "I yield my tribe to the Ruler of the World and to Elohim."

"Thank you, Grannus," Cerridwen said, taking the crown and putting it with the crowns of the kings who had already yielded.

"You're welcome, My Lord," Grannus replied, bowing in his saddle to Cerridwen and Arawn.

"This is unbelievable," Taranus said in a rage. "We're allies, Grannus."

"Times change, Taranus," Grannus said. "It's my choice, and I think it's long overdue.

Taranus fumed at Grannus. "We're supposed to be here to fight for the right to be the High King of Alastríona and decide which god we'll worship, and instead we're here watching this fool surrender to a stupid boy and a girl!"

"That's not why you're here at all, Taranus," Arawn pointed out. "The battle was never supposed to be between the tribes to determine who will be the king. Elohim has already chosen the Ruler. The real battle was between the gods who obeyed and the gods who disobeyed. That battle is over, and the gods who disobeyed have agreed to leave Alastríona and return to the purpose for which Elohim created them. All of the tribes will worship Elohim, and the universe will begin moving forward again according to Elohim's will and design."

"I can't believe that all of the gods have agreed to leave," Taranus stated.

"Believe it," Arawn said. "If even one of the gods continued to defy Elohim, the universe would have already been destroyed."

"What do you mean?" Ocelus asked, sounding aghast. "Elohim would have destroyed the universe including Alastríona unless the gods did as they were told?"

"That's exactly what I mean," Arawn replied. "There's a purpose for the universe, and Elohim created the gods to help fulfill that purpose. If the gods aren't doing what they were created to do, then that purpose remains unfulfilled. The day we retrieved the Kingstone was the last chance the gods were given to obey the will of Elohim. If any refused, then creation would have been unmade, and Elohim would start over. The gods wouldn't survive the unmaking of creation, just as we wouldn't."

"I can't believe that," Taranus said. "Mider would never let that happen."

"The only way Mider could stop it is by being obedient to Elohim,"

348

Cerridwen said.

"So the prophecy was about the gods battling to save or destroy all of creation?" Ocelus asked, sounding bewildered. "Then what's the purpose of the gathering of the tribes?"

Arawn nodded. "The peoples of Alastríona were never supposed to be separated by the gods into tribes. We are one people. We've been brought together in this place so the reuniting of the tribes can begin and so we can say good-bye to the gods and begin worshiping Elohim."

"No!" Taranus shouted. "No, no, no! It cannot be! I won't believe you! Mider wouldn't lie to me and my people."

"If he'd disobey Elohim, why wouldn't he lie to you?" Cerridwen asked. "If he told you that men were superior to women, if he told you he was the most powerful god, if he told you that your tribe was superior to the other tribes, then he has been lying to you for centuries. There is no superior tribe because Airmid made all people the same. Men and women are equal in all ways. Mider is just one of the twelve gods Elohim created to fulfill the plan for the universe. Elohim is the all-powerful god, not Mider. You were lied to by a god who didn't care about you or your people. Mider only wanted to be allowed to disobey Elohim without consequences, and Elohim could no longer tolerate that."

"So we have no choice?" Ocelus asked.

"You always have a choice, Ocelus," Cerridwen replied, "but there's only one correct option. The other options lead to war, death, loss, and the pain and suffering of your people."

"Tell me this," he said to Arawn. "Would you have really turned your dragons on my people?"

"Yes," Arawn said simply. "It would have pained me beyond measure, but yes. If you were determined to fight, I couldn't allow you to cause the deaths of those who are faithful to Elohim. To save them, I would have destroyed you utterly, and I would've mourned your loss until the end of my days."

"And if I yield to you?"

"Then there would be no cause for your destruction."

Ocelus looked at Arawn and Cerridwen for a moment. He reached up and removed the golden laurels that served as his crown. He handed the crown to Arawn to put with the crowns of those who had already yielded. "I and my tribe yield to the Ruler of the World. Lead the people well, and I will follow you."

"Thank you, Ocelus," Arawn said, accepting the crown. Turning to look at Latobius and Taranus, he said, "And what of you two? All other tribes have submitted to the will of Elohim. Will you submit, or do you want to face the dragons and the rest of us in a battle you can't win?"

"You're absolutely certain that no man is descended from a god apart from being created by Airmid?" Latobius asked.

"I can summon Airmid for you to ask yourself, if that would help you believe the truth," Arawn said.

Latobius looked at Arawn in disbelief at the idea of a human summoning a god, but he looked at the Kingstone and realized Arawn was probably the one man alive who actually could summon a god and survive the encounter.

Seeing no other course of action, Latobius removed his crown and handed it to Arawn.

"My tribe and I yield," he said.

"Thank you, Latobius," Arawn said as he took the crown and handed it to the escort to put with the other crowns. "And for what it's worth, I'm sorry to be the one to tell you what you learned today. I can't imagine anything more difficult than to discover that everything you've ever believed was untrue."

"Thank you, My Lord," Latobius replied, bowing to Arawn.

"That leaves you, Taranus," Cerridwen said. "For your crimes against us, you should be killed here in front of your people. But this day is about unity, not recrimination. If you yield, you may live and retire from the field in peace with the safety of your tribe assured. But if you resist, you'll never see another sunrise or sunset."

"Would you kill me yourself, girl?" Taranus asked, with as much bravado as he could muster.

"Taranus," Ocelus interjected, "be reasonable. It's over. You were wrong, and we've lost. If the Ruler of the World has been anointed to lead us, then cast off your pride and follow with the rest of us. It's better that we all learn to live together than to die fighting one another for some senseless reason."

"Join us, Taranus," Grannus said. "Don't let your people suffer because of you."

Taranus looked around at the other kings. He looked at Arawn and Cerridwen with defeat in his eyes. He reached up, removed his crown, and ran his fingers over the fish designs worked into it for a moment. Closing his eyes, he handed his crown to Cerridwen.

"My tribe and I yield to the Ruler of the World," he said quietly with his head hung low.

Cerridwen accepted the crown and handed it to the escort who placed the crown on the lance with the other crowns. Taking Taranus' hand in hers, she said, "Thank you, Taranus."

He lifted his head and looked into her eyes. In those eyes he saw forgiveness, rather than the triumphant look he expected. He realized how badly he had misjudged her, and tears filled his eyes.

Cerridwen squeezed his hand to reassure him that he had no reason to feel ashamed. "Thank you, My Lord," he said finally, pulling back his hand to dry his eyes.

Arawn and Cerridwen dismounted and motioned for all of the former kings and the general to approach. Those still mounted now dismounted. In the sight of all of the armies of the tribes of Alastríona, Arawn and Cerridwen embraced each of the former kings and the general as a sign of friendship, starting with the kings who had been opposed to the will of Elohim, and ending with General Thorsen who commanded the army of the Followers of Elohim.

"I hope we can lead the faithful as well as you've led its army," Arawn said to Thorsen.

"I have no doubt, My Lord," Thorsen said. "Those who have been touched by Elohim can do nothing less."

"So what happens now?" Esus asked.

"Now it's time for the gods to leave us," Arawn said. "I want all of you to stand here with me so the gods will see that the tribes of Alastríona are united once again."

Cerridwen and Arawn took off their halves of the Kingstone and placed them together. The Kingstone became one and glowed with a brilliant blue light in their hands.

Amplified by the power of the Kingstone, Cerridwen and Arawn's voices boomed: "I summon the twelve gods to this place."

The Kings Surrender their Crowns to the Ruler of the World.

CHAPTER 58

The gods answered the summons and appeared as luminous beings in a circle around the orphans and the former kings – standing in the exact same place where they had once gathered to create the world. The former kings, their armies, and their tribes looked in amazement at all twelve gods standing together.

No one other than the three orphans had seen the gods appear as they were now, and the former kings finally understood what Arawn and Cerridwen had told them about the gods being neither male nor female. Seeing the gods in this form convinced them that Arawn and Cerridwen had been telling the truth.

The orphans had heard the gods speaking individually before, but now they spoke in unison, and their chorus was the most beautiful sound anyone had ever heard before. "Good-bye, children of Alastríona," they said, loud enough for everyone at the gathering place to hear. "Our time among you is at an end. We leave this world in the care of the Ruler of the World. Follow them and obey the will of Elohim."

An instant later, all of the gods vanished except for Airmid.

"Where have they gone?" Cerridwen asked, startled by the sudden disappearance of the other gods.

"To the next world to be created. I must be there soon, but I've been given a few moments to speak with you before I must leave."

Airmid touched the Kingstone, and it made the familiar popping sound as it separated into two pieces. "Continue to guard the Kingstone. It will be entrusted to every Ruler who follows you until the time when it's no longer needed. At that time, Elohim will take it back. Until then, it will continue to guide you. Remember, it's in unity that great things are accomplished. Be ever inclusive, never excluding anyone. You never know the key contribution that each individual is destined to make. Look at yourselves, and you'll see that demonstrated clearly."

Arawn and Cerridwen nodded in agreement.

"One of your tasks will be educating everyone on the way Elohim wants to be worshipped," Airmid said. "Elohim is the Father-Mother of the universe from whom all life and purpose exists. Elohim gave life and has a plan for each and every creature that exists or will exist. True worship is acknowledging your role in the plan, committing to put aside personal wants, and acting in accordance with that plan, just as the gods have now done. Elohim doesn't want you to sacrifice *things*. Elohim wants you to sacrifice your selfishness and to live for others. That's the highest form of worship."

"Then I guess the best way to teach that to everyone is to live it ourselves first," Cerridwen commented.

"Well said," Airmid replied. "It's good for the Ruler of the World to lead by example. Your people will look to you for what they should be doing and how they should be acting. Being the living example of what you want the world to be is what Elohim intended for the two of you all along."

Turning to Amaethon, Airmid handed him a small scroll. "This is for you, Dragon Lord. Your destiny is intertwined with that of the Ruler of the World, but there are also other tasks that you must perform. Do not read this yet. You'll know when it's time."

Amaethon nodded, wondering if the scroll contained the prophecy that the dragons had mentioned.

"There's a word of caution I must give you before I go," Airmid added, turning back to Arawn and Cerridwen. "The gods taught man the art of war, along with jealousy, envy, and hatred. Man was never intended to learn these things. These are the seeds of destruction that could interfere with the plan of Elohim and keep this world from fulfilling its purpose. Only with unity, love, and compassion can their effects be neutralized."

Arawn and Cerridwen thought about what Airmid had said. "What do we do now?" Arawn asked, realizing that none of the gods would be around anymore to provide advice and counsel.

"Go and fulfill your destiny," Airmid said, vanishing as the sun reached its zenith in the sky. At the same moment, the fire from the dragons, which was still burning around the armies of the disobedient gods, vanished as well.

Arawn and Cerridwen put their halves of the Kingstone back around their necks and turned to face Amaethon and the former leaders of the tribes. From the looks on their faces, Arawn knew that they were profoundly affected by what had just happened.

"Are they truly gone?" Amaethon asked.

"Yes, they are, my friend," Arawn replied.

A sound coming from above caught his attention. The three dragons had left their place on the hilltop and were hovering overhead.

"Hail to the Ruler of the World and to the Dragon Lord," they said with their booming voices. "We pay homage to you and remind you that we are your servants should you ever need us." The dragons roared one more time, flew off toward the southwest, and disappeared into the distance.

"What are your orders, My Lords?" General Thorsen asked.

"Now we begin to learn peace instead of war," Cerridwen replied. "Go tell your tribes and armies that the gods are gone and there will be no more fighting between the tribes. Then return to this place. I think it's time we all started getting to know each other better."

That night, the leaders of the tribes camped together in the center of the gathered peoples of Alastríona. Arawn and Cerridwen wanted to begin the unification process immediately, and they felt that building trust and understanding between the former kings was the best way to start.

"It doesn't matter what has happened in the past," Cerridwen said as they sat around a large bonfire that had just been lit. "It only matters what we do from this moment on. For my part, I forgive anything that might have been done to me by anyone, and I ask the forgiveness of the living for anyone who may have been injured or killed by my hand."

"And I forgive what happened to my palace and my fleet," Taranus said. "I guess I don't need a palace any longer, and if we're truly unified I don't need all those gates in the city either. I hope you'll forgive me for my part in trying to prevent the prophecy from being fulfilled. Had I known what was at stake, my actions would have been different."

"I think all of our actions would have been different," Arawn said. "That's why we need to make sure that we stay unified in the future. If we're all working together as one, we can keep this from happening again."

"I'm guessing that trade will increase," Esus said. "It'll be good to share what we each have to offer."

"Just out of curiosity," General Thorsen asked, "Where will you live, now that you'll be busy uniting all the tribes?"

Arawn and Cerridwen looked at each other for a moment. Arawn answered. "We'll be spending a lot of time traveling to the territories to meet the people and get to know them better, but I think we need a place where all the people can meet, work out issues, and create opportunities for all of Alastríona together. It would be comprised of the best of what each of the territories has to offer. It would need to represent our vision for the future – built on the best of our past without being limited or defined by our past. It would also need to be centrally located to all the territories. We were thinking that this spot would be the best place. That way, we'd all come together where the gods stood when they created the world and where they left the world to its own destiny. I think they'd be pleased with the choice."

The former leaders of the tribes agreed with Arawn's suggestion and pledged materials, builders, and architects for the project.

Hours later, after everyone else had gone to sleep, Arawn, Cerridwen, and Amaethon were alone, sitting together and talking quietly.

Turning to Amaethon, Arawn said, "You've been with us so far, my friend. Are you ready to stay with us and help us change the world?"

"It would be my pleasure, My Lords," Amaethon said with his usual grin. "My place is with the two of you. The three of us are still bound by prophecy and destiny, and I think we have many adventures ahead of us. But can I do more than just summon the occasional dragon?"

They all laughed.

"You tell us," Arawn said. "You're the one with the scroll from Airmid. Any idea what it says?"

Amaethon held up the scroll and shook his head. "No, but the dragons knew."

"Do you think it's just about you, or does it involve the three of us?" Cerridwen asked.

Amaethon shrugged and put the scroll away. "I guess we'll find out when it's the right time to know."

"That sounds familiar," Arawn commented.

"Yes, it does," Cerridwen agreed, smiling.

Later, Amaethon stood up so he could get his bedroll and get some sleep. Arawn put his arm around Cerridwen's shoulder and started helping her take off her armor. She stopped him and took his hand in hers.

"I love you, Arawn," she said, giving him a kiss. "There's no one I trust more to change the world than you."

"I love you, too, Cerridwen," Arawn said, kissing her forehead gently. "When you spoke to Taranus after he yielded, I truly understood what Belenus, I mean Llyr, meant about bringing the peace. It made me love you even more."

"That's what partners are for," she said, letting go of his hand so he could continue unfastening her armor.

"Promise me that we'll always be there for each other like we were today," Arawn said.

"I promise, my love," Cerridwen replied, putting her head on his shoulder.

Arawn, Cerridwen, and Amaethon Arrive at the new Capital.

EPILOGUE

The gods left Alastríona behind and fulfilled the plan of Elohim, creating worlds and life across the universe. They never returned to Alastríona, nor did they tarry on any of the other worlds.

Cerridwen and Arawn did as they promised. They traveled to each of the territories, spending time in each so they could get to know the people and so the people could get to know them. For three years, they traveled constantly.

Once they had visited each of the territories, they returned to the gathering place, where their city was being built by workmen from all of the territories. It was a beautiful city that would eventually include all of the architectural and cultural elements from each of the tribes, integrated in a completely unique way. The city was dedicated to the unity of the peoples of Alastríona and included places for commerce, art and culture, and the sharing of ideas.

The center of the city, completed by the time Arawn and Cerridwen returned, contained the domed palace. This structure housed both the royal residence and the Council chambers where representatives from the territories met to help the Ruler of the World govern and lead wisely. Above each of the doors of the palace, there was a carving of the Kingstone. Directly below the Kingstone were two interlocking crowns and a dragon with its wings open wide. This design was reflected all around the city, including on the thrones in the great hall of the palace.

Arawn and Cerridwen worked tirelessly to establish ways to help the tribes work closely together. Ships were built to begin exploring the rest of Alastríona, using the best of what the Étaíne and Dunmaine had developed over the years. Colonies sprang up on the islands and lands that were discovered, and soon the people of Alastríona were migrating across the entire surface of the world.

In the fifth year of their reign, Cerridwen discovered that she was pregnant. She bore a son, and in honor of Arawn's surrogate father, she and Arawn named him Belenus. They had more children in the years that followed, as did Amaethon, who was joined shortly after Belenus was born. The three orphans had many adventures in their life, as did their children.

But that is another story altogether…

The End

ABOUT THE AUTHOR:

Award-winning author and publisher William Speir was born in 1962 in Birmingham, Alabama. He attended the University of Alabama, and graduated from the University of Alabama at Birmingham in 1984. He spent over 25 years in corporate America, serving as a management consultant, leader, IT executive, and HR/Payroll executive for top-tier consulting firms and Fortune 100 companies.

During William's corporate career, he published several articles on leadership and the human impact of organizational changes and technology changes.

His first experience with book publishing was with a series of ten textbooks he authored about field artillery in the 19th century. These textbooks were later consolidated into a single volume and re-published in 2015 as *Muzzle-Loading Artillery for Reenactors*.

In addition to his artillery manual, William has published 24 novels, including a 9-book action-adventure series (*The Knights of the Saltire Series*), five historical novels (*King's Ransom, The Saga of Asbjorn Thorleikson, Nicaea – The Rise of the Imperial Church, Arthur, King,* and *The Besieged Pharaoh*), one fantasy novel (*The Kingstone of Airmid*), one science fiction novel (*The Olympium of Bacchus 12*), one stand-alone action novels (*Shiko Unleashed*), one suspense novel (*The Day of the Dead*), three espionage/geo-political thrillers (*The Trinity Gambit, Codename: Mountbatten,* and *The President's Assassin*), and three Adult Fiction/Contemporary Romance Novels (*Love's Second Chance, Stealing Love,* and *Love Lost, Love Found*).

William is a 6-time Royal Palm Literary Award winner: 2014 Second Place Unpublished Historical Fiction for *King's Ransom*, 2015 Second Place Unpublished Historical Fiction for *The Saga of Asbjorn Thorleikson*, 2017 Second Place Published Historical Fiction for *Arthur, King*, 2017 First Place Published Historical Fiction for *Nicaea – The Rise of the Imperial Church*, 2017 First Place Published Science Fiction for *The Olympium of Bacchus 12* , and 2023 First Place Published Thriller or Suspense Fiction for *The Day of the Dead*.

For more information about William Speir, please visit his website at WilliamSpeir.com.

Progressive Rising Phoenix Press is an independent publisher. We offer wholesale pricing and multiple binding options with no minimum purchases for schools, libraries, book clubs, and retail vendors. We offer substantial discounts on bulk orders and discounts on individual sales through our online store. Please visit our website at:

www.ProgressiveRisingPhoenix.com

*If you enjoyed reading this book, please review it on
Amazon, B & N, or Goodreads.
Thank you in advance!*